The Call of the Beast

BY THE SAME AUTHOR

1. *The Marvelous Story of Claire d'Amour*
3. *Priscilla of Alexandria*
4. *The Angel of Lust*
5. *The Mystery of the Tiger*
6. *The Poison of Goa*
7. *Lucifer*
8. *The Blood of Toulouse*
9. *The Albigensian Treasure*
10. *Jean de Fodoas*
11. *Melusine*
12. *The Brothers of the Virgin Gold*

The Call of the Beast and Other Stories

by
Maurice Magre

Translated, annotated and introduced by
Brian Stableford

A Black Coat Press Book

ISBN 978-1-61227-653-3. First Printing. August 2017. Published by Black Coat Press, an imprint of Hollywood Comics.com, LLC, P.O. Box 17270, Encino, CA 91416. All rights reserved. Except for review purposes, no part of this book may be reproduced or transmitted in any form or by any means, electronic or mechanical, including photocopying, recording, or by any information storage and retrieval system, without permission in writing from the publisher. The stories and characters depicted in this novel are entirely fictional. Printed in the United States of America.

TABLE OF CONTENTS

Introduction

This is the second volume of a twelve-volume set of translations of Maurice Magre's prose fiction. It contains translations of his first three acknowledged works of prose fiction in volume form, *Les Colombes poignardées* (1917), as "Stabbed Doves," *La Tendre camarade* (1918), as "The Tender Comrade" and *L'Appel de la bête* (1920), as "The Call of the Beast."

Volume One, *The Marvelous Story of Claire d'Amour and Other Stories*, contains translations of early short stories, including the collection *Histoire merveilleuse de Claire d'Amour suivie d'autres contes merveilleux* (1903) and six other stories from various sources, published between 1901 and 1913.

Volume Three, *Priscilla of Alexandria and Other Stories* contains translations of the original version of the story collection *Vies des courtisanes*, first published in *Oeuvres Libres* 23 (1923), as "Courtesans' Lives" plus an additional story included in the version published in volume form in 1925, and the novel *Priscilla d'Alexandrie* (1925), as "Priscilla of Alexandria."

Volume Four, *The Angel of Lust*, contains translations of the novella, *La Vie amoureuse de Messaline* (1925), as "The Love Life of Messalina," the novel published as *La Luxure de Grenade* (1926), as "The Angel of Lust," and the chapter from *Magiciens et illuminés* (1930) entitled "Christian Rosenkreutz et les Rose-croix," as "Christian Rosenkreutz and the Rosicrucians."

Volume Five, *The Mystery of the Tiger*, contains translations of the novella *Le Roman de Confucius* (1927), as "The Story of Confucius," and the novel *Le Mystère du tigre* (1927), as "The Mystery of the Tiger."

Volume Six, *The Poison of Goa*, contains translations of the novel *Le Poison de Goa* (1928), as "The Poison of Goa," and the prose poems contained in *Le Livre des lotus entr'ouverts* (1926), as "Lotus Blossoms."

Volume Seven, *Lucifer*, contains a translation of the novel originally published under the same title in 1929 and the novella *La Nuit de haschich et d'opium* (1929), as "The Night of Hashish and Opium."

Volume Eight, *The Blood of Toulouse*, contains translations of the novel *Le Sang de Toulouse* (1931), as "The Blood of Toulouse," and the chapter from *Magiciens et illuminés* entitled "Le Maître inconnu des Albigeois," as "The Secret Master of the Albigensians."

Volume Nine, *The Albigensian Treasure*, contains translations of the novel *Le Trésor des Albigeois* (1938) as "The Albigensian Treasure," and the collection of vignettes "Communication avec la nature" from *La Beauté invisible* (1937), as "Communication with Nature."

Volume Ten, *Jean de Fodoas*, contains translations of the novel *Jean de Fodoas: aventures d'un Français à la cour de l'empereur Akbar* (1939) as "Jean de Fodoas" and the chapter from *Magiciens et illuminés* entitled "Le Mystère des Templiers," as "The Mystery of the Templars."

Volume Eleven, *Melusine*, contains translations of the novel *Mélusine, ou le secret de solitude* (1941) and the collections of vignettes "Le Côté d'ombre des âmes" and "Révélation des mondes invisibles" from *La Beauté invisible*, as "The Dark Side of Souls" and "The Revelation of Invisible Worlds."

Volume Twelve, *The Brothers of the Virgin Gold*, contains a translation of the novel *Les Frères de l'or vierge*, first published posthumously in 1949.

A long gap separated the collection of *contes merveilleux* that Maurice Magre published in 1903 from the next substantial volume of prose fiction that he signed with his own name. He did publish a small booklet containing two children's stories, *Les Trois métiers de Jeannet et Les Bon tours d'Yan* [Jeannet's Three Professions and Yan's Good Turns] in 1913, the first item of which is translated in Volume One of the present series, but the book is essentially trivial. His biographer Jean-Jacques Bedu, in *Maurice Magre: Le Lotus Perdu* [Maurice Magre: The Lost Lotus] (1999), also identifies Magre as the author of the erotic novel *Journal de Marinette, une femme curieuse* (1914), but the work in question is unobtainable and was probably hackwork written to commission. His most abundant work during the period was for the theater, almost all of it in verse, including the four-act lyric tragedy *La Fille du soleil* [The Daughter of the Sun] (1909), with music by Arthur Gailhard, the four-act verse drama *L'An mille* [The Year One Thousand] (1911) and a lyric drama in three acts and six tableaux *Le Sortilège* [The Magic Spell] (1913), again with music by Gailhard.

Also presently unobtainable is another book published by J. Fort, the publisher of *Les Colombes poignardée* and *La Tendre camarade*, issued between those two titles in 1918, *L'Art de séduire les femmes*, which Magre always included in lists of his works under the heading of fiction. Bedu does not include it in the bibliography included in his book, and presumably did not manage to find a copy for reference. It is not obvious why it is so scarce, given that it was reprinted twice, in 1921 and 1929, and I would have liked to include a translation here in order to complete the set of the author's acknowledged novels, but it proved impractical.

In 1908 Magre published two prose works supposedly based on his experiences since arriving in Paris from Toulouse. The first, *Conseils à un jeune homme pauvre qui vient faire de la littérature à Paris* [Advice to a Poor Young Man who Comes to Paris to produce literature], was swiftly reprinted as a supplement to the latter, a somewhat tongue-in-cheek guide to seduction entitled *La Conquête des femmes* [The Conquest of Women]. The preface to *La Conquête de femmes* states that when he was twenty-six years-old, while on summer vacation with his parents (i.e., in the summer of 1903)

Magre made the decision to cease the conventional search for a single woman with whom to form a long-term loving relationship and attempt instead to have sex with as many women as possible. The book ostensibly relates the results of observations made during that campaign—which, as he reports in his autobiographical text *Confessions sur les femmes, l'opium. L'amour, l'idéal, etc...* [Confessions regarding Women, Opium, Amour and the Ideal, etc.] (1930), rapidly became an obsession.

If that date implied by the preface is reliable, Magre must have made that resolution not long after completing "Histoire merveilleuse de Claire d'Amour," in which he had elaborated the argument that the light of amour was akin to the kind of lure that is irresistibly attractive but deadly, in the fashion of a flame drawing moths to annihilation. An example of that conviction is provided by the sad fate of the deluded Maurice in the story in question, who goes to Hell in quest of the eponymous heroine, even though she has told him that she does not love him and he has been advised of her faithlessness by no less a witness than Jesus Christ. The change of policy might therefore be regarded as an attempt by the real Maurice to overcome the kind of romantic illusions that had been leading him astray in his timid dealings with women.

The strategy did not work, as his subsequent fictional representations of erotic desire and his autobiographical reflections on that period of his life clearly testify. It was, however, an educative experience. Looking back on it in *Confessions*, Magre says that it was in that period he became sharply aware of the fact that there were two selves within him, and that his erotic impulses, their avidity and obsession, were the features of an inferior self whose sole goal was material enjoyment. The other, the higher self, was not orientated toward carnal pleasures but toward spiritual goals, aiming for a kind of purity that transcended material pleasures, and could be represented as an approach toward or union with, the divine. Magre routinely expressed that orientation as quest for "the ideal." The quest was supernatural, in a literal sense, attempting to rise above nature, beyond the material, and it is therefore understandable that the fictional spinoff from the quest was almost all fantastic in its content.

Many philosophers of the past, Magre recognized, had assumed that the quest to develop the superior self entailed the ruthless suppression of the inferior self. All of them, as he pointed out in "Le Côté d'ombre des âmes," one of the series of mini-essays contained in *La Beauté invisible* [Invisible Beauty] (1937; tr. in Volumes Nine and Eleven), had recommended chastity, although few of them had actually practiced it. Magre did not want to practice it either, and he quickly convinced himself that the division in his self was mirrored in the sexual attractiveness of women: that the beauty constituting the alluring flame also had a "pure" aspect, which belonged to the superior realm of the ideal. However, the simple notion that, as well as bad women like Claire d'Amour, there are good ones, like the mermaid Genofa in "La Fleur de jeunesse" (tr. as "The Flower of Youth" in Volume One), was exactly the kind of dogmatic cliché that Magre was always determined to avoid. In the first instance he attacked the problem from a very different angle, endeavoring to reach the ideal not by casting aside the carnal, but trying to work through it, to discover in sexual intercourse, especially in the crucial moment of orgasm, a kind of portal to the spiritual, to divinity. In *Confessions*, looking back from 1930, he explains that the endeavor in question was soon complicated by an attempt to attain the spiritual ideal of the divine by smoking opium.

Jean-Jacques Bedu was unable to identify exactly when Magre first tried smoking opium, and the chronology of *Confessions* is extremely vague, but it was probably after 1908 (opium is not mentioned in *La Conquête des Femmes*) and certainly before 1913. Although there might be reasons for doubting that the account of his early experiments with opium given in *Confessions* can be taken literally, there is no reason to doubt his fundamental assertions, which are that he first started smoking opium because he thought that lying scantily clad on a mat next to an drug-addled woman was a sure means of getting to have sex with her, and that a slight intoxication by opium—and he went to great lengths to stress that it had to be slight—achieved an alteration of his own consciousness that greatly enhanced the possibility, real or illusory, that the experience of orgasm would afford a glimpse of the divine. Indeed, he quickly came to think that it was the opium, rather than the orgasm *per se*, that provided the vital connection.

Confessions contains a long rhapsody, "La Messagère de la déesse" [The Messenger of the Goddess], in which opium is represented as a literal gift from the gods, a pathway not, as Baudelaire had once suspected, to "artificial paradises," but to the real one. By the time he wrote that rhapsody, however, and by the time he wrote the first of his four works of fiction in which opium-smoking and its fantastic effects are extensively represented, Magre had given it up. It did not take him long to witness, and perhaps to experience in moderation, the deleterious effects of addition and excessive inhalation. *Confessions* also contains a chapter describing the drug's destruction of some of his erstwhile smoking companions, as well as relentless assertions to the effect that, if opium taken in excess, the goddess ceases to reward its users and punishes them instead, setting them on a road to spiritual retrogression, in which the drug becomes the most degrading as well as the most dangerous of physical pleasures.

The attitude to the use of opium manifest in the four works of Magre's fiction in which it plays a major role—the first two, *Les Colombes poignardées* and *La Tendre camarade*, are included herein; the others are *Le Mystère du tigre* and *La Nuit du haschich et de l'opium*—is markedly ambivalent. All four pay homage to its revelatory role and the potential it has for functioning as a "messenger of the goddess" as well as a useful anesthetic, but all four also retain a keen awareness of its dangers. The most interesting of the four in terms of its extensive depiction of the effects of opium, and the most harrowing, is *La Tendre camarade*, which refers simultaneously to another cost of that experimental phase of Magre's life, which he apparently felt quite sharply.

In the chapter in *Confessions* entitled "Le Retour des morts" [The Return of the Dead], Magre detailed three deaths that continued to haunt him long after they had happened. One was the death of a friend of his youth, the second—detailed with embarrassed brevity—was the death of his mother, but the third, detailed at much greater length, was that of a woman he hardly knew, a prostitute named Elise.

Magre relates that he met Elise in a café, liked her, slept with her a couple of times, but actively avoided forming a continuing relationship with her, that not being part of his life-plan at the time. One night, however, she turned up at his apartment at four o'clock in the morning, in a state of extreme distress, presumably having had a nasty experience with a client. He did his best to comfort her, but she would not tell him what had happened or report it to the police, and in the morning, she left. Some time later, he received a letter from her, saying that she was dying, and would like to see once more the only man who had ever treated her kindly. He tore the letter up and did not go. Subsequently, he felt extreme remorse at that cruelty, but three months passed before he finally went to the address—which he still remembered in spite of having destroyed the letter—only to find that she was not only no longer there but was hardly remembered, a girl of that name who had died of consumption being confused with another who had simply gone elsewhere.

That remorse never quit him, and its legacy is obliquely echoed in both *La Tendre camarade* and *L'Appel de la bête*. In the latter novel the unnamed narrator behaves in a more honorable fashion to the prostitute who turns up at his apartment late at night in distress, but in *La Tendre camarade* the debt that the philosophical philanderer Jean Noël tacitly contracts to a prostitute whom he first treats kindly but then discards is left as tragically undischarged as the one that his opium-smoking companion, a former colonial officer, describes as the pivotal event of his life, and the one whose remorse has conditioned his opium-addiction. Jean Noël, busy pontificating about the search for the ideal via "tender comradeship," remains oblivious to the lesson that the colonial officer tries to teach him, but Magre clearly did not, and a belated awareness of the harm that he might have been doing on some of the women that he was using so casually and prolifically for his own ends might have played a role in convincing him that reckless promiscuity was an obsessive addiction he ought to attempt to break. The corollary use of opium, addiction to which he had always tried hard to avoid, declined too, his initial enthusiasm for the possibility of using it as a portal to the divine waning considerably as he became more familiar with its effects.

L'Appel de la bête, however, illustrates the fact that, having tried sex and opium as roads to the ideal and found them wanting, Magre found a further potential resource, in the occult underworld of Paris, to which he was apparently first introduced by Gabriel de Lautrec before the Great War, while he was still a thoroughgoing skeptic. That encounter is described in the opening chapter of the first of his autobiographical texts, *Pourquoi je suis Bouddhiste* [Why I Am a Buddhist] (1929), in order to illustrate the distance he has traveled since. The hostess of the salon to which he was taken to meet various belated adherents of the French occult revival, is named there as "Madame Doucenoir," but that is probably a pseudonym. The guest medium had promised to obtain a manifestation of "ondins" [water-sprites] but failed to do so, prompting Magre to criticize him sarcastically. The medium had also brought a book with him, at which Magre looked briefly: Madame Blavatsky's *The Secret Doctrine*, which was later to become one of the principal influences on his thinking and on his own scholarly fantasies.

That change of mind, however, and the replacement of his skepticism by a profound sympathy for occult ideas, does not seem to have taken place until after the Great War, which was not the only drastic change in his circumstances that took place between his early experiments with opium and the burgeoning of his interest in Theosophy and Buddhist ideas. In

1913, Maurice Magre married Jeanne Rosen, the daughter of a New York banker.

All mention of the marriage in question, and the fact that it produced a son, Claude, in 1917, is rigorously omitted from Magre's autobiographical writings, as if he were determined, quite literally, to erase it from the record of his life, although it lasted—technically, at least—for ten years, until it was dissolved by divorce in 1923. Bedu, reduced almost entirely to speculation, takes leave to wonder whether Magre simply married Jeanne for her money, referring vaguely to a substantial dowry, and finds it hard to believe that it was a love-match. He cites the curt brevity of the few surviving letters from Magre to his wife that he was able to locate—including some sent from Albi, where Magre was obliged to report for assignment when the Great War broke out less than a year after the marriage—as evidence of a lack of feeling.

Perhaps Bedu is right; it is perhaps noteworthy, that in both *Les Colombes poignardées* and *La Tendre camarade* the argument is explicitly put forward that the curt brevity of letters received by anxious lovers is not necessarily evidence of a lack of affection, but in both cases it turns out to be exactly that. On the other hand, Magre, ever prone to bursts of passion and always insistent on regarding love of gold as the source of all evil, does not seem to have been the kind of person who would marry for money, although he was certainly the kind of person who did not take long to have second thoughts about the wisdom of something he had done in the grip of an infatuation. Bedu found evidence that Magre had several affairs during the marriage, mostly with performers who appeared in his dramatic works—including a relationship with the singer Suzanne Parisis that lasted at least into the 1930s—and cites that as one likely cause of its dissolution, but it is unlikely to have been the only reason.

Whatever happened within the marriage that caused Magre to eliminate it so ruthlessly from his memoirs, it was certainly greatly disturbed in practical terms by the war, which inevitably disrupted his writing career as well. In retrospect it can be sent that Magre came through the war far more lightly than many others. The authorities spent months deciding whether or not to assign him for active duty, only deciding in December 1914 that he ought to have a non-combatant role in the auxiliary services, and then prevaricated over a specific assignment until April 1916, when he finally assumed duties as a medical orderly. That was an infinitely better fate than sending him straight to the trenches, as they might have done; nevertheless, his life was considerably disrupted.

During the long wait for assignment, Magre traveled frequently between Albi, Toulouse and Paris. Jeanne returned to her native America in the latter months of 1914, although she came back in 1915, and the couple were able to maintain a semblance of normal life in Paris during much of that year, albeit under a curfew that made social life difficult. Literary life was completely devastated, and very few writers managed to publish books during 1915 and 1916, the interference of the censors—"Anastasia's scissors"—becoming an oppressive presence, although the principal reason for the drought was simple economics.

In 1917, however, that situation changed, and numerous writers who had been silent for some time returned to print in a minor flood. Again, the release was probably mainly due to an easing of the economics of production, but it is noticeable that many of the novels contributing to the sudden abundance contained a forceful propagandist element, which often seemed to have been introduced arbitrarily into a pre-existent text, tempting the suspicion that the government lent some encouragement to the sudden renaissance, in the interests of maintaining public morale.

Les Colombes poignardées is one of the books that appeared in the context of that flood, albeit an atypical one, in that it is not only devoid of any propagandistic content but seems, on the whole, more liable to diminish morale than reinforce it. It calls attention to a social phenomenon that came in for a great deal of lamentation and scathing criticism in novels written after the war, and its ostensible praise for the actual attitude and behavior of Parisian women rather than the conduct and emotions that many people considered more fitting, would have seemed highly unusual in 1921, let alone 1917, when the situation was still critical.

It is probable that the author's unstable circumstances and lack of available time had much to do with the brevity of the work and its fragmentary quality, but Magre must have thought the narrative strategy in question rewarding, because he not only recapitulated it in *La Tendre camarade* but returned to it later in his career, employing similar patchworks to great effect not only in the novels *Le Trésor des Albigeois* and *Mélusine* but in the associated work of ostensible non-fiction *La Beauté invisible*. Even *L'Appel de la bête*, which was presumably written in more relaxed circumstances, retains a certain patchwork quality, introducing one substantial detour that must surely have been a separate short story before its arbitrary incorporation into the narrative. That was a habit that Magre never lost, and most of his longer works feature such intrusions.

The elimination of Magre's marriage from his autobiographical writings extends to his fiction as well, and none of the works of fiction he produced while he was actually married features a married male protagonist. In *L'Appel de la bête*, however—a novel that Bedu does not hesitate to describe in his bibliography as "autobiographical"—the unnamed protagonist does have a long-term relationship with his mistress, Rose-Thé, which is spoiled by virtue of the addiction to prostitutes that he deems to be a kind of demonic possession. Whether the psychological trauma that the narrator suffers after Rose-Thé leaves him reflects anything in Magre's own experience is, inevitably, a matter of pure speculation, but he does seem to have been able to identify with those feelings convincingly. Given that the account of the narrator's experience of his sex-addiction, although luridly exaggerated, has an evident connection with comments made in *Confessions*, and that the account in the novel of the protagonist's introduction to the occult underworld also echoes the author's own recent

17

fascination, it is tempting to suspect that there must be a connection of some sort.

On the other hand, when Magre did draw upon aspects of his own life in the design of episodes in his fiction—as, for instance, when he had dramatized his failure to reach his mother's death-bed in time to be present at her demise in "Histoire merveilleuse de Claire d'Amour"—his usual procedure of transfiguration involved extreme and lurid exaggeration; it would be dangerous to rely too much on his fiction as a guide to his real feelings.

That danger, of course, has never intimidated some critics. For instance, the subplot in *L'Appel de la bête* detailing the extraordinary career of the sadist Jean Lathème was adapted by at least one commentator to the decadent image that Magre had constructed for himself. The jacket copy of *Le Lotus Perdu* and Magre's Wikipedia entry both attempt to sum him up by means of a quotation from a review in *Le Figaro* in 1924: "Magre is an anarchist, and individualist, a sadist and an opium addict. He has all the faults, but he is a great writer." In fact, as Magre's autobiographical writing make clear, he had a horror of sadism, and after once feeling a twinge of sadistic pleasure when killing a lizard as a child, he reacted against it so strongly that cruelty to animals became a key symbol of evil in his mind and in his work, and sympathetic communion with animals became a central element of his notion of the ideal. (Furthermore, he was never addicted to opium and had given up smoking it entirely by 1924; his affiliation to anarchism had never been more than a tokenistic sympathy.)

It is notable too that in *L'Appel de la bête*, the narrator finds the idea of using magic as a means of seduction profoundly offensive, and that is echoed in several later novels featuring erotic magic. Unlike his discovery of the joys of opium smoking, which he hastened to combine with and fuse with his obsession with sex, his fascination with the occult underworld appeared to him, from its very inception, not to be a supplement to his temporary attempt to reach the spiritual via the carnal, but an alternative route from which the carnal ought to be excluded. In *Lucifer*, the uncanny gift for seduction that the narrator has had in the past is represented as essentially diabolical, whether or not it comes, as he suspects, from a literal satanic pact.

The narrator of *Lucifer* is belatedly named in an epilogue as J. N***, which links that novel to the three works collected herein, which all feature the character of "the poet Jean Noël," first introduced into Magre's work as a whimsical *alter ego* in "La Dernière sirène" (1905; translated in Volume One as "The Last Siren"). Although he is only central to the plot of *La Tendre camarade*, Jean Noël's presence in the other two stories is of some significance, as a curious kind of doubling of the author's implicit presence within the story—but as a version of himself of which the author had begun to disapprove by the time he wrote the three stories collected here.

As a continuing character, Jean Noël is not consistent, especially if one assumes that he is the J. N*** of *Lucifer*, but Magre was not consistent either, and seems throughout his life and career to have continually taken all manner of imaginative sidesteps in order to look at himself at a distance, evaluate himself and find himself wanting, sometimes harshly. He actually had fewer faults than the reviewer for *Le Figaro* was ready to believe, and perhaps fewer than he was occasionally wont to suspect himself—but he was a great writer regardless. The three works translated in the present volume find him still not entirely confident in writing fiction at length, feeling his way somewhat, paving the way for more ambitious projects, but there is no doubting their artistry and their force.

In all three works the intrusion of the fantastic is limited, confined to opium dreams in the first two and maintained in a strictly ambiguous fashion in the third. Magre seemed to have considered that attitude appropriate to prose fiction at the time, although his contemporary publications in other media are far more flamboyant in the use of the fantastic. The collection of the poetry he wrote during the war years, entitled *La Montée aux Enfers* [The Ascent from Hells] (1918) includes some striking supernatural narratives in verse, including "L'Incube et la vierge" [The Incubus and the Virgin], "La Fille de Luci-fer" [Lucifer's Daughter], "La Malédiction" [The Curse] and "La Vallée des larves" [The Valley of Ghosts].

Even more dramatic is the verse drama *La Morte enchaînée* [Death Enchained], first performed at the Comédie Française on 8 September 1920 with a cast featuring the cele-brated Gaston De Max, the poet Roger Gaillard, and the film star Jeanne Delvair as Death. Set in Greece in "the most re-mote epoch of mythology" in the city of Euphyre, which was to become Corinth many centuries thereafter, the story relates that King Sisyphe, having saved the beautiful Egine from the lustful pursuit of the god Ouranos, marries her, and then finds himself in competition for her love with his son Glaucos. When Glaucos and Egine attempt to kill him, Sisyphe con-trives to imprison Death as she comes to collect him, but that captivity is ended, with tragic consequences all round, when the lovelorn female slave Tyro is tricked into releasing her.

Magre made every effort to expand his endeavors in all directions once the war was over and normal life seemed to have resumed. In 1919 he collaborated in the founding of a new Symbolist literary periodical, *La Rose Rouge*, but it soon collapsed, as most Symbolist periodicals did, unable to com-pete with the solidly-established *Mercure de France*. The pe-riod of general enthusiasm associated with the war's end did not last long either, as its economic after-effects prolonged the catastrophe.

The separation of effort noticeable in Magre's work in the immediate post-war period, giving free rein to the fantastic in verse while keeping it captive on a light leash in prose, was decisively ended in Magre's work following the tentative ex-periment of *L'Appel de la bête*. Thereafter, the fantastic was liberated in all of his fiction, initially mostly in a malign role, but eventually serving much more various functions, many of them life-enhancing. The ambiguity maintained in *L'Appel de la bête* was increasingly compromised by more casual and explicit supernatural intrusions, and when Magre resumed writing novels after a brief intermission when he seems mostly to have written short stories, the novels in question were not merely wholeheartedly fantastic but flamboyantly so.

The translations of *Les Colombes poignardées* and *La Tendre camarade* were made from the London Library's copies of the editions published in 1917 and 1918 by J. Fort under the aegis of l'Édition; the translation of *L'Appel de la bête* was made from a copy of the Albin Michel edition of 1920.

Brian Stableford

STABBED DOVES

A Eulogy to Infidelity in the Manner of a Preface

It is a very marvelous thing that beautiful eyes can weep thousands of tears without their brightness or their color being depleted. And is it not necessary to be even more astonished that charming hearts have been able to contain treasures of amour and dolor, and spread untiringly the wealth thereof, without those treasures being in the least diminished?

It is not that women suffer less than men—quite the contrary—but what they throw to the devouring flame is a personal substance that gives a great deal of light, and a little heat, but is not consumed.

Let no one see in these little notes the slightest criticism of what has been called a woman's power of forgetfulness. Among so many beings who loved and were separated at the beginning of the war, women have not forgotten more rapidly, and if they were the first to betray, it is because they alone had the temptations and the facilities.

The war has shown us with a terrible evidence how fragile our affections are and how the individuals who appear to be the most similar and who are linked by a brief eternity can easily, at the end of a few months of distancing, become different, and strangers.

How many women will have discovered, after the initial terror of solitude, that the solitude in question has two faces, that of ennui and also that of liberty. They will have understood for the first time the gleam that there was in the eyes of the husband or the lover when he said in the evening: "I'm going to the club and might be late back." They will understand that if the kiss at the door was hasty, it is because the air-current of the stairway brought the breath of the solitary stroll, of the street where, preceded by the tiny light of a cigarette, one goes toward the thousand objectives of nocturnal life.

They too will have known the joy of dining in town whenever they please, of going to the theater without authorization. They will know the delight of the solitary awakening, they will lose the habit of the daily arguments by means of which the tyranny of those they love is exercised. They will employ that liberty and soon cherish it. And some of them will perceive that it is such a marvelous possession, and a companion with so much fantasy and variety, that they will no longer want to be separated from it, and that its charm, for them, will make the charm of domestic tenderness pale.

A powerful magnet will have summoned men elsewhere. They will have rediscovered in the depots, in the camps or in the auxiliary offices the primitive coarseness that is the foundation of their nature and which reappears as soon as they converse together freely. A coarse conception of life will have deformed their minds and altered their judgment of all things past. They will have plunged into the vulgar as into a regenerative bath. They will now only remember the former delicacy as one remembers a religion whose incense intoxicated but which deceived.

The two sexes will no longer die, each in its own fashion. They will live for new delights, which they will seek with all the force of their instinct through a few difficulties, a few hesitations, sometimes even encountering a timid remorse, in the same way that you encounter a shameful pauper on a street corner who looks at you sadly but does not ask you for alms.

Nature, with her invincible logic, will be the stronger, she will lead her children toward the paradise where they can satisfy their ancient appetite for happiness, and if, in order to enter that paradise, it is necessary to bite the fruits of treason, those fruits will inexorably be eaten; for, contrary to what moral people say, they are not poisoned, and even possess a delicious taste.

I am offering to readers a very light sketch of a tiny corner of a big picture that is yet to be painted. Do not search here for anything else. A few outlines are indicated here of women with their native virtue, their genre of courage, their sense of forgetfulness, their incapacity to struggle against duration. You will not find here, surrounded by ashes and deflowered bouquets, the antique altar that it pleases us incessantly to raise to Fidelity.

I do not believe that it is necessary to be afflicted by that. Under those graying tresses and her inexorable visage, that goddess was excessively honored by humans. She is the enemy of new joys, and the sadness of the times is too great for anyone deliberately to misunderstand the departure of hope for the future.

In any case, for an elevated mind, is fidelity such a precious virtue? Has not too much power been conferred upon it? Is there not room, close at hand, for another altar on which the crowns deposited thereon will bear the inscription: *temporary regrets*, for another goddess, whose visage, turned toward the rising sun, will assert that neither amour nor unhappiness is eternal, and who will be Infidelity.

She might also be called Consolation. The austere and mediocre individuals who establish moral conventions, the mendacious principles by which we live, will turn away on seeing her; but next to her, holding her hand, will be curiosity and desire, which are the virtues of those who strive to be superior.

At That Time

At that time, the low-cut dresses were hung up in wardrobes and the small sound of their sequins was extinguished in the apartments. At that time, the sheet music of new songs and the pamphlets from which roles were learned were thrown on to pianos as if, dead henceforth, their characters no longer had any meaning. At that time, jewels were locked away in their caskets, pearls suddenly tarnished and the red baton of lipstick fell from many delicate hands to make a little drop of symbolic blood on the carpet.

At that time, beautiful eyes that knew everything looked into the mirror of life with a sudden ingenuity, profound and somber eyes became as blue as the morning sky. At that time, the voluptuous became chaste and the bewildered lips of desire only any longer knew the kiss placed on the forehead. At that time, strange and fraternal conspiracies were formed between the chambermaids of the seventh floor and the elegant tenants of the first. At that time, the son of the concierge and the young lover of demi-mondaines became, by virtue of a sudden equality, sublime companions in adventure. At that time, gypsy violinists quit their operetta costumes for the red trousers and the blue jacket, and the last tango died away.

At that time, many women began a campaign in Paris in which there were also exhausting marches, dolorous retreats and mortal counter-attacks. It was necessary to take possession of the hill, bristling with humiliations more terrible than shrapnel, known as the Mont-de-Piété. It was necessary to wait for a long time to surprise the enemy well hidden behind a desk in the town hall, who hurled scornful glances and curt and incomprehensible words at you, which traversed you more effectively than Mauser bullets. It was necessary to sustain a heroic battle to bring back the modest booty of one franc twenty-five. It was necessary to confront insolent pity, hear the thunder of suppliers' demands, as deafening as cannon

26

fire, withstand the assault of all the creditors of your entire life. It was necessary to shiver in trenches made of one's own furniture, amid the sweat of solitude, beside the heater that the landlord had refused to light.

At that time, there were great hidden heroisms. Little hands from which all the rings had fallen clutched the ivory handle of an umbrella with the energy that is put into clutching the hilt of a sword. Exquisite faces that had only reflected amour put on the mask of courage. Slender bodies that had only known the passionate combats of lust, warm beds and perfumed baths writhed bitterly to battle misfortune. Under the armor of dresses, little avian hearts beat with an emotion stronger than that provided by the most desired rendezvous.

It was necessary to struggle with patience and resignation as well as courage. There was no hope of any sun of victory, no flag fluttered for the rally, and instead of military music nothing was to be heard except, in a distant courtyard, the heart-rending song of a lost musician with an accordion. There were incurable wounds, there were admirable unknown deaths and, in solitary rooms, the powers that watch over us must have pinned invisible medals on meager breasts chilled forever.

The Little Notebook

You loved him and he has gone. And for the first time in your life you find yourself unoccupied. You were one of those women who had a little notebook in which you wrote down appointments, and who always had a thousand things to do. That little notebook was connected to your purse by a little gold chain. What use will it be now?

Scarcely had the light entered your room, scarcely had you emerged from the sheets, than you planted a tortoiseshell pin in your hastily-twisted hair and you began a great battle with all your insignificant occupations.

In that battle you were always victorious. How, in the same day, were you to take on the hairdresser, the milliner, the lingerie-maker, to try things on at the dressmaker, to rehearse at the little theater where you were shortly to perform, to go to a concert with a friend who was initiating you into great music, take tea in three far apart places, public and private, to which you were summoned with equal force by amity and amour?

Now, there are no more friends, the tearooms are closed, even the hairdresser, that placid and loquacious fellow, has departed for the war and you have been obliged to expel shamefully the barbaric Auvergnat who presented himself as his replacement.

I leaf through the little appointment book and I look at the last written lines. *The Luxeuils, six o'clock; Bichara, six-thirty.* Then there is a blank page and then an address: 50th regiment, 3rd battalion. Afterwards I see a list that repeats. But no, it isn't a list. Monday: Marco, Marco, Marco, Marco, etc. And all week, on every page, there is Marco.

Marco is the name of the man you loved, for, occupied as you were, you still had time to love him. You no longer saw him, but rendezvous were necessary to your untiring activity, and you made a date to think about him in the precious little notebook, for every day and every hour.

The Broom

I rang the doorbell of Chinette's little town house and I waited. I waited for a long time. What! No domestic any longer! The house was deserted, the joyful house of nocturnal suppers, masked balls and tangos at five o'clock in the morning.

Finally, footsteps resounded in the distance, drew nearer, and the door opened slightly. I saw through the crack the face of someone inhospitable who had only come because of the possibility of a letter or a telegram and who had a strong desire to send the importunate visitor away.

That face was Chinette's, but it was a changed face, more serious, devoid of rouge and beauty spot.

I looked at her in surprise. In the house where she had once reigned, was she no more now than a servant? She was, in fact, wearing a white apron; she had a very simple corsage, her hair was tied back and she seemed to me, with her delightful face and her tiny feet emerging beneath her skirt, to be some modern Cinderella about to do the housework, on the threshold of a sleeping palace.

She recognized me and I went in.

She had no false shame.

"Yes," she said, "this is how it is. No more butler, no more chambermaid, not even a housekeeper. It's not that I'm afraid of finding myself entirely penniless, but how can I bear the thought of living as in the past, being served, having all my comforts, when there are so many men out there suffering and dying? And then, isn't it frightful? He, who was in such poor health in spite of his plumpness, who had only ever gone out in an automobile, being obliged to march all day, carrying a knapsack, making his own soup! How exhausted he must be! How unhappy he must be!

I knew that Chinette did not love the banker with whom she lived. I had been her confidant. She did not love him, she said, because he was too blond and too fat and she only liked

29

slim dark-haired men. She deceived him with all the facility of deception she had, which was a great deal.

Doubtless my astonishment emanated from my silence, penetrated the fixity of my gaze.

"When I lived with him he annoyed me, I couldn't bear him. His physique was odious to me. Then again, his excessive wealth put a barrier between him and me. It was like a perpetual testimony of the great injustice that makes some rich while others are obliged to work hard to earn their living. Now, since he's a soldier, since he's risking his life like all the others, I love him. It really is love. I think about him, I write to him, I wait for his letters. Once there was an obscure embarrassment between us. He had that sort of timidity, that lack of expansion of excessively rich men. With him, I retained all my pride, I was incessantly on the defensive. That's gone now. I feel him very near me. We're equals, lovers who are separated and who live in the hope of seeing one another again. Everything about him is dear to me, even his plumpness makes me feel tender. Isn't that curious?"

I replied that it was curious and, in order to know Chinette's soul completely, I asked: "And Paul?"

Paul was a young actor whom Chinette said she loved, before the war.

"Oh, him, I don't know. But he's young, he'll get over it. I don't feel sorry for him."

She fell silent momentarily in order to permit the image of Paul to fall forever into the abyss where forgotten lovers go, and resumed: "I would have liked to work, to suffer, like everyone else. But what can a woman do? I've tried to go into the hospitals, but it's necessary to pass exams, there are too many volunteers and they refused my help. Then I came home and I told myself that I'd lead the exemplary life of a poor woman here. I work all morning. In a little dress of no account at all I go to the market. I make my meals. I do my room, I sweep the house and I wash the floor of the corridor. In the evening I put the ordure out in the street. And in the big bed where I go to sleep, tired out, at nine o'clock. I savor a solitude that doesn't weigh upon me."

I felt that, amid the furniture whose golden feet could be seen protruding from beneath the dust-sheets, like those of lords in monkish robes, I represented a slightly shocking worldly element. The mere fact of knowing Paul and thinking about him rendered my presence difficult to tolerate for long.

I got up to leave. Chinette accompanied me to the stairway and in passing, mechanically, she picked up the broom that she must have set down when I rang. She held out her left hand to me and lifted it up in her right, with a sort of nobility.

That broom was, for her, the weapon that was going to defend her, to permit her to traverse that unfortunate period of her life without being humiliated by her conscience with the intimate pride that demands patience. On the threshold I looked at the beautiful oval of her face, slightly sad but resolved, her tied-black blonde hair and her soubrette's apron, and I saluted that unknown heroine who was battling destiny with a broom.

Trou La La...

I ran toward Montmartre in the hope of a familiar face, an individual with whom I might have been able to exchange a few words.

Night was falling over the terraces of cafés where men were reading the newspapers feverishly. People were also talking in animated groups, and I noticed that bearded men or those with long hair had suddenly acquired a greater importance, surrounded by a kind of aureole. Clean-shaven faces, on the other hand, slipped through the crowd insignificantly, trying to hide from the vague scorn of passers-by.

I raced across the Place Clichy and searched the sidewalk that forms the corner of the square and the Rue de Douai.

There, for many years, and whatever hour of the day or night I passed by, at midday, going to dine at a restaurant in the Avenue de Clichy, or four o'clock in the morning, coming out of the painter Dante's studio with a troubled mind, in the winter snow or the bleak solitude of summer vacations, I had always seen, immutably, braving the noise of automobiles and the gaze of policemen, a very old woman, almost shapeless, with atonal eyes, with no light but the gleam of a key he held in her hand, and I had always heard her hoarse and indifferent voice murmur as I went past: "Are you coming, dearie?"

I was often irritated that she dared to suppose that I might follow her. In my vanity, I would have liked her to recognize me, and mark me down on her mysterious tablets as someone too distinguished to enter her clientele, and to whom it was futile to appeal. She had often importuned me because I liked to look in the window of the nearby bookshop and, in that event, she stopped beside me, simulating a literary interest for the lined-up books, and repeated untiringly in a toneless voice: "Are you coming, dearie?" until I was obliged to leave the spot.

I had sometimes felt sorry for her. She had resisted all the changes to the area where she lived. An old house surrounded by trees, opposite the bookshop, had been turned into a school. A contemporary of old horse-drawn omnibuses whose upper deck one reached via a footstep, she had seen the advent of modern autobuses and electric trams from Levallois. I was accustomed to consider that creature as essentially eternal

The sidewalk of the Rue de Douai was empty. No footsteps resonated there. No key glinted.

I waited; I thought it was a mere change of habits. I went down as far as the Place Vintimille. There was no one there. I came back. For the first time, I could look at the books entirely at my ease. The bookshop was not yet closed, but I was not tempted to do it. The appeal to which I was accustomed was lacking. The creature had disappeared. All the potency of literature, with the fantasy of poets and the invention of novelists, that the bookshop contained, seemed extinct. The absence of the woman carrying the key had a profound significance. I started walking feverishly.

As I went past a bar whose door was closed, however, I saw with surprise through the window panes that it was full of people, and I heard an incomprehensible noise escaping from it.

I went in, and a singular spectacle struck my sight. Around the tables were assembled the fat matrons of Montmartre, clothes-merchants, procuresses from cheap hotels, seamstresses from music-halls in Sunday clothes, and fortune-tellers. There were also a few young women, regulars at the Moulin Rouge, a few failed actors who had become prompters or copyists and also professional gigolos, their heads supported by hands laden with tawdry rings.

But the women were wearing little or no make-up, the mannered gestures of the young men were somewhat false and awkward. Either by virtue of penitence, thrift or scorn for beverages, no one was drinking. The tables were bare.

And in a smoky corner, with a derisory gravity, as if they were accomplishing a comical and solemn ritual, all those hybrid beings, all those wrecks, were singing, with an infinite sadness periodically punctuated by coughing:

"Trou la la... Trou la la..."[1]

What ritual were they performing? What prayer were they reciting?

The dolor of that chant penetrated me, and I hastened to leave again. I went away. But after walking for some time, curiosity clawed me and I retraced my steps. Undoubtedly, what I had heard was merely a familiar refrain of that bar haunted by a particular society, which people must have been intoning at the moment when I went in.

I crossed the threshold again. Amazement! In the opaque smoke, the same individuals, immobile, were singing in a melancholy fashion:

"Trou la la... Trou la la..."

Was that the unexpected form by which all those spoiled beings, the refuse of the theater and gallantry, were participating in the general dolor? I don't know. But the tobacco smoke, the odor, the horrible gravity, the immobility of all those present and the incomprehensible chant gave the place a nightmarish aspect.

I sat down and saw beside me an old man who had a beard grown over several days, a dirty black frock-coat and a top hat whose silk was torn in places, and which he wore tilted back on his head. I recognized, without a doubt, some former leading man from a provincial troupe.

I looked at him more attentively, and I saw that large tears were running down his wrinkled cheeks and over his worn and excessively wide collar.

---

[1] The oft-repeated "*trou la la*" is the refrain of a popular *chanson paillarde* [lewd song] entitled "À l'auberge de l'écu." In that original it functions as mere gibberish, but in the context of the present story it is not irrelevant that *trou* means "hole."

But eight o'clock chimed. The street resounded with the noise of closing shutters and shop windows, and a pale proprietress clapped her hands.

The plaint fell silent; there were adieux and handshakes, and everyone left.

I followed the man who had been weeping, in the middle of a group. He was talking as he walked, stiffly and with a slight stoop, and from time to time he made an excessively grand gesture, as if he were deploying a cloak.

His voice was deep, moving and very youthful. I could only make out what he was saying partially, but I understood that he was talking about an only son who had departed for the war and of whom he had not had news.

The group stopped at the corner of the Rue Lepic. I saw that they were bidding him *au revoir* with an affectionate respect, and the man went up the street alone, with a long stride. I felt such a great pity for him that I was still walking behind him. In the sadness of that time, strangers approached one another to speak to one another amicably. I decided to say a few consoling words to him. I started to run, because he had a long stride and he was moving very rapidly.

The Rue Lepic was absolutely deserted. I drew almost level with him. I looked at him, and I perceived that in a whisper, gravely, with a great dolor in his expression, he was chanting:

"Trou la la... Trou la la..."

Then I went back down the Rue Lepic at a run, thinking how various the means of expression are of our hearts.

Martini Cocktails

Jacqueline has asked for a martini cocktail; she has taken a straw; she stares at the glass with her blue eyes, and she drinks slowly, gravely, as one performs a ritual.

There are beautiful things in the yellow color of the cocktail. There is a transformation of the place where one finds oneself, the amity of Madame Germaine, the landlady of the little bar where the cocktail is served, the satisfaction of the hat and dress one is wearing, the softness of twilight.

But when there is nothing more in the glass than a little disk of bitter peel and the fragments of the straw, broken by nervous fingers, one regrets those beautiful things and one asks for another martini cocktail.

The color of the second martini cocktail is more nuanced than the preceding one, its gold more sunlit; its taste is better, the fragment of bitter peel less bitter.

And there are things in it more beautiful than in the first.

There is the brevity of time, the sentiment that the war cannot last long and is temporary, that the French people are invincible, that all the men who have gone to fight will come back alive and uninjured: all the men, especially the one about whom Jacqueline is thinking.

That second martini cocktail produces such an agreeable effect that, in order for the effect not to be attenuated, it is necessary to hurry and ask for a third.

Splendid is the third Martini cocktail. It is radiant and it makes everything round it radiant. Madame Germaine's face is illuminated by a glorious aureole. The little chasseur in his blue uniform is like a naval officer about to board a submarine. The *Marseillaise* is murmuring in the distance; flags are flapping. By virtue of the miracle of the golden beverage, it seems that a few days have sufficed for the war to end and a young soldier named Marco to return to Paris covered in braid and medals because of the exploits he has accomplished. He only has one thought in the midst of his splendid deeds, that of Jacqueline... And now he is advancing toward her, leaning on a sword, and she goes to kiss him. In front of us, two women and an artilleryman are joking and laughing, for there are only happy events caused by the war, and an immense happiness penetrates the world.

"You're weeping, Jacqueline. I've just seen a tear fall into your empty glass; another is on the edge of your eyelid. Here's your little embroidered handkerchief; wipe it away quickly."

I know that among the beautiful thoughts and beautiful images that you've seen in the magical gold of martini cocktails there was no representation of my amity. That's of no account. I'll forbid you the fourth martini cocktail and take you home. It's a well-known effect of that marvelous beverage. It makes sadness come after the beauty. In any case, doesn't the one accompany the other in every aspect of life?

You reply to me that you have a horror of martini cocktails, but that you only drink them because of the memory, because Marco loved them.

Come on, let's leave the glass, where there's nothing any longer but the tear and the bitter peel.

What the Buddha With Golden Eyes Said

That evening, the Buddha with golden eyes that was on the mantelpiece of the little smoking-room in the Rue Caulaincourt spoke to the man lying on the mat facing him, and these are the memorable words that were spoken:

"Get up, former colonial magistrate. The days have come when mandarins must become warriors and put on the costume of samurai. O living sleeper, after years of an immobile life, moist with opium and dreams, you are about to be traversed by the sun, you are about to bear arms, you are about to strive to kill.

"You once brought me back, wrapped in a blanket, from Cao Bang, a remote little town on the frontier of Indo-China, where you bought me from an old bonze for a few silver coins.[2] That old bonze had sculpted my primitive image in the wood of a mangrove struck by lightning, and consequently designated by the Powers. That is why I am a favorable god. Since then you have taken pleasure in telling your friends that you stole me by night from a pagoda where I was the object of an ancient worship, at the price of a thousand perils. But I've forgive you that lie, because you cannot know how much more beautiful the truth of my origin is than your invention, which is that of the Occidental race.

"You have treated me with honor, you have given me the best place in your house; you have suspended over my forehead a little bronze lantern—bought, it is true, in a Paris ba-

---

[2] Magre mentions more than once in his autobiographical writings, most notably in the final chapter of *Pourquoi je suis bouddhiste*, being the proud possessor of a Buddha given to him by a physician returned from the Far East, who told him that he had obtained it from a bonze who had carved it from the wood of a lightning-blasted tree on the slopes of the mountain of Cao Bang. Naturally, Magre believed him.

zaar, but which is a sign of veneration. So I protect you and I will guide your jaundiced face and your wan shadow through the streets of towns, through country roads, amid the redoubtable ordeals that await you.

"For years now you have only left your apartment to go to a friend's smoking-room. From three o'clock in the afternoon, when you wake up, until six o'clock in the morning, when you fall into a vague semi-slumber, you smoke incessantly, your head supported by a hard leather cushion, among weapons, striped silks, incense-burners, lacquered boxes brought back, like me, from out there. Apart from the quality of the black drug that you absorb and the conversation of a small number of friends, smokers like you, everything is indifferent to you. You never read the newspapers in which the things happening in the Occident are written, you are unaware of and you fear the light of day; you have limited your life to the distance into which the swirling smoke of your pipe rises, and it seems that the great chimera embroidered on your door is defending you, by spreading its red wings, against the afflictions of the world.

"You have had enough strength of mind to resist the advice of your concierge, whose mind is not inclined to dreaming and who feels compassion for your way of life. You have been able to withstand the advice of a friend, a colonial like you, whose health is delicate and who, every time he comes to see you, discovers the stigmata of liver disease in your face. You have been able to laugh at another fearful friend who, several times, exhorted you immediately to destroy everything you use for smoking, including the admirable opium from Benares that is manufactured so expensively in London, because he claimed to know from a mysterious and reliable source that the police were about to search the houses of all the smokers of Paris.

"You thought that you would be able live until death in the wisdom of a perpetual dream, in the midst of friendly faces, among spirals of brown smoke. You are mistaken. The unknown Powers have decided otherwise, and millions of human destinies are about to be launched out of their way.

"Former colonial magistrate, how will you do it? It will be necessary for you to march for days with a knapsack on your back; it will be necessary for you, in the evenings, to lie down on the bare ground, without the familiar sizzle, without ruddy light, without black smoke.

"Then, this is what I recommend that you do:

"Men willingly agree to fix the term of the war at approximately fourth months. The anticipations of the gods ought to be in conformity with those of men. You can count on four months of war, four months during which it will be necessary for you to sustain a constant struggle against yourself much more terrible than with the enemy. An immense aspiration to smoke your thirty daily pipes will absorb your faculties. You cannot take with you either the tray or the lamp. So, you will replace those pipes by the pellets that you will absorb. Five will suffice per day. In three days, when you leave, you ought to have six hundred pellets in your bag. Thus, you will take your place as a man among men, and if it presents itself to your eyes, you will be able to look death in the face without weakness."

Thus spoke the Buddha with the golden eyes in the smoking-room in the Rue Caulaincourt.

At the same time, the painter Dante and a few friends of the former colonial magistrate were wondering anxiously how a man who lived lying down, who had not seen the light of day for a long time, and for whom opium was as necessary to life as bread for others, was going to be able, without transition, to make a soldier.

They went to his home to give him news of the war. They found him on his feet, calm and resolute.

"I'm on my three hundred and eighty-fifth pellet," he told them, smiling. "Soon, I'll have finished fabricating my provision of courage."

For the first time, he had drawn his curtains, opened his window and, with his lusterless eyes, he was striving to contemplate the friend that he had not seen for such a long time, the sun.

Voices in the Smoking-Room

The poet Jean Noël raised himself up slightly on the mat where he was smoking.

"That peoples are at war is the least of evils. As far back as we can go in the course of the ages, we see that men are natural warriors. At all times, nations have hurled themselves upon one another, not for the profound interest of races, but for the whims of sovereigns or the speculations of financiers. Millions of men fight and die for the interests of a minority, and do not protest. They even attribute a glorious meaning to that dupery. That's because war is a natural state. It's necessary not to be astonished or frightened by the extremity of its apparent evils, about which we hear talk. It's only necessary to fear its invisible evils."

The poet Jean Noël picked up a black droplet of opium on the tip of a needle, offered it to the flame of the ruddy lamp, caused it to swell and smoke, rolled it with amorous care, and, when it had adhered to his pipe, he went on:

"If men consent to die in large numbers, without any direct interest, without any immediate hope, it is because their instinct informs them, in default of reason, that life is miserable and that death is an intervention of no great importance that one can risk aimlessly because everyone running is the risk together, and because military music is intoxicating. The loss of lives is not what it is necessary to fear in war. Far more than machine-guns, the shrapnel of shells, incendiary bombs, torpedoes and floating mines, far more than tetanus, typhus, cholera and the other plagues engendered by great human agglomerations devoid of hygiene, we ought to fear the epidemic of evil that will spread in our souls. The small superiority that we have had so much difficulty in acquiring is dying and defeated. The selected sheaf of our sensibilities that we have cultivated within us with so much care is going to fade like a bouquet whose water has not been renewed. That which made us good, and artists, risks being destroyed by the evil wind coming from the war."

As if a cordial were necessary in order to remedy that moral destruction, the poet Jean Noël, having placed his pipe over the lamp, took several long draughts, the smoke of which he expelled slowly.

"It's my turn," said a woman whom no one knew, who had come several times before. She had never spoken, but smoked incessantly. "I seem to remember having known her once in the Latin Quarter," the painter Dante, who had brought her, had said by way of introduction.

Also there, lying on the divans or carpets, were Jacqueline, who hoped to find forgetfulness of her chagrin; two indistinct and shapeless individuals at the very back of the room; and a man of cheerful aspect who never smoked and only came, so he said, to make a study of mores, and in reality, in the hope of facile conquests.

Polly and Dolly were motionless, huddled together in a corner. From time to time, one of their ingenuous faces appeared from the shadows, stared at everyone with astonished eyes, and then disappeared again, and it was understood without seeing it that it was returning to the pleasure of a kiss.

The painter Dante, in an overly long kimono, was serving tea. Sometimes, he stopped and, pointing with an extended hand, either at the reflection of a Chinese lantern on ancient fabric, a bare foot emerging from a peignoir, or the ensemble of the things presented to his eyes, he said: "Isn't that a lovely color, eh?" And his habit of admiring the color of things in that place where perpetual shadow reigned was so great that sometimes, lying on his back, having just aspired a pipe and savoring it, he closed his eyes and repeated: "Isn't that a lovely color?"

The sound of cups ceased, a kiss given by Dolly to Polly passed like a little breath of tenderness, and the poet Jean Noël went on:

"From now on we're witnessing the renaissance of evil. Although the war has excited heroisms that are certainly admi-

43

rable, it has developed in the human soul a much greater power of evil. Our beautiful dreams of yore have been replaced by murderous and bloody imaginations. When I wake up at night, my wishes become images, and I see in the distance millions of Germans felled, cannons sowing death among them and entire fleets sinking with their crews. Those dreams are cruel and dolorous; they're a sign of passion and not of superiority. Haven't you noticed around you, in the petty actions of life, an unaccustomed activity of evil?

"Anonymous letters and denunciations are flooding from all directions. Many people, who are excellent patriots, are accused without the shadow of a pretext of espionage to the profit of Germany, solely because their face displeases the tenant who lives opposite their apartment. Others are obliged to go to the Commissaire of Police to show their papers, to establish that their father and mother are of French descent because their concierge has no sympathy for them. Hidden resentments burst forth, brooding hatreds are given free rein.

"People slander with more facility, accuse for no reason. People gladly announce that a friend has lost a leg, or that another is dead, and a secret joy is visible beneath a hypocritical affliction. Death has become familiar, catastrophe has become an element of the everyday, and instead of suffering in that element, humankind moves within it with an unexpected ease, seeming content with it and able to delight in it. All the hopes founded by humanitarian idealists have collapsed.

"Humans are no longer evolving toward the good. They are evil. In order to progress they have taken a road in error. We are on the wrong path. We are part of a failed humankind, since all the moral effort expended has ended where we now find ourselves."

Polly raised her tousled head, as if to testify by her surprise that evil had exceptions. One of the obscure beings in a corner and who was not visible said: "No, the war is a manifestation of amour."

Silence fell. An explanation was awaited. It was not forthcoming.

Jean Noël spoke again.

"If we want to retain the small sum of superiority that we have acquired, the precious wealth that enables us to savor the quality of emotions and the beauty of the arts, it's necessary that our minds remain inattentive to the horrible things of the war. I've decided not read the newspapers any longer and to run away when I encounter someone on the street who wants to tell me the story of a battle. I want the echoes of atrocities to expire on my doorstep. I go out as little as possible in order not to know more about the reversion of human beings to the savagery of their ancestors. I shall protect my old dream, and live with that alone, defending it against the sadness of the times. I'm determined to ignore the war."

Various and confused comments were exchanged on that point of view.

The man of cheerful aspect who was not smoking declared that he had put in his request for voluntary enlistment. A voice that emerged from the shadows said again, with authority: "The war is a manifestation of amour."

"But why?" asked the painter Dante.

There was no response.

Dolly and Polly had curled up in order to sleep, in the same peignoir. I had taken Jacqueline's hand; nothing could any longer be heard but the sizzle of the opium manipulated by the woman who was smoking incessantly.

Someone who stood up knocked over a teacup with his foot, and that made as much noise for the sensitive ears of the smokers as if an entire quarter of Paris had blown up.

"That light is hurting my eyes," said Jacqueline.

The poet Jean Noël drew the tray toward him and blew on the lamp like someone blowing on his wellbeing.

The Psychology of Letters

Jacqueline received letters from Marco. She complained that she did not receive a great enough number, but in sum, she received some. She consulted me about the import and the amorous meaning of phrases they contained. I wanted to please her and I strove to be a favorable commentator on texts that were often arid.

Barbas, my adjutant, is a decidedly charming fellow. We had an aperitif and then dined together yesterday... Barbas has assured me that we will be leaving the depot next week... I've very glad to be Barbas' friend... I hope that you'll meet Barbas after the war...

The last phrase, in particular, provided me with an argument.

One of the characteristics of amour is to want all the people who are dear to you to be united by a common affection. Marco has a new and great friendship, that of the adjutant Barbas. Since he wants Jacqueline to meet Barbas, it is because he loves Jacqueline.

Yes, but why are Marco's letters not full of marks of tenderness, as they once were? I strive to demonstrate that Marco's soul is undergoing an evolution almost general among the young men whose way of life has been changed abruptly by the war.

They have suddenly gone backwards a few years; they have become comrades again, beings made to live among men, with the pleasures of physical exercise, drinking, nourishment and coarse conversations. Their mistresses and Parisian life, the previous frame, are things at which they almost blush among the vulgar men who are presently their leaders and from whom they seek amity. It's necessary not to be alarmed by that. Amour will reclaim its rights later; there is a sort of truce of amour that will last as long as the war.

"But after all, in that depot at Albi, he might perhaps cheat on me."

"No, Jacqueline. It's a well-known fact that there are no women in the provinces, especially in the Midi. All the women are in Paris. Elsewhere, there are men and a vast human category in which one finds mothers, sisters and aunts, with faces in which there are qualities of foresight, wisdom, and goodwill, but it's impossible there to discover an oval with a clear complexion surmounted by a tiny little hat in the latest fashion that can make the face of a mistress."

Many a time, a few years ago, with the naïve illusion of youth, I disembarked in provincial towns and set forth along deserted sunlit esplanades, twirling my cane and darting inflamed glances right and left. Bleak families crossed my path. There were young women with overly pleasant but slightly red faces, from whom I was separated, in any case, by the abyss of social prejudices.

I was taken to see the manageress of the tobacconist's shop. Certainly, she seemed favorable to a fairly rapid conquest; but when one had made a provision of cigarettes sufficient for several months' consumption, when all of one's pockets were stuffed with boxes of matches and enough stamps for a year's correspondence, one perceived that one was at the same point, and that the engaging smile with which she offered you a packet of Gianaclis was the same for all the young men of the town, automatic and eternal.

I was shown in the music hall two or three women who had the reputation of having numerous lovers. But those lovers were the procurator, schoolteachers and town councilors, people established in the town who had been able to advance, for that conquest, an enormous capital of card games with the husband, walks with the mother, gifts and wasted time.

The traveler is irrevocably vowed to sentimental solitude. That solitude must be just as inexorable for the simple soldier who cannot act either by custom or the prestige of his situation.

No, Jacqueline could not be betrayed.

"However, I'm told that in every provincial town...for the soldiers...there's a house..."

I protest that Marco is far too delicate an individual. I remember a little antique side-street with brick houses, along the Tarn, over which the shadow of the cathedral extends, and on the thresholds of which stood two or three women in striped peignoirs, while an extraordinarily dirty corridor exhaled a whiff of garlic and cheap perfume.

A memory of college comes back to me. I think I can hear the out-of-tune piano, I see once again the cracked mirrors, the gaslight reflected therein, the faded velvet of the furniture. I think privately that those fêtes of the eighteenth year sometimes have singular returns in the hearts of men.

I know how weak the creature is. I imagine the sadness of Marco evoking, next to a body kneaded a thousand times over by an entire garrison, the tall and pure form of Jacqueline. And I pity him for that disgust, for that ordeal that one cannot escape, as inexorable as the draft board, or the journey in a third-class railway carriage, and it is with an immense sincerity that I repeat, while thinking of his treason:

"Don't worry; Marco loves you."

The Heroism of Chastity

From her Arabian slippers to her spread out hair, little Mariette formed, in the midst of cushions in the shadows of the smoking-room, a straight line of tense and quivering flesh. Sometime, that straight line became a voluptuous bow, and her clenched fingernails made a little noise on the satin they were scratching.

My friend Jean Noël had just picked up a somber droplet on the tip of the needle. I made a sign to him. He put down the pipe and the needle. He turned slightly, and with the gesture of someone looking for something he has just dropped, he paraded his hand over Mariette's hand and wrist.

Abruptly, the bow relaxed and released its arrow, which fell back in a spray of words.

"No, my lad, it's not worth the trouble. I've never been faithful, as you know very well. It's even my principle, my line of conduct, not to be. I acquitted my duties as a faithless mistress well enough with regard to Jacques, who knew me and loved me enough to forgive me for what my clumsiness sometimes let him know. But all that was before the war. Now I'm a good woman. It's a very new estate for me, and I won't hide the fact that I find it very difficult. But I've made it my point of honor to carry to the end the rifle and the knapsack of chastity. I too am on campaign.

"I shall be victorious. Certainly, it won't be without difficulty. Temptations have never been as numerous. Never, it seems, have there been so many men in Paris. And then, the absence of occupations and forced idleness inclines one more to amour. I won't mention my aviator comrades who bombard me with letters and whose uniform is so seductive. I won't mention the foreigners, even those belonging to neutral countries; their quality renders them slightly suspect. It's the wounded officers, most of all, who are difficult to resist.

"I tell myself that perhaps I'm committing a sin in remaining insensible to the sidelong glances of the young junior lieutenant that I encounter in the avenue of the Bois and who walks with crutches. It might be a kind of duty to console him a little. Who knows? Within a month his leg will have healed, he'll depart again and he'll carry with him the memory of my coldness. Out there he might think: *That young woman I liked so much turned away from me because I was wounded and on crutches.* So I might, without intending to, have aggravated the woes of that young man, who has shed his blood to defend us. Was I not wrong? But duty would then be too agreeable. It's necessary that it be dolorous.

"So I'm good. And when one is, like me, what you men commonly call a *temperamental woman*, one suffers. I'm content to suffer. I struggle with a powerful instinct that it within me. I sometimes feel a flame passing around my flesh as hot as that of cannon-fire, which envelops and sets fire to me. I resist the assaults of lust, I stand up to the explosions of desire, and I remain upright under the thunderbolts of amour. That's my fashion of making war. And when the man I didn't love enough comes back, I shall at least be able to offer him, in exchange for all the suffering he will have endured, a tiny drop of heroism, whose beauty he will comprehend because he knows the weakness of my flesh."

The tall Lucienne, who had not said anything thus far, but who was listening, leaning on the elbow of her bronzed arm in a slightly vulgar fashion, made a movement of indignation that caused her fake necklaces to clink, and exclaimed:

"That fashion of understanding life in wartime is stupid. Mariette is making herself suffer and she isn't giving any joy to anyone. Everyone is quite unhappy enough not to augment the sadness further by forging ideas that serve no purpose. For myself, I won't hide it, I've been the mistress of three military men that I didn't know, who have departed, and whom I'll probably never see again."

In the shadows, without seeing them, I sensed smiles of faces, expressing that, in everyone's mind, the number cited must be far inferior to the reality.

The tall Lucienne went into a long and scrupulous enumeration of details that I didn't hear. The upshot was that she had inspired three equally strong passions, the evidence of which reached her every day by way of a triple correspondence in inflamed terms.

"The duty of every woman," she went on, "in the present circumstances, is to be generosity itself. We contain a thousand joys in the lines of our beauty, we ought not to be miserly to those who might perhaps die tomorrow."

An invisible smile was still floating in the smoke-laden atmosphere, saying that the joys of which the tall Lucienne spoke did not number a thousand and were of a quality less precious than she seemed to be indicating.

"It's necessary to give ourselves," she insisted again, needlessly. "It's our true mission." And she extended herself lazily, as if a pose of abandonment might fortify the indubitable energy of her intentions.

Jean Noël made a vague sideways gesture, and his hand brushed the brown hair that fell in hard curls around the tall Lucienne's ridged forehead. He took a few wisps, which he rubbed between his fingers. But he turned away rapidly toward the lamp and the pipe, and as if he were speaking to those familiar objects and to me at the same time he said:

"When one does not have what one desires, it is vain to desire what one can have."

In The Home of the Seeress

"It's very well-known," Jacqueline told me. "The entire war was announced by a monk in the Middle Ages. My former chambermaid, who's now a manicurist, came to see me yesterday and told me about an extraordinary young woman who makes predictions and reads cards. There's no doubt that certain people have the gift of foreseeing the future. It's proven, even scientifically. I'd like to know whether I'll soon receive a letter from Marco. This is the address that my former chambermaid gave me. Let's go there."

I know that seeresses, desirous of contenting and augmenting their clientele, generally only announce fortunate things. I therefore content to satisfy Jacqueline's desire, and we set forth.

The extraordinary young woman lives in a very poor house in a very distant quarter. The staircase is wretched; an odor of rotten wood and cooking emanates from it, and I'm astonished as I climb it that people who have the power to know future events, the location of hidden treasures and the secret thoughts of men don't make use of those virtues to ameliorate their material lot slightly, and at least obtain the means of leading their prophetic life in less nauseating places.

A gilded paper star is stuck to the door to the right on the fifth floor. That star and, after the door is opened, the red turkey-twill that papers the walls of the antechamber, indicate to us that we have just penetrated into a magical domain.

"Only a few minutes," says a fat man of cheerful aspect, who resembles the idea one has of Tartarin.[3] My daughter is

---

[3] Tartarin de Tarascon, the eponymous protagonist of Alphonse Daudet's famous 1872 novel, a caricature of a supposedly typical inhabitant of the Midi, full of ludicrous braggadocio. As a proud and loyal son of the Midi, Magre must have found the portrayal extremely annoying as well as insulting.

busy with some people, very considerable people, who have come to consult her. She'll be yours shortly."

He has us sit down in a modest dining room and entertains us with his personal views on the war. I redirect the conversation and I ask him how he perceived his daughter's gift of second sight.

"It isn't second sight, properly speaking, its clairvoyance, the marvelous knowledge of past and future events that the elect soul possesses," he declares, proudly. "I was quite unaware of it until she reached the age of fifteen. One of my friends, who is a commercial traveler in wines, was dining with us one day. He looks at my daughter and says: 'I've never seen such eyes. I'm interested in magnetism and I'm sure one could put her to sleep.'

"'What's the point?" I reply.

"'Let's do an experiment,' he says. 'My wife has mislaid my watch and can't find it. I'll put your daughter to sleep and ask her,'

"He makes passes and orders her to go to sleep.

"'Where is my watch?' he asks.

"'It's at the Mont-de Piété,' says my daughter.

"'That's impossible!' cries my friend.

"'The receipt is in your wife's purse.'

"He laughs and wakes her up. 'Your daughter doesn't have the gift of second sight,' he says.

"But that same evening he came back. He'd found the receipt in the purse and his wife had confessed to having taken is watch secretly to the Mont-de-Piété.

"Since then I've put my daughter to sleep myself. You can't have any idea of the quantity of things she's been able to predict that have happened. So many very important people come to consult her. Her renown has increased, people talk about her, and they how come here from all over. One of the greatest bankers in Paris doesn't involve himself in any affair without asking my daughter what line of action he should take. It's absolutely forbidden me to reveal certain visits that I have at present. I can confide in you, however, because you seem to be very serious people. An officer of the general staff was in that very spot this morning. There are certain military operations that he's hesitant to undertake at present, and on which the outcome of the war depends. Is it necessary to carry out those operations? That's what the chiefs want to know. But I can't tell you any more, under any pretext."

The door opened and we were in the presence of a slightly well-built young woman with moist eyes and black headbands. She smiled on seeing us and showed us into a little room, also papered in red.

For his part, her father made a few vague magnetic passes and said in a low voice: "She's asleep, I'll leave you."

The young woman had taken Jacqueline's hand.

"You have a friend whom you love very much. Yes, you're surrounded by a great deal of love." Here, she interrupted the commencing ecstasy momentarily in order to dart a long glance at me. "It's necessary to love that friend. You'll receive business letters and you'll be entangled in your projects. There's a journey in prospect, and annoyances. But your friend's amour will assure you of triumph."

She darted a further glance at me, as the palm that would ensure that triumph.

Then she depicted Jacqueline's character at length, and in agreeable colors, and then the character of her friend, a very intelligent businessman who ought to lead her by the hand to an eternal happiness.

She punctuated every sentence with a glance or a smile in my direction, in order for there to be no doubt about the friend to whom those eulogies were addressed.

"But in sum," said Jacqueline, "does the person I'm thinking about love me?"

"I see love, success and happiness for you both," she said—and I believe that, in the certainty of our union, she was about to put Jacqueline's hand in mine and give us a supraterrestrial blessing.

We got up.

The power of the marvelous is so great over women that Jacqueline still had the naivety to murmur to me in a low voice: "Ask her when the war will end?"

I asked the question.

"I see great movements of men, much fire and much blood. I see the Emperor of Germany lying on the edge of a little wood in a field of clover. The war will finish between the twenty-fifth and the thirtieth of September 1915."

All that, with the salutations and amities of the father, only cost, as a wartime price, five francs.

In the dark staircase, Jacqueline said: "So the war is going to last another two months."

And on the threshold, she leaned on my arm and said and said again: "Isn't it funny—she thought you were my lover?"

And she laughed, pressing her shoulder against mine.

I didn't think it was funny, but I savored the sympathy that had come from her to me through the slight gap in the door of the marvelous.

The Dancer

We needed gasoline. The automobile stopped at the edge of a small village. While the chauffeur set out for a shop with his cans, we went on ahead a short way.

It was very hot and the shade of the plane trees only gave us partial protection. Behind a gate there was a kitchen garden and then a leprous terrain and a farmhouse of sorts.

A dog barked. We advanced with the intention of asking for milk.

A tall, slim peasant woman appeared on the threshold of the house. She stared at us with amazement, and then uttered a cry, waving her arms and running toward us.

The peasant woman was Pomone, the dancer from the Moulin Rouge, a friend of Jacqueline's.

"As you see," she said, "I've returned to the land. The war has returned me to the occupations of my childhood. I do gardening, I dig, I water the plants."

"What's become of little Luco?" I asked. That was her lover, a young dancer who performed little ballets or two persons with her.

"I don't know. He had no talent. The only good thing I've seen him do was miming fear when war was declared. I'll never dance with him again."

Pomone took us inside. Her grandmother, a very old peasant woman, was sitting in a rustic farmhouse room at a great wooden table.

"It's scarcely a month since I left Paris, and the life of the theater already seems so far away. I wanted to make myself useful. What can a dancer at the Moulin Rouge do? I thought that the best way to collaborate in some small way in the general effort, since I didn't have any capability to be a nurse, was to extract a few rows of vegetables from the soil."

We were at the table, with glasses of red wine that Pomone had served us, when we saw several aged soldiers, territorial guardians of the railway, who were at the door, wondering, on seeing us, whether they ought to come in.

Pomone laughed.

"They've come for the performance. What else can a dancer do when she's watered the cabbages or dug up the potatoes? She can dance. That's what I do for these soldiers. I'm giving them a show this evening. They're so bored! Then again, some of them had never seen a dancer in their life!"

Some fifteen soldiers had me in. They were timid, and spoke in low voices. The grandmother had taken away the glasses, and dusted the table. Pomone had left us, and we had heard her going upstairs.

She came down again a few minutes later, but she was no longer the peasant woman of a few minutes ago. She had swiftly put on make-up and she was dressed in a leotard and tutu.

"There's the orchestra," she said, indicating a slightly hunchbacked young man. "He's the pharmacist's son; he has a violin and he plays no matter what to accompany me. Anyway, you'll see."

Pomone danced as it seemed to me that she had never danced in her life. She danced heroism, amour, hope, the love of beauty and the desire for victory: the sentiments that were waiting in the depths of those simple hearts. And she had certainly never had an audience so contemplative, so religiously admiring.

The chauffeur came to tell us that he was ready to depart. The soldiers had retired, with bravos and effusions of admiration.

"You should stay here this evening. You could eat my rustic soup, and I have a bare room for you. The bed's narrow, but since you haven't been together long, you won't complain."

We refused, and we had a great deal of difficulty convincing Pomone, as we bid her adieu, that Jacqueline and I were not together.

"Well then, you're stupid," she said to us, as we left.

Embarrassed, Jacqueline started to laugh, and I couldn't help thinking that perhaps we were, in fact, stupid.

Friendship

"Friendship is a marvelous wealth," said the poet Jean Noël, leaning on his elbow amid Persian cushions. "To possess that wealth, it's necessary to deploy as much cunning, patience and courage as a poor man requires to become rich."

"That's very true, nothing is worth as much as friends," said Polly, abruptly showing a tousled head, which emerged momentarily from the shadows, only to return immediately in the direction of the delightful face of Dolly, the oval of which could be distinguished confusedly.

"Amity is far superior to amour. It's more disinterested, because it isn't based on preoccupations of a carnal order but on moral affinities. It's also rarer. The war, alas, is going to disperse the treasure of amity that we have constituted with so much difficulty. As more cities as bombarded and the cathedrals destroyed, that loss is irreparable. The two or three dearest comrades we possess will perhaps perish out there, and with them the pleasure of confidences exchanged, the companionship of the evening, and a certainty of fidelity, the best happiness of life."

"It seems to me that if I were a man," said the tall Lucienne, ingenuously, "I wouldn't have that opinion, and I'd love women enough while the war lasts, simply in thinking that some of my good friends who've departed might not come back."

"Veritable friendship," Jean Noël went on, "which is noble and great, can't exist in women, who are only linked by amicable thoughts as long as the troubled senses don't intervene."

Jacqueline raised herself up to protest. She was lying beside me. She had smoked a little. But just as she was about to speak, to affirm that women were as capable of friendship as men, she doubtless feared the resonance of her voice and she lay down again, and said to me in a low voice:

"That's absolutely false. Am I not your friend? Isn't our friendship based, as he said, on moral affinities and not on carnal preoccupations? Say so."

I had smoked a little, and that was a very direct and precise question for someone who, in the crepuscular red lamplight, was lying alongside a charming woman.

The charming woman was looking at me with bright eyes, without any hidden agenda—at least, it seemed so to me. Her kimono was folded over her bare neck, but insufficiently not to allow a glimpse of the birth of a perfect breast.

I remembered that Marco was my veritable friend, and I observed that Jacqueline's gaze really was devoid of a hidden agenda and I declared that our friendship, Jacqueline's and mine, was truly pure and noble among all friendships, and foreign to any dream of the senses.

"Thank you," said Jacqueline, a trifle dryly. "You're truly my friend, and then, you know how much I love Marco."

And having said that, without any apparent motive, Jacqueline drew closer to me—so close, so very close, that I felt the warmth of her shoulder and her slender body against mine.

Then she turned away and struck the pose of someone sulking.

I was thinking, in the vagueness of the smoking-room, how incomprehensible the human heart is, when I perceived that, without thinking about it, I had taken Jacqueline's hand in mine.

"Why are you sulking, Jacqueline?"

"Do you like this royal amber?" she replied.

"I like it in principle since you're wearing it, but I can't smell it."

"Well, I have it here on my neck."

I leaned over Jacqueline's neck. That royal amber was utterly exquisite.

It was in this restaurant where I'm dining with Jacqueline, talking about Marco, that I saw Jacqueline for the first time, two years ago.

She was sitting facing me, with her friend Rirette, of the Variétés; she was wearing a broad-brimmed blue hat and a summer dress that allowed her neck to be seen, and she was laughing in a slightly affected fashion, showing her teeth, and eating with a hearty appetite, shamelessly.

I asked Marco, who was next to me, whether he knew that two women, alone at a small table, one of whom was filling the restaurant with her merriment. Marco replied that all women were boring and that those were getting on his nerves particularly because of the noise they were making.

He had not even looked at them.

I insisted that he turn his head in their direction.

He declared that he knew little Rirette slightly, who was charming, but that her friend appeared to him to be, among all the beings it had been given to him to see, one of the most pretentious and most unbearable.

In order to express that judgment he had raised his voice slightly, for no reason, and by the flash of amazement that passed through Jacqueline's eyes I understood that she had heard.

A woman who is twenty years old and who has attained a certain degree of striking beauty only sees in the criticism of her physique a comical implausibility. She looked in our direction without anger, curiously.

I was distracted by her gaze as much as the notes of her laughter, which resonated again.

"Marco," I said, "since you know the friend of that delightful cheerful woman slightly, go and talk to her when she gets up to leave, in such a way that we can accompany them into the night. It's true that all women are boring, but those two will distract us this evening."

A flood of sympathy was pushing me toward Jacqueline, but I spoke thus because of a stupid self-esteem that obliged me, when I was with Marco, to share his opinion on the matter that women ought to be a mere pastime.

Marco began by cursing the evil genius that was driving me to seek out the company of women, the source of all ennui. We were dining, we were joyful and amicable; the infinity of the evening, with its idling, cinematographs and bars, was before us. He insisted that that solitude between comrades ought not to be troubled.

I insisted too, and he decided to go and say hello to Rirette.

A few minutes later, an automobile was carrying us toward the Bois.

"That woman," Marco said to me in a low voice, indicating Jacqueline, "is decidedly insupportable."

I replied: "Perhaps you're right." And as he listened to interminable theater gossip recounted by Rirette, Jacqueline and I chatted familiarly, having the delightfully banal conversation in which one finds similar tastes and habits, common manias, the love of the same books and the same actors.

And during the evening, in the paths of the Bois, where an odor of damp earth reached us, at Armenonville, before iced drinks, in the quivering of dresses, and all the way to the door of the house where we left Jacqueline, saying to her "Until tomorrow," her laugher rang out untiringly, as clear and fresh as the glasses from which we had drunk orangeade.

"How do you like her" I said to Marco.

"My opinion hasn't changed. She really is a horribly cheerful woman."

I replied: "She is, in fact, much too cheerful."

As he left me, Marco said: "Good luck for tomorrow."

And I made a vague gesture as if to indicate that all that was of no great importance.

I don't recall by exactly what coincidence it was that led Marco to come to take tea with Jacqueline the next day, and how he was able to condemn that cheerfulness that he found unbearable and I liked so much. But I remember that, in the following days, when I took Jacqueline to the Bois or the theater, when I initiated her to the painter Dante's smoking-room, where she drove all the smokers to despair with the sound of her laughter, either by chance or because he was too bored that evening, Marco was always with us.

I felt myself falling more in love with Jacqueline every day. A strange mental paralysis prevented me from telling her so. I sensed confusedly that she was alone, that she was bored, that she was at that turning-point where the proudest woman and most difficult to take belongs to the more audacious.

But Marco was always there!

One Saturday evening, we were all to spend the evening together at the home of the firmer colonial magistrate Miély. At the last minute I was obliged to go and meet my brother outside Paris and stay there until Monday morning.

The odor of the countryside, the melancholy of a beautiful property with very straight pathways, the river where men in short-sleeves were boating, gave me a great and abrupt desire for amour. I rehearsed everything that I was going to say and do to conquer Jacqueline. My memory drew up a list of favorable things she had said, consenting attitudes she had adopted. I went back to Paris full of fever, in haste to act very quickly.

Once I was home I wrote a first letter to Jacqueline asking to meet that evening, and a second to Marco. I explained to the latter that I was fonder of Jacqueline than he might believe and more than I believed myself. I told him that I wanted to see her alone and begged him to simulate, for the evenings that followed, occupations that would keep him away. Thus I would be able to hope to have the closeness to Jacqueline that the ironic surveillance of a friend renders impossible.

I had just finished my letter when the doorbell rang.

It was Marco. He was disheveled and had not shaved since the previous day. His gaze was full of the ingenuous egotism that is often the cause that attaches someone to his friend by the power he has to interest you in the smallest details of his personal affairs. He had scarcely come in than he had filled my room with the importance of the matters that concerned him.

"Why, you're writing to me," he said, perceiving the letter destined for him on my table. But he did not ask what the letter contained, because it was evident that it could only be about something that interested me, and his own preoccupation was, for the moment, the only thing that interested him.

"All women are boring, but life is even more boring," he said. "Between two evils, it's necessary to choose the lesser."

And he laughed.

You'd gone on a voyage..." He emphasized the last word to change my brief sojourn outside Paris into a long absence. "So, what had to happen has happened."

"What?"

"We had dined together. We had smoked together. It was at Dante's. There was only us, and Dante had a rendezvous at midnight. We were left alone. You understand..."

I did not understand, and the surprise was legible in my features.

"One doesn't know the true sentiments one has for a woman until one is lying beside her. A marvelous experience, and how instructive! On Saturday evening I took Jacqueline home. Oh, very sagely...she felt slightly ill. Then, yesterday..."

"Yesterday..."

"Yesterday, I went to see how she was. I have often told you that Jacqueline seemed to me to be too cheerful. Well, yesterday evening, she suddenly became sad. She had dined in bed. We talked about you. And that's how it all happened."

I remained silent.

"Given that nothing had happened between her and you, and that fundamentally you were no more intent on her than that, that you're like me, that you found her too cheerful, I don't feel any sort of remorse."

Marco's face did, indeed, express a joy devoid of reproach.

He was standing. He tapped me on the shoulder, saying: "I'm content. I'm very content. I've just left her house, and you can't image how charming a woman like Jacqueline can be when she ceases to be cheerful. My dear..."

But I stopped him.

When he had gone, I ripped the two letters into tiny pieces, a dust of paper that I crumpled between my fingers and began a fine rain through the open window on to the sunlit street, as light as my desire, a fine rain of the ashes of amour.

Pall Malls

"I assure you, Jacqueline, that these cigarettes are excellent."

But no, Jacqueline will not try them. She says that she doesn't like that tobacco, and that she can only smoke one category of cigarettes, in which it's necessary to hasten to go in search.

Those cigarettes are Pall Malls. And when the little box is finally brought be Jean Noël's stout cook, Jacqueline, with a smile of satisfaction, opens the packet with her light fingers, sinks back into the midst of the cushions on the divan and blows spirals of smoke toward the ceiling.

On the ceiling there is a Persian fabric, a ray of sunlight traverses the rising smoke, and Jacqueline's face is entirely distraught.

"Do you recall," she said, "the evening when we were here two years ago with Marco? He was wearing that green suit I liked so much, and he looked at me, with his eyes more ingenuous than usual in his willfully ironic face. In this very spot, he kissed me in front of you, and I don't know who said: 'They resemble Paul and Virginie.' It was stupid but, I remember that, at that moment, it gave me a very sweet pleasure."

Jacqueline put the extremity of her cigarette, of which nothing remained but a little cork tip, on an ashtray, and it seemed that she was following in the air the vision of Marco in a green suit, which dissipated with the smoke.

"Another Pall Mall, Jacqueline?"

There were further blue spirals and further images in the room.

"Do you recall," she said, again, "the Mortignys' masked ball. Marco had an incredible costume and he was furious with me because I'd made him wait for at least an hour in a carriage outside my door. That was still the blissful time when I made him wait.

"At the ball, we both repeated all the time: 'How tedious it is here.' It was only long afterwards that we were to learn that we had spent one of the happiest evenings of our life there. For that's the way it is with all happy days: one regrets them when they're almost forgotten, but when one's living them one says: 'It's cold...I have a headache...let's go...'

"I was in a paper dancing costume, multicolored and striped, and Marco joked: 'I'd like to light you like a match to cheer up this dismal soirée.'

"The evening was madly gay and I had forced Marco to dance. Then we smoked, slightly drunk. Then we went home. It was raining. There were no carriages. The paper of my tutu was in a lamentable state. We were soaked to the skin. A sad first light was rising when we arrived at my door. I was shivering. Marco said to me: 'I'll warm you up by taking you in my arms.' And immediately, the rain, the blinking gaslight, the desolate daylight, the decor of five o'clock in the morning through which the milkmen were trailing all became, for me, a splendid dawn."

And Jacqueline gazed at that dawn, through which masks of all colors were passing, on the ceiling, amid the luminous smoke.

"Another Pall Mall, Jacqueline?"

"Do you recall the fête at Neuilly, and the roundabout, and the argument that started between Marco and me because he no longer wanted me to mount one of the wooden horses? He claimed that there was a man who was standing there because of me, in order to see my leg in passing, and that I was drawing up my dress a little, deliberately. That was the blissful time when he was jealous. And I rode the wooden horse anyway, and the man stood there, and Marco, because of you, didn't want to let all his jealousy burst out.

"And afterwards, he repeated: 'What do I care, anyway, that a man was looking at your leg?' But afterwards, when we went home, he clasped me in his arms so tenderly! And that

67

evening he admitted to me that he had suffered because of the unknown man that I hadn't even looked at."

How many memories there are in Pall Mall smoke!

"Do you recall the scene with regard to the letter from his former mistress? And the restaurant in the Rue des Martyrs? And the evening at the Médrano circus when Gugusse threw me on the sand? And Lily's bar? And the engineer who made me a gift of a pocket electric torch?"

The blue spirals of the Pall Malls doubtless made that last image more precise, or the pocket electric torch reminded her of more intimate and sweeter memories, for there was a slight mist in Jacqueline's eyes.

"Marco only smoked Pall Malls," she went on, "so I only like those cigarettes. Do you think that he can find them in Albi?"

"The brand is very widely-distributed, and certainly..."

"If he's smoking a Pall Mall at this moment and gazing, like me, at the rising smoke, won't he be forced to think about the same things?"

"On what do you base that hope, Jacqueline?"

"On nothing. But I firmly believe that our minds can communicate through space via Pall Mall smoke, so I smoke them, in spite of the fact that the tobacco makes my voice hoarse and I don't like the taste."

And Jean Noël marveled and said "There's no point in feeling sorry for women when they're suffering from being separated from those they love, because they have unexpected and secret consolations that are only accessible to their light hearts."

Faults and Qualities

Amour is like measles or typhoid fever. Like those maladies it is communicated by the contact of a hand, an imprudent kiss or visiting someone already afflicted by the disease.

Thus, by dint of hearing Jacqueline talk about her love for Marco, I am gradually falling in love with Jacqueline.

I give her advice. I say to her: "When Marco comes back, it's necessary to be more coquettish with him. It's necessary, above all, not to tell him that you love him. Marco always says that he has a horror of cheerful women. In order to conform with that opinion you've diminished your cheerfulness, and your laughter, which once rippled like pure water between the white pebbles of your teeth, is now like a dried-up spring. You've gradually become tender and grave, similar to the ideal that Marco says he had of women. But that might have been an error. Men are contradictory and it's necessary not to take them literally. It was when you were too cheerful for his liking that Marco loved you. It's necessary not to lose that essential quality, which is your mental characteristic in life, in much the same way that if one has hair as dark as night, with a hint of brown, it's necessary not to use henna to produce a hybrid tint. Marco isn't writing to you much at present. To obtain the tender letter that you desire, believe me, don't write him long accounts of your sadness, but simple very short letters in which your fantasy is between the lines, and the frisson of a burst of laugher in the folded paper."

I give this advice in all sincerity. But a perfidious thought sometimes takes possession of me. I have a desire to push Jacqueline to unskillful steps that will make her lose Marco's love. I consider that Marco doesn't deserve the amour of a woman as charming as Jacqueline. I weigh him in a severe balance, and amity doesn't put any weight in the other pan to counterbalance his faults. I list for myself all the petty defects of his egoism, his egotism in regard to women, which ought to put him n the wrong in their eyes.

At the hazard of the conversation I sometimes remind Jacqueline of them.

Marco is sensitive to the cold. He lives in a studio to which a stove, always red hot in winter, gives a fantastic heat. When Jacqueline goes to see him, if she makes it manifest that she is too hot, instead of opening the window momentarily, he cynically stuffs his stove and says to her: "Well, take your clothes off then."

Moreover, Jacqueline sometimes does that, but if she's in a hurry, if she has errands to run or if she has put on a dress with complicated fastenings, she tolerates the heat.

When it's late at night, Marco doesn't like to leave his apartment to see his mistress home. He lives on a deserted boulevard and Jacqueline is afraid of going along it alone. Marco declares that one shouldn't be afraid, hat it's necessary to harden one's soul and even that it's an excellent schooling for that battle to go out after midnight. He adds: 'You have taxis a few paces away, and I'll keep an eye on you from the window."

He knows very well that the taxis are some distance away and when poor Jacqueline goes downstairs at a rapid pace she doesn't even hear footsteps to reassure her that Marco is opening his window.

I recall those petty aspects of Marco's character as jokes of no importance, in the guise of psychological observation.

I repent of it immediately because I see sadness in Jacqueline's eyes and I judge my conduct severely. Then, in order to make amends, I sing Marco's praises. Jacqueline approves, she overbids me, and it ends up as a hymn of eulogies.

And then, I'm entire vanquished when Jacqueline finally adds, blushing and turning her eyes away. "Marco has one quality above all, but I'd never dare to talk to you about that."

The Mystery of Hesitation

Jacqueline's love for Marco had become an unhealthy reverie, a kind of folly. She talked about nothing but him, and at the same time as she multiplies tender words and regrets in his regard, she never ceases to lavish on me all the coquetries a woman can lavish on a man she wants to tempt and by whom she wants to be loved.

To kiss a woman on the lips, even for a long time, when one is lying side by side in the painter Dante's smoking room clad in light kimonos in the midst of people who are also kissing one another on the lips is truly something of no importance, which it is appropriate to forget the next day.

But to kiss a woman on the lips when one is not becalmed in a smoking room, when one has not smoked, when one is simply coming back from the theater, when one is in a vehicle, is a gesture that has another significance entirely.

And if the woman has provoked that gesture by a pressure of the hand or various nuances such as the inclination of the head or the favorable movement of a shoulder, if she has participated in that kiss on the lips as much as a woman can participate, one can conclude that she is animated by a certain physical benevolence toward you.

Now, such things as that happened. I reproached myself. I was animated by hope. I criticized that hope. I subsequently judged it stupid. It was indisputable that Jacqueline loved Marco with an exclusive amour. And yet, there was that kiss.

The next day, there was a letter.

I had not seen Jacqueline all day and I was suffering from it. I wasn't due to see her that evening. I got home at about eight o'clock. She begged me in unusually tender terms to come to see her. She couldn't be alone that night, she said. She needed someone to whom she could talk affectionately. I was the only person on whom she could count. I had to come, even if I got home late, even if the hour was undue. In that case, I would find a key under her doormat. I had to come at all costs.

When one receives such an unexpected letter, of a formal character and which leaves no doubt as to the consequences that it implies, the best thing one can do is leave home precipitately and start marching along the street with great rapidity. That is what I did, and a few young seamstresses returning home burst out laughing when they saw me.

Delight, surprise, pride and dread were strangely mingled within me and were causing me pain. I went at hazard, and my initial momentum took me to the vicinity of the Parc Monceau, at the corner of the street where Jacqueline lived.

I stopped. I perceived her at a distance leaning out of her window. I could make out that she was in a peignoir, and seemed expectant.

I went back down the Avenue de Villiers, retracing my steps with an exact sentiment of the situation.

Jacqueline loved Marco. She only received rare letters from him, brief and insufficiently tender. Either out of spite, or ennui, or the desire to profit from the small sum of joy that life offers us, she had decided to cheat on Marco. She had chosen me because I was there, at hand, because she sensed that I was smitten with her. She would reject me afterwards with horror, and her love for Marco would only be more ardent. For such is the advantage, and simultaneously the defect, of deceit; it causes to stand out more clearly and magnifies the qualities of the person one has deceived.

No, assuredly, I ought not to fall into that trap.

I drew away rapidly, firmly resolved to going back to my apartment.

I stopped for a moment to light a cigarette; I studied a wall full of posters, and a splendid scene struck my eye.

I saw, traced by the brush of the imagination, Jacqueline's bedroom, with its delicate organization and its intimate disorder. I saw the blue eiderdown thrown back and hanging over the foot of the bed, and the dented pillows. Jacqueline's face was rendered more charming by blue rings around the eyes and a great lassitude; her hair was strangely undone, and she was lying next to me.

I felt myself blushing in the solitude of the street. I was no longer thinking about anything but that beautiful image and the possibility of realizing it. I took the path to Jacqueline's house again.

But as I was going along the Boulevard des Batignolles I nearly collided in the gloom with café waiters who were coming out on all fours under the metallic shutter of a restaurant that was closing. And among them there was a memory, and that memory loomed up before me and prevented me from going by.

Once, when I had a mistress that I loved a great deal, I had come to that restaurant with another woman. I had spent the entire time secretly listing the qualities of my mistress, comparing her to the other woman, and the comparison had been so overwhelming that I had been gripped by fury against that inferiority.

The memory of an odious evening rose up before my eyes, saying how pitiful the role of that companion of an evening had been: a role that I was about to play myself.

I resumed deliberating.

Everything is turned upside-down and the universe is depopulated by a great catastrophe. What will happen to us in such circumstances? The usual moral roles no longer count. The old reasoning no longer has any value. If a pleasure is on offer it's appropriate to take it, since we don't know what dolors tomorrow has in reserve for us.

With the light nocturnal breeze, an immense appetite for pleasure blew over me. Jacqueline appeared in my thoughts. It seemed to me that my mouth as about to make contact with her laughter and her teeth, and I resolved, definitively, to run to her house.

But I had wasted a great deal of time.

I arrived. The window was shut, and there was not the soft light filtered by curtains that is the sign of presence.

I cursed my hesitations a thousand times. I thought, however, that it wasn't late, and that Jacqueline had told me to come even if it was very late. Her key would be under her doormat.

I went up her stairway. The key was indeed there. I went in quietly.

I said: "Jacqueline!" in a low voice.

No one replied. I dared not witch on the electric light and, with a match in my hand, I gently turned the handle of her small drawing room. I saw by the light of the flame the portrait of Marco on the mantelpiece, a little table where there was a tea-cup, a book on the floor and two tiny slippers near the divan. The match flickered and went out just as my eyes went to look at the divan.

I lit a second.

And the second match showed me Jacqueline, who was asleep on the divan. She was deep in a delightfully peaceful and child-like slumber. Her face did not reflect any disturbance desire or amour, but a perfect serenity. The laughter of her admirable teeth was sensible behind her calm features, and the great peace of her heart and her senses. I had the invincible sentiment that if I advanced, if I took her hand, and if I sat down beside her, she would utter a cry of fright, would not remember her letter, and would throw me out angrily.

A bare arm emerged from the peignoir, terminated by a delicate hand. But I did not have the leisure to gaze at it, because the second match went out and left me in darkness.

And I saw clearly in that shadow, where Jacqueline's amber perfume reached me, mingled with that of her flesh, what it was appropriate to do.

And the third match illuminated an individual who was carefully replacing a key under a doormat and descending a staircase precipitately.

The Influence of the Depot on Amour

"I've never asked you for any favor," said Jacqueline. "Do this one for me. Leave right away."

It was a matter of going to see Marco at his depot in Albi, of finding out why he was no longer writing to Jacqueline, of finding out whether he no longer loved her, whether it was all over.

Albi is a distant town, and my conscience, with regard to Marco, was not entirely pure, for I reproached myself in spite of all my bad intentions. I thought that the step in question ridiculous for someone who was smitten with Jacqueline.

However, I went.

I was animated by a joyous illusion that the tedium of the journey would be compensated by the joy that I would cause Marco. A man who has been living a long way from Paris for several months, I thought, far from his mistress and his friends, would make a feast out of seeing a representative of his past life. How many questions Marco was going ask me! How many annoyances he was going to depict for me! How he was going to insist that I stayed in Albi for a few days!

And already, I had made up several excuses in order to be able, without lacking amity, to leave again the next day.

Like every petty provincial town, Albi is a marvel of silence, shadow and lassitude, and the experience of present days shows us that even a world war cannot succeed in troubling it. That force compounded of old town houses, venerable trees bordering avenues, paving-stones between which plants are sprouting peacefully, is immutable, and there is no human movement that can disturb its calm. The people participate in that peace, which is transformed in them into slowness and indifference. Thick mosses also grow between the paving-stones of their soul, and the avenues of their thoughts become long and cold, with a low shade that darkens them.

At the hostelry of the Grand Saint Antoine, into which I booked before I had succeeded in saying a word to Marco, two laconic lines from him told me I ought to be at the Café Glacier at five o'clock in order to see him.

At six o'clock I was still waiting for him to arrive, in a melancholy fashion, and I was wondering what punishment could have retained him when he appeared before me.

"Excuse me," he said. "That's an hour that I see you've found tedious. I was in the café opposite, over there, but, you see, I was having an aperitif with Barbas, my adjutant..."

"Barbas!"

"Yes, Barbas, whom I've often mentioned to you in my letters. We're intimates now. He's my adjutant and my friend. So I couldn't leave him."

And without asking me the slightest question about Jacqueline, about me, or about our friends, without even talking about the war and its probabilities, he delivered himself to long considerations of the importance of the amity of Barbas, about Barbas himself, about his intelligence, about the role he played in the barracks, about what he had done before being in the regiment, about his projects and about his mistresses.

The captain was a worthy fellow, of taciturn character, who didn't care about anything. Barbas defined him very well in saying: "Fundamentally, he's timid." But there was one thing that was very serious. The lieutenant didn't like him—him, Marco. For a long time he had wondered why. Barbas had explained everything in a confidential fashion: "The lieutenant doesn't like the sons of families, because he's jealous of them." Marco was the victim of the lieutenant's jealousy, there was no doubt about that, but in the end, the essential thing was to be Barbas' friend.

I strove to turn his mind toward other images, but he embarked on a topic of capital importance. That was the history of his relations with the major and the present state of his relations, as well as the major's psychology.

It was very long. I finally succeeded in mentioning the objective of my journey and Jacqueline. At that moment,

Marco's face, which I was studying, changed completely His eyes widened, his mouth opened, an expression of joy—slightly stupid joy—was painted on his features. Was it Jacqueline's name that had caused that change?

I thought so. It was nothing of the sort.

A shadow extended over the aperitifs that were in front of us. A soldier was standing beside our table. He was not clean-shaven; he had a long, thick, drooping moustache and a vulgar appearance.

"It's Barbas!" Marco exclaimed. And he introduced me to Barbas, who was glad to shake me by the hand and say: "You're passing through Albi?"

It happened, as he explained to Marco, that he was dining with the great Renée and had come to fetch Marco to have dinner with him.

Doubtless that desire was equivalent to an order, or an inestimable pleasure, an amicable windfall, for Marco leapt up, renounced without hesitation the dinner that we were to have together, and, careless of the long journey undertaken to see him, the things we had to say to one another, in memory of Jacqueline, he took my hand.

I insisted on seeing him that evening, saying that I was counting on leaving the next day.

He did not find my stay too short; he did not suggest that I could stay another day in order to see more of him, and told me that he would have half an hour to spare at half past eight before returning to the barracks.

"I can't refuse to dine with Barbas," he said to me, as he left.

But I understood, on seeing his haste and the sight of his back while he was drawing away with Barbas, that it was a matter not of an annoyance but a pleasure of a superior order.

"Old man," he said to me in the evening, "I'm very glad, in sum, that you've come. You can sort out everything with Jacqueline."

"What is there to sort out?"

"She's too cheerful a woman for me. If you recall, I told you that at the beginning. Jacqueline laughs too much. Now I'm far away and I'm taking advantage of it to break with her."

"But she loves you."

"That's not of any importance. What is desirable and marvelous about amour is to love oneself. To be loved is something it's necessary to dread. The amour that is given to you it's necessary to protect like a sacred fire, to transport it like a heavy burden, to watch over it like milk that might boil over and overflow. Jacqueline loves me. That's a peremptory argument that drives me to put an end to the liaison."

We had left the café and I was accompanying him back to the barracks. He was speaking with a confident cynicism.

"When one wants to leave one's mistress, what it is it that usually prevents you from doing it? The sight of her tears, the scenes, and also because one's habituated to her, the ennui of finding oneself all alone in the evening. None of those sanctions can be applied to me. I'm taking advantage of a unique opportunity."

I represented to him the extreme egotism of that theory.

"Egotism," he said, "is nothing but the ingrate and decried form of altruism. Wouldn't it be egotistical for me not to liberate Jacqueline from a lover who was agreeable to her yesterday but will be odious to her tomorrow, since I'm a different man, with other tastes, other ideas and who would probably displease her? At the price of a temporary dolor, I'm returning her to the unexpectedness of life, the possibility of new and greater joys. The rupture is, fundamentally, the most useful thing about a liaison."

We had arrived at the gate of the barracks.

"But for the moment, what will become of Jacqueline?"

A real surprise was painted on Marco's features.

"What? But aren't you there? Take her. I give her to you."

And he extended his hand to me.

A New Form of Camaraderie

What can you do when a charming woman passes by and smiles at you from behind her furs, except follow her in order to take account of that unknown sympathy? And if she is going the same way as you, it's appropriate to rejoice in that providence, which conciliates both your occupations and the unexpectedness of a pursuit.

There is nothing to deliberate if the charming woman goes into the same building to which you are going yourself, and if, in the obscurity of the stairwell she makes a sign, confusedly, that there is room for two in the elevator.

What can you so in that little errant cube in space, if you sense a favorable smile floating toward you and even if no words come to your lips, except take the risk of putting your arm under your neighbor's?

What can you do if that arm doesn't resist, if there is even a little pressure in your direction, if not move closer, to the point of feeling light hair next to your face?

Those are things that happened to me as I was going, with an exceedingly sad heat, to Jacqueline's heart in order to tell her about my journey and the result of my mission. I loved her too much to bring her the truth unsparingly and cause her a profound distress. I didn't love her enough to attempt to console her entirely, for my pride rebelled at the idea of taking a mistress who still loved my friend, and whom the latter no longer wanted. I was going to see her full of irresolution and without knowing exactly what explanations I was going to give her.

And when the elevator stops abruptly and one is in the situation I have described, what can you do except take advantage of that shock to kiss a neck in perfumed furs?

"I haven't asked you what floor you're going to," said the charming woman, with a burst of laughter."

"I'm going to the fifth."

"We're on the fourth. Come and have a cup of tea with me."

And I was beginning to have a very poor opinion of a woman who had such a great liberty of conduct when, only then, I recognized Chinette.

"Yes, I've left my town house and I've taken on a chambermaid again," she told me, while the latter was serving the tea. "What do you expect? The war is so long!"

I explained to her that I was going to see Jacqueline, who lived above her, but she assured me that there was no urgency, and I believed her.

"I welcomed you so coldly once, at the beginning of the war, that you didn't want to say hello to me today! As you see, I've become the Chinette of old again, and I no longer sweep my own apartment."

I asked her for news of her friend. She replied to me that he had a deferment, that he was in the vicinity of Paris, and that he was still a very tedious man.

What can you do when it's necessary to part company with a charming woman and you have no desire to do so?

I perceived soft footfalls moving about in the apartment above. They were Jacqueline's footfalls. There was impatience in their sound.

Chinette heard them too. "These new houses are made of cardboard."

I thought that my mission was very delicate.

"We're going to have dinner together and chat, and you'll only go up afterwards."

The dinner was full of the most amicable intimacy.

Jacqueline must have gone out, because I could no longer hear any noise overhead.

What can you do when you intend to go see someone and you know that they aren't there?

"Jacqueline won't be long coming back. You have only to wait. We'll have plenty of warning, for these ceiling are so indiscreet!"

It's extraordinary how certain women have, to a high degree, a taste for old furniture, and how competent they are regarding styles. That was the case with Chinette, and when she was on that topic, there was no stopping her.

"See how that little desk, which had no effect in my house, takes on value here. Don't you think that mirror is adorable?

I said "Yes" with sincerity, because it was her image that I was looking at in the mirror.

Perhaps Jacqueline had come back without me noticing it, because Chinette's comments on the furniture prevented me from lending me ear to any other sound.

It must have been rather late when went to see a delightful little dressing-table that was in her bedroom. It was situated by the window and, in order to see better, there really was no other means than to sit down on the bed.

That was what we did, and Chinette explained the beauties of the dressing-table to me.

What can you do to prevent a charming woman from going on too long about furniture, when it's late and you're sitting beside her on her bed?

Listening to Falling Slippers

One doesn't know what one is getting into when, while going to the fifth floor of a house, one stops on the fourth to take tea with an old comrade.

The war has created a new state of sympathy. Former comrades are no longer what they once were. They are much less occupied. Solitude and idleness have transformed them, and their camaraderie willingly takes on a sensual form.

I had gone in for a few minutes and I stayed for an entire week. Jacqueline's footfalls over my head beat time morning and evening to the remorse that I felt at leaving her without news. I said to myself: *I'll do it tomorrow*. And tomorrow, the charm of the hours still retained me.

You cannot imagine how difficult it is to maintain a tranquil heart when you are trying to interpret by means of sounds the life that is unfurling above your head. The apartments of modern houses are reproduced in a symmetrical fashion one above another; one knows that one's neighbors take their meals at eight o'clock in the evening, and once cannot doubt, the bedrooms being inexorably superimposed, that they go to bed at ten.

Now, every evening, in Chinette's bedroom, where I found myself, I felt my remorse aggravated by hearing the dull sound of Jacqueline's slippers, which she dropped before getting into bed. That was like two sighs of sadness. Those sighs were afflicted by the uncertainty in which she found herself regarding the treason of my friendship. They were like little regrets for things that had not happened, which she was letting fall from her slender feet into the past.

I would have liked not to hear them. I did my best to forget them. I paced back and forth, I moved objects, I chatted animatedly. What else can one do in a bedroom with an amiable comrade? But there were always a few seconds of silence, during which Jacqueline's slippers invariably sighed.

And one evening, when it was late, I was tired, and perhaps I had already been asleep, it seemed to me, without my being able to affirm it, that the two sighs of the slippers were followed by two further sighs, noisier, and two noises similar to those that two men's boots make in falling on to a carpet.

I listened, propped up on my elbow, with a passionate attention, but I heard nothing more, either in the night or in the morning. I told myself that if someone had been with Jacqueline, a burst of conversation would inevitably have reached me, and criticized myself for me evil thought. But I also told myself that Jacqueline might have employed a thousand precautions of silence in order not to inform of the presence of a man either her chambermaid or neighbors whose gossip she might have dreaded.

I was seized by jealousy, and then I suffered from my injustice. And the following evening, careless of the tender camaraderie of Chinette, I picked up a book and I listened. But Jacqueline was assuredly not at home, for I heard neither the click of a door nor light footfalls over my head.

Chinette fell asleep; time passed. Where could Jacqueline be at this time of night? With him?

And very late, almost in the morning, there was the sound of an automobile in the street, the hum of the elevator, and afterwards, melancholy, I heard Jacqueline's slippers whispering the great sadness of going to bed alone after having tried to amuse oneself, when daylight is about to appear...

The Intervention of Destiny

A moment always arrives when one goes home and one swears to oneself to lead a regular and laborious life henceforth.

That was what I did, and a few more days passed in the greatest uncertainty with regard to the conduct I ought to take with regard to Jacqueline; and those days were troubled by the memory of the sound of heavy boots falling alongside little slippers, without my being able to ascertain whether that noise was the result of a dream or a reality.

And one afternoon, while the problem was still agitating me, my doorbell rang and I saw Jacqueline come in.

Immediately, she stated weeping and fell into my arms.

Marco must have written to her, I thought.

And in her dolor, I distinguished a little solemnity, a little willful convention that immediately made me think that the dolor in question, although sincere and profound, was not forever incurable.

"Marco's dead! Marco's dead!" she repeated, on my shoulder. "And I want to die too. Yes, the day after your visit, his regiment left for the front. And the first day he was felled by a bullet between the eyes. I only learned it a few days ago when I went to ask his brother-in-law for news. A certain Barbas had written to recount how it had happened, and he sent back everything that Marco had on him. There was nothing for me, not a letter, not a word, nothing."

And Jacqueline wept with great sobs. She despaired with all the sincerity of a frivolous and amorous young woman.

Then, I understood how great and marvelous a lie is when it is the consolation of life, the color that permits the road to hope to be embellished and transformed.

And I said: "Marco adored you, Jacqueline. He hadn't written to you? Why? Because military correspondence is

84

monitored and he was afraid of having a black mark because of an irregular liaison."

I spoke without fear of implausibility, with an immense authority.

"Marco adored you. He spent an entire day repeating it to me. When I saw him, he knew that he was leaving for the front the next day, and his last words were: 'I've only ever loved Jacqueline, and if by chance I die in the war, you, our common friend, tell her that...'"

Different Ways of Dying

"Come right away," the chambermaid said to me. "Madame is having such a crisis of despair that she's going to kill herself. I came immediately to warn you."

I interrogated the simple individual who was in front of me. In spite of her evident simplicity, known to her mistress, that simple individual had been interrogated at length, an hour before, on the value of poisons, their power of rapid destruction and the difficulty of procuring them.

That simple being was, moreover, considering me without any sympathy. She estimated that I was one of the causes of the misfortune that had struck her mistress, based on something that she reported to me.

"She said, talking about you, that she would have been much less unhappy if you hadn't been so stupid with her one evening. She added that at present she was capable of anything, even throwing herself out of the window."

While hurrying to see Jacqueline I posed myself a problem. Would she prefer it if her lover was alive but no longer loved her, or dead and had always loved her? The solution did not appear to me to be in doubt, but there are problems that it is better not to solve.

Jacqueline had her hat on and was about to go out. The window was open.

She made me sit down next to her on a sofa and spoke to me with gravity.

"There's no longer a horizon before me," she told me. "It seems to me that I'm surrounded by a great sad and inexorable wall and that my hand encounters cold stone every time I try to take a step forward. The things that once interested me now fill me with sadness. I can no longer read novels, so insipid are their plots. I tried to play bridge the other day, and I had a headache after an hour. My friends' conversations are unbearable. The memory of the happiness I had, and which is lost, is a perpetual torture. So I've decided to die."

As if to plant that decision in her head, Jacqueline traversed her hair with a long nacre hat pin, with which she fastened her hat to her head. She gazed at the effect momentarily in the mirror, and continued:

"Everything is finished for me. I'll never be able to love again. As you can see, I'm very calm. I envisage things coldly, as they are. It's better to die than to live without love. I wanted to poison myself, but it appears that one suffers horribly, and I think I've had more than my share of suffering. The window is open because I leaned out of it just now with the idea that a vertigo might seize me and I could let myself fall. A few seconds more and perhaps it would have been over. What links things together? The doorbell rang. I went to open the door. It was a telegram inviting me to dinner. That changed my mind. I told myself that a woman crushed in the street must be a horrible spectacle. Then I found another means. I want to finish in a numbness, in an intoxication. I shall kill myself by drinking rapidly, with all my strength, the poison known as pleasure. All that life can offer of sensations, I shall seek out and I shall saturate myself with them until I'm consumed and death comes. Isn't that the finest way to die?"

Jacqueline got up.

"You'll excuse me, won't you? I have to go because we're dining early in order to go to the theater afterwards."

"Indeed, Jacqueline, there are different ways of dying, and that one is still the most acceptable."

Voices in the Smoking Room

Tears have flowed in great number, bursts of laughter have fallen silent, others have begin to resound, friends have left, others are dead, others have come back.

Leaning over the little lamp, Miély, the former colonial magistrate, fills a pipe with meticulous care, and his face expresses a calm wellbeing.

He has had a leg amputated.

Having spent several years of his life without seeing the sun and no longer knowing anything of the world than the silence of his closed apartment and the sizzle of opium, he was hurled into the furnace of the war and he fought heroically for months. He recounts how, in the course of a bayonet charge, wounded in the leg by a shell, he spent two days in a trench, and he owed it entirely to the pellets that he had taken with him that he had the mental strength to wait to be rescued.

Now he is tranquil and joyful.

"What a misfortune have I escaped," he says, "and what would have happened if, instead of a leg, it was an arm that had been taken from me? I wouldn't have been able to make up my own pipes. I would have been like a deaf musician or a painter gone blind. Before the war, I spent my entire life smoking, lying on my Cambodian mattress. I was obliged to listen to a thousand sermons from my friends exhorting me to go to the restaurant or the theater, and I sometimes had a certain remorse. Now I'm liberated from amicable discourse and remorse. Thanks to the fortunate suppression of that leg, my life has become just and normal for the first time."

And he aspired a large draught and made somber spirals swirl round the room, which rose toward the ceiling like a sign of gratitude.

Polly and Dolly lifted up their childlike faces and, addressing Jean Noël as if he were particularly qualified to respond, Polly asked:

"When will wars be suppressed?"

"Since humankind has reverted to its initial barbarity," he said, "the best means of suppressing wars, even the sole means, is no longer to give the world warriors, no longer to have any children. Thus amour would be purified, liberated from its only functional role. People could devote themselves, in complete liberty, to the highest of the arts, the one that summarizes all of them, voluptuousness."

"We're absolutely of that opinion," said Polly and Dolly almost simultaneously.

"We'd then be approaching the end of humankind, but it would be a splendid end. The race would be purified in diminishing. Toil would no longer be necessary, for humans would not be very numerous and the reserves would be sufficient to nourish them. Sometimes a child would still be born; its rarity would render it more precious and more refined. It would be welcomed as a belated witness of things concluding. Humanity would be distinguished in an apotheosis of intelligence, and might perhaps attain, in dying, that for which it was born, its maximum of amour and superiority."

Little Marcelle sat up and said:

"That's absurd. It's because there's a very great quantity of humans that there are chances of finding from time to time an agreeable intelligence and an almost possible physique."

"I'm part of the vulgar humankind that thinks that it's necessary to have a lot of children," said the tall Lucienne.

Then, in spite of the fact that her words had no connection with what had been said, Jacqueline, in a kimono that she had chosen deliberately because of its dark color, in order to be in mourning even in the intimacy of the smoking room, declared:

"In sum, during the war, it's men who are favored and women who are to be pitied. Men have the chance of having a varied life, of departing, of seeing the novelty of battles, even of dying. They go by in sky-blue costumes, enveloped by a heroic aureole; they're admired and pampered. But we, whether we're delivered entirely to ourselves far from those we love or because death has deprived us of them forever, don't play any role; we're condemned to an unbearable waiting and we'll find ourselves too numerous afterwards by comparison with men, the best of whom, in numbers and in choice, the war will have scythed down."

"Women have remained in the hearth," said Dante. "They pray that the men might live, but in the distance, the men are dying. The sage would think that the women have the better part."

"We're dying a little every day," said Jacqueline, "of the slow death of enervation and futile hope, and we'll die more after the war of disappointed joy, the time lost and the old age that will come more rapidly because of the harm we've sustained in loving."

"For myself," said Jean Noël, "what has astonished me most during the war is the prodigious facility that women have, if not to forget, at least to enjoy life as if they had forgotten. The marvelous power of pleasure is invincible in us. Scarcely are we overwhelmed by a great dolor than a desire for physical joy, for vulgar joy, rises up in our soul, and that desire is all the greater and of a more common species, as the order of the dolor is more elevated. That applies even more to women than to men.

"Just go to the Bois one morning and go up the Allée des Acacias. You'll see passing by, as of old, the delightful silhouettes of Parisiennes. Follow them for a few moments and you'll see that they're walking with the same lightness, that their little hats are posed just as elegantly in their hair, that their make-up is perfect, that their stocking are silk, that their skirts are as short as could be wished, in the latest fashion, letting their ankles show. Speak to them. Interrogate them. They all have a great wound in the heart, a great chagrin that they will relate to you at length, but you can invite them to tea, to dinner, to the theater. An immense avidity for pleasure possesses them. They have need of excursions by automobile, gossip in gathering of friends, the rustle of dresses in fashionable restaurants. Ask them what they thought and did before the war. The evolution has been the same for all of them and you will see that their ideas have changed in a matter of months, almost exactly as their girlish drams one changed. They began with projects of thrift, of high-necked dresses of the austere life. Like the schoolgirls of yore, they decided to go into a convent, to devote their life to religion. They wanted to devote the time of the war to chaste and religious waiting. But, just as in the days of adolescence, it only required a face glimpsed, a piece of music overheard, for the resolutions to vanish.

"I remember that when I went to see one of my friends at his property in the environs of Paris, when I arrived, I saw marvelous birds taking flight from the threshold of the house. They were immaculately white and they all had, on their quivering breast, over the heart, a large patch the color of blood. I thought for an instant that, mortally wounded, their plumage vibrant and their little bodies traversed by some invisible weapon, they were about to expire before my eyes. But no, they flew hither and yon, and soon came back to peck placidly, in spite of their splendid wound, the breadcrumbs that my friend threw them.

"'It's a species,' he told me, 'known as stabbed doves. It's said that those doves are incessantly shedding their blood, but they generally live longer than other birds of the pigeon family. Stabbed doves! Look at the beauty of their wings, the lightness of their flight, and how the sky is embellished as they traverse it!'

"It seems to me that many women are like stabbed doves. They peck here and there, they have a great bleeding wound, but they've very white and very beautiful, and they can fly very high."

THE TENDER COMRADE

I. The Jade Pendant

A young woman in a bar in Marseille has become intelligent. She has no idea how that has happened. It is as mysterious as the advent of a disease, but much more painful.

A bizarre power of sensation and understanding has taken possession of her; it became manifest, one day, suddenly, in the same way that the vomiting fits and vertigoes that she once had, when her typhoid fever declared itself after she had eaten oysters.

Books have the idea that it was because the organism of the oysters had remained too long in a park with polluted water. But it is better to burn with fever in a hospital and drink sickening tisanes, and to be plunged into baths of icy water, than it is to have knowledge of the relationships between individuals and to measure the miseries of her life.

At Malmousque one descends from the tram laughing, because it seems that the city ends there and that the sun and sea begin.

At Malmousque there is a path lined by carobs where the wind from the sea lifts up short skirts, and where it rains, during the month of September, ruddy fruits like drops of fine terrestrial blood.

At Malmousque there is a joyful painter who laughs at everything, because he has lived a great deal and suffered a great deal. He has the face of a benevolent faun, which lights up when Aline appears to his garden gate, her thin face slightly pink because she has climbed the hill at a run. She is serving as his model and he shouts to her immediately: "Get undressed!" before she has even opened the door.

When one comes back from Malmousque one gazes as the villas surrounded by palm trees, cork oaks and eucalypti, and one sees women sitting on the thresholds with indoor peignoirs, such as one would like so much to have.

When one comes back from Malmousque, one brings back the only money that one has not earned by the labor of amour, and that, if you think about it while the bloody carobs are falling around you, gives you a little pride, a little joy, and an inexpressible melancholy.

How many men there are that one will never know! One goes through the streets with a new dress, a little hat that suits you very well, and one crosses the path of quantities of men who do not look at women.

There are timid ones who prefer not to be in the presence of a desire; there are proud ones who dread their own fury if they perceive a disdainful smile; there are some preoccupied with their business affairs, others who seem to be crushed by their family life; there are poor ones whose poverty envelops them like an atmosphere.

One can lift a corner of the lip, offer the flame of the eyes, even bump into those blind men, but they continue to ignore you.

The sun, on the terraces of cafés, makes the aperitifs sparkle like so many multicolored beacons, but it is necessary to divine the meaning of those gleams. One vermouth-grenadine, with its orange glint, tells you to come and sit down at that table, another warns you to go on your way because of the dangerous reefs that are the evil sentiments of a bearded man. Subtle enigmas that it is necessary to divine in a second, little shipwrecks from which it is incessantly necessary to preserve oneself.

How many men there are whose acquaintance one makes immediately! One hears regular footsteps on the sidewalk behind one, and it is sufficient to stop at the first shop window to hear one of the two or three age-old phrases by means of which men accost you.

There are a large number of them who think that a second and an exchanged glance has been sufficient to seduce you, and who hope that you will follow them immediately and give yourself to them for amour.

There are a large number of them who talk about future dinners, evenings that will be spent together, the theater, and who draw away after a conversation full of promises, and who will never be seen again.

There are timid ones who address you familiarly at once in order to vanquish their timidity and proud ones who are respectful for fear of being put in their place.

There are some who immediately fix a sum of money and others who, either out of delicacy or avarice, allow a doubt to hover over that point.

There are some who take you home, others who don't want to go home with you because they fear some kind of trap, and the majority, who say: "Do you know a furnished hotel?"

If they only knew! There are rooms with numbers over the door whose thresholds one has passed over so many times, whose odor of mildew is very familiar to you! There are the peevish voices of proprietors that rend your heart, and there are dilapidated staircases that one has descended by night, without a match, groping, in order to flee the company of a drunkard.

How many unknown men in whose company one has undressed, how many grotesque, ugly and dirty men, of forms both similar and diverse, what an absence of joy, and what pain every evening!

Lucette lives in the room next door. She is pretty, humble and faithful. Men leave her no memory, and she has neither a liking not disgust for them. They are the useful accessories of her life, and she is complaisant, rapid and silent with them.

But the fidelity of her heart is immense. She is faithful to all beings who are not the men who pay her. She is faithful to her parents, who are in a village somewhere, and she sends them money every week. She is faithful to Mère Loute, her landlady, to whom she makes small presents of cigarettes and bottles of liquor. She is faithful to her dresses, which grow old on her because she likes the form and the fabric and because elegance has no price in her eyes. She is faithful to her room, which she would not want to change, to her furniture, to the photographs arranged on the mantelpiece, which are the modest gods of her simple life.

She is faithful above all to Aline. Often she has stuck her ear to the partition wall and wept, when Aline, forgetting the indifference of encountered arms and the almost unknown face above her, surrenders to the desirous genius of her flesh.

"It's noon, Aline, get up. It'll be two o'clock before you're washed, coifed and perfumed.

"I've slept so well, Mère Loute."

"A little while ago, Madame Rosalie, who has promised you fifty francs for this afternoon, came to remind you that you have an appointment at her place."

"O most charming of landladies, I was sleeping on the embroidery of my pillow and its design is imprinted on my cheek. Give it time to fade."

"Men don't like to wait, and one often misses a good opportunity by being five minutes late."

"Mère Loute. I put the tip of my right foot out of the bedclothes and it's gone cold. A few seconds more for it to warm up."

"Madame Rosalie doesn't always offer fifty francs."

"Did she say what kind of man it is?"

"She only told me the sum."

"What if it's a negro, Mère Loute?"

"There are genteel and well brought-up negroes."

"What if I don't go over there, Mère Loute. I don't need money at the moment."

"But you owe me two months' rent, wretch, and the price of your furs, which I advanced you."

"I can hear the mistral shaking the trees in the avenue. I sense that it's cold outside. Decidedly, I'll stay in bed and my body will be my own all day."

I was born in the village of Valentine, which has a horizon circled by mountains. The houses there are made of red bricks with slate roofs, and the Garonne runs limpid there over blue shingle.

There are leafy poplars there, hundred-year-old chestnut trees and pathways sculpted in multicolored stones, which rise up toward a region of ferns and wild mint, where flocks graze.

Have you noticed that all the women in the life are from another region than the one they inhabit. When one leaves one's village, one can't stop in nearby towns, because one is a minor and your parents, poor as they are, can have you brought back. Then too, one willingly believes that the further away one goes, the more beautiful life is.

I was born in the village of Valentine, of a poor girl and an unknown father. My first memory is of the great bright road under a burning sun, when I was coming back from a fair with my mother, who was staggering, and I was tugging her by the hand and weeping, because I was afraid that she would be run over by the hay-carts and traps that were going past.

One learns at a certain age that life goes on regardless and that other things will follow, but when one is a child, misfortune is devoid of consolation because one has neither a past nor a future.

O little village placed like a pink and white bouquet on the bank of the Garonne, delightful valley of pasturelands, apple trees and vines, I lived my detestable childhood there, and I hope I never see you again.

Mère Loute sells opium and favors the amours of her tenants. She has a good heart, and a little woman in an embarrassing situation always finds good advice in her house, a room on credit, and even a little money.

One glance is sufficient for her to recognize the face of a colonial to whom she can sell the yellow drug without fear, or that of a policeman who would like to catch her *in flagrante delicto* in illicit commerce. She smokes a little, she drinks a little, and, unlike other women's hair, hers is turning yellow instead of white.

She is a good administrator of her furnished house, but she sometimes says: "There's wind in the sails!" and she disappears then for two or three days. She comes back disheveled and fatigued, sometimes bearing traces of blows, and then she says to Aline and Lucette that she has appeased the beast that is in her and that there is nothing true on earth except giving oneself pleasure.

Mère Loute is joyful even when she argues with her maid, even when a tenant had left without paying her, and even when a passing mariner has sold her opium of poor quality.

At fifty, Mère Loute has two young official lovers; in the evening, in select company, she performs grotesque dances to cheer up her friends; she eats a great deal; she speaks familiarly to the local vegetable merchants, and when she sits on the doorstep in the sunlight she laughs by herself at others, at herself and the marvel that is life.

The city is traversed by a river that flows with gold. People crowd the banks, where there are cafés and shops, and everyone tries to collect the subtle errant gold, so difficult to grasp.

The gold circulates without any apparent law, and its possessor is not recognizable by any sign. An elegant woman whose feet bear sparkling ankle-boots and whose hands are jeweled might go along the river without being able to collect the smallest sequin, but some fat man with a thick moustache and a battered bowler hat might be a powerful custodian of that substance by virtue of trading horses or the possession of land.

There are secrets for making gold emerge from the river; but those secrets are not transmitted. They have to be innate. Egotism, cupidity and the absence of a taste for giving: those are the characteristic of the man who knows how to attract wealth. And it is necessary to add to them hard labor, patience and the rare virtue of never giving up.

But some come with a forehead wreathed with a crown of luck, and the current throws treasure at their feet of its own accord. Others are enveloped in a melancholy mist and all good fortune eludes them.

The waves of the river flow pitilessly and the bank is full of cries, appeals and rumors. A little woman is there in the great tumult of the seekers of gold; she does not know the secret law of enrichment; she is always leaning over where it is not, and her open hands only let sand flow through them.

In the mirror in the bathroom I can see myself entirely. A ray of sunlight through the window-panes makes the droplets on my body shine, and one might think that I am covered in pearls.

I have let my hair down over my shoulders. I admire their flexibility and breadth; I caress my breasts, which are straight and hard; I palpate the nap of my skin and I find the line designed by my leg harmonious.

O my body, with which so many men have taken their pleasure, it seems to me that you are as pure as that of a virgin, and when I gaze at you thus under a garment of evaporating water and then close my eyes, my mind loses the memory of all the embraces, forgets the forms, the odors and the cries, and I find an innocent soul!

If the door opened at this moment, and if arms caused my figure to curve by tipping it back, I would have the terror and the sensuality of the first kiss and the first self-abandonment.

But no one will come. I put on my linen chemise, my silk stockings, and my short dress. After having savored my fugitive virginity, I resume the costume and the aspect of a little woman who goes out into the streets and gives herself to men for a louis.

There is something like a great ladder that departs from the earth and rises all the way to the sky, and on the steps are women, differentiated by the emblems and appearances of their wealth.

At the very top there are those one never sees and perhaps do not exist, those who have several automobiles, pearl necklaces and a town house in which they have marvelous soirées.

A little lower down there are women who do not come into bars, or cafés, or smoking rooms: serious women who have serious friends and who live in comfortable apartments in bourgeois houses. They change lovers from time to time, but they do it without difficulty and without searching, by virtue of the natural play of things.

Then there is a vast crowd of women whose liaisons, by virtue of the mystery of their destiny, are marked with the seal of brevity; they only acquire small sums of money; porters and barmen give their addresses to clients who ask for them; they are always free for dinner or to spend the night.

They are an unfortunate population, elegant, perfumed, agitated, and a great distance separates them from women who are on the lowest rungs of the ladder. The latter are creatures of Hell, the grotesquely made-up demons, clad in garish clothing, who inhabit the dives of the old port, the whores of sailors and soldiers, perpetually menaced by a dagger-thrust from a drunkard, the police and the hospital.

A powerful hierarchy distances these beings from one another, causes them to hate and fear one another, for those lower down are jealous of those higher up, and those higher up do not even want to think about their inferior sisters, in order that the idea should never occur to them that they might one day descend as far as them.

A man with a jaundiced complexion, with a cap, follows Aline when she goes through the streets. He walks with his hands in his pockets, waddling slightly, and he sometimes approaches her and offers to buy her a beer.

She refuses and walks more rapidly. Then he sniggers scornfully and darts a glance of hatred at her.

One evening, in a dark street, he caught up with her, grabbed her arm and spoke to her very close to her face, saying that he wanted to have her and that she had to let him.

Aline saw his red wrinkled eyelids, his unhealthy complexion and respired his noxious breath. It was as if a sewer had sent him to her to call her a frightful creature, a kind of spoiled beast that he had trapped in passing.

She pulled free and fled. Since then, he has not dared to speak to her again. But sometimes she perceives behind her the man with the unhealthy face, with his red swollen eyes, watching her from a distance.

One goes up an interminable boulevard, one turns right into a street where there are only walls in front of which empty barrels are aligned, and one finds a poor little house whose unique ground floor window has shutters with an opening cut out in the form of a cross.

Aline sometimes comes that far at dusk. She goes to visit Père Donic, a workman who labors in the shipyards and goes home every evening to the room in which he lives alone.

He is from the village of Valentine and he knew Aline when she was little.

He is not astonished by the freshness of her face, the elegance of her costume or the incongruity that enables that charming form to appear in that sad domain of gray walls and lined-up barrels. He does not put two glasses on the table because he is sober. He says very little; he lights his pipe and he remains motionless, sitting in front of Aline.

They only exchange remarks of an extreme banality and sometimes they say nothing at all. Something, however, brings them together. The old workman never asks Aline to stay for dinner. Perhaps he would have liked to do so but has not dared, or is ashamed of his primitive manner of eating.

When Aline goes away and she looks back, she sees in the great sadness of the district the light that makes two red crosses on Père Donic's shutters and she knows that those crosses are the sign of a little amity that resides in the disinherited quarter of the city.

Once, only serious and discreet people came to Madame Rosalie's house, but the war has overturned everything, and now Madame Rosalie welcomes foreigners, English or Serbian officers, men that one will never see again and who stop for an hour of pleasure before embarking for Salonika or elsewhere.

Madame Rosalie flatters herself that she would be able to bring to her house, in accordance with the epoch and the price, all the women in Marseille, even those who are married and have an unassailable social reputation. In reality, she only disposes of a few little women like Aline and her friend Lucette, whom she passes off as the daughters of naval officers killed in the war.

Madame Rosalie has three rooms with three cabinets that she furnishes with an extreme magnificence, and in those rooms the daughters of naval officers encounter for an hour men that they do not know. In the first room here are so many mirrors that one cannot make a movement without seeing oneself under all aspects. That has the advantage, when one lies on the bed, of believing that one is not oneself, because one does not recognize one's own form. What is striking about the second room is the austere faces of Madame Rosalie's old parents, whose portraits are on either side of the lavatory door, as if to attest that that place is the abode of a respectable bourgeois society.

But Aline prefers the third room because that is the one where the electricity, because of a fabric lampshade, only casts a faint light. And she knows that gestures of amour that one has no desire to accomplish are a little less sad when there is more shadow.

And then, some unknown hand has engraved on the mirror a heart pierced by an arrow. And in spite of everything, that ridiculous emblem, when she looks at it and when she touches the design with her finger, evokes momentarily for her a genuine embrace and a genuine kiss.

O Lucette, how can a creature as insignificant as you weep so many tears? On the narrow and obscure landing where my door opens alongside yours, I hear you in the midnight silence of the furnished hotel troubled by the creaking of the stairs, stifled sighs and the sound of ankle-boots being deposited in a corridor.

I picture your solitude and I suffer therefrom, because it makes me think of my own. Should I knock and say my name? I know that you have lain down on your bed in your customary pose, your mediocre face lost in the pillow and your impeccable body offered without modesty to an invisible friend.

With what ardor you would embrace me immediately, O little friend, in such haste to taste the voluptuousness for which you do not even think of preparing by means of tender words. How can you hide so much sensual fury behind eyes so devoid of luster, beneath such an attitude always so modest?

I would like to console you for your chagrin and also avoid that which I shall experience as soon as I switch on the electric light and sense the weight of the darkness around my empty room. But why are you so hasty and so violent? I would like to sit next to you, to hold your hand, to speak to you as a good comrade and then leave you. But no, that would be impossible. Am I going to listen to the sound of your tears without pity, then?

The electric light goes out abruptly. I am even more alone in the darkness. I think about your smile of you when you see me and while my left hand strikes three little raps on your door my resigned right hand begins to unfasten my corsage.

At about five o'clock, in the little bar not far from the port, the gems of cocktails light up. Those temporary and multicolored flames are born, run and disappear, giving a brief warmth to the individuals sitting on stools.

There are English officers who come in search of women for the evening and who burst into hearty laughter at the slightest word on no matter what subject. There is a very correct man who engages in conversation very easily, who is a policeman who has come to catch the barman *in flagrante delicto* selling coco and opium. There is another one, very handsome and also very correct, who makes the most of his stature and the lines of his profile, who is like a god with a blond moustache and who is internally eaten away by money worries and the hateful desire to find a woman who will maintain him. There is a pale and rich young man who comes in leaning on the arm of a woman no less pale, who has short hair and is carrying a light cane. The woman sometimes goes away taking Lulu, the tango dancer, and then the young man draws away a petty actor who is there eternally and whom no one has ever seen on stage.

There are numerous and varied women. There are a few who are naturally cheerful but who become sad and weep at the first cocktail, but mostly there are sad ones who become cheerful when they have had a drink. The bar is the house to which one comes to buy crepuscular forgetfulness, the courage to dine with tedious people and to confront the uncertain and carnal things that the night has in store.

There is Lucette, who is the most insignificant; Totote, who is the most heavily made-up; Rosette, who is the ugliest; there is Jeanne the miser; Lydie, who goes with anyone; Julienne, who is sage; Marcelle, who listens perpetually to the hoarse cough that emerges from her chest; and Aline, who senses every day, through the smoke of cigarettes and the noise of conversations, rising within her, the cruel gift of clairvoyance.

Is there anything sadder that awakening by night and seeing in one's room the light of a street-lamp filtering through slightly-open shutters?

How tedious everything that is going to happen the next day seems then! What a lack of appetite for life one has! One has a novel on one's night-table, but it requires a good deal of courage to light the lamp and find the page at which one had set it down.

A common aspect, and common manners, that is what Aline reproaches in all the people she knows. She sees them file past in the tremulous light of the street-lamp, with their stout hands on which there are tawdry rings, their goggle-eyes and their excessively thick necks.

One gets used to the hotel room, to the restaurant food, to garments that are too tight or too large, why can one not get used to the vulgarity of people, and what is this dolorous gift of sensing it more every day? Why do certain stupid or vulgar words remain planted in the soul like little poisoned arrows, and why does her memory, with a kind of malignity, revive the wound by remembrance?

Where are the charming and delicate people that she imagines, and will she ever be admitted into that imaginary elite?

And when she goes back to sleep, at the hour when the street-lamp begins to pale, she carries into her sleep the sensation of a kiss that will be neither abrupt not brutal, and which will be confounded on her lips with the flight of tender phrases.

It is a fine evening for Aline when Miély, the former colonial administrator, invites her to his smoking room. The domestic he has brought back from Indo-China comes to tell her in the morning, and she never fails to go to that rendezvous, for she finds conversations that she likes and the physical and mental mildness that opium gives.

Miély does not talk much, but he takes pleasure, on certain evenings, in hearing others talk. He never leaves his apartment, and his life only commences at nightfall. He says, in fact, that daylight exercises a pernicious influence on the mind and that the wise ought to avoid, above all, the radiance of that excessively bright star.

He has large blue eyes, and a glabrous and slightly wrinkled face; he is gentle and indulgent. Clad in a long Chinese robe, he lives on his Cambodian mattresses with his books and his pipes, by the light of the little lamp in the smoking room.

He has lost a leg in the war, but one could visit him for a long time and not know that, because he is only seen lying down, under silks on which dragons are embroidered, eternally making up pipes with the same gesture, with a silver needle.

He is ignorant of the desire for women. He shows them an extreme courtesy when they visit him, but never, even very late, at the hour when opium has created a great sympathy, does he makes a gesture toward hem. It is said that there was once a drama in his life involving a Vietnamese girl that he loved dearly, but no one knows for sure.

"The love of a man for a woman," he says, "is, like the sun, a deadly element in the world. In order to be superior we ought to tend equally toward darkness and chastity."

But sometimes, in his bright eyes, for a second, a warm and vivid light appears, immediately extinguished by the blue and black smoke that he blows out copiously, like a memory.

"My little girl," said the painter of Malmousque to Aline, "don't go to the smoking room of the former colonial administrator Miély. When one is made like you, it's necessary not to tarnish your luminous skin in that opaque atmosphere, near those faces the color of tar. An opium sweat will get into your hair, penetrate the pores of your skin, and give you an odor of Chinese earth.

"Look out there in the garden, at that cork-oak from which the bark has been stripped. It's all white, like a young woman without clothing, with thickset body and a enormous head. If you only look at it for an instant, you only see a human caricature that nature has designed with a tree. But if you examine it more carefully, for longer, as one does with anything when one wants to see the life in it, you'll perceive that the cork-oak is comical and frightful, pitiful and good, that by virtue of the prestige of the light that bathes it, it evokes a thousand thoughts in you, and you'll love it.

"The sun makes the world lovable, because it enables us to see all its aspects. Woe betide the nocturnal beings who shun it and seek artificial dreams next to a lamp. The field of their thought is limited to the little room where they smoke and they become the prisoners of their obsession."

The painter Fortune stopped. He put down his brush; his faunesque eyebrows lifted, and he started laughing in admiration.

"At this moment I'm the witness to a miracle. The sun has rotated and is bathing your breasts and shoulders. You can't imagine what a roseate and yellow magic that makes. It's so dazzling, the outburst of such an unexpected prism, a beauty so great that I no longer even have the desire to reproduce it, so implausible is it."

He takes two or three steps, comes to touch the miracle, caresses it momentarily, laughing, and then says:

"No smoking room, eh? That's a promise. Dreaming, amour, it's necessary to do everything in the sunlight."

Either because he had only invited her or because the others invited had not come, Aline was alone that evening with the former colonial administrator.

They were silent but, thanks to the magic of the blue and black smoke, the silence around them was not heavy. And Aline knew that men are similar, even when they are supposed, like Miély, to have attained wisdom; she knew that their actions are the same when they are alone with a woman like her and that it is only the preparations that differ. She had smoked, her kimono was gaping, and the resignation as o what might happen was mingled with the softness of mild intoxication.

But the hours passed without her being able to calculate them, for it is an effect of opium to suppress the notion of time, and no caress troubled Aline's physical quietude.

And, very late, the former colonial administrator stood up and went to take from an old Chinese cabinet a little sculpted jade pendant suspended from a chain, which he put around his companion's neck.

"My friend Yong Lou," he said, "who was a mandarin, a relative of the Emperor and a great literate, gave me this little jade talisman. He often said to me: 'The unique and divine gift is the constant determination to acquire more intelligence.' Keep around your neck that insignificant object, but to which the age attached great importance, in memory of that assertion."

II. The Passage of Happiness

The face of the man with the square jaw was profoundly engraved in Aline's mind, as certain faces are engraved that one sees in a railway carriage, which one is inexorably obliged to contemplate during the hours of stupidity and baseness, and which reemerge thereafter from the depths of memory to obsesses you.

Aline gazed at the short-cropped hair, the fixity of the eyes, the overly large collar, the cravat in poor taste, and a great repugnance came to her for that inferior and evil being whose desire she felt upon her.

There was in the man's gaze the choice of the restaurant to which he might take Aline to dine, the estimation of the sum that the evening would cost him, timidity and villainy.

The atmosphere of the bar was dense and the odor of tobacco impregnated everything. Lulu's laughter was audible, as well as an argument over a card-game, the clink of glasses and bottles.

The opaque air was giving Aline a headache, which became a lassitude, a discouragement, in which disgust for her life as mingled with the desire to abandon herself to it entirely. One second more and she was going to respond by means of an engaging gaze to the mute invitation of the frightful man.

Then the door, opening, allowed a current of air to penetrate that made her shiver, and happiness, without warning, came into the bar and came to sit down beside her.

Happiness is an individual who speaks and tells you things that you know, since you have them within you, and to which you reply: "Yes, I'm like that myself...," and yet things that you did not know, since you have the sentiment that they have been suddenly revealed to you.

Happiness is an individual with an unexpected face whose gaze is familiar. He says new things that one marvels at hearing with all the more pleasure because they are beautiful, with a beauty in which one participates. He shows you that you are more intelligent, more sensitive and more charming than you thought. He elevates you in your own eyes. He parades over you a kind of light that magnifies your qualities and your faults. One could call him the illuminator.

And if he squeezes your hand a little, if he tells you on quitting you that he is glad to know you and that he counts on seeing you again, the banality of those words is adorned by a sort of magic, and you sense in your redoubled solitude that a noble and subtle element has disappeared, an element that evokes certain books, pieces of music, landscapes, something so rare and so ungraspable in such a poor life!

"You see, Mademoiselle, what we suffer from is not having the faculty of choice. When one thinks about amour for the first time, at the age of fifteen or thereabouts, one senses clearly that there is a host of individuals on earth that one might love, and with whom one might be happy.

"I recall that once, in the little town of Villefranche, there was the possibility for me of a charming mistress in almost every house. When I passed along the main street, the smile of the physician's daughter and the glance of the pastrymaker constituted certain promises, a flood of hopes. I lived in a rustic place, full of mediocre women, as upon a rich treasure of amour.

"But as one advances in life one becomes harder to please. The faculty of admiration is worn away by admiring. It's necessary to go to a great deal of trouble to find individuals susceptible of being desired, and when one perceives them in the distance, it often happens that one can't attain them. It's necessary for hazard to be good enough to put you in the presence of one of those charming individuals, who become rarer and rarer as the years pass.

"Who knows? Perhaps a moment will arrive when there are no longer any more than two or three women on the surface to the earth that it would be possible for me to love. And if one of them is in Australia, the second in China and the third has a lover she adores, what would become of me then?"

Aline's hand was near to his, and Jean Noël took it affectionately

"Everything goes well until the moment when day declines. One has occupations. One has lunch. There are cigarettes. There are books. But when night is about to fall and one goes out into the streets, along with the clack of the shutters of closing shops, the flight of little seamstresses away from workshops, there is a collapse of resolutions.

"To dine alone is impossible, dining with one's friends appears odious, dining with serious people or one's relatives seems monstrous. One requires a feminine sympathy at all costs. But at seven o'clock in the evening all the sympathies are organized and the solitary man can only have hope in the unforeseen.

"Do you believe in the unforeseen, Mademoiselle? It's a very capricious power which is only manifest very rarely. Just now I made a sign to a cab-driver and I gave him the address of one of my friends. Did he mishear, or was he, beneath his overcoat and muffler, the modest conductor of a beautiful hour that was about to come? He set me down outside the door of this bar. I renounced my visit and I came in, seeing it as a little indication of destiny. I saw you and I had the sensation that you were waiting for me and that I was late for a rendezvous that had been fixed or me by subtle words that no voice had articulated and that instinct nevertheless perceived."

Aline's hand made a movement as if to withdraw, but Jean Noël held on to it and squeezed it lightly in his own.

"It's a marvelous thing to have a little hand like that. One only has to take off one's glove and place it negligently on the table to make it known around oneself that one has a nervous and tender nature, and that one belongs to a refined race.

"Chiromancers see in the form of the fingers and the lines of the hand the influences that the planets exercised over us at the moment of our birth. Assuredly, I could tell you your character in the slightest detail, and make a thousand predictions for you, if I examined that little hand with care. It has sufficed for me to feel its warmth to know that it contains anxiety and sensuality.

"No, I know what you're going to tell me and what you aren't going to tell me. The hand is a curious summary of the entire being. One cannot take anything with a hand; one can only give. Whatever is the best in us, we transit it by means of the hand. For as long as yours remains in mine, a current of sympathy will come to me, an unknown radiation by which I will be bathed. And when you take it away, I shall suddenly be alone and abandoned.

"Already, you say, and in such a short time? And you laugh. Time doesn't exist. One knows in an instant or one never knows. That that is why I feel this evening that I am next to a childhood comrade with whom I've often played hide-and-seek and I've already kissed frequently."

And Jean Noël lifted Aline's hand to his lips.

"I've sometimes heard it said that a seller of little balloons for children had been lifted into the air, on a very windy day, and that it was necessary to call a sharpshooter to burst the balloons one by one and permit him to descend without danger.

"I too sold little balloons and I've been lifted by them into the air. I've floated in the clouds. I've traversed the rain and been transpierced by the sun. Now I'd like to come down again without crashing to earth and I'm looking for the sharpshooter who would like to burst my colorful illusions one by one, and very prudently.

"I beg you, throw the few pebbles that you hold captive in the palm of your delicate hand, skillfully, and bring me back down to earth with all my threads, which are no longer holding anything but the dead skins of my burst balloons."

Aline withdrew her hand gently, not in order to throw a stone but to put on her gloves.

There were stormy raindrops in the street that went *flac!* behind her, and Aline ran. She did not know whether she as running away or whether she was going precipitately toward a delightful goal where she was awaited with impatience. She was simply going home. No one was waiting for her. She was not in any hurry. And yet she was running. It sometimes happens that people start running without reason, under the influence of a rather sharp emotion, either because they think they are hastening the march of time, or in order to put their body in unison with their soul, which is going so quickly itself!

"Where are you going, Aline?" said a little woman named Georgette who was gazing into a perfumer's window in spite of the rain.

The air was very heavy and very damp. The evening clouds were low. The storm was charging the air but did not burst. It was very hot.

Aline remembered that she had to buy rouge, and also matches, but she did not stop, either at the perfumer's or at the tobacconist's.

"Where are you going, Aline?" said Mère Loute, who was turning the corner of the avenue.

Evidently, she was going home. But who could have said where she was really going?

III. The Advent of the First Kiss

"I know him," replied the painter Fortune. "His name is Jean Noël and he's a poet. That title ought to be a recommendation of sorts for you, the assurance that it's a matter of a bourgeois individual of tranquil mores and a timorous and faithful character; for in the times in which we live, the characteristic of poets is that they're good husbands and they go to bed early.

"This one is different; and I can't tell whether I like him more because his ideal differs from such a mediocre ideal. I can't compare him to any other man, and when I'm with him, I don't know whether he charms me or whether his ever-unexpected words are disagreeable to me.

"But as regards you, I'm sure of one thing, and that is that you ought to stay away from him. Why? Because he's a man who loves women and who has ideas about them that are personal to him. For a woman to be happy with a man, it's necessary that he have a constant desire for her, a vague scorn and a visible sense of his superiority. I'm afraid this new friend won't be sufficiently scornful of you and will consider you as an equal, and I'm afraid of what might result from that in your heart.

"Anyway, the words that I pronounce are vain. One asks for information about someone that one is going to love in order to take the opposite part, and the more deleterious the information is, the more the desire is increased. You won't take any account of my advice, and I give it to you with the same sentiment that I experience when I make a gift of a painting to someone who won't have it framed and will relegate it to a corner."

The first sign of amour is that one thinks, if one goes out into the street, about encountering by chance the person that one loves. Two people can spend an entire lifetime in the same

113

city without ever meeting, but a nascent amour willingly bases its foundations on the impossible.

As she opened the door of the patisserie at tea time, Aline avidly scrutinized all the groups. She had not come for the cakes, nor for the tea, nor for the petty intoxication of five o'clock. She wanted to continue the conversation of the previous evening with the man she liked.

He wasn't there. She sat down and she waited for him. The cakes were good, the tea too sweet, her patience infinite. And when, later, the patisserie emptied and she was certain that no one was coming, she experienced a disappointment mingled with a little anger at having been all alone at that rendezvous that no one had given her but to which her appetite for good fortune had brought her, her desire to see a beautiful hazard realized.

For a woman like Aline, who gives herself to everyone with the greatest facility, there is nevertheless one man to whom she would like to refuse herself, and that is the man she is going to love.

It is difficult to refuse oneself when one does not have the habit of it; but Aline senses clearly that nascent desire is a flame that is not ruled by the law of ordinary flames and that it will perish instead of burning if it is fed.

So, when she emerged from the bar at about seven o'clock and she ran into Jean Noël and he asked her "What are you doing this evening?" she replied that she was meeting her friends and that she regretted it but that she could not get out of it.

She saw in the distance the evening that she had to spend all alone, like a desolate plain on the far side of which there was a staircase in a furnished house and a sad bed. But a profound instinct advised her to do that, and she went into that plain smiling, without looking back.

In the poet Jean Noël's smoking room, on the tray with silver incrustations, there are two little statuettes to the right and left of the lamp.

One is a completely white statuette of Aphrodite. Her right arm is raised to the height of her shoulder, her hand is holding a flap of her veil, which she is about to let fall in order to appear naked. She has a rose in her left hand, and there is a split pomegranate at her feet, a fruit consecrated to her because there are as many seeds within its rind as the amours that one can have in one's heart.

The other is a statuette of the Buddha. He is seated with his legs crossed; he has a broad rectangular face, and one cannot tell whether he is weeping or laughing, because he expresses wisdom and, viewed with the eyes of a sage, the joy and dolor of the world are confounded.

The statuette of Aphrodite is in marble, that of the Buddha in jade. The forms of one are perfect, whereas if the other were stripped of his green and black veil, he would seem a risible caricature.

And both of them, so different from one another, on either side of the ruddy lamp, like either side of human desire, consider one another without hatred, for they know, being gods, what invisible thought unites them.

When Aline saw the two statuettes, Jean Noël asked her: "Which of them do you prefer?" She was about to reply, immediately, that it was that of Aphrodite, and Jean Noël was about to smile, but she reflected and hesitated.

And he said to her: "Who could choose deliberately between them? One launches oneself first toward voluptuousness as toward the most valuable thing on earth, and then one stops because of thought.

"Here's a peignoir that harmonizes with the color of your skin and slippers that come from Tunis. Put them on and come and take your place here."

He had indicated to Aline the cushions with yellow embroidery that were on the other side of the tray with silver incrustations.

Like any woman who is coming to a man's home for the first time, Aline thought about the fashion in which the evening would end, and sought slight indications of that end in the disposition of the place and the phrases of her host. When she was installed in the flimsy peignoir amid the soft cushions, only separated from Jean Noël by the narrow tray, she thought that he had only to put down the ivory pipe he was holding and hold out his hand in order to take hers.

Then a great timidity and a great fear came over her. She pulled the flaps of the peignoir down to her ankles. She had the sentiment of neither being pretty enough nor shapely enough. She was ashamed of the words she was about to pronounce, and the form that she was about to uncover.

Having launched puffs of smoke toward the ceiling, Jean Noël put down his pipe and Aline closed her eyes.

But the doorbell rang.

"I've only invited two or three friends," he said.

Whether there were two of them or a large number was all the same to Aline. And it seemed to her that she had escaped a great and delicious danger, and she did not know whether she was disappointed by that or glad.

The friends were charming because they were smiling as if they were accomplices of an invisible action and were saying: No, put yourselves on the same side, next to one another.

And the mild night flowed slowly over the little recumbent group, and slow words took flight, and a languor penetrated the beings, and Aline was very close to Jean Noël, so close that she had the light weight of her head on his shoulder.

But by virtue of a delicate miracle, in spite of the fact that they both felt that a few affinities united them, there was no other tender rapprochement throughout the night than that head posing lightly on that shoulder.

And when, having dressed again in the morning, Aline bid Jean Noël *au revoir* on the threshold of his apartment, she sensed clearly everything that she had left there of herself, and that that night of chastity had been worth more than any caresses.

There are only five minutes that are truly exquisite in all the amours on earth. In the same way that a little before sunrise, during the days of spring, the air takes on, for a few moments, a color and a fluidity softening by virtue of its extreme beauty, that will no longer be discoverable during the day, the atmosphere of amour is only truly pure during the few minutes that precede the first kiss.

The vehicle had traveled for a long time in the dust and the sun. But the first kiss cannot be born among elements that are contrary to it. So, during the first hour of the excursion it was not manifest, although Aline and her companion nevertheless sensed its subtle presence around them

Now they had to their right accumulations of barrels among which raged children were running and shouting. The noises of the port reached them, prolonged by the evening air, and they were cradled for a moment by an Italian song intoned by mariners seated in their boat.

The breath of the first kiss enveloped them at a bend in the road, but it was dissipated by the racket of an electric tram that brushed the vehicle and overtook it. Had it departed never to return? That was possible, for it is a breath of such capricious essence.

The light of the evening became darker and it happened that the vehicle passed alongside a garden from which a tree protruded over the wall. For a second there was a little more freshness and a little more darkness. And under the foliage of that tree where it was so mysteriously nestled, the first kiss abruptly allowed itself to fall, and penetrated Aline and Jean Noël with the softness that they would never find again.

IV. The Unavowed Confessions

"A cigarette?" said Jean Noël.

"She's a charming woman, but she sleeps with all the men she knows."

"All of them?"

"It's a manner of speaking. I mean with all those that are possible for such a thing."

"Do you know that it's the woman I love about whom you're saying that to me?" said Jean Noël, smiling.

The other apologized, and the conversation turned to another subject.

I was born in the Village of Valentine, out there at the foot of the Pyrenees, of a poor inn servant and a father I never knew. I always thought that he must have been a vagabond, for when my mother had been drinking she willingly gave herself to men of the road.

Yes, my mother drank and one can't know what infinite misery that represents for a child. I knew nothing, in the early years of my life, but sad and base things, painful chores, blows received and rebuffs, and I had the sentiment of being, in the scale of beings, inferior to an animal.

I had no humiliation in consequence. The humiliation only comes later, when anyone is attributed a value. And it's perhaps because they have never thought about themselves, because they have never situated themselves relative to others, that the unfortunate are able to support their misfortune.

I even stood, for the fair of Saint-Jean, with a branch of laurel in my hand, in the main square of Saint-Gaudens. I didn't know then that the laurel was the symbol of glory. At that moment, it symbolized for me that I was for hire as a farm servant for thirty sous a day.

Was it because of my paltry appearance? I don't know, but nobody wanted me. I was very sad that evening, still standing in the square, with my laurel branch, which the sun had withered.

I remember that all the money I possessed I had spent to buy a hat and get my railway ticket. The station was sunlit and I looked at the young women who had parents and a house, and who were going home for dinner.

I was carrying all my miserable possessions rolled up in a napkin; my entire fortune was a few sous, and I was going alone, God knows where.

Two horse-dealers who were waiting alongside me on the platform were looking at me with eyes gleaming with desire. When I respired the odor of travel and humanity in the third class carriage my heart failed and I nearly went back. But the newsvendor waved bonjour to me with his hand and his face brightened with sympathy when the train pulled away. That was a great comfort for me, and I thought that the world wasn't absolutely evil.

The horse-dealers had got into my carriage. They didn't take their eyes off me. They were fat and breathing heavily. I was impatient to arrive in order not to hear that panting. I didn't know then that I was condemned for my entire life, to have beside me, in trains, in the streets and in hotels, men painting with desire, like dogs.

People who have not known extreme poverty know nothing of life. They don't know shame, they don't know terror, they don't know bodily dirtiness, and they don't know the greatest evils. They can only have an obligatory pity for misfortunes that have no measure for them.

I wonder how I've been able to descend into the utmost human depths and not remain entangled there. When I cast a glance at the years I've just passed, I see my life as a long road that departs from a little mountain farm alongside a laundry, under the poplars, and ends, after having traversed crossroads where there are furnished hotels, in a brothel.

The great turning point of my life was the moment when a man with hands laden with big rings offered me a hundred francs in a café to go into a house. He showed me the hundred franc bill, and ordered drinks incessantly, talking up the happy life that I was going to lead.

Compared with that danger, neither the police, nor the man who chased me one evening with a knife in his hand, nor my typhoid fever, were anything.

I'm telling you everything, even the base and ugly things, because I have a great need in me for sincerity. I'd like you to perceive my present thoughts and the unfolding on my past life as your own thoughts and your own life.

I'm not afraid of falling in your estimation. It seems to me that your sympathy has washed away the pollution of bad memories from my twenty years.

Because, instead of offering me money and taking me home with you, you spoke to me courteously; because, instead of the gesture of buying me, you made an effort to please me, it seems to me that I've become another woman. I have more value in my own eyes. A door has opened for me which over-looks a beautiful unknown domain, a domain whose existence I suspected, but whose beauty I never knew. I run there now with delight, and it's you who have shown me the way.

I had a lover who made me do the seaside towns. That was the year when I made a lot of money. He took the greater part of it from me, it's true. I gave it to him gladly, because the empire he exercised over me was a form of love.

He beat me at the slightest pretext. He landed great blows on my back, which made me feel very ill, and a friend told me last year that if I had had bronchitis the year before it was because of the beatings I'd received.

He was never tender with me and he never told me that he loved me. But he sometimes had depressions, slight savage sorrows that brought me closer to him and made me love him in order to console him. I knew that he wasn't bad, fundamentally, and that he only beat me because he had a violent nature and he lost consciousness when he was angry.

I left him voluntarily, not because I despised him for living with me, but because I sensed that he didn't love me.

I wouldn't like to run into him. I know that we wouldn't be able to live together again, but I might be able to follow him once.

When one has led a miserable life during one's early years, one keeps the memory of that misery afterwards like a burden that it's necessary to carry, which is very heavy and drags you down.

If I walk along the street without thinking about anything, and someone bumps into me, I look up, and instinctively, I have a desire to put my arm over my face to ward off a blow. In a second, I've become once again a humble little country girl to whom everyone gives slaps.

I sometimes have within me desires for elegance, for success, and I sense a determination to realize them, but I have a chain that binds me to poverty and prevents me from launching myself forward. And if I try to explain to myself why that chain exists, I think that it's because, deep down, I love the poverty that one curses incessantly, which oppresses and causes suffering, but which gives you a taste for life.

I've known a time when nobody loved me. One has bad periods like that in life. No lover, no friend, and even intimacies in one's quarter, in the café where one goes, which contribute to giving you a sensation of general hostility.

Then I had a great stroke of luck. I went into a furnished house in a little street in Nice, and the landlady took a shine to me. She said that she would have liked me to be her daughter. She mended my lingerie, gave me warm wine in the evening and gave me such good advice!

She was a former prostitute who'd retired, bought a furnished house with her savings and a family boarding-house for little women with no furniture and no family. I'd never felt a truly disinterested affection in my life. I loved her for her kindness and I still love her. I consider her as all that life has given me of a family, and when I write to her I put at the head of my letter, not without tears coming to my eyes: "Ma petite maman."

But Aline did not say the things that were pressing on her lips. She was not certain enough of the marvelous power of the truth. She did not know how divine sincerity is, even when it uncovers evil and ugliness, on condition that one does not waste it on the mediocre or the malevolent.

She did not recount her life. She even strove to imagine another full of banality. She described a happy childhood in the home of with parents, then her abduction by a naval officer who subsequently left for Indo-China. He had loved her a great deal and he sent her an allowance ever month, but she no longer loved him at all.

And Jean Noël listened distractedly to that story, either because he had heard similar ones, or because the past of others did not interest him, or simply because he was thinking about something else.

V. Prayers in the Blue Smoke

I would like my beloved to remain there, beside me, for a long time, without touching me. I would like to be able to think entirely at my ease about the happiness of having someone who is my beloved. But that thought is fleeting, and, at the moment when I try to grasp it and savor it, it slips away.

Perhaps I haven't known the greatest happiness in life, and that's why I'd like to think about that happiness in order to fix it more firmly within me. But it is a rule for happiness to be rebellious to the knowledge that one can have of it and to float around you formlessly and without measure.

And then, one is never very certain that happiness really is happiness, that it isn't going to be suddenly transformed and that one is not going to feel very unfortunate in its atmosphere. Thus, there are stormy days when one looks at the heavens and one sees them very bright and very pure but with a slight mist that only adds to their beauty. A few moments pass, one raises one's head again, and one perceives that the sky, previously so blue, is thickly laden with clouds.

I would like my beloved to take me in his arms quickly, in order to be sure of grasping my happiness.

What relationship can there be between a jade Buddha that comes from China and a little woman like me? In the blue smoke, however, it seems to me that the Buddha is smiling at me.

I would like him to start to talk to me and introduce me to the mysterious things there are on the far side of the world. All the men I have known who have lived out there have reported different thoughts, another mentality than the men of France. Certainly, they're no less vulgar with women, but I've had the sensation next to them that their vulgarity is attenuated by the sentiment of the vanity of things, and by a kind of resignation. Undoubtedly they have learned that from the ugly god with the singular smile who is worshiped in Asia.

A great wisdom emanates from him. I sense the indulgence of the jade smile upon me, and the consolation procured by the sense of the immense order of things.

I would like the Buddha to tell me why I'm here and whether I ought to love the man I love.

I would like my beloved not to forget that I've exchanged the flowers that he offered me for the three roses that I had in my corsage. We were in a restaurant and he bought me a bouquet of violets from a little girl. When we got home I gave him my three roses and said to him: "These are for you."

He put them on the mantelpiece negligently without attaching any importance to them. I could have got up, put water in a vase and placed them in it, but I didn't want to have the appearance of caring too much about that little sentimental gift and I'd like it to be him who had thought of it.

But the roses are there, and I sense that they're withering in the smoke, and that they'll be dry and dead in the morning.

And I remember then that he said the other day, half-smiling and half-serious: "I detest flowers. They are to the beauty of the world what the bounty of the sou that one gives to a beggar is. In the same way that the sou dispenses us from any other good deed, flowers with their faded hues dispense mediocre souls from any other love for beautiful things."

I would like my beloved to tell me that he loves me. He hasn't said it to me yet, but that's no reason or him not to think it. There are so many things that are within us that we keep hidden, that we cannot, and don't want to, reveal to the one that appears to us to be the most precious.

He must have said it to a lot of women, through the same blue smoke, in similar nights. The words must be worn away on his lips by dint of having been pronounced. Who knows? Perhaps their sound will be sufficient to evoke for him other faces and other bodies. I don't want my beloved to tell me that he loves me.

His caress doesn't resemble any other. It carries me far away, it cradles me and makes me happy. I see on his face then the furious magic that pleasure gives. But afterwards, when he releases me and I remain beside him, immobile and exhausted, I sense that he look at me covertly and I surprise in his eyes neither fatigue nor sadness, but only curiosity, and then, I would like so much for my beloved to tell me that he loves me!

At about six o'clock in the morning, he lit a cigarette and he wept.

I asked him why and he replied: "Daylight is appearing."

"There's no other reason?" I said.

"Isn't that one sufficient?"

But I persisted, believing that I had done something to offend him.

And he said to me: "There's no sadder folly than smoking a cigarette at daybreak. The smoke is bitter then and memory has lost the beauty of its mirage. One is a prisoner between the fatigue that grips you without you suspecting it and redoubtable slumber. One senses thought escaping you with every blue spiral and symbolically, one deposits little gray ashes, like those of one's dead soul, in the minuscule tomb of the ash-tray."

VI. The Night of the Good Deed

"Only one good deed in my entire life," said Jean Noël. "Is that enough. That's what I thought, and I only accomplished one. But it was a truly good deed, because it wasn't useful to anyone, or to myself.

"When it has been raining and the weather has been cold in Paris for three months, a beautiful warm sunny morning is a delightful thing. One doesn't know that spring as so far advanced, and one suddenly perceives it. *It's stupid*, one says to oneself, *it's arrived without anyone knowing!*

"Imagine the odor of the leaves, a little breath of nature, and the joy of the earth along the fortifications. I was walking with an incomparable intoxication when, in front of a door that I knew, I was witness to an unexpected spectacle.

"A concierge that I knew and whose frightful face, full of evil sentiments, made me turn my head away when I perceived her in the morning, was outside her door, leaning on her broom. And her face, habitually charged with acrimony, appeared to me to be different and transformed. It was the same one, but had become human and sensitive, with lips that trembled and the gleam of two tears under the eyelids, and a magnificence of pity on her jaundiced features.

"And I stopped, wondering with amazement what could be the cause of such an astonishing transformation.

"On the sunlit boulevard a funeral was going by, but a funeral such as I have never seen, and which had to belong to the lowest class of burials. No cortege was following it. No mortuary functionary was preceding it. There was no wreath and no black sheet. There was simply a coffin placed on a cart.

"The cart was jolting, which gave it an even more wretched appearance. It was hastily taking, to I know not what cemetery, an individual who must have died in a unparalleled solitude. Poverty and the absence of amity represent the greatest evils on earth. The sad vehicle was the symbol of it, and its poorly-greased axle had a low and resigned whine.

"My gaze met that of the concierge and, without speaking to me directly, rather speaking to things and to the gods, she expressed her principal thought: 'The poor fellow didn't even have a concierge, then.'

"Then indignation replacing pity, she added: 'Or that woman is a wretch to have let him depart all alone.'

"In that concierge, whom I knew to be a propagator of calumnies, active in malevolence, treacherous and venal, there was, therefore, a professional honor that was never exercised in the domain of material things, since she handed on letters irregularly for the sake of persecution and made false reports to the landlord in order to have people thrown out, but which existed in the realm of pure ideas and which involved respect for the dead, pity for a poverty that she could not have seen.

"I measured that superiority in seeing the precious tears run down the frightful face. That concierge, who had been for me the very image of villainy, was setting me a good example, My dry heart opened to I know not what affectionate tenderness for the unknown person who had died alone, and I started to run to catch up with the jolting cart.

"In the splendor of the sunny day, I went toward a distant suburban cemetery. And the streets had never been so animated, the trams had never made such a racket, life had never been so vibrant.

"Couples whose arms were linked, young men marching in bands, having in their eyes the visible signs of the joy that amity gives and families displayed in doorways attested at the passage of the remains of the solitary individual that there is only happiness in the communal life in which all human effort consists of fleeing solitude.

"And we passed by, he and I, without being noticed or saluted, and we arrived thus at the solemn portal of that beautiful and sad garden of the *Thousand-and-One Nights* that is the cemetery of Saint-Ouen. And without my wondering specifically who the person might be that I was accompanying, and image came to my mind, an image that my imagination did not create and which seemed to me almost to have the reality of a memory.

"The coachman increased his pace and I walked with long strides along an immense driveway bordered by marble and cypress.

"I saw a tall individual, poorly dressed, although in a sufficiently correct fashion, but in clothes that were too large, which seemed not to have been tailored originally for his usage. Zouave trousers and rather long hair gave him the vague appearance to which the humble aspire whose ideal is to be an artist.

"A former laborer who would have liked to become a painter or singer in Montmartre. Timidity and the absence of talent had prevented him from succeeding. A natural goodness keeping away all evil deeds, he had not been able to raise himself up either by virtue or by sin. A charming man, in truth, who had gone past everyone without daring to stop. He had within him treasures of love for people at whom he only gazed from afar, treasures of gratitude for benefactors that ill luck had prevented him from encountering; in addition, a man who inspired no great sympathy because he spoke little and had no definite profession.

"Like everyone, he had had a history. I could only make out the end of it confusedly, an extreme poverty characterized by these symbols: a furnished hotel closet at fifteen francs a month and a total absence of underwear, but habit prevents the suffering of the poor from being agonizing.

"The absolute solitude that had come to him slowly and mysteriously, as old age comes, had been the most terrible evil for him, because the remedy was behind all the doors of his hotel, in all the shops in the streets, on every threshold, and he had not been able to attain it.

"There were, however, two men dressed in black who were waiting for us, chatting, sitting on a bench, in the depths of the cemetery. And I experienced a slight consolation in thinking that by virtue of the administration of matters of death, those two men were placed there in order to occupy themselves exclusively, for a few minutes, with the fate of the unfortunate man that I had accompanied.

"I feared for a moment that they might ask me whether I was a relative, or address some question to me. They did nothing of the sort. The men acted as if I did not exist. They picked up the coffin and he cart drew away rapidly.

"I took a few steps behind them and I saw that they deposited the coffin in a very wide hole. The unknown would only have a narrow place in an abandoned corner. He would repose in a vast grave in common with other human forms. For the first time, he was about to know the companionship of other beings, his fellows, in an amicable tomb as large as the immense earth.

"And I sometimes see the poor and timid man smiling at me from afar in the misty fluidity intermediate between dream and apparition where we imagine that the vain shades of the dead are wandering.

"'You enabled me to taste,' he says to me, 'the sweetness and regret of consolation. What remains of us, contrary to what is believed, retains the paltry human vanities, albeit enfeebled and diminished. Thanks to you, I have been able to take pride in a small cortege that walked behind my remains. In my turn, shall follow you in life, not to protect you, for I am even more timid and futile among the dead than among the living, but in order that you can sense around you, in the great solitude of life, the invisible amity of one who can do nothing. And that will be a great deal.'

"I am very proud of that humble protector. I like to see him marching in my thought, with his frayed collar and his zouave trousers. He represents a good deed so perfect that I have never wanted to accomplish any others."

Then the former colonial administrator Miély raised himself up on his elbow and said: "Actions have consequences that are unknown to us. Who can affirm that the deed one accomplishes that one thinks good might not become, by virtue of unexpected consequences, a creator of evil?

"Good has the same essence as happiness—by which I mean that it is likewise changing and perishable, that it also has its bitterness and its ugliness. In the same way that when one is happy it only requires a word overheard or a memory or the happiness to be effaced, when a good deed in accomplished, one perceives that it has a very sensitive quality, that it is modified in accordance with the warmth or the transformations of the soul, that with an extreme facility, it can become an evil deed.

"And that is why I think that it is necessary to refrain equally from good and evil, as one is protecting oneself from two redoubtable powers that do not exist.

"Near a little lake in Hanoi, on one evening of pleasure, I was able to believe that I was accomplishing a good deed. It was a very long time ago and I had not attained the wisdom that the combination of opium and the years has given me.

"Under the veranda of the procuress Thi-Ba-Sen we were drinking champagne, and everything, apart from the slightly darkened eyes and amber skin of the con-gái, bore a fairly close resemblance and Parisian soirée. There had been dancing, a piano and communal joy, and the avidity for immediate pleasure blossomed in my companions.

"I noticed one con-gái who as making the gestures of amusing herself without appearing to obtain any pleasure. Her distant gaze seemed to surpass the horizon of the little lake and to be contemplating an imaginary landscape. She had very beautiful and very profound eyes and, at a given moment, she rested them on me as if to express her solitude and her sadness.

"I thought so, at least. It was doubtless my solitude and sadness that I saw in her eyes. But on the gaze depended a new life, for that very evening, and forever, I took the little con-gái away with me.

"A little con-gái that one takes from Thi-Ba-Sen's is worth no more than the few piastres that one gives in exchange for her. She is a servant in the house, a companion on the mats on the smoking room, a sensual comrade in the hours of the siesta. One takes her and one gives her up, after a few months or a few years, as one takes a woman for an evening in Europe.

"Now, it happened that my little friend Thi-Nam spoke French fluently, had read books and allowed to appear in her words a soul similar to mine The daughter of a prostitute enriched and married to an interpreter, she had been raised by the sisters, and had learned our customs and thoughts. But her mother was dead and the interpreter had gone away, abandoning Thi-Nam to her destiny. That destiny the procuress Thi-Ba-Sen had taken charge of directing. My little friend claimed that I had arrived at the exact moment of her debut in the life. Naturally, I didn't believe her. I estimated, with reason, that it didn't matter, and that the essential thing was that Thi-Nam was charming.

"She was. I was astonished by the extent to which she was. I admired her facility in understanding everything. Then a notion of duty entered my mind. I resolved to develop Thi-Nam's intelligence, to raise her toward me and make her my true companion.

"It is a great mystery that there are beings who aspire to rise in the human scale, while others descend. It is also a great mystery to know whether the effort toward greater intelligence and knowledge is essentially sublime or whether ignorance and simplicity of the heart lead us more directly to what we believe to be the verity of life.

"Is it necessary to develop thought with what it entails of desires and suffering or, on the contrary, to limit it, because there is a great deal of evil in it? Is there a goal to be attained, a torch to carry further on?

"This happened in the time of my youth. I firmly believed that we ought to go toward comprehension of the world by means of an active mind, as on a sacred path that is enlightened as one advances along it. I had not yet seen the tombs that border it And I did not know that for a few tremulous lights there were great dark spaces.

"Little Thi-Nam wanted to advance along the sacred path and I thought I was undertaking the great good deed of my life in leading her there by the hand.

"The first magical effects of opium are linked for me with the pleasure I had in educating Thi-Nam in the things that I loved. Opposite me, behind the lamp, I saw her extend her thin body in a ke-hao of black silk; I saw her silky chignon, her narrow forehead and her glittering eyes. I savored the profound pleasure of speech that is understood, of a thought that is magnified because it is shared.

"The room in which we were smoking, at Cao Bang, where I had been appointed administrator, was prolonged by a great veranda after which one saw a garden of extraordinary vegetation. Behind the wicker trellis, coconut-palms, rubber trees and areca palms were crowded. The odor of opium mingled delightfully with the vegetal saps. And during the first part of the night, for as long as I talked, the garden was motionless and silent.

"But when we had smoked a great deal, when it was late, our bodies were light and a great voluptuousness came to us from a pressure of hands, then the garden became strangely noisy, the trees agitated, and spoke, and all of them in their voices, which had no precise meaning, were contradictory to what I had said. It seemed that their murmur came from very far away, from the heart of the great Asiatic forests, where the putrescence of roots and wood makes the air thicker, and

132

where there are millennial accumulations of dead vegetation. And that murmur, after the hours in with I had recounted my narrow European wisdom, pronounced a more profound wisdom, inherited from innumerable centuries of the impenetrable Asia.

"Thi-Nam was Catholic, but in the manner that people are out there—which is to say that she mingled in a singular fashion the cult of the Virgin with that rendered to the ancestors.

"In the room, among the ebony furniture, the porcelain, and objects bought here and there, stood the altar to the ancestors, and she sometimes went there to burn little sticks of incense. She deposited presents on it: bananas, a phial of choum-choum and a bowl of rice.

"She also went to mass. She was perpetually filled with terrors. She dreaded Hell, and also dragons, the spirits of the sky. She alternated *Paters* and *Aves* with magic formulae to dive away evil spirits.

"And I went into battle against all those celestial and infernal powers. I elaborated metaphysics for her usage, a history of religions that she could understand. I told her about the long struggle of humankind through the centuries against the gods that did not exist, and its future victory. I informed her that she had within herself the seed of all wisdom and she looked at me with wonderstruck eyes that sometimes seemed to open to a new world.

"She no longer went to mass. The bananas dried up on the altar of the ancestors and she no longer filled the phial of choum-choum that the boy had drunk.

"But in the evening, when we had smoked a great deal and the trees agitated beyond the veranda, then she huddled against me, and I sensed that she was prey to ancient superstitions, the old legends of her race, and I defended her with my arm against the thousands of terrible forms surging from the profundities of the forest.

"Above the areca palms and the rubber trees, however, my voice made itself heard every evening for Thi-Nam's childish soul. She read the books that were dear to me and which I had brought; she renounced without realizing it a thousand details of Annamite fashions; she became similar to a little Frenchwoman in her language and her manner of loving.

"She said that she loved me but I didn't believe her. I had never been loved in France, because of my timidity, my lack of fortune, my mediocre physique. The mere appearance of her love gave me an illusion that became sweeter to me every day. I lived in the happiness that I doubted. My skepticism diminished. I exaggerated the mental prestige that I had acquired over Thi-Nam and the importance of my role.

"Then time passed. Habit created invisible and powerful bonds between us. Gradually, I perceived that I loved the little Annamite girl. The optimism that happiness gave me also made me believe that she really loved me. I had the pride of having animated a bronzed Asian statuette, of having created a companion for myself.

"That lasted until the day that I discovered that she was deceiving me with a sergeant in the militia, and had never ceased to do so since the first days of my arrival in Cao Bang.

"But I considered then that my life with Thi-Nam as a good deed. Having knowledge of that good deed I had respect for it and I set it ahead of my anger, my pride and my dolor.

"I did not throw Thi-Nam out after beating her, as custom demanded. I even kept her next to me. I explained to her that I forgave her, estimating that the movements of our senses are temporary and ought to be considered as vain compared with what our minds had decided.

"And I didn't act thus out of egotism, because I wanted to keep my mistress at any price. On the contrary, my limited experience of women, my absence of reflection didn't permit me to support without disgust the idea of having been deceived. I loved her less. She loved me more. I attached myself forcefully and dutifully to perfecting the soul of that instinctive creature, in spite of the bitterness that was henceforth mingled with it for me. And that was the culminating point of my good deed—I mean, what I thought was a good deed."

The former colonial administrator fell silent, and everyone waited for the continuation of the story of Thi-Nam. But he launched several puffs of smoke toward the ceiling, and contemplated the spirals for a long time.

In that smoke he was doubtless gazing at an amber face with its pulled-back chignon and frail shoulders under a colored shawl, and seeing thuyas and coconut palms agitate, perceiving another, lighter smoke agitating, which was that of sticks burning before the altar of the ancestors.

Perhaps he had the desire to say something more about Thi-Nam. He prepared a pipe in silence, making a gesture as if he would continue when he had smoked it. But after that he began another, and then another, gazing every time at the blue spirals rotating above him, the light spirals swirling the clouds of his memories.

And he did not say any more, either because it was sad to recall the past, or because a few more pipes had reminded him of the vanity of speech.

"And you, what good deed have you accomplished, Aline?"

Aline was very confused, because she had looked hard into her past and saw nothing but a long sequence of bad deeds. All the petty actions of her existence seemed to her to be ugly and sad, as she imagined evil to be.

She was not sufficiently clear-sighted regarding her life and he lives of others, and was not proud enough to say that she had accomplished a great many of them, that every night spent in the arms of a man was illuminated by the sun of true purity, because she had given them a great deal of pleasure without receiving any herself.

135

VII. The Night of Tender Camaraderie

"Amour is a great mystery," said Jean Noël. "No one knows why people are attracted to one another, why they seek one another ardently, seizing one another furiously only to reject them subsequently.

"What is the power that makes people of different sexes devote themselves to a thousand schemes that all end in one unique result, to lie down in the place that serves them equally for sleep and to embrace one another, for a variable time depending on force and desire?

"Nature and human wisdom inform us that those actions are only accomplished with the goal of reproduction, and that the beauty there is in amour, the sentiment of superiority that we glimpse there for a few seconds are only clever tricks that wily nature has prepared in order to reach her goals more easily.

"But it is permissible, in that case, for us to tell ourselves that the means are perhaps more valuable than the end. A traveler who is going by night along a beautiful avenue of palm trees toward a dirty and dilapidated inn would to better to sleep under the beautiful stars than in the unknown room where the ugliness of the décor would poison his night.

"Since nature dupes us, why should we not dupe her in our turn?

"For nature is not sublime. People incessantly make use of her to defend or excuse a thousand absurd or ugly actions. To obey the law of nature would be to revert to the condition of savagery. Everything within us that is noble and superior strives to struggle against the monstrous ends of that unkind mother devoid of reflection and sensibility.

"Nature has found the mirages of amour to incite us to have numerous children. Let us have the appearance of entering into her views, but let us play the trick of not going to the end of the course. Let us pause at the admirable and rapid moment when, by the exchange of mutual sympathy, we arrive at a magnification of ourselves, a possession of the divine that, for all that it vanishes promptly, nevertheless seems to be the best thing there is on earth.

"The quest for the perfect minute that the individual, forgetful of the survival of the species, realizes in amour is the true goal that it is necessary to pursue.

"The English eccentric who is the habitual hero of Jules Verne departs, I believe, in I no longer know which of his novels, to search throughout the world for a miraculous ray that the sun darts as it sets, under certain atmospheric conditions, over seas of a particular phosphorescence. For only a single second, all the colors of the rainbow in a magical prism inundate the earth and the sky with an incomparable dazzlement.[4]

"Only a single second!

"Amour is like that magical ray. With a fervor equal to that of the English eccentric, it is necessary for us to pursue it throughout the world.

"But instead of boarding ferries that are shipwrecked, of traversing tropical vegetation with caravans, encountering numerous cannibal tribes, followed by a faithful and comical servant, it is alone, in the voluptuousness of bedrooms, next to a recumbent woman, before the enigma of her smile or her tears, that it is necessary for us to search for the light of the ray.

"Sometimes it shines. It is made of the silence of the night, of the certainty of not being disturbed, of the warmth of the atmosphere, of delicate perfumes, of the nobility of the

---

[4] The reference, although the plot summary is slightly inaccurate, is to *Le Rayon vert* (1882; tr. as *The Green Ray*). The eccentric protagonists are actually Scottish.

place where one is lying, of the harmony of the objects and fabrics that surround you.

"It is made of the beauty of the face, of the contour of the body in the lamplight, of the softness and the duration of the caress.

"It is made of a subtle physical communication that is established with the woman who is next to you, with the consequence that if you simply join your hand with hers, a gentle warmth comes to you in the body and the soul, which is simultaneously sensuality and tenderness.

"It is made of the desire that is born, of the possession that is imminent, of the ardor of the senses that is combined with an equal impulse of the imagination.

"It is made of the sentiment that no obligation binds you to one another, of the power that one has to take oneself back after having given oneself.

"That quest is difficult, for we are blind, having over our eyes the blindfold of conventional ideas, and we do not know in what direction it is necessary to extend our arms.

"Amour is the most interesting thing on earth and we do not have for its practice any organization, any artfully-prepared location, nor any favorable furniture. It is even considered as an evil element, permissible only when it has been weighed, classified and supervised in marriage. For the greater number of men, behaving badly is synonymous with making love.

"And even those who are liberated and who have understood the importance of amour attribute to it a clandestine character and only give themselves to it with a vague remorse. In any case, they only seek it like a superior pleasure, which is a manner of debasing it.

"The sympathy of a man and a woman affect different forms that are more or less appropriate to bringing us closer together at the divine moment.

"Passion is dangerous, for it tends to enchain being in a unique amour. Now, it is a bitter and rigorous law that determines that the splendid light fades away as amour is prolonged, to be replaced by a uniform gray clarity. It is necessary to be able to renew that passion incessantly, and the poverty of our nature, the lack of opportunity and the force of habit render that renewal very difficult.

"Carnal desire alone is impotent, in the rapidity of its satisfaction, to enable us to attain the goal, and the sentimental amour of the fifteenth year only has incomplete resources.

"Amity, which is a marvelous rapprochement between individuals who have recognized and chosen one another among thousands, places sympathy on another plane and distances us from the desired path.

"And it goes without saying that our instinct guides us and that if we love passionately, it will be impossible for us to slide that passion toward a different sentiment.

"It is evidently more convenient to consider as admirable everything that we have within ourselves and to yield to it without control. But that is a convenience for which one pays dearly, for one condemns oneself by that strategy to ignore the sublime contribution that amour might make to life while remaining the dupe of its ridiculous and dolorous illusions.

"One can orientate one's sentiment toward the path one wants to take. In the same way that one can diminish the suffering of jealousy by reflecting on the absurdity of jealousy, one can mingle sensuality with amity, or amity with passion, in accordance with what one judges necessary to happiness or to the ideal one has traced.

"Above passion, there is amity; above amity, there is affection, and above affection there is the tender camaraderie that is the most perfect form of amour.

"Passion makes us suffer; it is exclusive and limited. It limits the horizon of life to one being. Amity deceives us because it hastens to betray us as soon as passion makes a sign.

Affection wearies us because it has monotony for a companion, because its breath is insipid and its face reflects too much kindness.

"But only tender camaraderie, which is voluptuous and fraternal at the same time can give us both the pleasure and the superiority of amour.

"One is the slave of a mistress or a legitimate wife. Such women subordinate amour to the general conditions of life, to their dignity, to their material situation, to their future. The tender comrade might have a dignity, a material situation and a future about which she thinks, but they are elsewhere, in another domain, and she is unaware of a reciprocal effort upon amour when she is with you.

"The tender comrade does not have a key to the apartment because she knows that happiness cannot go everywhere every day, that it is necessary for it to present itself unexpectedly in order to be recognized as happiness, instead of being named habit. The tender comrade does not make jealous scenes, and nor does one think of making any, in the same way that if, in the course of a walk, one washes one's hands and face in a stream, the idea does not occur to you of accusing the water of being unfaithful.

"The tender comrade, when she arrives, always brings a perfect virginity, that of her good will, and when she is about to quit you, there is in the gesture of her extended hand the possibility of an eternal adieu.

"The tender comrade wears the bright costume of youth, of which she is the most qualified representative; she is the messenger who does not know the secret of her mission, the blind bird of paradise; she is the frivolous and temporary companion who permits us to attain the divine by way of voluptuousness."

Aline leaned over Jan Noël with an infinite tenderness. By virtue of the marvelous effusion of her heart, she lived incessantly beside the man she loved the divine minute of which he had spoken.

The former colonial administrator shook his head as if he were about to declare the vanity of speech, and how vain and deceptive amour was, in whatever form. But as he was smoking with a certain avidity and postponing his words until after the next pipe, he remained silent, for the next pipe was always on the immediate horizon of his desire.

Sometimes Jean Noël looked at the time on the watch that he had around his wrist, as if he were waiting for someone. Then Aline asked him:

"Who are you waiting for, to check the time so often?"

He replied with simplicity and a question mark:

"Haven't I told you yet that my mistress is arriving this evening on the train from Paris?"

For a few minutes, Aline was like someone who has received a violent blow and is wondering whether they are gravely wounded.

"Your mistress!" she said. "What am I to you, then?"

"You're my tender comrade," replied Jean Noël.

And Aline remained silent, for she did not know whether she was like those functionaries to whom one gives an honorary title at the moment they are rendered destitute.

VIII. The Enemy Friends

"When one has a mistress and hazard or your own initiative gives you another, is it wise to introduce them to one another and make friends of them?"

"It's wise and practical, for one avoids a host of lies, one doesn't have to divide one's time into two unequal parts that one always offers awkwardly and are always judged insufficient. One then has a life that forms a double and harmonious whole that has nothing to distract or modify it."

"But the two mistresses won't take long to engage in a merciless struggle that will poison the harmonious life and soon render it impossible!"

"Nothing of that sort happens if they have a liking for one another, whether that penchant is natural or one provokes it by telling both of them to love one another reciprocally. But it's appropriate, above all, that there is one of them who is the one that one loves more, the true mistress, and that the other only occupies a secondary situation, because she came along afterwards and brought a lesser contribution of amour."

"How do you weigh that contribution and what happens if she loves you and suffers?"

"Haven't you noticed that it hardly ever happens, and there's hardly anything that doesn't sort itself out after a time?"

"She's very pretty," said Jocelyne, taking Aline's hand, while the vehicle jolted in the dust along the coast road.

Jocelyne smiled, showing all her teeth, which were superb. She talked about Paris, theaters, her friends and her clothes. She had the faculty of changing the topic of conversation abruptly, with no apparent reason, and she allowed that faculty to develop within her because of the convenience it has.

Having declared that Aline was pretty, she immediately talked about something else, instantly giving insignificance to the declaration, and the subjects of the conversation were things and people that Aline did not know. From time to time, Jean Noël and Jocelyne tried, by means of some banal comment, to attach her to their group and relieve her sentiment of solitude, but that solitude was only aggravated as the vehicle rolled on and the sun became hotter.

"How amusing it will be for the three of us to have lunch together!" said Jocelyne.

The vehicle had stopped. Aline shook her mantle, which the dust of the road had covered with fine gray ash. She would have liked to be able to shake her soul, on to which a rain of ash had also fallen.

We're almost the same age, and I admire you for having gone so much further than me along one of the roads of life, the most beautiful, the one that rises, for there's another that snakes into the lower depths, which is very dark and which I know better than anyone.

Out there, there is the great mystery that Paris is for me, with its prodigious boulevards, its hotels vibrant with orchestras, its dazzling teas and costumes, and I admire you for penetrating that with ease, emerging smiling, having retained the most delicate perfume in your clothing.

In spite of the frankness of the gaze, the simplicity of the desire, the determined amity of all your words, I fear you slightly, because you're drawing me somewhere and I can't tell where.

How can I like you? It's from the moment when I knew that you existed that the luminous atmosphere of sorts in which I was moving was suddenly veiled.

"I annoy you with my advice," said the painter Fortune to Aline, lighting his pipe, "and that's why you no longer come to see me.

"A painter ought to live with is brushes and his colors, he ought to have models for mistresses and other painters for friends. A little woman like you ought to frequent other little women of the same sort, and your lovers ought to lean their elbows on the tables in cafés, play cards while chatting and have provincial faces. It's an essential condition of happiness to remain within one's environment, to occupy a narrow place there, to be oneself."

The painter Fortune blew a great puff of smoke, and, in accordance with his custom, he began to laugh heartily.

"And then, there's a means of traversing life without suffering; that's to laugh at everything, for everything is joyous and it's not worth the trouble of doing oneself harm for anything except painting, which ought to be the goal of life."

Aline was about to reply that she was not a painter, but Fortune was already throwing a hasty sketch of Aline on to a canvas and rejoicing in such a natural pose in such a beautiful light.

"It's necessary not to be jealous, Lucette, since I don't love you and I don't love that woman that I don't know either. I take you in my arms more to console you than to console myself for the sadness of my life. You weren't jealous of the men that I didn't love, you haven't been jealous of the man that I have loved, and now you are, this evening, of a woman who is nothing to me.

"If I'm abandoning you in your room without a kiss at the hour when you're ordinarily so tender, it's not because of her but because of him.

"I'll come back all alone. You'll be able to hear my footsteps in the corridor, my door closing, and you'll even be able to listen later to take account of my solitude.

"I'll lie down on my bed, I'll put my hands over my eyes, and I'll have lowered the lamp in order to try and see more clearly."

"At one time...," replied Jean Noël, "but why speak of the past when the present is there with its pleasure and its ennui, and when the future is soon going to appear with its mystery, unveiling itself at every moment?

"What a charming soul is that of that little woman who surrenders herself with all her heart! It's necessary to render her amour for amour. That's what I would have thought, at one time. But isn't it vain to ask oneself what one would have thought at one time, when it's so difficult to know what one thinks at the moment when one is speaking?

"You ask me if I love her. That word has so many meanings that I daren't make use of it. Yes, I love her. But that doesn't answer your question, because I strive, on principle, to love everybody. You ask me whether I don't fear hurting her. It might be the case that I do that, but I don't fear it, and she fears it even less.

"At one time, I would have thought, above all, of making her happy. One is, in passing through life, a different person every year. The young man that I see in looking backward was already an egotist. Anyway, you tell me that I'm an egotist. It might well be that I'm not. We can't measure the range of sympathy and know whether it's the bad that we're keeping to ourselves and the good that we're giving generously to another without doubting it, and without doubting ourselves.

"And then, let's examine the following facts. There are two women, one of whom has been my mistress for a long time, the other for a week. I've told them that and I haven't hidden anything from them. Sincerity, the absence of the unknown, has deprived their jealousy of any aliment. They aren't jealous, or almost not.

"Let's suppose that they find one another reciprocally charming, that they sympathize with one another, that they become two friends. Holding the first with my right hand and the second with my left, I walk between the two of them without knowing whether there is one that I prefer to the other.

"By virtue of the intersection of those three sympathies, won't there result a greater happiness, a greater richness of amour? To attain in amour a subtle degree that hasn't yet been attained, isn't it worth the trouble of making delicate instruments vibrate, in an unaccustomed fashion, even at the risk of drawing out some discordant note, because the instrument is mysterious and one doesn't know its harmonic possibilities?"

IX. At Antheor, not far from Agay

At Antheor, not far from Agay, the rocks are red, there are parasol pines what resemble suns, eucalypti that resemble young women, and cicadas that make so much noise that one might think that the entire earth were sighing in the heat.

At Antheor, not far from Agay, after an all-white lighthouse in the middle of blue pines, the road goes along the sea shore, and while roses spring from pergolas, one sees such calm little bays between such tormented rocks, in such a magical light, that one would like to be a navigator of dreams landing in those minuscule ports.

At Antheor, not far from Agay, the pine needles squeak underfoot, the perfume of dried algae mingles with that of fresh flowers, with the consequence that one doesn't know whether the source of one's intoxication is the salt of the sea or the essence of terrestrial plants.

At Antheor, not far from Agay, there is a little villa with columns, which is posed like a bouquet of stones at the edge of the waves, and in that villa happy days dwell, and in that villa anguish dwells, and the face of happiness smiles perpetually alongside that of woe.

"Which do you prefer?" said Jocelyne to Aline, placing alongside a white rose the pearl that she had on her finger.

"It seems to me that there is more splendor and life in the rose, and it embalms too.

"The pearl has lived at the bottom of the sea. Far away, in an ocean, a man has dived in order to find it. A jeweler has worked on it. Women have suffered in order to possess it. How beautiful it is, a pearl!

"But when one looks at it closely, what a sadness there is in that dull gleam!

"See how fragile the rose is," said Jocelyne, and with the tip of her little finger, with a curt gesture, she strips off all its petals.

Aline regretted the beautiful dead rose, but, on the sand of the pathway, it seemed to her that the scattered petals designed, crudely, a great melancholy face.

In the villa at Antheor, everything is bright and new, the furniture is painted in a thousand varied colors, and in the big room that overlooks the sea the lanterns that are lit in the evening seem to illuminate a puerile fairyland.

In the villa at Antheor, Jocelyne plays the piano in the morning, she utters bursts of laughter when she is not playing the piano, and at other times she dances, with her hands behind her head, and a grave and distant expression then passes through her gaze.

Into the villa at Antheor Jean Noël has brought the jade Buddha and the little statue of Aphrodite; he has placed them facing one another on the silver tray, where they exchange silent words that never end.

In the villa at Antheor there are many kisses, many caresses that the sun burns, that the nocturnal wind causes to evaporate, and Aline gets up every morning with hope and goes to sleep with renunciation.

"When I see both of you with your orange turbans and your violet slippers on that high balustrade that overlooks the sea," Jean Noël said, "it seems to me that you're two sultanas from the *Thousand-and-One Nights*.

"Then I hear the cries of caravaners who are arriving in the dusk, the appeals of dervishes who are responding to a subtler music, those of feminine reveries scattered in an invisible city.

"Sitting on the bench, among the cacti and the mimosas, I sometimes think with passion that you're about to enter the palace of your absent master and that you'll embrace there on colored mosaics, for the amours of sultanas are primarily composed of mutual kisses.

"At other times the marvelous mildness of the air engenders within me a dream so profound that I no longer want to quit the shade of the mimosas, and I recall the Arab poet Tahir, who saw his wife fall into the sea from a similar balustrade and who neglected to run to her rescue, so beautiful was his inspiration."

The orchard of Agay is surrounded by a wall so high that one can scarcely see the crowns of the apple trees with their crowns of flowers and the little drops of blood that are cherries.

The orchard at Agay is an old orchard planted by a miserly former master of that great marine domain, who constructed that high wall in order not to abandon anything to pillaging children and to shelter his fruits.

When one goes past the closed doors alongside the worn stones, and one sees, high above, the tops of the trees whose trunks and foliage are invisible, one recalls the fairy tales of one's childhood, if one has a soul that is even a little inclined to the romantic.

There are magical fruits in there, and a captive princess, and in order to free her it would be necessary to confront a dragon that launches fire from its mouth.

If one does not have a soul inclined to the romantic, one knows that the magical fruits are sold in the marketplace in Saint-Raphael and that the dragon is a mild old man of the Midi who reeks of garlic and who does not launch fire but a jet of water enveloped by a rainbow from the spout of a watering-can.

There is a hill from which one can see the sunset. One can, in principle, see that from any hill, and even from any point on the earth, but on that particular hill, there is a stone from which one can gaze at it with the emotion that creates memory.

"Sunsets," said Jean Noël, "make one think about death, immortality and Lamartine's *Meditations*. There is a sun that is setting in me, a nuanced and slightly timid sun that does not resemble this splendid and grandiloquent landscape."

"Personally, I have a desire to weep, I don't know why, on seeing the night rising slowly from the pine forests and gradually extending toward the sea."

And when we go back along the road along the seashore, I can't understand how it is that Jean Noël and Jocelyne are talking indifferently about a thousand futile details of their life in Paris. One might think that the moving beauty has not affected them, or has merely stirred their curiosity. They're the ones who are artists, and I'm not, but it's only me whom that beautiful landscape moved. Are their souls above nature? Am I a poor little fool who weeps for nothing?

There is a violet room with a large white bookcase that is full of books. It's in that room that the most beautiful hours pass for me, because the mysterious sea of thought has come to bathe me there.

That sea is deeper, more colorful and more various than the Mediterranean that my eyes behold. It has raised up more tempests, it nourishes more monsters, it is inundated by more suns and moons. It comes from further away, all the way to the little ignorant girl that I am, and who reaches out her hands fearfully, at random.

Because he has indicated a book to me, because he has clarified with a word the meaning of another, because he has made me understand the beauty of certain thoughts, because he has believed in my effort, why am I linked more solidly to the man I love than by amorous words or the pleasure of caresses?

He has held out a mirror to me and he has shown me my soul; he has come with a magic wand and he has caused hidden springs to gush forth; he has informed me of everything there is within me that is susceptible of elevation. I'm dazzled by that new gift; I wouldn't want any longer to renounce it, but I also know how much I shall suffer from it.

"You see, Aline," said Jocelyne, "When it's cold, one lights pine-cones in the fireplace; they make a high and joyful flame. But at present it's spring, it's warm, leave your body unclad."

"Have you noticed, Aline, the large hooded cape that is hanging in the antechamber? When it's cold and the wind blows, I put it on to go out into the rocks. It comes down to my heels and from a distance, I resemble a customs man or a lighthouse-keeper. But at present it's spring and we can walk around in a short, bare-breasted, in the tamarisks."

"You see, Aline, in the winter one takes the mosquito-nets off the beds, and folds them up in the cupboards. But at present it's spring, and one replaces them. They're dazzlingly white and still a little stiff, because they've come from the laundry. I want to see you naked on the bed through their light gauze, as if through a transparent dream, a subtle robe that doesn't ouch you."

"When you both go to bathe," said Jean Noël, "I remember the story of the sirens. There are several of them. There's that of Ulysses, which is the best known. But what folly it was on the part of that hero to have himself chained to the mast when the sirens sang! Why did he not think that if those marine and artistic beings appealed to men with their irresistible voices and drew them under the waves, it was in order to enable them to share their pleasures in their palaces of nacre and opal? Life with those goddesses must have been infinitely better than a problematic return to Ithaca through a thousand perils.

"I knew a man who, having heard the sirens once, immediately raced to follow them and stayed with them for a long time. When he came back to the land, his wife had remarried and his children had become bearded men who didn't recognize him. But that was perfectly all right with him. He had conserved from his sojourn a taste for very refined arts and a great philosophy, and he said voluntarily that existence is, in sum, only possible with the sirens.

"I'd risk drowning myself if tried to go under the water with you when you bathe. But you can certainly sing to intoxicate me when you come out, streaming with droplets of water, and dry yourselves in your peignoirs. Then you draw me by the hand into the bedroom where the large divan is, the fabric of which is impregnated with perfumes, and is worth as much as any grotto."

This evening he drew me into the garden while Jocelyne was playing the piano, as if he wanted to be alone with me and say things to me that she ought not to hear.

We had been walking for a few minutes, but he hadn't said anything. The sea wasn't making any sound, the shingle wasn't squeaking under our feet, the trees weren't agitated by the wind, there as a harmony of silence and immobility.

Then he kissed me on the lips, but a kiss that seemed to be given on the sly, that had the implication of a secret between the two of us.

And just at that moment, a toad, from the direction of the land, began to croak, and a mimosa branch fell at our feet.

We returned to the villa. The piano had stopped playing. The secret had flown away.

O ancient fig tree, why do you remember so much another old fig tree in Gascony; how can such different terrains cause similar trees to grow?

When I look at your blanched trunk, low and twisted, and your broad leaves, it seems that I have become a little girl again; I see the village of Valentine in the distance, outlined in the depths of a valley, and I hear the hiccups my mother had when she'd been drinking.

O aged fig tree, you shelter at present a creature very different in appearance from that little girl. And yet, just as, when I was afraid and when I felt bad, I once ran to take refuge under the shade of your brother on the bank of the Garonne, I've come to your foot again today to listen to my soul, which is afraid and feels bad. I was very abandoned once, very alone, devoid of amour. I'm no longer alone now and a great deal of amour envelops me. Is it the same thing, then, since I'm under the old fig tree again, all tremulous again?

The life of women who live in Paris has complications of which those who live in other places are unaware. Jocelyn has to depart abruptly for Nice on her own, and won't come back for a few days.

At first I didn't believe it because of the happiness that burst forth within me, and which seemed to me to be too great. But the car had already arrived in to which her traveling bag and her hat-boxes were carried in haste.

We went as far as the gate and I didn't understand how she could leave. She loves very little, or she loves with a great certainty, or she thinks very little of me.

Was there a kind of jealousy in her most tender kiss to bid me adieu, or was her indifference manifest herein, with a slight regret for the days that we were going to spend together?

"*À bientôt.* Don't get bored without me."

The car drew away. Jocelyne only looked back once and waved. No, she wasn't jealous. At least, it seemed so to me.

X. The Night of the Aphrodite and the Buddha

That evening, as the night was mild, as the murmur of the first cicadas had fallen silent, as the moonlight came in through the open door to the terrace, and Jean Noël was smoking in silence, it seemed to Aline that the objects placed on the silver tray were animated by a strange life.

The statuette of Aphrodite lowered the right arm that she had raised, smiling, and cast aside the flap of her veil that she was holding. She thus appeared completely naked, took two or three steps amid the metal needles and the talismans spread around the lamp, and she smiled with a perfect ease that was not pierced by the slightest modesty. Then she advanced deliberately toward the jade Buddha that was on the other side of the tray and fixed him as she marched with her gaze, in which there was delight, irony and an incomprehensible desire.

Aphrodite agitated the rose that she was holding as an amorous appeal, stuck out her perfect breasts, then bowed and fell backwards, but the jade Buddha remained immobile, with his hands folded over his enormous belly.

And Aphrodite said: "It's me who leads the world by agitating my rose. The pleasure I give is the foundation and the reason for being of everything. Morals change in accordance with times and peoples, religions are born and die, the afterlife with its recompenses is an uncertain hypothesis, but I don't change; since the commencement of the worlds, I've been the sole certainty of happiness.

"O sensual lust, which is simultaneously the intoxication of the soul, what better and higher thing has been found? You reveal the beauty of the human form, you are the obedience to the law of penetration of beings.

"Fortunate are those who are consecrated to me from the first awakening of their bodies in adolescence! They have been able to take from life all that it can give. Fortunate, if they have avoided the traps that fidelity extends for faithful souls, that religion extends for credulous souls, that toil extends for laborious souls! They can, when they are old, look at their existence in memory without regret.

"And as for those whose faces have taken on coarse expressions because they wanted to ignore me, to those who have cultivated what humans call virtue, what a bitter dupery their lives will have been, since they will have spent them rejoicing in embracing the wind!"

The rectangular face of the jade Buddha became animated without it being possible to distinguish whether it was joy or sadness that it reflected. And he said:

"You have expressed a truth that has its place among other truths, and which is neither more false not truer. Pleasure ought to be put above duty, for duty is nothing but the law imposed by the strongest egotism. But above pleasure is the love of everything, above that love is the wisdom to know its vanity, and above that wisdom is the void.

"The beauty of the body and the sensuality of the flesh only augment our desire to live in order to savor that beauty and sensuality again. Everything that we can grasp escapes us, everything that intoxicates us deceives us. The perfume of your rose, Aphrodite, does not make me shiver, and the warmth of your flesh against mine leaves me insensible. After having striven to cherish the universe equally in all its forms, including yours, I am striving to destroy within me the ability to cherish. I prefer immobility to movement and ugliness to beauty because they make us desire less.

"That is why, with my arms folded over my ridiculous belly, I gaze without budging at the ruddy lamp that does not illuminate, I respire the smoke whose intoxication extinguishes the senses, and I enter a little more every day into the consoling void."

With a delightful freshness, with a slight perfume of marine algae, pines and mimosas, with a vague crepuscular light, the morning penetrated the dormant room and spread over Jean Noël and Aline.

The latter, on awakening, immediately looked at the silver tray. The statuette of Aphrodite was in its place, and the jade Buddha was sitting facing it.

The little lamp was flickering and about to go out, and it seemed that it was not so much because of lack of oil as the contact of the morning that was brushing it.

Then Aline told Jean Noël about the dream that she had had and the words she thought she had heard. And he replied;

"Human folly would be nothing if the folly of the gods were not still on earth."

XI. The Days of Waiting

Happiness, so brief in itself, flies way even more rapidly when one knows that it will soon finish. And the knowledge one has of its imminent conclusion contributes to precipitating that conclusion.

And Aline was conscious that a desolation was emanating from her fatal to amour, a power of suggestion that acted unknowingly on Jean Noël in the direction contrary to the one she would have desired.

She was like someone rolling down a slope. She could not stop herself. There was, involuntarily, a sad gleam in her gaze that seemed to the staring at the debris of her broken amour, and every kiss that she gave had the savor of being the last.

She took account of the fact that she might have been able, with a more joyous conviction, with a certainty that might have emanated from her gestures and her words, to prolong her happiness, to render it more vivacious by giving it the aliment of her own faith.

But she did not believe it, and she had too much love for Jean Noël and not enough for herself.

"When one departs in a car through the mountains of Esterel," he said, "One goes alongside beautiful scorched forests, one traverses valleys where there are only the houses of guards and one arrives, at the end of a road, at the Auberge des Adrets.

That inn is like all inns, with one sad room and an arbor beside it, into which chickens come to peck. But there are old trees all around it and the prestige of its name adds to the charm of the place. If the weather is fine, well set forth tomorrow, the two of us, and we'll have lunch at the Auberge des Adrets, and we'll come back at dusk when freshness descends from the trees and simultaneously rises from the ground.

Aline promised herself a great enjoyment in that excursion, but the next day the sky was laden with cloud.

"We'll go to the Auberge des Adrets tomorrow," said Jean Noël.

Tomorrow! Tomorrow! What folly, when life is there, preparing all its traps to prevent the charming tomorrow from ever arriving!

The next day, a car came to a halt outside the villa. It brought Jean Noël a telegram obliging him to leave for two or three days.

"You have the books. There's the silver tray; there's the sea. I confide you to the gardeners and Jocelyne's chambermaid, who are excellent people. Don't be too bored. Tomorrow, you'll have a letter.

Tomorrow! Tomorrow!

I have gone all alone along the sea shore to a little beach where there are sometimes fishermen. There I sat down with a book that he has told me to read and I waited for the gardener to come and fetch me for dinner.

When one is bored, time is a pitiless tyrant, but a tyrant always vanquished. I know that the hours will pass in the end, but there's no reverie bright enough to struggle against presentiment.

I've watched the slow progress of the waves over the stones; I've interested myself in the children playing; I've seen a boat land and two men get out with fish in a net. I read, and then I closed my book, and then I gazed at bizarre forms in the clouds.

When the gardener came to fetch me and I went with him, he said: "You're all alone this evening, Mademoiselle."

There was certainly no pity in his voice. He was simply observing the fact in order to say something, but how dolorously his words resonated within me!

There was indeed a letter, but it was so vague and so short that it would have been better if there had not been.

It's true. I tell myself, in order to console myself, that there are people full of affectionate sentiments who only write brief and dry letters, and it's necessary to know how to consider those hasty words as evidence of hearts that have difficulty revealing themselves.

I try to write a letter in which I shall reveal my whole self, my life, my thoughts and my amour. How difficult it is! I'm afraid that he'll laugh, because of my faulty French, because of the naivety of what I'm expressing. I strive to form an elegant handwriting, I apply myself, I begin again. Then sincerity takes possession of me and I write, I write for a long time and I sense that the true things, said simply, take on a great force.

I'm truly content with my letter. When he has read it, he will have a better idea of me. Who knows? He might come back sooner. He might love me more.

But when I have folded the letter into the envelope, I suddenly think that he hasn't left me his address.

The gardeners and the chambermaid surround me with cares; they're full of amiability for me, but I'd prefer it if they had less. I'm sure that it's an effect of my imagination that always makes me think that they feel sorry for me. However, they give the impression of trying to compensate for a wrong that has been done me, of looking at me to see whether I might be weeping.

Why should they feel sorry for me? Am I not very fortunate? They don't know that I've always been poor and that the life I've been leading for a few days represents for me the discovery of a luxury that was unknown to me. They don't know that I'm in love. When they see me reading they think in their simplicity that I'm toiling and they can't suspect that in the magnification of my soul that the books procure, there's a source of new joy every day.

Oh, I'm very fortunate! Three days pays so rapidly! The cicadas are singing, the sea is blue, I walk and I dream. But how dolorous that good fortune is!

There is a great joy distributed in nature. One hears it in all the sounds, one sees it in the purity of the light, and one touches it with the dampness of the evenings.

Behind the gates the dogs are barking; they're summoning one another for play, they're voicing the joy of obeying their instincts, the satisfaction of aimless movement. The birds fly in an eternal pleasure in the midst of the azure. There are insect amours in the grass.

The roses testify the pleasure that plants have in growing. The trees sway with satisfaction in the air, benevolently opening their great gnarled arms. Fruits abound, a symbol of wealth. Gems run over the trunks like sensual tears.

There is a great joy distributed in nature, when one gazes at it, telling oneself that one will be in the arms of one's beloved that evening.

As the train arrived at Agay at six o'clock, Aline thought on the evening of the fourth day that she go along the road to meet Jean Noël. He would certainly arrive that evening, the gardeners had said. And it seemed to her that she had a joyful presentiment that announced that arrival to her.

She put on a pink dress that he had thought pretty one morning. She redid her hair several times. She suspended the jade pendant that the former colonial administrator had given her around her neck.

The road had never been so bright between the somber blue of the pines. She stopped several times to listen, to see whether the noise of the cicadas was mingled with the bells of a carriage.

"Bonjour, postman. Isn't there a letter for me?"

No, there was nothing.

"Is the Agay train not late?"

"No, it went through a while ago."

She sat down not far from the lighthouse. Perhaps Jean Noël would come on foot because of the mildness of the evening. The evening was very mild, and darkened gradually. The cicadas had fallen silent. A neighbor who must have arrived on the six o'clock train had gone past a long time ago.

Aline saw a flock of birds rising from the other side of the bay, which seemed to be heading for Antheor. They formed a black patch in the sky, where stars were twinkling here and there. She picked up her umbrella, which she had dropped. She walked back slowly, very slowly.

The next day, at six o'clock, the same train would go through, and Aline was on the road in the same pink dress, with the jade pendant around her neck.

Pergolas extended roses toward her; their air as motionless, arm and heavy with perfumes. Aline sensed overhead the magnificence of the evening and of nature, and in her heart there was hope that was fleeing and distress that was arriving.

"Bonjour, postman. Isn't there a letter for me?"

No, there was nothing. The Agay train had gone through long time ago. Night had fallen completely. Aline went back to the villa, but things had taken on a different aspect for her, she gazed at them and understood them with another soul.

The barking of the dogs behind the gate had something heart-rending about it. It was the plaint of blind souls enclosed in bestial unconsciousness. The flight of birds was rapid and fearful; they were exchanging signals to warn one another of the approach of birds of prey. Insects were devouring one another in the grass. The trees were tormented by the sun, the rain or the wind, and the contortions of their branches testified to their obscure dolor. The sap that moistened their bark was a sweat of despair.

The entire earth was suffering, like her and she moaned softly as she talked, carrying her delicate pain of amour in the midst of the moans and the inferior pains of things.

In Aline's room, under the columns of the terrace, in the baskets of the garden, something had changed. While descending the staircase, while walking, while breathing the air, she felt the pity of the gardeners and the chambermaid floating around her.

And behind that pity she seemed already to see a little hostility, the sentiment that she was a guest for whom they could have less respect, with whom they could be more familiar.

She went from one place to another, not having the strength to read, nor having the strength to remember, not having the strength to anticipate. She was like someone who has constructed a beautiful edifice and has suddenly perceived that her work is no longer anything but ruins, without being able to explain why.

But when evening came and there as the noise of a train in the distance, Aline marched hastily along the road, scrutinizing every bend carefully until night fell, for hope is tightly bound to our hearts.

The sound of the bell at the gate. What novelty, what promise there is in the sound of a bell resonating across a garden.

"Bonsoir, postman,"

"Yes, there's a letter. It's necessary to sign for it."

What a worthy man he postman is! But why is it necessary to sign? She signs. The postman smiles beneath his moustache, A letter on which *Value declared* is written is always a good letter, which gives pleasure, and it's agreeable to give pleasure to a charming young woman.

The postman doesn't go away. He remains standing before her, as unexpected and vulgar as destiny. He talks about things and people. Perhaps he'd like to drink a glass of wine? He would. Aline hastens to fetch him one, hugging the letter against her body.

She finally reads it. That is quickly done, because the letter isn't very long, Jean Noël isn't coming back. He can't. It's because of very important reasons. They'll see one another again. There are two or three truly polite phrases. She can stay at the villa as long as she wishes. Everything is at her disposal. If she has any need of anything, etc. etc.

No, she no longer has any need of anything.

XII. The Night of the Bad Deed

"Certainly," said Jean Noël, "I've accomplished many bad deeds in my life, but I don't have any remorse about them. Perhaps those bad deeds only enclosed a tiny drop of evil. Only one makes me suffer when I think about it, in spite of the fact that it did no harm to anyone and I know that I've done worse.

"When one has just arrived in Naples an one asks the porter in one's hotel where one can go for a stroll for an hour or two, he indicates a place above the city, the name of which I no longer remember, where there's a museum, or a church, or a viewpoint for contemplation, or perhaps all three. That's what happened to me. I spotted a cab passing in front of the hotel, I gave him the name of the promenade in question, and we set forth.

"Naples was enveloped by clouds that day and I was in a very bad mood in not seeing the sunlit beauties I had imagined. It was a somber city that I was traversing. I perceived the profile of the coachman in front of me. He was astonishingly thin and old, with a short and singular beard. His garments were very poor. As for the horse, it was a creature even thinner than its master and more fleshless, whose like I had never seen before. Its trot was exceedingly slow, and the entire vehicle was creaking as if it were about to break.

"My ill humor was augmented by traversing the city in such a grotesque rig.

"As we were climbing a rather steep street, he meager horse stopped, exhausted. Then I saw the coachman, instead of using his whip, or even cracking it, get down from his eat and go to talk to his horse. I didn't understand what he said to it. He spoke to it softly, and sometimes darted a timid glance at me to make sure that I was tolerating the stoppage without anger.

"He must have saying to his horse: *We're both old and ugly, poor among the poor. We make people laugh, and it's a miracle if we find one or two distracted clients a day who permit us to earn a few oats for you and a little bread for me. I know that the hill is rude and that you can't do any more, but think how great our poverty is. Humans are pitiless, I fear that the man who is sitting in our carriage will quit us. Come on, make an effort, my brother.*

"People were looking and laughing outside a shop. Sitting in the carriage, I felt quite ridiculous. Doubtless the horse heard what its master said, because it set off again at a slow pace.

"A little further on, however, it stopped again; then it set off of its own accord. But then, with a spontaneous movement, the coachman jumped down from his seat. I thought it was to lead the horse by the bridle. Nothing of the sort. He started pushing the vehicle with all his might, and he had on his desolate face of a poor old man the fear of my discontentment and pity for his sad companion, as well as the need to help one another.

"It seems to me now, by way of memory, that the sight of that spectacle ought to have wrung tears from the hardest heart. Nothing of the sort. The people we passed were mocking ostentatiously, and I was like any man engaged on the path of evil sentiments, I had a blindfold over my eyes, I was sinking further by the minute into egotism and the absence of pity.

"Instead of getting down and pushing the carriage with the old man, I smoked a cigarette in a negligent pose, or I even smiled scornfully to make the passers-by who were mocking understand that I could see all the ridicule of such a scene, that I was a stranger to the city, that it was a consequence of scorn that I had taken to transport me that carriage of the lowest order and that lamentable coachman.

"I went so far as to voice complaints about the slowness of the mount and murmuring that I was in a hurry and that it would have been honest to warn me.

"At no time did the grandeur of that fraternity of the poor touch me.

"And when we had arrived at the church or the museum—I don't know—I put on my face the expression of a man who is exasperated, who has been duped and who is about to make a legitimate execution.

"Instead of keeping the coachman in order to go back down, I asked him severely how much I owed him. He stood before me, cap in hand, out of breath, very humble, as if defeated. He fixed himself, poor fellow, a derisory sum, in a low voice. And I, the egotist, counted it out for him parsimoniously, only adding an absolutely insignificant tip, for which he thanked me, saluting me several times.

"While we were coming up, fog had accumulated over Naples. The coachman plunged into it and disappeared, as if into a sea of distress. All the forces of evil possessed me at that moment: the imbecile vanity of appearance, the incapacity to understand the fraternal soul of the poor, avarice, and the misconception of pity.

"I believe that from that spot the entire panorama of Naples and the sea ought to unfold, but nothing could be seen but clouds. I took a few steps, and suddenly, a light appeared in that mist, an interior clarity of my soul more resplendent than the sun over the bay of Sorrento.

"I tried to launch myself in pursuit of the coachman, but either I mistook the route or, by virtue of an irony of destiny, the horse was able to run after quitting me, and I did not find him. I didn't see him again during the three days I spent in Naples. My bad deed was accomplished forever."

"The only sin that appears to me to be unpardonable is a sin against the mind," said the former colonial administrator, in the course of a long silence. "I can't remember whether I've talked to you about my little friend Thi-Nam, whom I loved and I believed I had rendered more intelligent. It was against her that I accomplished the greatest sin possible, and that sin was all the greater because it was exercised at the same time against myself.

"I was then one of those people who pursue a goal with a great apparent sincerity but in which, deep down, they don't believe themselves, not having faith in the goal that they're pursuing.

"I had been in Indo-China for too long, and an immense nostalgia for France had overtaken me. For the noise of areca palms I wanted to substitute the sound of the acacias and plane-trees of my own land. I wanted to see once again the long rows of cypresses that shelter farms and the red bricks that cover them.

"I had the right to a leave. I decided to return to Europe. I abandoned Thi-Nam. It's true that she had been transformed in my company. But fundamentally, she was only a little savage, who would find, when I had gone, a greater happiness. That, at least, was what I tried to persuade myself. Hadn't she deceived me, in any case, with a sergeant in the militia?

"I swore to her that I would come back after six months, that I wouldn't forget her, and I left, having charged one of my friends, a customs officer, with giving her some money a short time afterwards and telling her, carefully, that I wouldn't be coming back.

"One always has the right to quit a person that one no longer loves. The amour that she has for you and her suffering in being left are not sufficient reasons to retain you. But what is unpardonable is to have raised her up, to have given her a spiritual element that she can no longer do without, and then to cast her back into an inferior life.

"The crossing, the arrival in Marseille and the pleasure of seeing France again, were a kind of daze for me, which prevented me from thinking about Thi-Nam, I feared remorse and I avoided it.

"I went to spend some time with relatives in Salon. It was in the purity of that Provençal landscape, on the great straight roads, under the giant plane-trees that the image of the little companion with the amber skin and the tied-back hair reappeared to me. Perhaps I missed her because of the ennui and the solitude In the midst of people who did not have my ideas, perhaps because I found her, by comparison, much more intelligent and more refined than all the women I saw. I waited with impatience the letter from my friend telling me what Thi-Nam had thought of my abandonment.

"The customs officer was a worthy fellow who liked me, but who was rather vulgar and considered women as an element dangerous to amity, which he placed above everything. I only received a letter after several months. Thi-Nam, he told me, had taken things very well. Abandonment, for a con-gái, was so natural. She was consoled. It was unnecessary to think about her any longer.

"I felt resentment at first, and then a great melancholy. Then I thought how just and fortunate it was, since I had left her, and that augmented my sadness further.

"On the bed in a little white room in Salon, in Provence, with the sound of trees audible through the open window, I was smoking one evening, on my own. Hours passed and I remembered. And when I had smoked a great deal, memory vanished and as confounded with the present.

"I closed my eyes from time to time, and then the sound that the trees were making in the garden reminded me, unmistakably, of the voice of the Asiatic forest out there, behind the veranda at Cao Bang.

"In that voice there were desperate appeals of suffering souls, the flutter of the wings of the spirits of the sky, the mystery of accumulating vegetation, the words spoken by the stone dragons motionless before the portal of the paradise of Lao-Tsen.

"And sometimes, a particularly profound and human cry mingled with those confused voices. It was the plaint of a poor little being lost in an immense forest, trying to find her way, afraid and weeping: the plaint of Thi-Nam, whom I had abandoned in the great Asiatic forest.

"And it seemed to me that she was on the other side of the tray, lying down as before, with her interrogative eyes, her pulled-back chignon and her amber skin. But the expression on her face was no longer the same. It reflected the fear of solitude, the sadness of being betrayed by the man she loved, an infinite pain. Her cheeks were hollow and there was something like two tear-ruts beneath her eyes.

"And she said: 'You have extinguished in me a bright and sacred flame that you had lit. The appetite for learning, the love of books: all that left me with you. I am descending again now to a road where there is no longer any happiness. You have killed that which you loved, the work that you had created with your thought, that you had modeled in your image. It is a little of yourself that has disappeared. Never more, henceforth, will you know the sweetness of long nights while you smoked, enrapturing the soul of your little friend Thi-Nam, who loved you so much, in her manner.'

"A few days later, I received several letters from friends that told me about the despair that Thi-Nam had felt in losing me. None, however, criticized me. I was told that she had left Cao Bang and returned to Hanoi.

"Remorse had taken possession of me. Before my leave was over I embarked in Marseille, swearing that I would find her. But the events of life are like a river that flows and never goes back toward its source I found out on arriving out there that when Thi-Nam had learned of my resolution to quit her, her first concern had been to reestablish the altar of the ancestors that she had long since ceased to honor. She had brought bananas and bowls of rice to it again. She had stayed motionless for entire days in the smoke of incense sticks that she burned. She had been seen again two or three times with the sergeant of the militia, and then he had quit Cao Dong abruptly, all alone, to return to Hanoi.

"Cau-Dong is a daughter of Heaven who broke a jade cup and was expelled by the king of Heaven. She came back to earth and led such a perfect life there that she obtained immortality. There is a pagoda in Hanoi that is consecrated to Cau-Dong. It's a sort of convent of Buddhist nuns and a few poor women led a miserable life there, receiving alms from foreigners who come to visit the pagoda, and burning incense before the image of Cau-Dong.

"It was there that Thi-Nam had gone to seek refuge. I can only explain by the excess of dolor that backward return of a mind that had become intelligent and liberated from superstition. A nun at the pagoda told me that Thi-Nam had been taken to the hospital, very ill, and then had died of pneumonia. She had been buried in an Annamite cemetery on the road to Hue. It had been, I was assured, a very appropriate ceremony. All the nuns had followed the coffin.

"There is a multitude of hillocks along the road to Hue, giving the impression of a great sea, and every wave in a little mound exactly like all the other mounds, and all the dead there are anonymous.

"Under one of those mounds was Thi-Nam, whom I had loved, whom I had only raised up to allow her to fall into a more primitive religion, and only a few ridiculous old Buddhist nuns had accompanied her when she was dead, when I ought to have carried her myself, pressing to her my heart like my cherished child."

Miély made a gesture that embraced the objects placed before him, the pipe and the lamp, the smoke and its spirals, and which also embraced the objects of the past, other pipes and other lamps, and a more ancient smoke.

And he said: "It's since that time..."

Everyone was silent, and then they talked more about good and bad deeds.

"What do we know about things?" said Jean Noël. "Perhaps Thi-Nam found among the ridiculous priestesses, in offering a bowl of rice and bananas, a consolation that embellished the end of her days more than European intelligence and even more than amour."

Miély, who was following his own thoughts, went on, addressing himself directly to Jean Noël.

"Don't you think that other men have done harm to other Thi-Nams and that there are among the living other cemeteries as sad and as anonymous as the little mounds on the road to Hue?"

Then the doorbell rang. The rustle of a dress was heard, and Aline appeared on the threshold of the smoking room, very hesitant and very intimidated.

"Excuse me," she said. "I thought that I could…that I might be permitted…"

XIII. The Descent

When life has written the final word to the sequel to a story of amour, whatever it might be, it is very difficult to erase.

The individuals almost always see one another again, they sometimes spend a night or two together, but they never rediscover the unique perfume that they have respired.

Tender camaraderie! Aline would certainly have liked to be a tender comrade. But above all, she would have liked not to be suffering. She did not have enough experience and had too much tenderness to know how to change her pain into sensuality.

And then, if you does not live continuously with one another, everything collaborates in separating you. On the fragile monument that one tries to build there is a wave every day that deposits a layer of sand. There is the wave of friends, there is that of money, there is that of journeys, there is that of new liaisons. And when many waves of sand have accumulated, one perceives one day that over the happiness, over the memories, over everything one has loved, there is nothing but sand.

"I loved him because he had raised me toward him, because he had made me understand why one book is better than another, because he had talked to me about things unknown to me until that day, such as the sympathy people have between them, the philosophy of the Chinese, and the charm of the arts.

"I loved him because, when we were chatting together, he strove to let me believe that he was speaking with someone as intelligent as him and of the same quality.

"I loved him because he sometimes remembered and sometimes forgot, because he gave the impression, when he looked me in the eyes, of looking further than me, into the region where my soul was born.

"I loved him because he only loved me a little, because I was afraid of losing him. I loved him for other reasons."

"You see," said the painter Fortune, "in order to triumph over oneself, it's necessary to develop in oneself the joyful genius of life.

"I don't know any place on earth more frightfully sad than a certain street in Paris, which ends at the Réaumur-Sebastopol Metro station, at midnight. A commercial district, when the shops are closed and it's deserted, offers an image of incomparable desolation.

"I recall that, passing through it once, I witnessed and extraordinary spectacle. In front of the entrance to that Metro station, the most frightful of them all, a man and a woman, modestly dressed, were standing enlaced, waltzing and humming. No music was drawing them along. They were not impressed by the solitude and the ugliness. I thought that they were preceding some joyful band by which they were stimulated, but there was nothing of the sort. They were alone. Possessed by their interior joy, they had been urged to manifest that joy in movement.

"I admired them for a long time. I've often thought about them. They had the joyful genius of life. Let them be, like me, an example. Without music, without friends, it's necessary to be able to dance in front of the Réaumur-Sebastopol station."

One recalls how joyful one was to be rising up. One descends.

One recalls how a little more luxury, a little more superfluity, the quality of boots and gloves, had been agreeable to you because they were the symbols of a better life. One goes back to old boots and old gloves.

One recalls how one has suddenly seen unfolding before one a new horizon, and what sweetness there was in feeling more indulgent to everything because one felt that one was loved and that there was a little more good around you.

One recalls how the road that rises was beautiful because the people one encountered there were more intelligent and finer than those one had seen before, and how, in darting a glance backwards, one had a horror of the ugliness and evil traversed.

And yet one descends again without wanting to, without being aware of it at first, since one doesn't want to believe it, since one doesn't want to think about it.

And there comes a moment when one recalls less because the memory wears away, and one descends more rapidly, because life is pitiless.

Out here, at the extremity of an outlying district, in a street full of empty barrels, there is a poor little house whose unique ground-floor window has shuttered with and opening cur in the form of a cross. It's there that an old workman lives who is from the village of Valentine, and whom Aline went to see from time to time before being happy.

She goes back there. She traverses the Hell of dust, of lined-up barrels, of gray walls. The old man is still there. He has her sit down and they sit there facing one another, almost without saying anything.

While gazing at the sculpted face of the peasant from her homeland who has become a laborer, she evokes involuntarily the land out there, the vines that are attached to the apple trees, the apple trees that are broad and low and where cuckoos sing in spring, the lush meadows, the paths that go uphill under the chestnut trees, the shepherds with their brown capes, the flocks with their capes of wool, the water of the river, the freshness of the valleys.

That old man is like her. He is an exile, he wanted to live in the city. They are both miserable, rejected and solitary. And when she goes away, she sees in the distance, when she looks round, in the great sadness of the district, the two ruddy crosses that the light makes in the shutters, the two crosses, as insensible and inexpressive as the pity of the poor between themselves.

Now it is necessary to go back to Mère Loute, to listen to her advice about men and about life. It is necessary to see Lucette again, to submit to the gaze of her faithful eyes, to resist her caresses. It is necessary to go and sit down again in the little bar, not far from the port, to listen to the arguments of Totote, Rosette and Jeanne the miser. It is necessary to go back to Madame Rosalie's house to meet English officers and tell them while undressing that one is the daughter of a naval officer killed in the war. It is necessary to go up into hotel rooms where one finds a familiar odor of mildew. It is necessary to submit to common men that one does not know. It is necessary to make a perpetual addition of petty sums whose total is never sufficient for the budget of her life. It is necessary to go and come along the same melancholy and loveless route where one always encounters the man with the jaundiced complexion, who walks with his hands in his pockets, waddling, and exhaling a noxious breath, like the appeal of the utmost depths.

There was a charming woman who kept a family boarding-house in Nice, who liked Aline a lot, and whom the latter called her "petite maman." They wrote to one another regularly, and Aline thought that she might perhaps find a refuge with her.

Yes, they had written to one another regularly, but not for some time, naturally; that is always the way. But a petite maman remains a petite maman whatever happens.

And Aline went to Nice. One was very glad to see her. But the family boarding-house had prospered, all the rooms were taken, and there was no place for her at the moment. The petite maman was very busy, and afterwards, she devoted all her free time to a young man who had become her lover. One falls in love at any age, doesn't one? Aline would live elsewhere and come often to say *bonjour*. She had had chagrins? She will tell her all about them some day. But everything passes. It's necessary not to torment oneself. Go on, *à bientôt, ma cherie.*

Petite mamans who keep family boarding-houses are no better than the others.

I had to leave the furnished house, the bar, and the street. I found my life tedious and miserable, certainly, but when I imagined another more beautiful, I didn't know that it was also nearby and that I could grasp it.

Now it's too sad. I can see what I might have been and what I shall never be. And I can also see what I'll become, and it's that clairvoyance that makes me suffer. It wasn't necessary to talk to me about good and bad deeds, of religions in which the people of Indo-China believe, where they go forth under the thuyas, where there are noisy forests near verandas and everything makes one dream and think.

I've drunk a poison. Perhaps it's like all poisons. At a certain dose it can fortify or intoxicate, but at another, it kills.

I shan't die. One talks a great deal about dying, but it's difficult to die. I've drunk the poison that renders one more intelligent and gives one disgust for one's own existence.

Thi-Nam, you are my sister. But I can't erect in my furnished room an altar to the ancestors where I can burn perfumes and to which I can bring offerings, as you did. I could only honor there one sole ancestor, my mother, who drank. I don't know any others. And then, I don't have faith in that religion. Sticks of incense only remind me of evenings of amour, and Mère Loute would come to drink the bottle of liquor that would replace the choum-choum.

Thi-Nam with the pulled-back hair and the bronzed complexion, you are a more favored sister, since you repose beneath a little mound, alongside a road, while it's necessary for me to lie down without repose in many beds, to earn the poor living that animates me, to have the right to my little mound.

This evening, Aline is holding in her hand the jade pendant that she wore round her neck attached by a little chain. It was Miély, the former colonial administrator, who had given it to her. He got it from a very wise mandarin, a friend of the Emperor, and she had attributed to that pendant the value of a talisman.

She is walking very rapidly along a deserted little street. Her heart is empty and she feels ill. She reaches the harbor and turns left. There is a canal there with stagnant water, where there are old boats beyond usage and where drains terminate.

Oh, no, the mandarin friend of the Emperor was incorrect. Perhaps he was speaking for beings of another race, or only for a rich elite. Or perhaps he was an old fool who didn't know what he was talking about.

She recalls his words, which Miély reported to her: "The unique and divine gift is the constant determination to acquire more intelligence." Oh no, that gift isn't divine. It causes too much suffering. It is, on the contrary, the sign of the curse on earth for poor girls like her.

She throws the jade pendant into the stagnant water of the canal, and without looking back, she goes back to her life.

This story was told to me in a café in Marseille, one very hot afternoon, by the painter Fortune, a joyful man and full of pity, whose face is like that of a faun.

He showed me Aline, who was sitting among other women and laughing with them. She must have been pretty, and still was in a way, but she had the elusive mark of women who stay up late and have too many lovers.

"It seems to me," I said, "That she's laughing louder than the others and putting her elbows on the table more causally."

"That's true," Fortune replied. "Perhaps she's even wept less than the others, but there are qualities in dolor, and tears are not always its expression."

"It also seems to me that she's drinking more," I said, on seeing that she had several small glasses in front of her, "and that there's more true cynicism in her gaze when she looks at the men passing by."

"That's true," said the painter Fortune, "But the greater the height from which a stone falls into the mud, the deeper it plunges, and when it's a matter of a soul, it disappears to the point that one never finds it again."

THE CALL OF THE BEAST

Chapter I

How did it come about within me? I seem to remember. It was not by virtue of a slow sequence of desires, an evolution of my soul. It appeared to me abruptly, one evening in my life, like a new road that one discovers at a crossroads, where there are more trees and where it is more agreeable to walk.

When I stopped in front of the kiosk of the Toulousan florist and I look a large bouquet of carnations in my hand, I was still similar to myself and I did not know what magic there was in those flowers.

I smiled at the toothless merchant because I recognized her, she had no more changed, in fifteen years, than the low, bright houses of my native city, its avenue, its side-streets and its canal. I remembered that she had previously been a procuress as well as a florist, but in the manner in which one is in the Midi, more to render a service to good girls than out of personal cupidity. Doubtless she still was, and at the same time as the dusty flowers of her display she had a desire to offer me a young friend—but she did not. She wrapped the stems of the carnations in paper and held them out to me.

Dusk was about to fall. It was summer, and the atmosphere was very heavy. A thousand impressions of my youth came back to me, emerging from familiar doors and stones once trodden.

I walked joyfully, bouquet in hand, toward the cemetery, for in truth I was enjoying my pious action, the victory that I had won over my egotism by devoting two hours to carrying those flowers to my mother's grave—two precious hours, since I had arrived that morning and was departing again the following day.

A tram stopped beside me. I thought about boarding it. Perhaps my destiny would have been different if I had done so. But the weather was warm and I knew that men of my race, gathered together in a vehicle, emit a disagreeable odor of garlic and sweat. I hesitated. The tram set off again. In any case, the distance was not long—at least, I thought so. It was, in reality, infinite, since I was never able to reach the cemetery that evening.

Memories are linked to sounds and odors. When I heard the saws of marble-cutters and an odor of stone mingled with the perfume of my carnations, I immediately relived a melancholy All Souls' Eve, an excessively heavy shirt the knot of a blue cravat with white spots displayed on my breast, and an infantile conversation with a child named Robert. And I walked with all the more contentment for having honored the past.

The monumental mason's shop overflowed on to the avenue with all kinds of model tombstones. And as I bumped into the corner of I know not what eternal regrets, laughter rang out, and I saw a woman at a ground-floor window,

She was a joyful she-wolf with gilded ears of May corn in her brown hair. She was leaning idly on her elbows and I could see her breasts jutting over the window-sill.

My hesitation lasted a second, during which I wondered to what social category the woman might belong. As soon as the next second, however, after her laughter had resounded in my ears, I was fixed on that point and I could, without fear of being mistaken, estimate the woman's value in monetary terms.

She was a twenty-year-old she wolf who was offering her warm form to a passing bearer of flowers, extending her teeth to bite and laughing by virtue of natural gaiety. Her corsage was unfastened, there was a laziness in the movement of her shoulders, and one sensed in the inclination of her body a natural desire to undress.

I was like someone sitting on a seesaw who falls abruptly to the other side of life. The attraction of a vulgar room that I glimpsed, of an unfamiliar bed on to which I might push a cheerful and venal young woman, mingled within me with lust and the heat, the dust and the heavy blue air. I leapt over a cross and I offered my flowers to the woman, thus introducing a slight sentimental character into an affair that was not.

She continued to laugh, while staring at me. I saw a veritable sensuality in the green reflection of her dark eyes, which filled me with desire. My heart beat a little more forcefully, I sensed my blood circulating harmoniously and, like a wave coming from the end of the avenue, I received an impression of the beauty of things. The canal that I had followed, a barge towed by a horse, the white stones of the monumental masons, the wreaths of artificial flowers, a line of cypresses in the distance that dominate a white wall, and even the bottles of a small pharmacy, all seemed to me to be the chosen frame of a unique evening that my destiny had arranged for me.

I threw an invitation to dinner into the balance of an a ready-certain success, She responded with an acceptance—and I perceived, in observing that she had almost no southern accent, that all the coincidences were favorable to me and that I was fully gratified by fate.

I opened the door of the room with delight. I had no regret for my interrupted pilgrimage. Was it not, in sum, a vain manifestation good for simple folk? Was it not sufficient to honor the dead mentally?

In reality, that shaky ground-floor door did not only open to the room of a one-louis little woman; it enabled me to enter a new region of life that I cannot say was either less beautiful or less dolorous; it enabled me to connect with a long corridor of which I could not see the end, with an infinity of other rooms where there were low lamps, turned-back beds and naked forms, where I was to pursue for such a long time the youth of pleasure that does not want to die.

Chapter II

When I plunged my key into the lock of my apartment it seemed to me that the key turned with difficulty, as if, during my absence, it had been damaged by rust I dropped my valise, but not with the satisfaction of a man who finds himself at home after twelve hours in the railway and half an hour in a taxi. On the sofa there was a handkerchief, an open book and a paper-knife, and a small slipper on the carpet, all of which gave me the image of a disorder that seemed annoying. By contrast, an unaccustomed order on my work-table appeared to me to be an assault on the materials of my thought. The light was less rosy through the lampshades. It was too warm.

Immediately, I heard Rose-Thé's voice calling to me.

"It's you, finally!"

In those syllables there was all the pleasure she felt in seeing me again, but I was not touched by it. Finally! She had, then, been waiting excessively, I was too late, my voyage had been too long. She was already reproaching me.

I opened the door and I saw Rose-Thé, stark naked on the bed, supporting herself on her left elbow. Her skin made a long blonde patch against the violet wall-paper. There was a natural abandonment in her pose, mingled with a slight effort to make the line harmonious. I savored that unexpected beauty keenly, for Rose-Thé was beautiful and that had been the original reason for my amour. I also savored the surge of affection that pushed her toward me and the quiver of her being as she kissed me.

But I savored it in a new fashion and I was internally astonished to receive familiar impressions so differently. It seemed to me that I was a stranger who was watching a play, who was seeing a traveler return home after a few days' absence and find his mistress naked on his bed. I heard the banal words they exchanged.

"How long you've been away. What have you done? Have you had a good time? Have you cheated on me?"

"It was horribly hot. I haven't done anything interesting. I've been in the train since seven o'clock this morning."

I looked around at the furniture and the walls of my narrow room. There was not a corner of the carpet, a pleat of the curtain or a design on a cushion that was unknown to me, that was not like the testimony of my existence, my desires and my thoughts. And I perceived that all those things surrounding me were bizarrely detached from the past, existed in themselves, with a life of their own to which no memory was linked. The cushions no longer attested that Rose-Thé's slender body had sunk among them; there was no memory of a delicate hand over the ash-trays. The mirror was mute, as if no image were reflected in its cold glass.

I was penetrated by a disagreeable impression, and I wanted to efface it as quickly as possible.

It was as if the wellbeing that I did not utilize because of its continual presence and its certainty, while continuing to be present and certain, had evaporated round me, by virtue of a subtle mystery that is not appropriate to wellbeing. I wanted to grasp it, to assure myself of its indisputable possession.

I took Rose-Thé in my arms and I kissed her lips. They were warm and tasted simultaneously of milk and fruit. I touched her breasts, which were perfect in form and firmness.

But then I thought of other, less perfect breasts that I had seen crushed on the sill of a ground-floor window, in a white avenue rising toward a cemetery. I thought about a heavier human contour, a mouth from which an animal merriment burst forth. I saw again an entire banal evening in which I had intoxicated myself with vulgarity.

We had dined in a restaurant that she had chosen because she was known there, where the waiter gave her a familiar wink. Then she had a desire to go to the cinema, because of a film of which she had seen the first part the previous week. There she had met a man who had a black moustache and wore a bowler hat and trousers without a crease, and who had come up to her, addressing her as *tu*. Then he had perceived me and had moved aside.

"Pardon me—I didn't see that you were with company."

"He's a pharmacist, you see," said my new friend, laughing, "and it's very useful to know a pharmacist, because he sells you all the drugs you want."

Then we had been in a bar, where she drank several cocktails, as much by taste as to conciliate the proprietress, a fat Jewess obsequious with men and severe with women.

Then, excited by the drink, the music of a tango, the cries and the laughter, my friend had become truthful and realistic.

"You see that fellow," she said, showing me a young man dressed like an illustration in a fashion magazine. "I was with him for six months, and I've also slept with the fat man who's with him, but only once."

And I thought that she had also slept with another, powerfully built, who had just sat down on a stool and had said *bonsoir* to her without looking at her, with a little twitch of his jaw.

And I relived the impression of unhealthy disturbance that had gripped me, in that atmosphere of provincial partying, next to that woman that I had desired, and whom all those men had had before me and would have in future.

Roe-Thé smiled at me with her beloved mouth and I had before my eyes the teeth of the she-wolf. I perceived an alcoholic breath.

I wanted to rediscover the richness of every evening, the possibility of pleasure that seemed to flee from me. I folded the offered body of Rose-Thé against the bed. Her perfume rose from warm sheets, and it seemed to me that I was breathing an odor of rain and dust, out there, in a room where the clock was covered by a globe of glass and where, from the sky of a wooden bed, floral curtains fell.

The life of a man, his wellbeing and the march of his destiny, depend on the riches he possesses and those of which he disposes.

In that epoch, I was rich. By that I mean that I had no money, or very little, but that all the other goods for which a man searches had devolved upon me in abundance. My friends were numerous, they pressed me incessantly to go and see them and they were visibly glad when I went to surprise them in order to spend the evening with them. My apartment, without being vast and luxurious, possessed the atmosphere that comes neither from furniture, nor fabrics, nor the disposition of the rooms, nor the light, but from a special life proper to apartments, which ensures that one is at ease there and one has no desire to go away rapidly when one has gone in. I say that I had no money, but I had enough for a moderate existence with modest pleasures, which was sufficient for me. A few people said that I must have talent. I enjoyed a certain consideration. I had the reasonable and clear-sighted appearance, the facility of entering into an understanding with people, that immediately attracts the sympathy of concierges, taxi-drivers, post office clerks, and which enables one to move in the streets as in a familiar element.

I was only familiar with the ennui that one can measure and limit—which is to say, the ennui that one experiences in an antechamber when evil destiny obliges you to go and solicit an official personage, or the ennui of waiting, when one has a rendezvous, for someone who is late. But I was unfamiliar with the profound ennui, inherent to your nature, which grips a man by the temples when he wakes up and makes him see the emptiness of his existence.

I had not read all the books. I even discovered, perpetually, a great number of them to which I had never even given a thought, but which were very interesting. I even obtained a new pleasure from them, that of having them rebound and collecting them.

I loved traveling and railways. The frame of a railway carriage pleased me because of the moving solitude one finds here. I did not know many countries, and the ever unrealized desire to see them gave me a kind of reserve of fortunate possibilities that I might draw upon when the moment came.

The theater cost me nothing. I didn't go there, because it sent me to sleep, but I knew that I could go there easily, because I knew artistes everywhere with whom it was permissible to chat for an hour.

I had no taste for nature, and I found it redoubtable because of its powerful sadness, but I knew that, strictly speaking, by confronting it and struggling with it in the confines of some beautiful property where I was invited to spend the summer. I would succeed in mastering it and extracting joys from it.

I could wander for a long time in unknown quarters, enjoying the variety of shops that were always similar, finding picturesque details of life in side-streets where there was nothing in particular. Sometimes, the mere appearance of a café encountered on my route and where I sat down was sufficient to give me pleasure. And on those days, everyone appeared to me to be interesting and worthy of being studied, simply because they were clad in human form.

A long way away, in the charming town of Saint-Gaudens, I had a happy family who were alive, and I knew that they would be even happier if I went to live nearby. I didn't go, but I knew that I could. And my family was, for me, like nature, a possible resource for bad days, a grave, respectable wellbeing to which one could have recourse any time, with a little effort.

I worked regularly, and I liked to work. I was content with small successes that enabled me to hope for great ones. I said that the most absolute liberty is indispensable to life and, as I thought that I was free, I was. I had no stomach aches and I slept well. No religious thought tormented me. I was not followed by the specter of any evil deed.

And there was also the morning air when I went for a walk in the Bois, the pleasure of the port drunk at six o'clock in a bar in the center, where the number of comrades and women whose hands I shook gave me the sensation of being a very popular man. There was the warmth of the little restaurant into which one goes when one is hungry, the silence of midnight when one returns home and the impassioning book over which one goes to sleep.

Finally, there was Rose-Thé, whom I loved.

I was not entirely sure of loving Rose-Thé. Sometimes, I said to myself: "Do I love her?"

And at other times I said to myself: "I've loved her a lot. How long will I love here?"

But those were questions to which I did not reply, because I knew full well that I only asked them in order to deceive myself.

When one meets a woman and one begins to walk with her, one can take several roads. Some of them are short, some of them long. Some are sunlit, some are rainy. There are some where there are trees and others where one continually stumbles over stones. Some are bordered with charming little houses and others in which all the doors open to shady furnished hotels. There are some that only go to Asnières and others that take you to China, and even further.

The one that I had followed with Rose-Thé began in the Bois de Boulogne, beside a table where here were two cocktails, before which we were sitting. It plunged under the acacias, amid the heavy summer heat; one saw couples enlaced on benches there, and one was sometimes blinded by the headlight of an automobile traveling at top speed. In truth, we had no idea where that road led, but we found it full of an immense charm, because we had not yet reached the period where one holds hands. That period arrived very rapidly, however and was surpassed as soon as the road turned and brought us back toward the Porte Dauphine.

The road led to places where one takes tea at five o'clock; it made zigzags in the environs of Paris, traversed the fair at Neuilly, stopped at shooting-ranges and menageries and plunged into a dazzling fourteenth of July to vanish into the Gare de Lyon.

The road went along the quays of Marseille; it turned through the old quarter of that astonishing city's port, paused for the time to have lunch on a terrace of the Réserve and continued along the sea shore. Then it was shaded by parasol pines, buried beneath enormous mimosas that overflowed from florid properties, crushed beneath the leaves and petals that rained down from rose-bushes. It traversed towns, rolled through Nice, returned to Grasse, a lands of perfumes, reached the high rocks of Estérel, in order to bring back those who were following it to their exact point of departure, at a table in the Bois de Boulogne where there were two cocktails.

But the road didn't stop there. Then it took a rather uniform trajectory. It made little curves in Paris, to end every evening at the same place, at the door of the house in which I lived. And in spite of that uniformity—or perhaps because of it, who knows?—the road continued to have its charm and poetry.

I sometimes walked along it with delight, when I had the luck to perceive that I was happy, at other times with ennui, for one always thinks, foolishly, that present happiness is depriving you of a greater happiness that one imagines, and which could be realized in other circumstances.

I was not entirely sure of loving Rose-Thé, but in reality, I loved her. I loved her, first of all, for the habitual reasons that enable one to love someone. Because of the efforts I had initially made to conquer her, which are like a capital that one has invested, which one does not want to lose, and which one wants to see fructify into durable happiness. Because of her face and her body, which corresponded well enough to the ideal that I had of beauty. Because of her appetite for sensuality and a physical harmony that existed between us for pleasure. Because of her mental facility in conforming to my tastes, my ideas and my reading, a facility that is often what we call intelligence in others. Because of a spontaneity and an exaggeration of her instinct, which made her laugh for little things and weep for even less, which made her participate with an extreme ardor in the smallest events of life in which she was involved.

But in addition to those reasons, I loved Rose-Thé for a host of petty actions, tastes and spoken words, which formed a kind of chain composed of rings of different form and color, a chain of memories by which I had held her.

Long ago, at the beginning of everything, there was an attitude of simultaneous timidity and curiosity.

Then there was a comical dance to mark her satisfaction one day when I had announced that I would spend three entire days with her.

Then there was an evening at the home of friends when she had really drunk to much champagne and on the way back, on foot, in the street, when she wept softly against my shoulder, manifesting an infantile remorse and promising me not to do it again.

Another time, I saw her at the window, one day when I was late; the wind was scattering her hair and there was an anxiety so full of tenderness in her features.

She had broken a little vase of no value. I opened the door and before I had had time to express my indifference to that minimal event, she fell to her knees, begging my pardon.

One day when she was laughing in loud bursts, she stopped abruptly in order say to me passionately: "You are my life!" And afterwards, she had resumed laughing, without my being able to grasp the transition between hilarity and amour.

But I loved her above all…and in truth, I was never able to explain the profound reason for it…because she had known difficult days in her childhood and the quotidian drama of momentary need. Perhaps it was because of my habit of weighing in a mental balance the suppose merit of every person and honoring each according to the sum of effort. Perhaps it was because of the contrast that I established between such a delicate and beautiful creature and evocation of the poor lodgings, the miserable meal and the absent fire. Perhaps it was simply because of the magnificent charm of poverty.

But something else entirely had gripped my heart. It was the relationship between Rose-Thé and her parents. Every time I had had a mistress I had tried hard never to see her parents.

The mothers resembled their daughters too much; the aged image of the person one loves is suggestive, to the point that one no longer finds in her anything but a youth permanently deteriorated. One is embarrassed before the fathers, who, in any case, rarely exist.

Rose-Thé had almost never spoken to me about her parents, except to mention that they lived nearby; but one day when, exceptionally, I went to find her at home, I saw them.

Two timid old people were sitting in a modest dining room. They were framed by the shadow of a walnut dresser; and it seemed to me that they must always have lived there, that they were immobile and immutable, in the radius of that item of furniture, which only contained a few plates, no silverware and where the provisions were lacking in abundance that the lowest shelf was garnished with books.

One sensed that the genius of financial affairs had been far away from them, that they had shown little initiative in their lives, and a great deal of resignation to an ordinary fate; that they had not attempted great enterprises, he remaining in his role as an employee, she not seeking to develop a very petty commerce in lingerie. But qualities radiated from them of the tranquil depth of race, disinterest and probity, and a certain moral purity, which cannot be expressed in words, enabled by their confidence in life and good will.

It also seemed to me that they marveled with a constant wonder, that they could not get used to the idea that they had put into the world a being so blonde, so luminous and so created for elevation as the smiling Rose-Thé.

And when I quit them, after banal remarks, as I went downstairs with my mistress, I had the sentiment that I had made a discovery, that I had just heard, for the first time, a harmony that I had never perceived before.

And I also loved her more for not acting like a thousand other women, for not making any excuses for the poverty of the house, for not talking to me about a great fortune and great situation lost, for being, with an easy loyalty, devoid of reticence or regret, comfortable with her family and her past.

We had turned on all the electric light-switches in order to make the apartment more cheerful. Something was separating us, a shadow that I wanted to dissipate; and for that I enlisted the aid of light, thinking that all the illuminated lamps might perhaps induce a little clarity in us.

There was a power cut at that moment. After having waited for a few moments in darkness, we decided to remedy the cut, but our lack of foresight meant that we only possessed one single candle.

We placed the unique candle in an ugly medieval candlestick that had been relegated to a cupboard, and a wave of ill humor emerged from the fabrics and the walls and passed through us, because of our lack of foresight. A short argument followed, to determine which of us had been at fault in not thinking about buying candles.

Then we each took a book and sat down to read, our two heads close enough to touch, beside the little flickering flame.

But I wasn't reading. In my mind there was the obsessive memory of the prostitute with the teeth of a she-wolf and the breasts squashed on the sill; I respired the perfume of tobacco in her hair; I heard her obscene laughter on the bed; I perceived in the most minute detail the slightest gestures she had then made with me, the fall of her ankle-boots, the dress that she had taken off, the hairpins that she had removed.

I wanted to chase that vision away and find affectionate words within me in order to reestablish a current of warm sympathy with Rose-Thé.

I found exactly what it was necessary to say. I nudged her with my elbow. But she was reading a novel and had reached the most dramatic passage.

"You're annoying me," she said. "Let me read."

I waited a little. I saw that she had finished a chapter. I took her hand. I was about to speak. Then the candle threw out a large flame and went out.

Rose-Thé uttered a cry of anger. She had not been able to read the last few lines, which were of capital importance.

We got undressed in the darkness, which is an infinitely melancholy thing. In order for Rose-Thé to let her hair down, I lit a match, and then another. As she did not consent to hurry, I was obliged to confess to her, at the sixth match, that by an inconceivable stroke of bad luck, I had just burned the last one in the only box.

That was not calculated to modify her humor. I postponed my impulse of tenderness until the following day, not knowing that in that order of ideas, words that are not spoken are never rediscovered.

Chapter III

It was in our twentieth year.

People called us the four Don Juans of the Rue de Cha-lets, because it was in that street that two of us had our student rooms, where we met up to celebrate our good fortunes noisi-ly. Those good fortunes were the unique objective of our ex-istence.

At twenty, almost all men are simultaneously at the summit of their intelligence and their stupidity. They have just finished their studies and they have an enlightenment regard-ing everything that will decline because of their lack of effort. On the other hand, they are intoxicated by a breath of im-measurable hope, a puff of vanity that makes them behave basely, animating them with a maximum of stupidity.

My three companions and I, in the days that are called the happiest in life, therefore mingled in Toulouse the specula-tions of thought with the obstinate and blind pursuit of all women.

Verdelle was the one of us who had the most experience and devoted himself most exclusively to amour. He was sup-posed to be writing verses, and even a novel, but that only had a secondary importance in his eyes. One saw little of him. Perpetual rendezvous summoned him hither and yon. Even in the morning, very early, one was not sure of finding him at home, for there were little seamstresses that one could only see at eight o'clock, before they went to the workshop.

He was mediocre in his person, like the majority of men who torment the desire of women, for it is noticeable that those whom nature has created very handsome only make use of that beauty to please occasionally, when circumstances im-pel them to do so.

Verdelle was not a seducer but a lover. He fell in love, he suffered. He was a sentimentalist, obstinate in addressing him-self to women who were not predisposed to sentiment either by their nature or the conditions of their life. He was conscious of that error, but he fell back into it incessantly. He rapidly gave a melancholy form to every liaison, enveloping it with an atmosphere of romantic sadness that was fatal to it. In any cases, that sadness disappeared quickly, to be replaced by another. His amours succeeded one another, and he brought the same ardor to them. He had the faculty, he said, of loving several women at the same time and suffering from that equally. But all those despairs were conceived and expressed in joy, and through the inexhaustible series of his dolors he remained a cheerful and facetious companion.

Very different was Hallu, who had a slightly crooked mouth, and curious bristling hair, hard and straight, planted furiously on his head, which it framed lightly in spite of the immense efforts he had not to let it be seen. He was a student of philosophy and was already passionate about the occultism to which he was later to devote himself. A violent lust, always unsatisfied, was the secret of the state of anger in which he lived. He was irritated, firstly at being submissive to the tyranny of desire, a secondly at being unable to obey that tyrant.

He detested women because he was obliged to think about them, to solicit them, to pursue them in the street and because he received humiliations from them. He was scornful of them because of their intellectual inferiority and because they did not honor the title of philosopher with which he adorned himself. He said that the most beautiful ought to be locked up, in order not to trouble the thought of sages and artists by their sight. He compared them to precious vases containing a beverage of insipid taste. It is necessary to drink if one is thirsty and then throw the precious vase away with disgust.

In reality, as his pride was immense, and he lived in the perpetual dread of being rejected, he only addressed himself to inferiors, and for him the precious vases were waitresses in restaurants and hookers in alleyways.

Hallu never ran out of sarcasms and bitter remarks against the fourth of the Don Juans and the Rue des Chalets, who was the robust and placid Plaignier.

Plaignier was not a student like us. He had not been to the lycée. He was a son of peasants, but who had an education and a natural culture. He was an Occitan writer, and he sometimes recited verse in dialect, which seemed to us to be particularly harmonious because we did not understand them. In spite of the very small resources at his disposal, he envisaged life with serenity. He was tall and he had beautiful honest and calm eyes. He was the one of us who pleased women most because, to his natural seduction—which came primarily from the lack of seduction—he added an irresistible gift. He sang dialect songs in warm and full voice, and there was no doubt that his voice had a powerful magical effect on the women to whose amour he aspired.

Several years went by with the pleasant mildness of amity, when it shines upon several friends with shared hopes, and the confidences one makes in the evening while walking through the streets, when the shops light up like the infinity of desires, and one goes on indefinitely until one is exhausted by fatigue, with the gatherings where one drinks a great deal, the suppers where one has only one plate and one glass for two and even for three, the Sunday excursions to the country, accompanied by mistresses, with everything there is of the common and intoxicating warmth of the amity of young men.

But it came about that Hallu fell in love and thought that he was loved. He only appeared among us any longer accompanied by a woman named Paulette, who did not seem predisposed either by her life or her character to be the lover of a philosopher like Hallu.

She belonged to the category of women who have an innate liking for deception and complication. She had seen a group of four friends and had said to herself that by becoming the mistress of one of the four friends she would have every facility for passing from one to another and enjoying an atmosphere of secret intrigue that she was seeking.

I ought to say that none of us resisted, that we even facilitated Paulette's desire singularly. We were not exceptional in that. In spite of their protestations, even their love of fidelity in amity, there is a donjuanesque vanity in the heart of every man, and they strive incessantly, even when they refuse hypocritically to admit it to themselves, to please their friend's woman.

It was with Plaignier that Paulette commenced, because of the prestige of the singing, and at first, nothing called attention to it except the frequency with which our friend sang and the pleasure he seemed to experience in it.

She continued with me, making me swear, as she had done with Plaignier, to maintain the most absolute secrecy.

Finally, after a few days, she was Verdelle's mistress, and he extracted such vanity from it, made so many veiled allusions to it and had so many reticences that it would have been necessary to be blind not to perceive it.

An interior force obliges seducers, or those who believe themselves to be such, to recount their seductions, even sometimes to the person whom they are offending by their exercise.

Those four men who possessed the same woman told one another, and proved it to one another by means of intimate details—details that they found frightful, and the knowledge of which tore their hearts.

They swore that their strong intellectual amity must not be broken for a vain matter of a woman. It was their quadruple mistress who was insulted and expelled. She was unsurprised by that and went away smiling, for, by virtue of manipulating jealousy, she knew its fury.

But the friends had caused a subtle charm to fly away. Confidences became bitter henceforth. Hallu, who was the most afflicted, did not receive any balm from philosophy. His natural bitterness increased. He experienced even more the need to please women, at the same time as the desire to debase them in speech. He became almost unbearable.

The first vacation was a pretext for separation. I left for Paris. I learned that Hallu had done likewise. Plaignier got a small job in Toulouse. Verdelle had been carried away by the breath of amour.

The true value of men has nothing to do with the degree of their success and the situation they attain. Those who seemed in my youth to be the most intelligent almost all orientated themselves toward mediocrity and have not quit that road. Perhaps it is because of some hidden passion to which they consecrate all their efforts, some secret god that demands all their energy in sacrifice. Perhaps hazard has played a greater role.

One leaves one's friends on the road. One loses them, rediscovers them, replaces them. But amity gives almost all its warmth once only, when one is twenty years old. Afterwards egotism, interest and women obscure and limit it. One is desolate to find withered trees where flowers and fruits once grew. One shakes for a long time a hand that does not try to pull away, one has a desire to open one's heart to a hurried individual, who has a rendezvous, who cannot dine with you this evening, who is busy all week, and next week too.

Old friends are like mirrors in which one looks at one's past image. One would like to linger, to rediscover oneself, to halt the years. One extends one's hand to the person one was, and one encounters the icy glass of the mirror.

Old friends are sometimes glad to see you again, because they honor and regret their youth. But they have changed. They have usually become bourgeois, with frozen brains. They immediately want to give you advice, and they give it. They want to modify your life in the direction of theirs; without having received a mandate from anyone, they have become directors of conscience. They are severe because they think they possess the truth and they are acting for your own good.

One also encounters old friends who have not changed. By virtue of a strange power they have kept the habits, the manner of speaking, the hairstyle and even the face of old. They say the same things, in the terminology of the college.

197

They have stayed with the same books and the same ambitions. They no longer fear the headmaster, but they have created another who has almost the same powers, and if one offers them a cigarette they go to smoke it in the toilets.

But those old friends are not the best.

Verdelle got up joyfully when he saw me and extended his hands to me. In the bar that I had just entered there was an odor of tobacco that, in combination with the face and voice of my old friend, evoked forcefully the atmosphere of the cafés of my youth.

He was almost the same, although I had lost sight of him twelve years before. I told him so and he blushed with pleasure. He had aspired to be handsome when he was twenty, and now he had passed thirty I sensed that he invested all his pride in appearing to be very young. He had the same appearance of insignificance and lightness, and bright eyes that gazed over your head, which is the sign of a vivid imagination.

In the time of our amity he already possessed the gift of confusing what he dreamed with reality, and I saw rapidly that he had not lost it, and that it had even developed.

Immediately, we said: "What are you doing? What's become of you?" and the other things that one as when one meets a friend. And we added: "And women?"

Verdelle smiled and made a gesture. He wanted to say that that was his thing, the domain of his knowledge, and that he was not a child, as of old. When I talked to him about Rose-Thé his eyes glinted, I sensed that he was weighing my value, that I had become very light for him and that he was rejoining internally because that woman still unknown was about to be inscribed in the number of his imminent conquests.

"You ask me what I'm doing in life and whether I'm working," he said. "You see, my dear, one can't occupy oneself simultaneously with literature, business affairs and amour. There are several routes in life; it's necessary to choose. Some are ambitious for glory, they achieve it if they strive for it; with average qualities and patience, one always reaches one's goal. There are avid individuals who desire a great deal of money. They're insensate, because it isn't fine apartments, automobiles and dinners in fine restaurants that make you happy. I saw immediately where happiness is found, and I devoted myself to that. It's in women. A town house and servants aren't necessary to be happy. Two small rooms suffice, provided that there's a flower in a vase, a cup of tea at five o'clock and that the staircase is appropriate for an elegant woman to be able to visit you without traversing an atmosphere of poverty.

I agreed with Verdelle enthusiastically, firstly because I think it culpable, in principle, to disparage someone's way of life even if it is different from yours, and secondly because what I imagined Verdelle's life to be had an impact on my imagination.

I made another two or three allusions to the situation that Verdelle might occupy in life, but each time he made a broad gesture, as if to wave away an importunate image.

In Paris, when one knows how things work, when one has connections, one has no need of a situation to live. A little publicity, a little commission, and one can make in five minutes, which chatting over a beer, what a model employee takes a month to earn by his obscure work in an office.

"And you live alone?"

"Do I live alone? I certainly do live alone. The moment one is married, or completely stuck with a mistress, you can say that the doors of life are closed to you. In any case, solitude is only a word, a scarecrow with which one makes oneself afraid. In reality, we're never alone in the midst of the variety of the world. As soon as we wake up, we have the housekeeper, the man from the gas company. Then there's the concierge, the waiter in the restaurant, the friends one meets, the female friends one is going to see, those one finds in bars and finds again in theaters. How can one be alone? One can't, even if one wishes. There isn't any true and redoubtable solitude except the one experienced when one has a faithful companion perpetually by one's side. One also has the housekeeper, the gas man, the friends of both sexes, but it seems that one is on another plane than that familiar humanity, that one is passing through them, that one has lost the faculty of radiating in their direction. One thinks that one is coming and going as one pleases, but nothing of the sort. It's a phantom of oneself that is coming and going. An invisible thread binds you to the woman who shares your joys and your troubles, and when one begins to participate in life, she tugs that thread from afar and one is abruptly snatched from the place where one is and where one has begun to enjoy oneself."

Hazard dictated that I glanced at the time at that point in his speech.

"You're an example of it," he told me. "You've found an old friend, you're content to chat with him, but I the distance someone is pulling a thread and there you are, ill-at-ease, thinking that it's seven o'clock and that you need to go home."

I assured him that it was nothing of the sort, while having the frankness to admit to myself that he was right.

Two little women with short hair advanced toward us smiling. They were young and had a family resemblance. One hastened to loosen her coat in order to render the birth of her neck visible, where there was a pearl necklace. The other, a little less pretty and not quite as well dressed, followed all of her friend's gestures with admiration.

They sat down next to us.

Verdelle ostentatiously addressed them as *tu*, and his conversation was exclusively devoted, to begin with, to showing me that he was an intimate comrade of the two little women.

There was then a question the purchase and sale of a ring, and then a third woman, who knew the other two, and who had been Verdelle's mistress.

A cocktail had followed a port, and had given way itself to another cocktail. Many people were coming and going. Women were laughing and questioning one another. They were of all sorts and they all seemed desirable to me. The one who was beside me and whose neckline and pearl necklace I

200

could see, had an odor of human flesh, youth and heliotrope every time she moved her arm, which intoxicated me. She had crossed her legs and one could see her silk stockings all the way to the knee.

And suddenly, I had a sensation analogous to the one I had had before the Toulousan prostitute while climbing toward the cemetery through the marble slabs. I was capsizing on a slope of desire. A wild sensuality took possession of me, as if a wave departing from the depths of my being were spreading, after having burned me, over the glasses, among the tables, over the bartenders and the drinkers.

I saw the faces around me being transformed. As if every cocktail had been a powerful aphrodisiac, and a force were springing from their prism, those who were drinking them seemed possessed by a spirit of lust. The men took on an appearance of bestiality. In their parted jaws one glimpsed their teeth shining. Their hands were larger and squatter, only agitating as if to seize. Everything they said had an obscene double meaning.

The women were moving around them in order to excite their desires. Their gazes recalled the hours in which they had been taken, reproducing the voluptuous poses, every detail of their activity in the service of pleasure. One sensed that they were naked beneath their dresses, and they made gestures as if to take them off. They offered themselves to me indecently by the movement of their rumps and the narrowing of their eyes, staring at me with a flame that became red. It reached the point where I was obliged to master myself in order not to grab them by the legs as they passed by.

Others entered, smiling and wild, who all made the same movement to throw back their cloaks, falling into armchairs with the gesture of a woman abandoning herself, her eyes half-closed, in expectation of the embrace.

They were all sliding past one another, brushing one another, sniffing one another, exchanging signs or lingering over pressures of the hand, obtaining rendezvous for the night to come. The man and the woman going out arm in arm were certainly going to throw themselves against one another in the semi-darkness of the auto that would carry them away, or they would go to the nearest furnished hotel in order to slake their desire there.

Thus, I was alone in not participating in that general sexual excess. I had the sensation of being the dupe of my stupidity. Far away, as if at the end of a very long road, I perceived the image of Rose-Thé, who was waiting for me. The thought of being awaited irritated me. Verdelle was right. I was bound forever by a thread that my mistress could pull at her whim. I was a kind of chained puppet.

I paid for the drinks. I invited Verdelle and his two friends to dinner. All three happened to be free. They accepted.

As we went out, Verdelle tapped me on the shoulder, laughing. I sensed that he was desirous of being a pimp, of demonstrating had power over women.

"You can go if you want, you know, if you need to. The moment you have a friend..."

Chapter IV

Rose-Thé and I went to see the painter Martial in his Montmartre studio—a man of genius but as yet unknown.

He lived with a little woman by the name of Zette, who realized that *tour de force* common among little women, of being the mistress of a great artist who has no money, of having none herself, and yet being elegantly dressed, having silk stockings and a fur coat.

Without being Zette's friend, Rose-Thé took pleasure in exchanging with her the vague words that women exchange, and I didn't dislike the limited pride, mingled with a joyful conception of men, and the world, that characterized Martial.

He set before us the following problem:

"Is it possible to receive the rich director of a gallery in a glacial studio, when the weather in very cold and one has neither any coal nor capital to acquire any?"

"It's impossible," said Zette immediately.

"You don't know life. To succeed, it's necessary to appear rich, to have an interior, to give receptions. Lévy-Bloch will give me a commission all the more brilliant, he'll buy the two canvases I want to sell him, if the elite of Parisian society is here and if he has a sensation of great luxury. You'll reply to me that he can't have that sensation of great luxury if the stove isn't lit. That's what proves that you don't know life. All is illusion. It's sufficient to create the belief that it's warm, and the guests will be warm. I'll put a candle in the stove, which will shine as if it were stuffed with coal, and you'll see that the temperature will seem very mild. Thus, the rich people will be duped and that will be a great pleasure for the poor people we are. I'll add that, caught by the ambient illusion, even we will be warm too, and that will be a further gain."

Zette did not, in fact, know life, for she didn't raise the objection of the staircase, nor that of the absence of chairs, nor that of the skylight through which the rain sometimes came in.

Rose-Thé and I affirmed that the soirée would be one of extreme magnificence.

The painter Martial was enjoying it in advance, and he listed the people he intended to invite.

I didn't know that, among the names he was throwing out at random, there was that of the man, unknown to me thus far, who was to have so much importance in my life.

It was November, and the evening was exceptionally severe. It was snowing, and I wondered with anguish how, in his studio open in all directions, Martial could struggle against the power of the elements with his little candle.

Fortunately, the elite of Parisian society is crowded into Martial's abode. It is a young elite, almost exclusively devoted to the arts, which is worth more in hope than in reality. I can see three or four people who did not belong to the milieu, and who have come to see the artists.

In order to give more glamour to the ensemble of his gathering, Martial introduces everyone as the most remarkable and the greatest in his profession. Scarcely has one crossed the threshold than one ceases to be mediocre. An architect is the greatest architect of all time, a poet is a modern Homer and even a man who does nothing becomes the most intelligent dilettante he knows.

I perceive a face that is well known to me

"There," Martial said to me, "is the most curious individual of our epoch. He's a magician. He predicted the war six months before it broke out, the exact date at which it did so; he predicted its end and also knows the date of the next war. When he pleases, he can read your thoughts like a book."

It was my old friend Hallu. We shook hands affectionately; he seemed to have quit me the day before.

As I spoke to him about myself, he gave the impression of being up to date with my affairs.

"I haven't lost sight of you," he said, meaning that he had followed me in life in an occult fashion.

But it is in a real fashion that his eyes are following a young woman who seems to me to be very pretty and is laughing at everyone in a corner, with the poet Jean Noël.

I said to myself then that Hallu had retained his old soul.

I examine the women who are there impartially. I make a mental competition. They are sitting in a circle, with Martial's paintings for a backcloth. Unknown to her, each of them is presenting to the silent jury that I am her feet, the birth of her legs and her animated hands; each one is bringing the grace of her features and the weight of her hair—and it is Rose-Thé who wins the invisible first prize.

Yes, Rose-Thé appears to me to be the prettiest, and also the most desirable, but it is my reason alone that observes that before the sage jury that I have instituted. By an inexplicable effect of my nature, it is the others that I admire and desire. I observe that bizarrerie in myself without being able to remedy it. I am astonished by it and I suffer from it. I would like it to be otherwise, but I can't do it. It seems to me that a stranger has slipped into me and taken possession of my senses. He is the one directing me, staring at the women, speaking to them in a low voice, striving to transmit a message of desire to them. I was not like that before. Mentally, I go back over the road of recent days. It happened all of a sudden, as if I had drunk a philter, as if I had been possessed. I remember clearly. I breathed the scent of ensorceled flowers one evening in Toulouse. Then a carnal being entered into me.

I stand up and take a few steps, because I sense that otherwise I will arrange a rendezvous with my neighbor for the following evening.

Zette is triumphant. She runs to the right and the left, smiling, and her soul, that of the mistress of the house, is entirely reassured by the splendor of the reception, thanks to the presence of a table tottering under several bottles of cheap white wine, which, combined with cold tea and lemonade, makes a delightful beverage.

All the glasses are not of the same format and they vary from liqueur glasses to champagne flutes. Two or three cups and a large bowl complete the variety. I even believe that there is an empty jam jar playing the role of a glass.

Anyway, everything is going very well.

For its part, the candle is playing the role of ardent coal marvelously. The stove is very luminous, even too luminous. It is putting out a light that is too uniformly dazzling.

But the elite of Parisian society seems satisfied, either because it is does not have the habit of being warm, or because it carries within it an interior warmth more potent than that of an ardent stove.

Lévy-Bloch, the art-dealer, is also delighted. He has taken off his pelisse. He is a very fat, red-faced man. He is eyeing the women, smiling stupidly. Martial nudges Zette with his elbow to show her that he is panting and very warm.

He has brought a Russian with him, who is a blond man with a little moustache. He is parading slightly glaucous, humid and cruel eyes over everything. He has also taken off his pelisse—and Martial has just said that everything will go well, since the Russian gives the impression of being satisfied with the temperature. According to him a Russian must be colder than men of another race.

Zette's beverage is working wonders, and all the guests are praising it, and drinking a great deal.

Two poets recite admirable fragments of their works, with great success. Annie, who should have been admitted to the Conservatoire years ago, recites verses by Baudelaire. Lévy-Bloch affirms, very loudly and gravely, as if he were pronouncing historic words expected by the crowd, that he likes Martial's paintings enormously, and that he will make something of the fellow. And I hear him murmur with much less solemnity to Zette, but as if it were the logical continuation of the preceding historic words, that he finds her charming and desires to see her again soon.

"Everything's on the right path," Martial says to me. "We're truly in society, and there's a certain atmosphere of luxury."

But why the devil can a match not be found at the right moment, when Lévy-Bloch wants to light a cigar? It is as rapid as a catastrophe. Zette has bounded forward, holding out her cigarette. Too late! Lévy-Bloch has approached the stove without fear of being burned; he has opened the little metal door and leaned over.

Martial and Zette look at one another with horror, and suddenly feel the cold accumulated in the room penetrate them profoundly.

Lévy-Bloch has seen the candle burning sadly in the empty stove, the symbol of poverty.

When he straightens up with his cigar lit, he does not have the astonishment that one might expect, nor the irony. But he is cold. He puts his pelisse back on.

Oh yes—all is illusion.

Martial sees the hope of a sale vanishing. He will not be treated like some rich painter that he knows and who sells his works for the sole reason that he has no need to sell them. His forehead darkens; he darts a melancholy glance over the soirée, which is deprived of all its splendor. He sees how disproportionate the jam jar is beside the liqueur glass. He feels the wind that is blowing through all the cracks in his windows. The winter cold chills his bones. The difficulty of life overwhelms him.

Fortunately, Zette knows one side of life. She knows that it is necessary to attenuate the unfortunate effect of poverty, and she knows how to attenuate it. She draws Lévy-Bloch and his pelisse into a corner and speaks to him in a low voice.

I see her smile. It's not a sacrifice that she's making, or, if it is one, she is making it joyfully. Lévy-Bloch is ridiculous, fat and red-faced. My God! There are more tedious things in life, and men fatter and more red-faced. Yes, yes, it's understood; she will bring him the two canvases herself, tomorrow.

And when we have gone and she finds herself alone with Martial, they will blow out the candle in the stove and she will tell him that the paintings are sold.

And as youth has a great power of belief, Martial will imagine that Lévy-Bloch has not seen the candle, that he has been seduced by a reception in the abode of a rich painter who has talent, and he will cry: "I was right, you see!"

He was right. All is illusion.

We are going down the Rue Lepic in the winter night. Rose-Thé is talking to Annie, the future pupil of the Conservatoire. In front of us, Jean Noël is walking alongside the young woman he has not quit all evening, and whose bursts of laughter we have heard at times. Hallu is beside me and he is looking obstinately at his feet as if he were concentrating the effort of his will on them.

I turn round abruptly, like someone who senses that he is being observed.

Lévy-Bloch and is Russian friend are coming down behind us, and I do, in fact, see the man's glaucous eyes fixed upon me. They are moist, as if he were about to weep, but one might think that they are never dry.

Why is that Russian looking at me?

It seems that Hallu is magnetized by his feet. I touch his arm. He makes no response. As we arrive at the Boulevard de Clichy, I question him, asking him what he is thinking about.

He seems annoyed to have been interrupted in his reverie, and finally stops looking at his feet, but regretfully. I consider them and have a desire to tell him that they are not worthy of such long examination and that it would even be better not to pay any attention to them, because of their considerable and almost deformed appearance.

He points at Jean Noël and his friend, in front of us.

"I was trying to carry out an experiment. It didn't succeed, but I'll have my revenge next time. Come and see me and I'll explain everything."

Hallu disappears without saying *au revoir* to anyone. People shake hands. The Russian's green-tinted eyes are still posed on mine and I feel glad to be finally rid of his presence.

Rose-Thé and I walk on a little way, and comment on the soirée and the people we saw there.

How curious women are!

Rose-Thé finds Lévy-Bloch very sympathetic, and not too bad physically. And I have the satisfaction of hearing her say that the Russian disgusts her and has the effect on her of a reptile.

Chapter V

Hallu lived in a little apartment in the Rue du Delta, on the fifth floor, an apartment of the kind that has a milk jug on the landing and where a lock removed a long time ago leaves a hole in the door that is stuffed with paper. A number five, poorly traced in chalk on the wall, reminded distracted visitors that they have reached the fifth floor.

Hallu came to open the door himself. He was wearing black velvet pajamas with white edges, singularly funereal, ragged and stained, and I saw immediately that he had retained, in spite of his affectation of clairvoyant realism, a great deal of the puerile romanticism of our youth. Willfully ill-assorted objects cluttered a little hallway. There as a stuffed bird, a turtle's carapace, a Japanese mask, a halberd and dusty volumes.

I penetrated into a small drawing room in which the vivid sunlight of two o'clock in the afternoon was replaced by the tremulous light of an oil lamp. Curtains, once bright red, were imperfectly drawn, and in front of the window the daylight struggled sadly with that of the lamp, refusing any harmonious fusion.

More dusty volumes cluttered the floor, the table and the seats. In one corner, there was a divinity of sorts, which was not a Buddha, nor a goddess of good fortune, nor a Virgin, nor an Egyptian statue, and which appeared to me to be rather curious. On the table I perceived a photograph of Mademoiselle Stevens, the young woman I had seen in Martial's studio and who seemed to me to have preoccupied Hallu greatly. Several little wax figures were lined up on the mantelpiece and seemed to be maladroit sketches, making me think that my friend was devoting his spare time to sculpture.

"Yes, it's her, you recognize her," Hallu said, on seeing me looking at the photograph. "Perhaps you think that she's the mistress of the fellow she was with the other day?"

"In general," I said, "When a woman leaves with a man, there's every chance..."

"Nothing of the sort," said Hallu, in a tone that brooked no reply, "and there never will be. I can tell you one thing, of which I wasn't sure a few days ago but of which I'm certain now, which is that she'll be my mistress in a short time."

I remembered that in the course of Martial's soirée, the young woman in question had not cast her eyes upon Hallu and that she had said *bonjour* to him very coldly when he arrived. I remembered her slender and supple silhouette, her sea-green eyes, her feline grace and the sound of her laughter, and, considering the unkempt Hallu, with his hair like an uncultivated forest on his head, his mouth twisted by envy, in which a missing tooth made a gap, the reek of an unwashed man that his person emitted, I hoped that his certainty had no basis.

And as the memory of the philosopher's ancient confidences came back to me, his base sensuality and particularities of his physique of which he boasted, I was seized by disgust and said to myself that if there was a harmony in creatures, it would be destroyed by that union.

Hallu surprised my thought and said, bitterly: "One never wants one's friends to succeed in that matter. But that doesn't matter. I believe that in a few days I'll have made a discovery that will give me the power of which we dreamed when we were twenty."

I made a sign that I didn't understand.

"It's not a discovery, for a host of wise men have practiced what I'm searching for and have profited from it during their lives. How many have known the secret of casting the spell and have made use of it without anyone knowing! It's a matter, of course, of casting the spell of amour, that which consists of making oneself loved by the woman one desires. I'm not thinking of practicing the other, although it would be just as easy, and even easier. It's easier to kill by means of magic than to make oneself loved."

211

I looked sat him with astonishment, but with an apparent credulity, for I wanted him to continue talking. I was not taken in by my expression.

"You're like all the men of your time. You don't believe in that nonsense. Fortunately, moreover. It's thanks to that development of human stupidity, because of that reign of skepticism, that I can work peacefully and recover the traces of a science that's almost lost. Whatever I do in that order of ideas, and whatever result I obtain, no one believes me. But you, such as I know you, after having laughed and thought: 'My friend Hallu is mad,' you're going to say to yourself: 'Who knows? What if he's right? What if that belief, which goes back to the remotest ages of antiquity, had a basis of truth? What if the practices that the Assyrians and the Chaldeans knew, those peoples far wiser than ours, gave positive results? What if it's only a matter of finding the formulae, and that madman Hallu were on the point of finding them?' To make all the women one wants to come to one's bed, even the most chaste? What a fine secret, when one has hair that's beginning to go gray!"

Speaking thus, he almost touched my temples with his black fingernail, causing a little triumphant laugher to resound. Then he passed his hand through his hirsute black hair, as if to affirm his superiority over me in that regard.

But he was right. I said to myself: *More extraordinary things have been seen—wireless telegraphy, for instance. Why shouldn't influences act at a distance, why shouldn't they be provoked? Weren't the magicians of old the initiators of modern scientists?*

"Tracked and persecuted through the centuries by ignorant and limited men," Hallu said, "Magicians didn't write down their secrets directly. They transmitted them in the form of symbols, of which it was necessary to possess the keys. Or, when they confessed them under torture, they only confessed them incompletely, in such a way that they would be unusable. The greater number of the magical formulas we posses come from witch-trials, so the formulae have a bizarre and even

212

comical character. They're almost always false. It's necessary to recover the truth from among a host of deliberate errors and mystifications.

"In addition to that, there's the material difficulty of carrying out experiments and the near impossibility of procuring the indispensable elements. Where could I find, for instance, the heart of a weasel, the testicles of a leopard—which, strictly speaking, could be replaced by those of a three-year-old billy-goat—the fish known as squilla, the catochitis stone and the satyrion herb? And even if I knew where that herb is, it would still be necessary for me to pick it on a Friday at midnight, when the moon is full and I can do it clad in white and walking backwards, without exciting the suspicions of passersby. And if all those things are in my possession, there would be the difficulty of making the person on whom I want it to act drink the beverage I've composed, or to wear around her neck the talisman composed of those ingredients that would influence her by magnetism."

"You once had a scientific mind," I said, "positive and little inclined to the marvelous. Do you really believe in the influence of a weasel's heart, the fish known as squilla and he catochitis stone?"

"What's marvelous about it? You admit that there are sympathies and antipathies between beings. They always have physical causes, a carnal basis. Why, by virtue of a principle unknown to us, shouldn't those physical sympathies be transposed by means of a vehicle as physical as them? Why shouldn't desire, which is a disease itself, be transmitted by absorption or contact like diseases?"

"It would still be necessary for reality to confirm those hypotheses."

"But it's not a hypothesis, it's a certainty. I've already achieved surprising results. Do you know what tying the shoulder-knot is?"

"Yes—it's provoking amorous impotence at a distance, and the naïve Middle Ages punished with death people accused of troubling nights of newlyweds in that fashion."

213

"Well, it's a power that I possess. René Stevens isn't mine yet. She soon will be. But in the meantime, she won't be anyone else's. Whoever the man might be with whom she lies down, the circle of coldness with which I envelop her at a distance will act upon him, and she'll only have beside her a ridiculous lover who won't be a lover."

I was skeptical, but I did not make it manifest. Hallu had stopped and was thoughtful. The bitterness of his mouth was further accentuated.

I said to him: "Admitting that you have a woman by occult means, you only have her body, the pleasure that you can get out of it. She gives herself to you, but doesn't love you for that."

For a second, his face reflected an expression of sadness, which was followed by a coarse satisfaction, the base desire of a brute.

"That's already a lot," he said. "And then, if you want to make a woman love you, the best means, the one that gives you the greatest facility, is to begin by bedding her. One can then find psychic means for a bewitchment of thought."

I got up to go. I was experiencing a certain disgust, mingled with a vivid curiosity about my old fried. He sniggered bitterly on the landing. A deformed figure five was displayed in chalk before my eyes, and I suddenly saw again the expression of simultaneous pride and tenderness that Mademoiselle Stevens' face had, her slender neck, the birth of the shoulders, and I thought privately that if wishes had any occult power in the invisible, mine would prevent her from climbing that staircase.

Chapter VI

I cannot explain how, having invented the plausible pretext of a journey, I was able to quit Rose-Thé, whom I loved, and whose charm was exercised on me in a permanent fashion, in order to go and find some prostitute, quite pretty, admittedly, but who went to bed with anyone for a little money.

The reason could not be an ordinary lust. The pleasure I had had with that woman, named Paula, a habitué of the bars of Toulouse and the treat of petty provincials on the spree, was only, in truth, a pleasure of the most mediocre order. Why did it exercise upon me that spell, call me back to her with such force?

Sitting on the train that was taking me to Toulouse, I did not sense the ordinary joy that I had in movement, and yet, I knew that I was responding to an appeal of my instinct and that a dolor would take possession of me if it had been necessary to go back. And I couldn't help thinking about Hallu and wondering whether it was not a kind of bewitchment, whether I might be the victim of some secret maneuver, whether the fat proprietress of the bar where I had drunk might have thrown the dried skin of some enchanted animal into the martini of a cocktail instead of lemon peel.

When I had braved the sadness of a station at seven o'clock in the morning on a day in November, the inexpressible odor of dentifrice, linen and dust of a provincial hotel room, and I had respired the amicable odor of the stones of a city where the climate is warmer, I launched myself rapidly, without bothering to buy flowers, toward the avenue near the cemetery.

I knocked in vain. No one replied. I knocked again and called out. Eventually, from the courtyard behind the house, where a broken pump, an empty shed and a leafless fig-tree made a desolate landscape, an old woman emerged, like the sordid fay of that mediocre place, broom in hand.

She was jovial and obsequious. She bowed. She desired to enter into conversation, to be useful, to execute commissions, to recount her life-story. Paula had gone. She didn't know anything else, except that even the postman didn't know her new address. That's what little women are like. No foresight! They don't think that they might have very agreeable visits. But a little woman could be found. If one didn't find that one...

I left. My desire to see Paula had just increased a hundredfold. It was further augmented by my forced solitude in the immense deserted cafés of the morning. Finally, the hour that many people call the hour of aperitifs sounded, and I ran to see the fat Renée-Marie, who opened the doors of her bar.

Yes! She knew Paula's address. And could one refuse to reveal it, when one manages one's own bar, to a sympathetic man who takes a glass of port with you and will come back in the evening with friends and have many more? What a nice little woman Paula was! She had everything necessary to succeed. The grand bicycle merchant in the Boulevard Carnot was interested in her for a long time and wanted to put her in his furnished flat. Paula, it's true, had no dress sense, but she had a good figure, one couldn't refuse her that. It's an enormous advantage for a woman to have a good figure. Unfortunately, there was that dirty fellow. Who could take her seriously when she was with such a man? There was no doubt about it, he was living on her. If he had even been a handsome fellow! But no. He was a brute. As for being embarrassed to go and see her because of him—ha ha! That's good one! On the contrary, he'd be delighted. The more friends Paula had, the more content he was, the more she brought him. All in all, an utterly dirty fellow.

It was in the Minimes that Paula lived, and that was the quarter in which I'd spent my early childhood. Renée-Marie welcomed newcomers with a broad smile on her jaundiced face, and I leapt on to a tram.

It was an open tram, for the day was fine and was warm. It went slowly, without haste, in the manner of a provincial tram, and was carrying almost no one. A woman with a basket signaled to it. It stopped, and set off again indolently. And as it passed the Rue des Chalets, a curious phenomenon was produced. I saw myself, with a gripping reality, emerging from that street, where I had once lived, with a large black hat slightly tilted over the ear in order to give me a conquering air, and a light cane that I was twirling in my right hand as I walked. And behind me, with an equal precision, I made out my companions: Hallu, Verdelle and Plaignier, young, dressed without elegance but preceded by their hopes, which seemed to be playing fanfares before them. And there were also other faces, a little less clear, emerging from the neighboring streets and filling the Rue des Chalets. There were young seamstresses, bourgeois demi-virgins, Paulette, who had been our common mistress, the faces of students of that era, and an old housekeeper named Rosalie who made up our rooms and liked us a lot.

And suddenly, it all vanished. The tram had gone past the Rue des Chalets. I perceived that someone behind me, who was singing in dialect, had just stopped singing.

I turned round. I looked at an individual who was sitting there, and whose voice had evoked my old memories, and I recognized Plaignier.

It was him. He still had that air of powerful tranquility, but his face was wrinkled. He had something slightly vile about him, and a little grave. He was poorly and negligently dressed.

He recognized me, and we shook hands affectionately, asking one another the habitual questions about our lives.

We had arrived at the Minimes. There, two columns loomed up near a canal. Not far away there was a sluice-gate surrounded by bare ground, and beyond, the Toulousan suburb extended with an inexpressible sadness, further aggravated by the splendor of the autumnal sun.

We walked a little way, linking arms in order to show our mutual contentment at finding one another again.

"Shall we have something?" I said, showing him a minuscule café of shabby appearance.

We had almost arrived at Paula's house, and I wanted to quit him beforehand.

He smiled, and there was a momentary embarrassment, which dissipated immediately.

"It's me who has that little café," he said. "It's not a brilliant business, but after all, one has to live."

Inside I saw two heavily made-up maids with red corsages and very low necklines. I understood that they were half-servants and half-whores, and that the little café was one of those little cafés of which there are many in the outlying districts of the cities of the Midi, welcoming soldiers emerging from barracks and humble men who have finished their day's work.

As one of them served us, Plaignier glimpsed my expression and said: "Don't think that…they're maids. I have a delightful mistress."

I hastened to tell him that I didn't doubt it, that this business was as good as another and that, in life, it's necessary to do what one can without worrying about the opinions of others.

He talked to me about his mistress. According to him, she was the prettiest girl in Toulouse. She was twenty years old. She was extraordinarily elegant.

"Does she help out with the café?" I asked, without knowing why.

"Certainly not. She doesn't work. She really is a very chic woman. She goes to teas, to the theater. She's only seen there."

And as the warmth of friendship circulated between us with evoked memories, I told my friend that after being faithful to a mistress I loved for a long time I had come all the same to Toulouse to see a little woman with whom I had already passed one evening me time ago.

218

Plaignier appeared to show a vivid satisfaction.

"And what's she like?"

"Pretty enough, but not very. Rather vulgar and modest in appearance. A Toulousan woman, like so many others. Her name is Paula and she was living at that time near the cemetery. Do you know her?"

Plaignier's eyes had creased. His smile had taken on a slightly fixed expression.

"Yes; this is a small city, you know. Everyone knows everyone."

He looked around for a moment, as if the canal, the two columns, the shops and the low houses appeared to him with a character of great sadness, as if he were seeing the ugliness of things and the misery of life for the first time.

But that didn't last. The natural serenity of his face reappeared. He was a simple man who liked simple situations.

He started to laugh and tapped me on the knee. "It's my mistress you're talking about," he said. "Except that women are different, depending on the point of view at which one places oneself. She lives over there. The three of us will have dinner together."

I sketched a gesture of refusal.

"You know very well," he said, drawing me toward the house, that I've never been jealous."

An evening with a woman one desires in provincial bars and cafés is long when one is not sure of the outcome of the evening. One knows deep down that the stake isn't worth the game that one is playing. One would like to have the whole affair concluded, and even not to have started it. But the persistence of desire and one's own sluggishness obliges one not to turn back.

Paula's hair, black at the roots and gilded thereafter, fell from her head in sheaves. In the restaurant where the three of us had dined she had eaten gluttonously, she had laughed, she had drunk and she had stared at all the men who passed by, including the waiters, with shiny eyes whose lashes fluttered.

She belonged to an inferior race, devoid of delicacy and without any limit on her instincts. She spoke about many of the men of the city who had been her lovers, and insisted expressly, in order that it should be clear to me, that Plaignier, who lived with her, was aware of her liaisons.

I suffered from my friend's baseness, but he did not seem to be aware of it. On the contrary, he insisted cynically on what his mistress said. He seemed to have passed on to another plane than the one of which ordinary men live, from the moral point of view. And I wondered momentarily whether that was not a great superiority, and whether Plaignier had not attained a high degree of philosophical wisdom.

Now, in Renée-Marie's bar, Paula was going from our table to the neighboring tables, where comrades were sitting, getting up to dance, stopping dancing in order to laugh uproariously because of something said in passing, incessantly showing her brilliant teeth and her low vulpine brow, tinted blonde.

She had left us for quite a long time when she came back precipitately to tell us that the jeweler's son was there.

"He's the son of a rich jeweler," Plaignier told me, calmly.

Paula departed again immediately in order to go and dance with him. He was a young man, very personable and very correct, who danced the tango with gravity, as one accomplishes a pious ceremony.

I thought, on seeing the fashion in which Paula swooned languorously against his shoulder, that the result of the evening, already very dubious because of Plaignier's presence, was decided, and that I had only to beat a retreat with as much dignity as possible.

I was wrong. Plaignier assured me of it.

"Paula throws herself more or less at all these brutal businessmen," he said, designating the generality of the audience.

But suddenly, Paula discovered the existence of an intimate friend who was among the three musicians of the orchestra, whom she had not noticed until then. The three musicians were huddled on a stage so tiny that it was a miracle that they could play.

While dancing, Paula made joyful signs at a brown-haired violinist, who sometimes looked at her with a blasé smile. She spoke to him volubly and, as another musician picked up a plate in order to make a collection, I saw Paula recommending to the jeweler's son and his group not to forget the orchestra. The orchestra, presenting itself before everyone with a plate, and remaining there for a few seconds, could not be forgotten under any pretext. Paula approached us in order to make a similar recommendation, but Plaignier seemed discontented by it, and that was his sole shadow of ill humor throughout the evening.

I noticed, in addition, that, either by distraction or for some other reason, the musician did not present the plate to my friend. After that neglect, I experienced a vivid satisfaction in seeing the plate advancing toward me, and with an ostentation of which I was not the master, I threw a handful of coins into it.

Saucers were rising up over the tables like fragile monuments commemorating the victory of alcohol over man. All the young men were causing animal cries to resound. A woman had hiccups.

I saw Paula in a corner giving explanations to the jeweler's son, and I thought I understood that she was introducing me as an exceedingly rich foreigner who it was necessary to handle carefully, her situation and future being at stake. The jeweler's son resigned himself easily to such a natural fatality.

All three of us were on the boulevard, in the blue nocturnal air. I said that I was going back to my hotel and certainly, seeing the false serenity of Plaignier and his humble expression, I ought to have done so, out of pity for him and for the memory of friendship. But I was marching on the road of desire.

"The weather's fine, come back with us," said Paula squeezing my arm. And she added, in a low voice: "Make a semblance of leaving us and come to join me later."

It was impossible that Plaignier had not perceived her whispering.

The sad columns and the water of the canal appeared to my eyes. Then we arrived next to the little café, before which there were four laurel bushes in wooden pots.

There, I learned that everyone was going their own way, Plaignier into the little café, Paul to her home.

"I have a room up there," said Plaignier, showing me a mansard window while Paula winked at me ostentatiously.

I shook their hands and made a semblance of going away. I was still under the shadow of the columns when I retraced my steps, knowing full well that I was wrong and that I was acting badly.

Paula was waiting for me, laughing, on her threshold. The window that Plaignier had shown me was now illuminated by a faint light. He would only have had to look through it to see me, but he did not, for he was doubtless only too certain of my return.

Paula put an arm round my neck.

"Come in, Coco," she said.

I was already in the corridor when I stopped.

In the distance, in his room, Plaignier was singing a melancholy song, in dialect. In the silence of the night, over the bleak suburb, it took on an unexpected importance. Was that a sign of his indifference? Was he singing for the maids in the neighboring bedrooms? Or playing his last card? Did he want to recall Paula to him by the means of seduction with which he must have charmed her originally? Or was he saying to his old friend that friendship ought to be honored, even when a friend has come down in the world, and that it is only then that fidelity truly has merit?

Paula's warm face was against mine. I sensed her odor of youth and I followed her.

The problem of desire seems to me to be insoluble. Why do two beings precipitate themselves upon one another frenziedly, in order to obtain a pleasure that they could, in sum, have with others? Why that electricity of the gaze, why that appetite, sudden and violent, to be devoid of clothing, to have one's skin against the warmth of another skin, of such a color and such an odor, to swoon there and not elsewhere?

A week went by, for me, of an almost animal existence. I did not even have the power of knowing the remorse of living among vulgar, base people and suffering from the invisible harm that I was causing my friend Plaignier. And yet I knew that the harm is all the greater if one is inflicting it on someone who has lost his nobility of soul and taken the descending path. I knew that it is unpardonable then, because it is exercised against the most pitiful.

But in the blind satisfaction of our passions, an instinct in nevertheless on watch, and urges us not to sacrifice everything to those avid beasts. There was no reason for my mind to decide to take the evening train to Paris on the seventh day rather than any other. I remember that I was like a man who has sat down to a meal in order to satisfy and indeterminate hunger for vulgar dishes and who eats until they stop being served.

Before quitting Toulouse, I went to say *au revoir* to Plaignier.

I went through the main room of the little café where a maidservant with a puffy face was asleep, her elbows on the marble table stained by wine, and I went into the little garden in the rear.

There, Plaignier, in his short-sleeves, was devoting himself to some cultivation or other. He had a spade in his hand. He put it down on seeing me and waited, calmly. I had not seen him for two or three days, and he few seconds of silence that preceded the banal phrase that I pronounced seem very long to me.

"I'm leaving, my dear," I said to him, with a grand bonhomie, "And I've come to shake your hand before leaving."

He said "Ah!" moving his head slightly and letting a new silence fall.

"I'm returning to the land, you see," he said. "I've already become a peasant again by the hands and feet." And he showed me his hands, yellow with mud, and his feet shod in gross clogs. "And I'll end up going to labor in my homeland, being a peasant entirely."

"What! You're going to leave...."

I was about to say: *You're going to leave Paula*. I stated again;

"You're going to leave this little café?"

Plaignier smiled.

"It was an illusion I no longer have. One doesn't live with women when one's a peasant like me. I put the three thousand francs I possessed into this café. It's a very bad business. The maids steal from me. They have a capacity for drink that you can't imagine. The barracks are some distance away. There are broken glasses for which no one pays. In sum, I can't recover."

"And you'd have the courage to go back to the country?"

I thought about a very poor house, at the very edge of a village, in the Pyrenees, and a square of land bordered by a hedge. I had once stopped there for an hour, during the vacation.

"Yes, I'll go back to my little field, and that will be my salvation. There's a well out there, and a single tree, which is a cypress. But a single tree is sufficient, you see, when one has finished with the ridiculous hopes of youth. I remember that in summer, when I was a child, I lay down in its shadow, which covered me exactly. It shrank at midday and became enormous in the evening. Well, that was a symbol of my life. I'm now in the middle of the day, and the shadow is very short, but as my life advances in the little field out here. I'll have the shadow of the cypress before me, longer and longer."

I told him, and I thought it, that perhaps he was right, if he didn't fear the ennui of a life to which he was so dishabituated, and where it would be necessary for him to renounce the women for whom he had such a liking.

"Not at all! I'll marry a peasant woman, who'll labor with me."

I shook his hand in order to go.

He added: "I hope you'll come to see me then."

Our gazes met. I thought that he was putting a certain irony into his words—but no, not in the least. And he shook my hand very affectionately.

Chapter VII

Rose-Thé told me that during my absence Lévy-Bloch had come to see her with the reptile with the glaucous eyes that accompanied him everywhere and who was Russian. I learned that the Russian was named Pavlichef, that he had been smitten with a warm amity for me and that he was awaiting my return impatiently in order that we could dine together with Martial and Zette, in whose home we had met, and other friends.

I was astonished to have appeared so sympathetic to someone who had not addressed a word to me and, in sum, did not know me. But I told myself that the laws of sympathy are mysterious and that in that order of ideas, anything is possible.

I accepted, in spite of Rose-Thé's ardent insistence, who would have preferred not to go to that dinner because of the repulsion that the Russian inspired in her.

I even remember that, when evening came, she declared to me that she had a headache and, contrary to her habits, she insisted that I go alone. Contrary to my habits, however, I also insisted that accompany me, and she came.

The dinner took place in a new restaurant that had just opened, and was also a dance-hall. We found the painter Martial at the door, who had arrived in advance and who was waiting, preferring to go in with friends, he told us. He was clad in a loose black jacket, according to the formula of artists who are not rich, and he was wearing a blue lavallière cravat with white spots that seemed new. He had difficulty disguising his joy at dining with Lévy-Bloch and that joy was only tempered by his timidity at penetrating into a luxurious place. Zette arrived late, coming from who knows where. The Russian had the icy cordiality of a naturally cold man. And there was also the poet Jean Noël, with Mademoiselle Stevens.

I admired the latter. Her bright green eyes seemed to be the reflection of a pure and sad soul whose gaiety is politeness. Her translucent shoulders emerged from a tulle dress almost the same color as her eyes. Her hands were little jewels, and there would have been a perfect modesty in all her movements if a certain feline quality hand not revealed a hidden sensuality at times. Nothing in the young woman's attitude indicated that she had the slightest familiarity with Jean Noël. I felt detestation for Hallu, remembering his words and his desire.

Lévy-Bloch could not conceive of a meal without a great abundance of wines and he served everyone generously. The guests shared that manner of seeing. The imprudent Zette sometimes insisted that a dish was brought to her again, as if she were hosting the dinner. Then, Lévy-Bloch laughed with pride.

The radiant Martial talked about his works, tracing lines in the air with his thumb, and ate enormously, bent double over his plate. He emptied his glass as soon as it was filled and I perceived, after the desserts, that Zette touched him on the knee to stop him from drinking the finger-bowl containing a slice of lemon, which he carried to his lips in his furry of absorption.

The Russian heaped me with maladroit politeness, which, with the warmth of the meal, I no longer attributed to anything but a real amity, but I only replied confusedly. I no longer worried, either, about his moist eyes fixed upon me.

In spite of the effort I made to take part in my friends' delight, to enjoy the intoxication one moment and Rose-Thé's smile the next, I became disinterested in the place and the people as the meal went on. I saw something else; beyond the tables brilliant with crystal, between which the waiters were running, I distinguished other images, and I was their prisoner.

The auto that had brought us had climbed the Faubourg Montmartre for a few seconds. I had breached its air, and I could not detach myself from faces rapidly perceived by the light of little bars under which the humanity of prostitution swarmed.

I imagined the intense and moving pleasure that I would have had in quitting my companions, leaving and walking along the road full of whores, respiring the breath of cafés and the exhalation that comes from the depths of the corridors of furnished hotels. I imagined one of those hotels that I knew, in the Rue Geoffroy-Marie, which had an ancient wooden barrier near the door and where the rooms were hired by the hour at an exceedingly cheap rate.

I had gone in there once, years ago, shortly after my arrival in Paris. A woman I had encountered had told me to go to see her there. Her name came back to me: Lucie Blomet. I had asked a fat bare-headed maid for her, who had said in a thick voice to someone in the hotel office: "Someone's asking for Lucie."

"Well, she's in eleven," someone had replied.

The fat maid had told me: "She's in eleven," showing me a corridor, and I had felt that she followed me with her eyes as if something was about to happen.

I had knocked on the door of eleven. Lucie's voice had replied to me: "Ah! It's the grogs!"

She had opened the door slightly and I had seen her on the threshold in her chemise. Behind her, in the part of the room I could see, there was a bowler hat and two large boots, worn and gaping.

"Oh, that's annoying!" Lucie Blomet had said, calmly. "I can't let you in. Come back anther day."

And she had closed the door. I had heard her say: "It's not the grogs yet."

Why did that memory return to me with such a singular precision while the orchestra was playing, while Rose-Thé was searching my face for my personal impressions in order to formulate her own judgment on the occasion, and I ought to have had a thousand other subjects of thought?

Why did the memory of other whores, other places where one encounters them, the cafés where they wait and solicit, like beasts in a market, haunt me with such force?

I tried to detach myself from it, to watch the couples who were dancing the tango in front of me, to follow Pavlichef, who had invited Rose-Thé, and to measure their value as dancers.

I did not succeed in that. I was there, among my friends; I pronounced banal words; but my veritable soul was wandering in the Faubourg Montmartre, rubbing shoulders with shady nocturnal individuals, stopping in front of cinema exits, approaching women, brushing their bodies, respiring their odor.

And sometimes, a face emerged from the confusion of images, appearing to me with a gripping verity, and it was always the face of a whore with her head slightly sunken into the shoulders, who resembled a blonde she-wolf.

It was late. Pavlichef proposed that we go to his residence to have a glass of champagne, as all people do who consider that the night is an enemy that one must kill by means of theaters, suppers and belated gatherings.

We went. He showed us his apartment with an affected indifference. I noticed that Rose-Thé was more affectionate than usual and pressed herself against me with a sort of affectation. Mademoiselle Stevens was in haste to go home because her parents were waiting for her. The green of her eyes had an unequaled purity. The dinner, the music and the champagne had not communicated to her the animation the rest of us had. She remained proud, smiling and distant, and I told myself as I looked at her that neither Jean Noël not Hallu would attain their objectives.

Pavlichef had continued to send me, via the intermediary of his moist gaze, a sympathy that did not succeed in obtaining mine. He told me that he hoped that I would like to spend similar evenings with him in future.

And suddenly, when we were in his antechamber, I understood.

He was holding Rose-Thé's coat while she arranged her hair in front of the mirror. Of, certainly, he was no longer thinking about me! His legs slightly bent, his eyes, extraordinarily devoid of luster and bulging from his head, fixed on

Rose-Thé, he gave the impression of a stupid beast ready to pounce. A tenacious and violent desire emanated from him.

He did not pounce. He helped Rose-Thé to put on her coat with a cold politeness.

I was irritated with myself for not having understood sooner. But as we were walking along the street I heard my mistress talking to me again about the disgust that the Russian inspired in her—and I concluded that there was no need to exaggerate the importance of all that, and that Rose-Thé loved me too much.

So many men are insensate!

Chapter VIII

Nature does not act insensibly, as people say and as they believe. Evidently, one does not see children growing visibly, but there are plants that have an extraordinary growth in a single night. At every moment we are witness to phenomena that seem to have been created uniquely to disconcert us. We are used to that, but on reflection, we are obliged to agree that nature has incomprehensible eccentricities in her laws.

Children have two ears that develop simultaneously and in an imperceptible fashion. It is the same for the fingers and the hair. The teeth, however, do not follow that regularity of development. One sees them spring forth one by one in childish palates.

In the order of natural phenomena the seasons follow one another but do not give way to one another harmoniously. In October, without regard for the delicacy of our organisms, a sharp cold suddenly appears, to be immediately replaced by an abnormal heat. One goes out without an umbrella; a diluvian rain replaces the sunlight without transition. It takes five minutes for a tidal wave to be unleashed and devastate a shore.

It is the same with human passions. They surge forth within us like the tidal wave, and when they pass they destroy the moral edifices that we have built with so much care. We do not know where they come from or where they go. We are obliged to observe their violence and submit to it.

I had been subject to a storm. It was followed by a clear spell. A tempest came that bowled me over. And this was the first sign of it.

I had turned the corner of the Boulevard des Batignolles and was going up the Rue de Rome when I crossed the path of a woman whose eyes were shiny and who looked me directly in the face while lifting the left-hand corner of her lip. In her right hand she was carrying inn a visible manner, almost solemnly, a key. She raised it like a weapon, like a symbol, like a

231

sort of professional sign. Thus she suppressed uncertainties and explanations. She gained time on the brief and hard life of the street. Everyone knew, when she raised that piece of iron, that her bedroom as hospitable to everyone and that one only had to follow her to penetrate into it and enjoy her body.

The woman's face was anonymous, similar to all the faces of women of that category. That was what I thought, at least. I still believed at that moment in my life that all women were nearly alike, externally and in the soul. I was only to realize a little later their dolorous diversity and human profundity.

I perceived as I went past that the woman was limping slightly, and a single glance over my shoulder confirmed it. She was walking behind me. Had she changed her mind about her direction? Had she perceived a possible desire in my gaze? I don't know. But she had turned round and, in truth, she was following on my heels.

As we were alone on the street I heard her footsteps on the sidewalk, which were hastening in order to catch up with me.

I felt disgust for her and an unjust anger. What! That woman, who must hook men every evening in the environs of the Place Clichy, whose path I had crossed in front of a tobacconist's shop and who had probably chosen that place because the commerce of tobacco attracts me, that bearer of the key offered to all and sundry, was confounding me in her wretched clientele! She took me for a poor clerk, a solitary stroller in quest of modestly-priced pleasure!

I hastened my steps. I heard the limping hooker behind me walking a little faster. Then I experienced a bitter joy in walking more rapidly, in outdistancing her. Her irregular footfalls had became distant. Two autobuses went by in succession with a horrible din, and I no longer hard anything.

But suddenly, I stopped. From my inner depths, a heartbeat increased, and I sensed a sudden warmth in my brain. I had deceived myself. The form of the limping woman appeared to me singularly agreeable and full of sensuality. Her torso had inclined slightly as she passed me, with a movement that troubled me. I remembered that her face was young, that her eyes were not wrinkled, and that her hair was abundant.

She must inhabit either a hotel room or a small apartment among the thousand obscure streets of the Batignolles quarter. The key that she had caused to shine in my eyes was the emblem of immediate hospitality, curiosity immediately satisfied.

I went back rapidly, sounding the obscurity of the lamentable Rue de Tome, but I understood that things were contrary to my desire, for just at that moment a passing train released a thick jet of smoke, by which I was enveloped. And when that jet had dissipated, the tottering silhouette was no longer within the circle of my gaze.

I had the sentiment of a sensual opportunity lost, a pleasure that it would be difficult for me to rediscover.

And from that day on, it was as if an almost perpetual desire was unleashed within me, but a desire that was not exercised on the pretty and veritably desirable women that I might encounter, a desire that only enveloped with its heavy mist the mediocre creatures of the street, those who seek out and offer themselves to passers-by by means of their eyes and their whispered words. It seemed to me that since Paula in Toulouse I had abruptly tumbled down a descending ladder to the bottommost steps.

The boulevards, which I had always detested for their breathless and commercial crowd, which I had carefully avoided in my excursions, took on a great charm for me. I can even say that I discovered their beauty. I became their guest every evening. I knew that it was the place on earth where there was the richest human soil, the most abundant and the most various. I took pleasure in sitting down on the terrace of some café, in looking around and the provincials at the tables, neighboring thieves in quest of coups to bring off, with idle aged retirees, with whores fatigued by their comings and goings, and with men similar to me, tormented by sexual desire.

I gazed, dazzled at the rivers that the Faubourg Montmartre and the Boulevard de Strasbourg are, which carry indifferently businessmen, pimps, autobuses and the perennial lost children. After having paused on the banks formed by the cafés, where there is so much foam and detritus, I left myself drift in their waters, and dived delightedly into their errant mud. I became accustomed to recognizing, in a matter of seconds, among the lone women, those who were bearing within them the intention of making the acquaintance of a passing lone man, either for an immediate sum of money, or for future advantages, or with a disinterested thought, by virtue of ennui or laxity. I became expert in those distinctions. I was astonished by the prodigious quantity of beings submissive to hazard, who come out every day at the same time and go forth without knowing where, but with the certainty that before the evening is over they will have followed another unknown being and that the mystery of desire and form will have been revealed to them.

I was also astonished that there were so many pretty and cultivated women who were condemned to that wretched métier, that quotidian uncertainty. Experience informed me that the destiny of certain women was marked by an eternal bad luck, while others, who were neither more beautiful not cleverer, struggled incessantly from the dawn of their life to quit a lover or break a liaison, being a center of attraction;; the former were always abandoned, or never attracted anyone, not because of their personal faults but, it seemed, by virtue of the natural play of things. And a slow descent, the mediocrity of chosen lovers, resignation, the sight of the street where encounters were possible, also led them to try their luck at crossroads, or the window through which one appears to be gazing, in order to permit the timid to speak to them.

There were others who might have been able to triumph over men and existence and who were astonished to see themselves reduced to that miserable labor. Those wore the glorious crown of amour and put all their effort into hiding it. They extinguished the flame in their eyes and made their bodies languid in order that no one would discern that they were prey to one unique thought, that of an exclusive amour. Mistress of a poor lover, they procured luxury, and even a daily meal, rapidly and furtively, between five and seven o'clock, before going to render to the man they loved a body that no embrace could prevent from remaining virginal.

There were bourgeois women who aspired to give the temporary adventure, although venal, a sentimental character, who took the twenty-franc bill without looking at it, while talking about their social life, or who crumpled it into a ball like an unimportant piece of paper. And there were other bourgeois woven who took pride in equaling the whores in the crudity of their language, the absence of modesty and the audacity of caresses.

And there was the innumerable host of professionals, who seek men as one accomplishes labor, at the same times, who naturally do not expect any pleasure therefrom, but a fixed return, wary of accidents and enforced unemployment.

I ought to say that those had a profound attraction for me. My reading, my education and my life had accustomed me to consider amour, its gestures and its physical manifestations under their aspect of beauty. For years, I had mentally decorated the image of two bodies coming together for the pleasure of an unequaled prestige. I even said, in conversations with friends, that the most elevated and most moving manifestation of our sentiments is in the movements of the female body.

So, walking alongside a woman belonging to the most vulgar category of hookers, but the lines of whose body had an undeniable harmony, I shivered on hearing her speak with simplicity of what her métier involved, the number of men she went with every day, the fatigue that resulted therefrom, the choice of hotel and the haggling over the price. And the emotion I felt, a kind of laceration of the spirit, was voluptuous.

And a little later, when she asked in a natural tone whether it was necessary for her to undress entirely, when she removed her corsage and her skirt while talking about the particularities of the room, the drinks that it was necessary to have sent up and the heater that was working efficiently; when she lay on the bed like a clever animal about to accomplish a trick, my heart beat, I felt faint, having the sentiment that I was committing sacrilege toward a god that I had created myself and who, because of that, was all the more divine.

And I extracted from that sacrilege a tortuous pleasure that I had no difficulty in satisfying because the field where I could encounter it was as long as the streets, as profound as the Metro, as multicolored as the evening cafés, and as vast as Paris itself.

Chapter IX

And it was in the same epoch that my habitual egotism was traversed as if by an arrow. That came as abruptly as the temptation of the Toulousan prostitute, like an eddy of disinterest in the soul, and it also agitated images of the past within me.

I learned that my friend Jacqueline was very ill. I was linked to her by years of an affectionate camaraderie. Once, I had suffered a little because of her; then I had lost sight of her. We had found one another again with great pleasure and had both sworn an oath to see one another constantly from that day on—but months had passed without either of us making the slightest effort to meet up.

The idea that she was ill caused me a pain that surpassed anything I could have anticipated. I ran to visit her, I saw her, and I was afflicted by her condition. I came back often at first, and then every day.

Nothing would perhaps seem more natural to an ordinary man, in whom duties and pleasures form a natural equilibrium. But for me, in whom egotism had gradually suppressed in life everything that is tedious, to the profit of that which is agreeable, it as an extraordinary thing.

It was extraordinary because I did not visit her for the pleasure of seeing her, or by virtue of the solicitude of affection that makes you incessantly anxious for those one loves. I had no pleasure in seeing her, and even suffered from it. Her mind had become confused. She was the disturbed and deformed image of a beautiful painting whose color and thought I had loved.

But Jacqueline, who had recently lost her lover, was all alone. She had manifested a great desire to see my visits renewed. I knew that I was bringing her, with the sentiment of amity, a moral support. And in spite of the little time that I had, because of my work, and Rose-Thé, and above all because of the crisis of vulgar lust into which I had recently entered and which possessed me entirely, I did not let a day go by without imposing on myself the duty of going to spend a little time with my sick friend.

I took account of the fact that, for my nature, with the new preoccupations by which I was animated, that represented abnormality. But I accomplished the actions to which I was impelled as one obeys a new law, as I had once obeyed in Toulouse the instinctive law that had told me to give to the she-wolf leaning on the window-sill the bouquet bought for my mother from a maleficent old woman.

And it was in the same epoch that the habitual tranquility of my soul, its joyous establishment among material enjoyments, was penetrated by a subtle atmosphere of meditation, orientated subsequently by a small event toward graver and more metaphysical reflections.

I lived within quotidian life, without any care for matters of the beyond, no longer thinking about dead friends and vanished mistresses, similar in that regard to the majority of men. A ray of light reached me, a ray that left within me a glimmer, faint at first, but which, instead of disappearing like all radiance, was to grow and extend.

Hallu had sent me a note telling me to go to collect him, and he would take me to witness some rather curious experiences. I did not fail to do so, and we departed together for the Boulevard Saint-Jacques.

There, in a little house preceded by a garden, we were received by a stout gentleman of jovial aspect, and an old lady of whom one could see nothing except and enormous tortoise-shell fan. Hallu told me that the stout gentleman, who was externally reminiscent of a commercial traveler, was a notorious spiritualist, the author of several remarkable pamphlets on that subject. He greeted me cheerfully and indifferently; he declared that he had all sorts of reservations about the results of the experiments, because of the presence of an uninitiated newcomer, and paid no further attention to me.

A very mild and timid man, who was a great medium, arrived thereafter. He easily obtained levitations, the displacement of objects, and apports of singular circumstances sprung from the invisible. With even greater facility, he evoked spirits by means of tables.

"Of course, we can expect almost nothing today," said the jovial man, darting a glance at me that rendered me personally responsible for that.

A little side-table at which we had just taken tea was cleared, the lamp was lowered, and it began.

I shall not recount the details of the soirée, similar to several others I witnessed at various moments of my existence, and to almost all soirées of that sort. The table delivered a thousand raps and said a host of things; but I could not help thinking that I had once amazed a credulous assembly by directing an experiment and forcing the table, by the natural means of my fingers, to strike the number of blows that I dictated to it.

That evening, it rapped in the same fashion—but I was full of good will and I strove to convince myself that, this time, it was under the empire of an occult force.

It was late when the old lady with the tortoiseshell fan, sensing that I had been a rather neglected guest, asked me out of pure politeness whether I did not also have, either a dear individual or a famous one to interrogate, who could be invited to come to the little table.

I was about to recuse myself when the memory returned to me of a charming female friend who had died a few years before, with the need to address a pious thought to her. Then, influenced by the sincerity of my companions, the strangeness of their speech and the nervousness that resulted therefrom, a doubt took hold of me and I wondered whether the room might be full of subtle ghosts, vain shades that were crowding around the table, avid to express themselves, like the shades that had once enveloped Ulysses when he had accomplished rites of evocation, with wine and a sword, on a sea shore.

I therefore said that I would be glad to speak to my friend Cora Leger, who had died six years ago.

Immediately, the evokers, their eyes fixed and hands extended, had far less difficulty than Homer's hero might have had, in accomplishing their summoning task.

"The lady's spirit is here," said the medium. "Would you like to speak to her?"

Nothing is more difficult, more intimidating and more moving than embarking on a conversation in the void in that fashion, with an individual one cannot see. I did not have the authority given by the habitude of such experiments that my friends had. They expressed themselves without the slightest embarrassment and sometimes allowed themselves to question, brusquely and with vivacity, certain dead people with whom they were discontented.

Thus, I stammered things that were not very clear, to which the replies were incoherent, and I glimpsed a pitying smile on the face of the jovial spiritualist.

I collected myself, however, and I asked: "Are you happy?"

Yes, but...

And a silence followed. There was a reservation in that happiness.

"Do you desire anything, and can I satisfy you?"

Yes.

"What do you desire?"

The word *banana* was articulated clearly.

"Is that all?" I asked.

I'm cold.

"Where are you at this moment?

Far away, on the planet Venus.

"Can I do anything to prevent you from being cold?"

The word *coal* was articulated clearly.

That was all. Raps were then struck at random and my companions concluded that the experiment was terminated.

I have not reported that here as a curious phenomenon, since it is very similar to all those that are attempted in that order of ideas, and can only be distinguished from them by its banality. It is solely because of the influence that it had on me and the reflections to which it gave birth in my mind that I mention it.

It was late. We hailed a taxi and I told Hallu that I would drop him at his house.

"However," I said, on the way, "if these communications corresponded to a veritable appeal, we have to wonder whether they're plausible or useful. If my friend is on the planet Venus, what's the point of making me aware of her desire for a banana or coal?"

"You only see things that are within the radius of your wretched knowledge. The ancients, who were infinitely closer than we are to the verity of the problem of death, brought wine, milk and fruits to the tombs of lost individuals—everything that they supposed that the dead might desire."

Hallu said no more, scornful of my ignorance. I left him, and paused in a restaurant in Montmartre whose manager I knew. I ordered a drink, and when the waiter interrogated me as to whether I wanted something to eat, I asked him for a banana. He brought one.

My ideas were clear. I was like someone who has a mission to accomplish and who is only thinking of that.

I explained to the amicable manager that I needed a few small lumps of coal. He smiled at that whim, but went to the kitchen and brought them to me, wrapped in newspaper.

I went home. Rose-Thé was impatient at my lateness. Spiritualism appeared to her to be an absurd folly into which she did not want to see me fall. She nevertheless asked me, with a vague dread, whether I had seen any spirits.

I replied that I had not. The packet that I had under my arm intrigued me. She thought for a moment that it was something for her. She unwrapped it and looked at me in amazement.

"Why the devil do you have that?"

Fortunately, she fell asleep.

I deposited the banana and the coal at the foot of the bed, near the door, which stood ajar, as modest funerary offerings, and did not seek any further to understand whether there was an unknown possibility that they might be agreeable to my dead friend and bring her some pleasure in her invisible existence.

Chapter X

Hallu greeted me with a keen satisfaction, as if he had perceived the distress that was animating me and that had led me to him that day.

It was about himself and is affairs that he talked at first. Almost all men are like hat. Even when one comes to consult them on some point, when one has come especially to tell them a story, it is their own story that they are avid to recount, as the only interesting thing on earth.

He rubbed his hands. He paced back and forth. He was content. He was about to succeed. His latest experiments were conclusive. He had just discovered the true meaning of an ambiguous text and he was certain now, not only of paralyzing his rival Jean Noël in the fashion most shameful for him, but also of having Renée Stevens when he wanted her—and he was about to want her.

"It's not everything to have a woman," he told me. "It's necessary to have her in certain conditions. It's a matter of a young woman who is certainly a virgin. Her ignorance might deprive me of all pleasure. Well, thanks to my magic, I shall have a virgin who will be a bacchante with me, a vicious being, a monster of perversity. Oh, I shall be well avenged for her pride, even her disdain, for I can confess to you that, in sum, she has disdained me."

I made a vague gesture.

"You find that very natural, because it's me. But personally, I've never been able to explain it to myself. Women are so odd! They prefer some imbecilic dandy to an intelligent man who will elevate them in the order of thought. Why? It's stupid. Perhaps they believe that they'll have more pleasure. How wrong they are! Doesn't sensuality come from the brain? Aren't intellectuals always the greatest sensualists? Women are victims of heir blindness and it's rendering them a service to enlighten them."

Hallu had a smile in which a repulsive conceit was shining. His eyes creased; for a moment his face took on a faunesque expression.

"You can't imagine," he went on, "the results that one can achieve. The world would be changed if certain secrets were divulged. All the same, there are a lot of people who know them. It's also necessary to defend oneself. Would you like me to give you some good advice? Whether you're ill or not, never allow blood to be drawn from you for any reason whatsoever. It's now a habit of all physicians: at the slightest pretext, an analysis of blood. Remember what I say: never! Never!"

I said that there was no question of my allowing my blood to be drawn, and asked him for an explanation of his words.

"When one has someone's blood and one possesses a little of the true science, it is as if one had his life. I can't think without a shiver of envy of all the possibilities that opens up to certain hospital doctors, and for the directors of laboratories where analyses are carried out. They have around them hundreds of labeled bottles in which invalids have deposited their blood, and if they knew, there would be as many destinies in their hands, passions to which they could give birth, or deaths that they could provoke. Some of them must know. When I go past one of those large pharmacies were there's a notice saying *Analyses of all kinds*, I tell myself that perhaps there's a magician there who is delivering himself to terrible practices, and I see the lost flames of the enchanters of the Middle Ages glinting in the bottles in the window. And I regret not having chosen that career long ago."

There was a silence. I did not add any faith to what Hallu said, but I was deeply troubled by it.

He had stopped pacing back and forth in the room and was contemplating his disgraceful feet, which were slightly turned inwards, in a meditative pose that was familiar to him.

"No, evidently, I don't have Mademoiselle Stevens' blood. How could I have acquired it? Oh, if only I had it!" His face took on a terrible expression and he clenched his teeth. "You'd be able to see her at this moment running naked on all fours in this room. I didn't have any blood, so I've employed more ancient, more rudimentary methods—the methods of the Romans, which are those of the Renaissance."

He moved aside a cloth that was over the fireplace and I perceived two little yellow-tinted statuettes that had been made of wax and were bizarrely clad.

"You've read a thousand descriptions of that in all the books that deal with spell-casting. A wax statuette, a few hairs, or pieces of the fabric of the garments of those one wants to bewitch, magnetic passes...all that's insufficient. It's necessary to have the secret. Finally, I have it."

I asked him whether, if he succeeded fully, he would have any remorse.

He burst out laughing.

"It's necessary to be very young to have remorse. I've passed the period in life when I was still susceptible to have any. And then, can you tell me where the harm is? Why should Renée Stevens belong to Jean Noël rather than me? Because it's him that she chose yesterday? It's me that she'll choose tomorrow, apparently of her own free will. I'll only have modified the causes. The result will be the same and she won't complain about it."

I evoked the sad eyes, the slender neck, and the translucent color of the young woman's shoulders. A desire gripped me to leap forward and break the magic dolls. But I reflected that it was infantile to add faith to the tale. In any case, supposing that it were true, I would be running the risk of causing unexpected harm by doing violence the maleficent figurines.

After a pause, Hallu went on: "If you need my collaboration for yourself, I'm at your disposal. Where are you from the amorous point of view?"

The obscure impulses by which I was agitated had causes too incomprehensible for me; Hallu's theories had impressed me too much for me not to have a keen desire to know what he thought of my case.

"Might there not be," I said, "an ensorcelment less direct, which is not caused by the will of an individual but by an ensemble of influences, by memories, by landscape and by people from one's past?"

"What do you mean?"

"Then I told him about the evolution, the fashion in which I loved Rose-Thé and with what mysterious force the desire for other women had taken possession of me in spite of that love. I told him about my journey to Toulouse, the bouquet of flowers that I had bought one evening with a pious thought, the Toulousan prostitute who was laughing amid the tombstones, my sudden appetite for her, and then that sort of descent toward increasingly vulgar pleasures, women increasingly inferior within the circle of prostitution.

Hallu listened to me with passion; his eyes shone with an immense interest. To the pleasure of knowing that I was unhappy was added that of examining my curious problem.

"How good and evil are linked and mingled, following one another and confounded with one another, is a subject to which I've always been strongly attached. Good and evil! In any case, that's a manner of speaking. Where does one commence and the other finish? On what principle can one rely in order to tell the difference? If one takes as a touchstone one's own suffering, does one not perceive that continued woe becomes, at length, a glad state, much as quotidian happiness often oppresses you like a prison? There is in you an appeal of obscure forces, of inferior instincts, which is the call of the beast—of evil, if you wish. But are we sure that if you follow that beast, it will not lead you, through the obscure forest of desires, to a region more luminous than the one you know?"

I replied that we were, indeed, not sure of that.

"It was once said of people like you that they were possessed by the devil. They were exorcised. In order to be sure of their demonic status, needles were plunged into their bodies."

I made the remark that the experiment was futile.

"They were then burned, because that epoch was simplistic, but Satan wasn't burned. He developed all the more. The fire increased his power. You're possessed by the devil, my dear in the manner of those in the Middle Ages. Except that the devil might be a charming and very superior being. The fallen angel only fell because of his effort toward knowledge. In our case there is also an effort to attain the extreme depths of amour. Do you know that Simon Magus, who was an immense genius, only loved a single woman, named Helen, whom he called the divine thought, and whom he had chosen, he most wretched among the wretched, in a brothel in Tyre?"

I said that Simon Magus was entirely unknown to me.

"You can descend as well as rise. That depends on you—or perhaps not. Who knows? It depends on the encounter with the divine thought, and it is not found in all brothels. But I'd like to know one thing. At the same time as this crisis, did you not feel ideas developing within you of another order entirely—a taste for philosophical study, for example, or an unexpected disinterest in which your egotism was sacrificed?"

"Indeed. That has been a need within me, and I have observed it with astonishment. Why do you ask?"

"You're a man, you're subject to the crisis of humanity. Remember the legend of Hercules. It's not at twenty that it makes him encounter vice and virtue, but later, when he's already a celebrated hero. He follows virtue. We don't know what would have happened to him if he had followed vice, or if, by virtue of his power, he had been able to keep both goddesses with him. That double splendor, that simultaneous force, if the combat of our soul, which desires to expand. Plants have a stem that goes toward the sun, and roots that spread out through the soil. It isn't given to all men to encounter vice and virtue."

Hallu started laughing and I began to get annoyed. But he went on, with an attentive thoughtfulness in his gaze that prevented me from doubting his seriousness: "You might well be the victim of a sort of natural spell in which an old woman selling flowers played the unconscious role of witch. She

247

didn't have your blood in a bottle, but she had your past scattered around her. There are so many forces that we don't know, so many secret influences! Those forces might have grouped together of their own accord. You took the bouquet, you gave it to..."

He stopped. "Do you remember," he went on, Jean Lathème, who was at school with us?"

I didn't remember him.

"His story is curious, and has something in common with yours."

"Jean Lathème was certainly a man very different from you: more intelligent would be saying too much, but more instinctive, more rapid in the realization of his ideas. Our families were acquainted, and we were comrades when we were ten years old. I remember that at that time, his greatest pleasure consisted of catching flies, sometimes bees or other insects, and tearing off their wings so that he could catch them subsequently, dragging themselves along miserably, suffering and struggling. He found an incessantly renewed pleasure in that game, and sometimes devoted entire afternoons to it. When he went to the country he brought back grasshoppers in his handkerchief, and especially butterflies, because they had the faculty of living for a long time nailed to a wall with a pin through the body. He told me that he put them next to his bed in the evening, that he went to sleep listening to their wings buzz, and that he had a sharp sensuality in waking up with the little sound of the pain of wings beside him.

"In spite of the natural cruelty of children, I disapproved of that sort of play and I turned him away from it as often as possible. It goes without saying that when he grew older he renounced it, and even became, violent as he was, an entirely good and very mild person. When I was preparing for my degree in philosophy at the faculty of Toulouse, which is the time you and I became linked, he came to borrow books by Renan that I had—reading that is always the sign of a moderate culture.

"However, his parents being acquainted with a newly-appointed governor of Indo-China, one day he came to tell me that he was leaving with him for Saigon and that he intended to enter the colonial administration and make his career therein.

"W remained in correspondence. He returned to France after three years and spent almost all the time of his leave with me, for his tastes were carrying him increasingly toward philosophical studies. He gave me enthusiastic descriptions of Indo-China and made me promise to go and see him there.

"I decided to make the voyage, but I let two or three years pass during which his letters became exasperated and reflected certain changes. I had not had news of him for quite a long time when a rich uncle who sold wine in the Midi and had been given the Agricultural Merit award on the recommendation of a friend offered to pay for the voyage to Indo-China, about which I had always spoken to him as one of my most pleasant dreams.

"I only spent six months out there and I'll tell you another time about that prodigious country, where there is both the beauty of the earth and the wisdom of the mind, and where I was to obtain the little true knowledge that I have, as a result of curious events that have nothing to do with the present subject.

"Finding myself in Hanoi, I resolved to visit Lean Lathème. He was a functionary in the small town of Na-Nham. I took the train as far as Phu-Lang-Tuong and traveled aboard the Company river-launch to begin with, and then on horseback, to my friend's abode. I passed through beautiful landscapes that were spiced in my eyes by a hint of danger. It was the epoch in which De Tham controlled the bush. I don't know whether you remember what the French newspapers said about it; I don't think they talked about it much, but all of Indo-China was agitated by it.[5] He held the government and

---

[5] Hoang Hoa Tham, aka De Tham [Colonel Tham] was the leader of the 1890 Yen The insurrection against French colo-

their flying columns of riflemen and legionnaires in check with a small band of pirates. With an unusual audacity he moved around with a rapidity that seemed to make him ungraspable. No one dared denounce him, for he terrorized the villages, subjecting indigenes he suspected of having denounced him to frightful tortures, and extended those tortures with improbably refinements to their wives and children."

"I do, indeed, vaguely remember having read what was published on that subject."

"At the time when I went there, Na-Nham was in the center of the region in which De Tham operated. The group of militiamen with whom I was traveling were not at all reassured, but we arrived safely one evening when the sun was setting with a particular splendor over the rice-fields and the plantations of pepper-trees, and the distant horizon was closed by the somber line of the forest.

"I had announced my arrival to Jean Lathème. To my great surprise, for I knew that the arrival of a European is a considerable event in a remote little town, he was not there to receive me. One of his friends, a physician, was charged with welcoming me in his stead and doing the honors of his house until the following day. Dr. Romillet was a charming man, polite and timid, with the face of a pale child framed by a stiff black beard, crushed by an immense colonial helmet. He lived in the same house as Lathème, whose constant companion he was.

"He was an opium-smoker. He made no attempt to hide it and immediately after dinner he took me into a room of which the characteristic is to be devoid of furniture apart from a wooden chest, mats and small leather cushions, square and very hard.

"He invited me to smoke but I refused sharply, for I already hated everything that is susceptible to weakening the will. I installed myself beside him and we chatted. He was

---

nial rule in northern Vietnam. He fought a guerrilla campaign for a quarter of a century before being killed in 1913.

rather interesting, something of a litterateur and something of an artist, but without order and superficially, as men of weak character can be.

"I asked him whether Lathème was also a smoker. 'No, unfortunately,' he replied.

"I couldn't help telling him that I didn't share his opinion and that I thought that all a man's intellectual faculties were abolished by the habit.

"He explained to me at length that it was nothing of the sort, and that, at any rate, in the present case, for reasons that he could not explain to me, opium would have exercised the most salutary influence on my friend.

"I remember that there was a heavy and humid heat by which I was overwhelmed. Droplets of sweat were pearling on the doctor's brow and he told me that he would smoke more that evening because he considered opium to be refreshing. It seemed to me, by the fashion in which he talked about Jean Lathème, that the latter exercised a sort of intellectual domination over him in which fear was mingled.

"He was restless and nervous. He continually raised himself up on his elbow and listened anxiously to the noises from outside. He gave the impression of being fearful of Jean Lathème's return and, at times, he fell back, his head on his leather cushion, murmuring with a groan: 'As long as he comes back! As long as he comes back!'

"But the hours passed, and Jean Lathème did not come back.

"Nothing was more anguishing than those hours of waiting spent in an unfamiliar house in an unfamiliar land with a weak and frightened man—increasingly frightened as the night went on and as I sensed his lucidity decreasing under the influence of the drug.

"In the end, I could not bear it any longer and I demanded that he explain himself clearly. He contented himself with shaking his head silently. He had recovered a sort of calm, even indifference, and in spite of my urgent questions he re-

251

mained motionless, his eyes fixed on the ceiling, not taking any account of what I said.

"I ended up going to sleep at daybreak. But the next day went by without bringing anything new. Romillet introduced me as a friend of Lathème to an officer, Captain Rivière, who came in the morning and had a long conversation with him. I thought I discerned that he was rather cold in my regard, as if the title of being Lathème's friend was a mediocre recommendation in his eyes.

"The evening went by in the same fashion as the previous one, and the night commenced similarly, in the scantly furnished room, on the Tonkinese mats.

"Several times, the doctor got up and went through a veranda that gave access to the garden, to listen for footsteps in the night. Knowing me a little better, he became more loquacious. He talked to me about Lathème.

"'He's a very intelligent man, he told me, but what doomed him was his sojourn in Hué with King Tan-Thai.'

"I remembered that my friend had indeed been the secretary of the resident in Hué. I asked in what sense he had been doomed and what that had to do with King Tan-Thai, but he refused to continue and started talking about De Tham.

"'Do you know what that pirate's latest exploit was? It happened some distance from Phu-Binh. He burned a little village of twenty houses. But that's nothing. Troops that weren't far away saw the fire at a distance. When they arrived, none of the pirates were there, only the inhabitants of the village remained—but in what a state!

"The young women—there were four of them—had been nailed to walls, but only after their breasts had been cut off. As for the men and the old women, some had had their feet cut off, others their hands, this one an arm and that one a leg. They learned from one of the survivors that their torture had lasted a day and a night, during which De Tham and his companions had forced those unfortunates, by pricking them with their swords, to walk on all fours, aiding themselves with their mutilated stumps like insects whose wings had been torn off.

That survivor, who died shortly after the arrival of the soldiers, had also lost his reason, for he added things that surpassed the imagination and could not be believed.

"I asked what kind of man De Tham was, to give proof of such an astonishing cruelty.

"'A man who, it appears, has a great enough occidental culture, an intelligent man but fanatical and attained by the sadism that ne sometimes finds in the Chinese race when it is degenerate. The French government, desirous of conciliation, had once accorded him a kind of feudal fief in Yen-The, where it was understood that he had absolute power, and no one would any longer pay any heed to him as long as he renounced all agitation in the country. What might have happened in Yen-The during that period, no one will ever know. Many of our compatriots knew then, including Lathème...'

"Dr. Romillet's eyelids began to flutter more rapidly. 'Since then, he's gone back to the bush, and the suzerain of Yen-The, who gave royal feasts, has become an errant savage. When I say savage, it's a manner of speaking, for a savage as refined in cruelty is very close to being civilized.'

"We began to indulge in endless dissertations about sadism, and he told me about King Tan-Thai, who had been deposed because he tortured his wives. He claimed that many more people than we believe conceive the sensuality that accompanies cruelty, in a more or less conscious fashion. I told him that he was exaggerating and that those cases, which are sometimes manifest, are quite rare.

"'Well,' he said to me, 'your friend Lathème has made confidences to me that I would rather he had not made, on that subject. It appears that when he was a child, he experienced an extraordinarily great sensual pleasure in tearing the wings and feet off insects and making them walk thus. Since then, he has affirmed to me, the pleasure of amour has been linked to those memories, and every time he finds himself with a woman, he is unable to prevent himself imagining her without hands and feet, walking on her stumps.

"Dr. Romillet had fallen silent and as looking at me, but at that moment, I could not divine what he was thinking. 'Now,' he went on, I don't believe in sorcery, so I haven't given any importance to what Lathème has said to me on the subject of a cornelian pendant that King Tan-Thai gave him, and which exercised a sort of sensual charm upon him.'

"I interrupted him to tell him that personally, I had faith in certain matters of sorcery, that I believed to some extent in the power of talismans and that he would give me pleasure by telling me what he knew about that pendant. But he started to laugh and told me that he didn't know anything, except for that vague indication of Lathème's part.

"It was a little later that we heard someone walking in the garden, and Jean Lathème appeared on the veranda.

"He shook my hand as if he had seen me the day before. He pronounced a few vague words in order to explain to me that his functions had retained him outside Na-Nham. He was much aged. He seemed very weary. He only addressed a few words to the doctor, and asked our permission to go to bed immediately.

"I saw him the next morning. We chatted for quite a long time, but he was scarcely interested in the news of Europe that I could have given him. He only asked me what I was doing out of simple politeness. He seemed distant, separate from me, like a man who was living elsewhere.

"That day, we learned successively of several sensational events relative to De Tham. He had ravaged another village and tortured the inhabitants by cutting off their limbs in the strangest fashion. But this time, he had also tortured a French woman, the young wife of a customs officer from Than-Nguyen, who had been taken prisoner in the bush. That had taken place during the first night of my arrival. But it was to be his last exploit, for we learned that a few hours afterwards, a Chinaman in his band, tempted by the lure of the promised reward, had cut off his head during the night and brought it to the officer in command of the flying column of legionnaires launched in his pursuit. That column ought to be on the point of arriving at Than-Nguyen.

"That news was naturally welcomed by everyone with great satisfaction. Jean Lathème appeared to be neither astonished nor impressed by it. That was about six o'clock in the evening; but when Dr. Romillet and I went to table for dinner we learned from his boy that he had departed in horseback.

"Immediately, the doctor said to me: 'It's not worth the trouble of waiting for him. He won't come back'

"I asked him what he meant. The he made me party to his suspicions. A survivor of one of De Tham's massacres had said that a Frenchman had presided over the latest tortures and had even been their instigator. His declarations had been attributed o the madness of pain. But since a Chinaman, a companion of De Tham, had betrayed and killed him, there was no doubt that people in Than-Nguyen were being informed at that moment of the details of the recent massacres and the presence of a Frenchman while they were being carried out. There was no doubt either that it would be known that the Frenchman in question was Jean Lathème.

"I protested. 'It's certain,' said the doctor. 'I've spent nights meditating about that and hoping that I was mistaken. How can his absences and his attitude be explained otherwise? And then, two or three times, here, while I was smoking, he was talking loudly in his sleep, and what he said was frightful. He's run away because he thinks that the Chinaman who killed De Tham is going to reveal everything in his regard. Now, thanks to what series of coincidences and events was his sadism, obscure at first, revealed to him? How, after having imagined it, did he dare to enter into the path of realizations? Did that process begin in the company of Tan-Thai, by virtue of the sight of blood, when the latter, during the festival of spring, went at midnight to an esplanade of white stone, to sacrifice an aurochs in accordance with an age-old ritual and sprinkle the audience hereafter with the shed blood? Was it his more secret celebrations, to which he succeeded in being invited? Or was it later, with De Tham? Did he incite the latter to the cruelty to whose attraction he was subject? That's what we'll probably never know.'

"He added: 'And I have no doubt, if I recall the stories he told me about certain lusts of his childhood caused by the torture of flies and butterflies, that he obtained, like a return, a suggestion of that past.

"Needless to say, I did not linger in Na-Nham. I had no reason to stay there. Before leaving I encountered Captain Rivière, and his almost invisible manner of saluting me confirmed me in the opinion that a friend of Jean Lathème was not recommendable *a priori* by that quality alone.

"However, what the doctor had told me appeared implausible. By the time I arrived in Hanoi, I was convinced that I had been deceived by the absurd reveries of an opium-smoker, and regretted leaving so precipitately. I inquired about Jean Lathème but could not learn anything about him, except that a replacement had just been appointed. Silence was maintained over that affair. On my return to France I learned that my friend's parents had been informed of his death."

"That story is very curious," I said to Hallu, who was gazing at me with a smile of satisfaction, "and I'm glad to know it. But I don't really see what connection it can have with mine. As far as I can go back into my childhood, I've always had a horror of doing harm to animals, even flies. I only impaled a single butterfly with a pin, on the pretext of collection, but I recall that the flutter of its wings inspired me with a vivid pity, that I crushed it in order that it would not suffer, and that I swore never to do it again. As for women, it has never entered my mind to cut off their hands or breasts, of which I love the form and feel so much."

"I'm convinced. I've only told you Lathème's story because, in his case as in yours, there was a mysterious return to the past that impelled both of you to abrupt actions in order to satisfy a pleasure. There are only analogies between you. You took a bouquet from the hands on an old woman one day, and that bouquet probably exercised a magnetic action upon you.

In Lathème's story too, there was a cornelian pendant that exercised an influence upon him. For him it was a king, for you an aged procuress, who were the intermediaries, and the effects were different."

I was now sorry that I had spoken to Hallu with so much sincerity. I found his explanations ridiculous because they did not bring me any enlightenment.

I got up to leave.

"You don't believe me," he said, accompanying me. "And you'll go on to the end. You'll suffer the fate of the bewitched individuals of the Middle Ages. You won't be burned because times have changed and the Inquisition has disappeared, but you'll bestride a broomstick and you'll go to the Sabbat one night soon—and who knows? Perhaps you'll burn yourself thereafter."

I shook his hand rapidly on the landing where the figure five was still chalked. I went down the stairs as quickly as possible and heard him laughing and shouting to me over the banister:

"To the Sabbat! You'll soon go to the Sabbat!"

Chapter XI

A great distress had gripped me. The light of five o'clock filtered through the drawn curtains. I was half-lying on the bed, scarcely unmade. There was a dress making a circle on the floor. I gazed at the garish luxury of the bedroom, the furniture fatigued by so many temporary guests, and I felt that they were engraved in my empty brain, in the manner of certain series of faces contemplated for too long in a railway carriage, which come back to haunt you afterwards, persistently.

I was obliged to turn my eyes away from a gilded page leading against the frame of a clock that was not going. I was gripped by anger against its ugliness. My foot brushed a pale blue eiderdown. An unhealthy curiosity almost impelled me to look to see with what stains it was soiled. But as I lifted it up to do so, I reflected upon the pointlessness of imposing that disgust upon myself.

On the marble of a small table there was a hairpin. A cigarette-end had been forgotten in the fireplace.

Another couple had passed that way only a few minutes before me. I had only been separated from them by the time to change the sheets and open the window to expel the odor of tobacco. They too had experienced that embarrassment in the midst of the hostile furniture, they had looked at themselves with astonishment in the mirror that had reflected thousands of people, and they had embraced one another on the wide bed.

Who were they? The group of a random encounter, like the one I formed with an anonymous woman? Perhaps people who loved one another, brought together by an ancient desire. Separated by life, they came furtively to find one another again for an hour, and when, what did he décor matter, the sadness of the furniture and the venal bed? They had thrown themselves upon one another with the fury that pleasure gives when one is about to attain it, when one knows that its depths will not be bitter, because it will have the aftertaste of tenderness. In this same place, they had exchanged caresses without lust, sweeter than the caresses of pleasure. They were saddened by seeing one another so infrequently, had lamented their separate existence, and had formed projects.

I envied that imaginary couple. I imagined the woman, tell, with slightly sad blue yes, hair that she had let down and spread over the pillow, her gray silk stockings, her hastily unlaced ankle-boots, her docility in the gestures of amour.

It was that woman that I ought to have encountered. Perhaps it was her that would have retained me irresistibly. We were made for one another, but inharmonious hazard had separated us. She had been there a few minutes before with someone else and I would never see her.

The noise of water had resounded. The door of the toilet opened again. The anonymous woman reappeared on the threshold. For a second, I had the sensation that someone unknown had entered the room. It really was someone unknown, in fact, but with whom I had nevertheless had a few moments of abandonment on the bed.

I felt a great lassitude at the idea of words to be exchanged, of the chambermaid for whom it would be necessary to ring for the departure, the money to hand over, the difficulty of getting change, what it would be necessary to say in the street in order to quit her. I thought privately that perhaps, if it only depended on a wish to formulate, I would consent, in order to find myself alone, to that woman being suddenly projected into the Gobi desert or the middle of the Sahara. And the idea of the sufferings that the unfortunate woman would be obliged to endure by thirst, fatigue and the temperature in those terrible places was insufficient to soften me.

Or, I imagined, the woman might open the window, she might suddenly change into a light vapor, and disappear into the air without leaving any trace. I compared those absurd inventions with those I had on certain days when, contrary to my present impression, I felt an excess of life, a joyful delight. That was ordinarily in the morning, after a good night. I gazed at some fat woman walking along the street, very bourgeois and very solemn, and I imagined her stupefied face if I had advanced, laughing, and give her a slap on the behind. Or, seeing a man clad in black and having the appearance of a grave magistrate, I thought of what might happen if I snatched his hat and ran away with it.

In the present case, the woman was not transported to the Sahara, she was not mutated into vapor, and she even came toward me with the disagreeable objective of stroking my face with her hand. But she stopped, stood still, and started to laugh. She gestured to me to listen. In fact, I perceived a slow sound analogous to a lament, which was coming from the next room.

A simple partition undoubtedly separated us, for I now heard the monotonous plaint rising, becoming louder, decrease and recommence. All the mystery of houses of rendezvous, the unknown couples who came into these superimposed, sym-metrical rooms to embrace rapidly, to enjoy and exclaim, and who returned thereafter to their lives, was in that regular la-ment, in that little song of a voluptuous woman abandoned to the genius of the flesh.

Then there was a cry, a few words, and silence. And my melancholy was greater in knowing that, behind that partition, alongside me, two beings were lying who had conducted their own passion there. I thought about Rose-Thé and I had, if not remorse, at least the regret of not having her in my arms.

Now they were talking in the room next door. There was sometimes a burst of laughter and I thought I recognized the sound. I stood up and listened. I made a sign to my companion to keep quiet and I waited. The partition was truly very thin, for I had heard the sound of ankle-boots being put on again, the foot tapping slightly, and I imagined the couple in front of the mirror, putting their hats on, ready to leave. And my heart beat faster when I perceived, divining it as much as hearing it, the phrase, grateful and lascivious in its ingenuity, that she pronounced, doubtless leaning toward him for one last kiss.

I had a violent desire to make sure that I was not mistak-en, that I had not been deceived by a similarity of voices. The couple emerged from the next room. I heard their footsteps in the corridor. They went past my door and I opened it softly by a crack as they reached the staircase.

No, I was not mistaken—it really was her! She had already resumed her attitude of proud modesty and there was something in the languor of the neck that might have made one think of what she had been doing a few minutes earlier, the audacity of her words, and the entire abandonment of her body.

It was Renée Stevens who was going down that staircase, the road of hidden pleasures, her little hand still clasping the arm of Jean Noël, as if she had wanted, in leaving, to hold on to a little of his flesh and knead it with her fingers.

Chapter XII

"Why do you call that Russian a serpent?" Rose-Thé said to me, with a certain ill humor. "He's a charming man, who doesn't make one think of that animal at all."

I looked at Rose-Thé with surprise. But I reflected that all women are like that, and that their opinions change rapidly. I was no more astonished a little later when she declared that he was one of the rare men who had been sympathetic to her from the first day. And as I was marching at a deliberate pace along the road of blindness, I told her that as she was taking tea with him in the afternoon, she ought perhaps to invite him to dinner for the following day. And that was agreed.

Now, as events are connected with a powerful force and determine one another in order to produce what we call coincidences. I met Verdelle, whom I had not seen for a long time, apparently by chance, on a street corner.

He took me by the arm, drew me into a café on the boulevard where he had, he told me, a rendezvous with a delightful young woman, and he immediately told me, adding a great abundance of details about his very numerous good fortunes. He must, in truth, have been painting his dreams, the adventures that he imagined, but my stupid credulity rendered them real and as he saw my admiration and even my envy, he multiplied his accounts.

"In fact," he said, "the tall Lucette is gathering a few friends tomorrow evening to her house. I ought to be the only man, along with a certain Jaubert, and it might perhaps be amusing. Would you like to come? I'll take you."

I replied that I would be difficult for me because I was having a few friends to dinner myself. But in sum, Verdelle could very well come to dinner too and take me away thereafter, under some pretext, when my guests left.

"Still in the same situation, then! No liberty!" said Verdelle bursting into laughter. And a sincere pity appeared in his gaze.

It was agreed that he would come and that we would do it.

"I'll sort it out, and there won't be a scene." And he tapped me on the shoulder, as if it were the shoulder of a poor slave.

"I'll tell Hallu that we'll pick him up on the way," he added, "in order that it will remind us of our youth."

When I remember the little events of that evening, when almost nothing happened, the words that were spoken, which were almost all of an extreme banality, I think that I could have determined for myself, that evening, with other little events and other banal words, a different destiny. A series of things were to commence then, which I would have been able to impel in another direction—on that evening and no other—and by accumulating thereafter ten thousand speeches and ten thousand actions, I could no longer prevent what I could have prevented on that unique evening simply by not saying these few words:

"I'm going to go out with Verdelle this evening."

And it certainly seems to me, on reliving those hours many times over and despairing of them, that I had even then a confused sentiment of my folly, that I was acting while a muffled voice inside me was saying that I ought to do the opposite of what I was doing, a muffled voice that was speaking through a thick fog to a second consciousness of my being.

So, everything was simple and banal. Jean Noël and Renée Stevens were there. Verdelle was there, who talked incessantly. Pavlichef was there, whose immeasurably glaucous and empty gaze filled my soul with terror, but without my being able to suspect it as yet.

We did what people always do when they gather together after dinner. We had coffee, a liqueur, we chatted, someone played the piano, we smoked innumerable cigarettes, we chatted some more. My friends talked about going; I told them that

263

there was no hurry, while being avid to see them depart and to depart myself. At one moment, they even stood up like people absolutely determined, and Pavlichef had picked up his hat and struck the pose of someone about to bow correctly.

Assuredly, at that moment, there was no afterthought; he was only thinking of leaving. And it was me who, guided by a limitless folly, took his hat, placed it on the piano and insisted that he stay.

Verdelle made me a sign, and it was then that I found, for which I have the sole responsibility, something that sprang from me like an admirable inspiration.

I was obliged to go out with Verdelle, I explained. We had to see someone at midnight, after the theater. How amiable my friends would be to stay for a while, to keep Rose-Thé company, while smoking another cigarette!

I should have known and understood, though! It was obvious that Pavlichef desired my mistress with all the force of a wild beast without consideration. I was not unaware, when Renée Stevens declared that she could only stay for a little while longer because her mother would be anxious, that she must be desirous of running, either to Jean Noël's house or some nearer hotel, in order to be taken on a bed and to cry out with pleasure. I could not doubt it. I had heard her, a few days earlier, I had seen her, base and voluptuous, go down the hotel stairway afterwards. It was very easy for me to foresee that, five minutes after my departure, she would leave with Jean Noël and that Pavlichef would remain alone with Rose-Thé. I did foresee it, in fact. But what harm was there in it, in sum, I said to myself, determined to deceive myself, as I was determined to deceive others?

I saw clearly that Rose-Thé did not find anything annoying in that nocturnal rendezvous and did not express any discontentment. But I obeyed the law that the more one deceives a woman the more one is possessed by an immeasurable confidence in her regard.

And I went out, joyfully, into the night. listening to the discourse of a fool, to go to see women I did not know in a distant apartment—and whom, because of that, were ornamented in my eyes with great charm.

Hallu, forewarned, was waiting for us. At first he was cold and bitter because he divined that Verdette and I had dined together and thought that he ought to have been invited. But afterwards he softened, his mood became cheerful, his little eyes started to sparkle, and as we went along the Avenue Tridaine on foot he tapped me on the shoulder familiarly with the air of someone sharing a joke with me. At one moment he even bestrode his cane as if it were a horse and preceded us, at a trot, limping in such a grotesque manner that Verdelle leaned toward me and said: "Our comrade Hallu is already drunk."

In the Rue des Martyrs, in the home of the tall Lucette, the party was in full swing. A freakish individual, half child and half mature man, was playing the piano when we arrived. Four women were dancing together, laughing and jostling one another, in the drawing room and the dining room, which were connected by a large glazed door that was wide open. The person that Verdelle had named as Jaubert, a vulgar man with a goatee, was in his short-sleeves; he had put a napkin around his waist and, simulating the mannerisms of a maître d'hôtel, he was serving liquor to two other women, who were laughing uproariously and drinking without pause.

We were welcomed by cries of joy and immediately surrounded by sandwiches and glasses of liquor, which we drank in order to put ourselves in harmony; but that harmony was incessantly elevated, and we had a great deal of difficulty rising so high.

The freak never stopped playing the piano, as if he were a mechanical man. From time to time he turned round, and one saw a sickly face cleft by a burst of laughter. Doubtless he was conscious of being the cause of all pleasure by means of music, and that must have been sufficient for him. The tall Lucette brought him, at intervals, champagne or liquor, which he absorbed in a single draught, almost without pausing.

The heat was infernal but a very young little woman named Niche had kept her coat, which had a fur collar, hermetically buttoned up. The others had insisted that she take it off, but she gave the pretext of a special nature that meant that she was always cold. She had been dancing and drinking and sweat was running down her cheeks, removing her make-up. As they continued to insist, she sensed the fragility of the reason that she had given and confessed that she had no blouse. There was general hilarity. She took off her coat and, as a skirt without a blouse was declared inharmonious, she also took off her skirt. Hazard dictated that she was charming, with perfectly pulled-up stockings and a very short chemise.

Another woman, jealous of her success, immediately imitated her, and offered a les agreeable image to our eyes. She threw her combs across the room while dancing, and long brown hair began to swirl, spreading an animal odor.

Everyone continued drinking. It was late. The tall Lucette had turned down the electric light and only one lamp still remained, over which a blouse or chemise had been thrown, which tinted the entire room with a vague ruddy light.

A woman had drawn Niche into the bedroom. They had not closed the door and were visible on the bed. The freak played a slow waltz. Women were heaped up on the divan. A violent odor of ether suddenly rose up and filled the room. Jaubert had thrown cushions down in a corner and was confusedly entwined there with one of the women.

Hallu was radiant. I saw his little eyes sparkling beside me.

"Well," he said, "you've come to the Sabbat, as I announced to you. It was inevitable. Don't you have a desire to walk on all fours, to bark, to howl, to crawl like a snake or to leap hither and yon like a monkey?"

I started to laugh without pleasure and asked him what he meant.

"But, according to what you told me yourself, you're possessed by the Beast. It's got you and it won't let go. You've come here to worship it, like all the others who are lying here, in fact. If you and I were more clairvoyant, we'd perceive that the lamp that is illuminating us is held by

266

Haborym, and we'd distinguish his deformed belly and sniggering face in the wall. We'd also perceive that the ridiculous little piano player is none other than Belphegor and we'd see his short wings palpitating under is jacket. The tall Lucette, by virtue of the spirit of pollution, must have hidden hosts in the creases of her body, and that Jaubert, who retains his goat's beard in life, is nothing but a monstrous goat to satisfy the witches. We're blind, otherwise we'd discern the Beast, above all these forms, with his horns and his frightful muzzle, the lips of which hang down over his breasts, and his double sex, the adoration of these creatures. It's here, assuredly, invisible but powerful, and joyful in seeing its faithful obscenely prostrated before it. Perhaps, with a little effort, an exteriorization of our thought, we'd succeed in distinguishing it, there, in front of the mirror. Look hard. Can't you see the contour of an enormous head, which seems to be leaning over the piano?"

No, in truth, I could not see anything. I was gripped by anger against Hallu. I had a desire to seize him by the shoulders, to shake him, to shout at him that I had had enough of his stupidities, that al his magic was nothing but stupidity, and that his savant spells had not prevented the woman he loved from going to lie with a man and fill a house of rendezvous with her amorous cries. But I remained silent, for my disgust was now overflowing.

The freakish musician had abandoned the piano and as in a corner, pressed against a woman. The odor of ether was sickening. Grunting was audible. A bottle of champagne placed on the floor and then knocked over was making puddles on the floorboards. Only Niche, naked and fainted on the bed, was showing with her body a line of perfection, like a symbol of beauty, which persists and shines in flashes in the darkest festivals of lust.

I astonished myself by picking up my hat, and I fled. It was now raining torrentially. The streets were deserted. I could not find a taxi. It was necessary to go home on foot. When I reached the vicinity of my house I was mentally and physically exhausted.

I heard the sound of a door being closed, but softly, as if by someone taking precautions, ashamed of leaving so late. I saw a silhouette drawing away rapidly, and thought I recognized Pavlichef. I was too tired to make the effort to call to him and run after him.

I looked at my watch. It was six o'clock in the morning.

Chapter XIII

I have always been struck by a curious phenomenon that is produced from time to time in old houses.

The old house is there with several stories, pots of flowers on widow-sills and an ancient stairway that goes up in zigzags. It is old, certainly, but all in all, it does not seem any older than many others that are alongside it or a little further away, placidly living the existence of old houses. There is a shop on the ground floor, tenants on all the others, and a happy animation fills it.

And suddenly, without any kind of preparation, the old house collapses. No shock has shaken it, there has been no hurricane, and in any case, it is solidly wedged against the others. The old house has folded up of its own accord. Doubtless by virtue of a slow and invisible labor, its materials have disaggregated and it has crumbled, rushing the shop and the tenants sitting in the security of the superimposed apartments.

I remember, as a child, going to see one of those houses that had just fallen into ruins like that. It had made a vast cloud of dust, and the firemen had come running with the chimerical hope of find inhabitants trapped under the debris. And everyone was greatly astonished because a blue pot containing a geranium had come through that collapse without being broken and without the geranium being injured in the slightest.

It was thus, abruptly, that the edifice of my happiness collapsed. Doubtless a slow usury had undermined its substance. It must not have existed any longer except in a state of appearance, but I believed in my unperspicacious soul that it was a solid happiness in which one can repose and sleep.

It collapsed with my being able to foresee it, crushing its charming tenants, who were habit, affection, the pleasure of seeing a beautiful face and savoring the qualities of a charming heart. It crumbled without my even being able to find under its debris the geranium that had been flowering on a window sill.

No, it was not very long after the soirée that I have reported. Perhaps it was a fortnight thereafter. Rose-Thé was already asleep and I was reading, sitting in an armchair next to a lamp. I could hear her respiration on the other side of the door and I stopped reading to admire the purity of that sleep.

And then, without any reason, a singular thought occurred to me. Perhaps it was because Rose-Thé had embraced me very distractedly or because she had fallen asleep too soon or because something foreign was floating in the atmosphere in a subtle manner. For the first time, the thought occurred to me that Rose-Thé no longer loved me and that she was deceiving me. For the first time, I examined the possibilities, I dared to confront the enormous improbability that my vanity had erected against that idea with my reason.

And immediately, I was obliged to admit that nothing was more possible, more normal and more just. I did not believe in an immanent justice, but it was in the order of things, given my personal conduct in her regard, that Rose-Thé was deceiving me. It was in the order of things, I said to myself, but that order was exceptionally disturbed in my favor, either because of Rose-Thé's faithful nature or because of the powerful charm that I exerted upon my mistress.

Having reassured myself, it happened, as I was pacing back and forth, that I perceived Rose-Thés handbag. It was made of an old embroidered fabric; its golden chain was dangling, and its lock was open.

Now, during the years that I had been living with Rose-Thé, it had never occurred to me to search her handbag, both because of the scorn I professed for that action and my extreme confidence in Rose-Thé.

But that evening, seeing the bag open, I was gripped by a violent desire to examine its contents, all the more so because I could see several letters in the corner. I told myself that it was an unnecessary action, in view of the fact that if Rose-Thé

270

had a letter to hide she would not have left it in evidence in her handbag; but I also told myself that my confidence might have given her a complete security, and that the imprudence of women is infinite.

I picked up the bag, and felt my heard beat faster at its contact.

Feverishly, I seized a letter on which I had recognized a man's handwriting. It was from Zette, with a comical orthography, containing nothing but banalities. There was a printed invitation to an exhibition of paintings, a Metro carnet and a piece of paper with addresses written in pencil. I was confused and triumphant.

However, I opened another interior pocket and I seized along with a louis d'or conserved as a fetish, a minuscule photograph. Then my confusion and my triumph increased, because that photograph was mine. I looked at it complaisantly, and even tenderly. I had given it to Rose-Thé a long time ago and I was there, younger than at present, and I found myself very sympathetic.

I rendered full homage to Rose-Thé, reproached myself for my suspicions, and was ashamed of having searched the bag.

I was about to replace the little photograph where I had found it when I perceived that there were two, of exactly the same format, enclosed together. I looked at the second and recognized that it was a photograph of Pavlichef. She had cut it with scissors so that it would be the same size, and as it had doubtless been larger, only the head remained, which seemed enormous, from which the eyes bulged and occupied a disproportionate place.

I looked at that photograph for a long time, stupidly. My first thought was to wake Rose-Thé up brutally, demand an explanation and reproach her. My second thought was to give a normal and inoffensive cause to the presence of the photograph. While taking tea, for instance, with other friends, there had been talk of photographs, Pavlichef happened to have one on him; he had shown it to her; he had said "Would you like

271

it?" and mechanically, out of politeness, she had put it in her bag. Or, when he had come, it had slipped out of his pocket and Rose-Thé, having found it on the floor, had kept it in order to return it to him. It was improbable, but possible.

My third thought was to seek the light of verity a little. And it appeared to me that my conduct with regard to my charming mistress was unworthy and had no excuse but the mystery that was dormant in my soul and my senses, a mystery that could not be perceived by others. Assuredly, she knew, in part or entirely, via the conversations of friends, that I was deceiving her, and in what wretched fashion. What was astonishing, in that circumstance, about her thinking of deceiving me in her turn, and even that she had already deceived me?

A certain wisdom extended over me. I replaced the two photographs in the bag, in the place where I had found them.

I remembered now. Rose-Thé had changed. She was colder with me. She seemed preoccupied. My entire life with her in recent times was illuminated by a light in which I had not yet seen it.

But it might be that nothing was yet irrevocable. I had wronged her repeatedly. I would change direction. I would right those wrongs. I would try to reconquer my mistress by patient effort, by constant solicitude. I sensed treasures of persuasion and tenderness in myself. I resolved to employ them the very next day.

Such was my stupidity and indifference in her regard! Rose-Thé affirmed that she had explained to me about her mother's illness and that she had told me several times that she was leaving to take a cure at Luchon. I had forgotten that because nothing concerning her interested me any longer.

How mistaken she was, as I was about to explain to her!

But there! At the precise moment when I had resolved to act, at the precise moment when I sat down to warn hr that I was going to speak at length, as I was raising my finger to stress the importance of it, saying: "Listen..."

The doorbell rang.

And the envoy of destiny, the occult instrument of everything that was about to follow, which signified the misfortune with which I was about to be struck, the bearer of the lie, the announcer of the unexpected event, had donned the costume and appearance of a young telegraph employee. He resembled neither Oedipus nor the Comte de Monte Cristo. He was childlike, with blue eyes; he was indifferent, above all, indifferent. He did not think of commenting on the text of the telegram or of mocking me. He handed me the telegram and he went away, hopping down the stairway on one foot.

No wink or conventional signal had been exchanged between Rose-Thé and him, because he was in truth a veritable telegraph employee, not a child paid to play that role. And the telegram was authentic and bore the place or origin and time: Luchon, 16-30. And it announced in an irrevocable fashion that Rose-Thé had to depart for Luchon that evening. She was to depart that evening, without being able to put it off, even to the following morning, because the imperious telegram had in its few laconic words the mystery of malady and the prestige of filial sentiments.

Her mother was ill in Luchon and demanding that she come immediately.

Oh, how rapidly she packed her trunk! How ready to hand everything she needed was! In truth, the laundress must have known about Rose-Thé's mother's illness and foreseen her aggravation, and also thought that one cannot go to see one's sick mother without silk chemises, because, that morning, in spite of the fact that it was not her day, she had brought back the silk chemises that Rose-Thé loved so much and received felicitations because of it.

The force of blindness still inhabited my soul and I made recommendations regarding the hotel where it was necessary to stay on arrival and a physician that I knew and whom she ought to consult.

But as the afternoon passed in those preparations, a sadness invaded me that was not the normal sadness of being separated from one's mistress for a few days. And Rose-Thé, who had initially painted on her face all the anguish appropriate to that maternal illness, seemed to become detached from it, and smiled, going back and forth, glad of that precipitate departure.

It was only when the taxi was outside the door that a presentiment came to me, as the same time as a resignation to events. Then I perceived that the gaze that Rose-Thé cast as she left the apartment was melancholy. Yes, that gaze, the veiled gleam of which I saw again a thousand times thereafter, in memory was a broad circular glance cast over the furniture, the books and the cushions; it was a farewell glance, the glance of a good person whom destiny is bearing away, but who owes gratitude to a place where there was a little happiness. I was not mistaken; there was a tear in that glance. Rose-Thé, I thank you for that little gleam in your eyes, which enlightened me further...

From that moment on I knew, but without yet admitting it to myself. I would have liked to ask Rose-Thé why her trunk was so heavy and why she was taking so many things for such a short absence. But I didn't. Every minute gave me a fuller understanding. And when I went on to the platform at the station, when I had taken the pillow and the blanket, then what had to happen became known to me and I foresaw with certainty the letter that I would receive in two or three days; I even imagined a few of its phrases. The thought that a fatality was being realized, of which I was culpable by virtue of my actions, prevented me from pronouncing any of the words that might perhaps have averted it.

Rose-Thé was sitting in the compartment, her eyes fixed on the net in which her small traveling bag was placed, but it was not the bag she was looking at. One might have thought that she was seeing things that were very far away. Was it the past or the future?

I imagined for a few seconds the joy I would have had in departing with her, in being one of the travelers that one sees heading for the Midi with their mistresses. I imagined awakenings in unknown stations, the hand one presses under the blanket, a brioche that a merchant hands you through the window in the morning, the fraternity of the train in which there is a profound pleasure. But that was too painful for me, and I pushed those images away.

And when it was all over, when I found myself alone on the platform in the midst of the passengers who were waving, I saw the sequence of events with a horrible clarity. I had become clairvoyant. I glimpsed the solitude of life without yet imagining its dolor. Projects for the next day and the following days had merely become pale and blurred, becoming less interesting. My entire life was suddenly enveloped by a mist, light at first, but which would become denser.

I left the Gare d'Orsay. The melancholy Seine was gleaming in places. The Louvre continued to deploy its bleak grandeur. I raised my head. The night was splendidly serene, but the stars gave the impression of having recoiled to a distance greater than usual. I looked around. An autobus seemed an errant monster in quest of people to absorb. The Tuileries were like a cemetery. All the passers-by were sad and ugly.

I lit a cigarette and I walked slowly, not thinking about anything, in the immense emptiness of the streets.

Chapter XIV

For a poor painter who is going to receive three hundred francs from an art-lover, the acquirer of a splendid canvas, nothing is more legitimate than taking a taxi. Evidently, that will cost four, perhaps five francs, for the art-lover lives a long way away, in the rich quarters, a long way from the Metro station. That sum is considerable, and one can imagine all the things that might be done with it; but it is nothing compared with three hundred francs. Then too, it is easy to imagine that one has only sold the painting for two hundred and ninety-five francs, and thus the taxi is free. Finally, when one is an artist, should not one know the marvelous sensations of luxury, will one not obtain inspiration therefrom?

So, that morning, the painter Martial, having taken Zette by the arm, invited her coolly to take a taxi.

He did it without ostentation, as an indifferent matter, because, when one is called upon to become famous, it is appropriate to familiarize oneself with the great advantages of life and to seem not to be impressed by them, even before the woman who shares your poverty.

More practical, Zette made a movement of anxiety and amazement. A life unknown to Martial had familiarized her with taxis, expensive restaurants and even certain falsely luxurious interiors. The proposition appeared less beautiful to her than he was able to believe. And Zette had the certain knowledge in her mind of their mutual lack of money at that moment. The previous evening, they had spent their last francs on cinema tickets.

It was too late. With a gesture, Martial had stopped an individual with a surly face who, his eyes on his steering wheel, seemed plunged in a meditation whose depth prevented him from perceiving the world.

The address had seemed very distant to that individual, but Martial's sovereign ease and his fashion of opening the door had subjugated him and he had contented himself with proffering a few unintelligible complaints.

Immediately, Martial perceives that he has made a mistake. He has departed too early. There are few people in the streets. There is little chance of encountering anyone. It is excellent to be seen in taxis. He thinks about one of his comrades, who is a sculptor and who claims that he often goes to the races. The races! Isn't that risible! He's a poor local sculptor who is devoured by jealousy and doesn't even go to the Luxembourg because of the state of his suit. What a revenge it would be for Martial for the many nasty comments he has received from that sculptor!

There is also the pharmacist in the Rue de la Gaieté who is often on his doorstep and who would think: *Aha! That Martial! He's taking taxis; he's beginning to succeed.*

It's the same for a few people who are petty creditors and who would see that ease as a good omen for an imminent payment.

When they go along the Rue de la Gaieté, fatality dictates that the pharmacist is in the process of sticking on a label. Martial leans over ostentatiously. He is intoxicated by the morning air whipping his face. He would like to stand up in order to be visible at a distance.

How fast one goes in a taxi!

"It's quicker than going on foot, eh?" he says to Zette.

And he also notices the difference between the houses in the rich quarter of the Étoile and his own dwelling, but without bitterness, like someone participating in that wealth.

"Wait for me for a few minutes," he says to the driver, while Zette remains in the vehicle; and as the driver declares that he has only been hired for one journey, he adds: "You'll get a good tip."

Neither Zette nor the driver would have time to get impatient. Martial has seen in the mirrors a painter full of authority and genius going up a staircase with a thoughtful expression. He possessed three hundred francs. A taxi was at his disposal at the door. He sees in the same mirrors, a painter coming down struck by destiny, who has nothing except the profound sentiment of his imprudence. The buyer has left for the Midi the day before, forgetting Martial and the three hundred francs.

Martial lacks presence of mind. He is crushed. He is on the point of telling Zette everything in front of that man, who now takes on terrible proportions. She stops him. She has understood. She hurls the address of a friend at the driver.

She dies not say: "It's your fault!" She makes no reproaches. She is thinking about what to do. The friend lives in Montmartre. He will not have gone out yet. He will lend her the taxi fare.

"And the tip?" adds Martial. We aren't talking about breakfast, of course.

A cruel jest of destiny! The friend has gone out earlier than usual. It's the first time in a long time, the concierge remarks, laughing.

The chauffer has lit his pipe and is about to raise his flag, so certain is he that the journey is concluded. It's necessary to stop him. It's necessary to ask him, incoherently, to go somewhere else. But where? Martial and Zette suggest names. But one is traveling, another has a job that requires him to leave home early, a third is sleeping with his mistress, whose address they do not know.

"You'll have a good tip."

What is the driver going to do? Is the going to explode? His eyes swell and seem to be about to pop out of their orbits. Perhaps an attack of apoplexy will strike him down. Martial thinks that that is the only solution that might save him.

No, he doesn't die. He calms down. He sits there, murmuring redoubtable things, mingled with threats and imprecations. They go toward a new address on the Left Bank.

Destiny is pitiless. No one home again. Consternated, Marital reappears on the threshold, having lost all courage. Zette is ready to burst into sobs. They raise their eyes toward the driver, timidly. Assuredly, the drama is about to commence.

What's happening? The monstrous driver has changed his appearance. He's an ordinary driver, who simply says: "Where to?"

They play one last card and head for the Place Periere. But they are very anxious about that change, which seems to them to be more frightening than fury. And abruptly, a thought occurs to them. Isn't the driver taking them to the police commissariat? Might they not go to prison for having used him without being able to pay him?

They watch anxiously to see whether he will stop outside a house above which there is a flag. They imagine the mysterious faces of policemen behind desks. They tremble.

But the driver goes faithfully to the indicated address, and the last card, naturally, is lost.

Now the driver is completely transformed. Powers of humanity have taken possession of him. He is standing next to the vehicle benevolently, very meek and humble, still in silence, for he lacks means of expression.

He finally speaks. He has understood. He knows that his clients have no money and that they're in search of some. It's difficult to get money and to part with blood if one has none. He, now a driver, has been in extraordinary situations before. He will give credit. He will come to Martial's home in a few days to collect what Martial owes him.

Martial and Zette have a desire to weep. They would like to offer the worthy man a drink, but they do not have the necessary sum.

And that is when I arrive, like Providence, to offer the drink, to pay for the trip and to give a good tip.

And when the driver has gone and the humorous side of the affair begins to appear, I ask Martial who the art-lover is who owes him three hundred francs and has not given them to him.

"It's the Russian," he tells me, "Lévy-Bloch's friend. He left yesterday evening for Luchon."

Yesterday evening! I accompanied Rose-Thé to the station yesterday evening. They have departed on the same train.

Chapter XV

Misfortune is rapid, but mental dolor is slow. It does not come like a revelation. It infiltrates gradually. If an arm is torn away, we howl, we bleed, we fall; but if a part of our soul is torn away, we smile and we chat as before, sometimes even more agreeably, unaware that that redoubtable operation has taken place.

That is what happened to me at first. I did not know that something had been detached from me, which was the best part, the charm and the great beauty. I did not know that I had lost the best reason for being in my life.

I shall not retrace the events that marked my rupture with Rose-Thé; I ought rather to describe the absence of events. I received the letter that I had foreseen; I replied to it; I did not receive a further response. I waited. The temporary clairvoyance I had had on the eve of the departure of my mistress disappeared. It was replaced by the chaos of hesitation, of hope, of remorse and absurd thoughts, succeeded by crazy thoughts.

The sentiment that dominated me at first was that Rose-Thé had loved me too much and could not do without me. She had acted on impulse, she had wanted to punish me for having received her, she was now beginning to suffer, she would come back repentant. Only a false self-esteem prevented me from writing. But in my turn, it was necessary that I punish her. I would not write to her again, and that would hasten her return.

But what then? Was I going to take back a mistress who had left me? Was it not a unique opportunity to break a liaison that was an obstacle to the expansion of my life, without having the responsibility for it and without regretting my good luck?

But gradually, other, more veritable sentiments came to light. An immense appeal was within me, an internal clamor that demanded Rose-Thé and, if not her past love, at least her presence. I was ready to excuse everything, I would consent to anything, I would beg her pardon, provided that she was there, that I could talk to her.

And it was at dusk one evening at the beginning of summer that I had a singular encounter, at the same time as the extent of my dolor was revealed o me.

Desirous of fooling myself and making myself believe that I was still the same, I had recommenced, after a brief interruption, pursuing the quest for vulgar women that possessed me like an illness.

I had dined early, and without knowing why, I had gone to the left bank in order to stroll in the Latin Quarter. I had sent my early years in Paris there and it was full of memories. Like all men who have lived in a place and who return there some years later, I was afflicted by all the changes that were presented to my eyes. The Café Vachette, where I had wasted so many hours, had become a bank. The Boulevard Saint-Michel had been pierced, and a broad road now cut through the Rue Monsieur-le-Prince and troubled the meditation of its shady hotels and old bookshops. I asked myself seriously whether severe laws ought not to forbid touching things, changing the destination of shops and mutating cafés into banks, in order to perpetuate memories more precious than speculations.

The iron grille of a wine-merchant where I had eaten for a long time consoled me slightly when I found it immutable and, as I was going back toward the Place Saint-Michel, I crossed the path of a solitary woman and stopped in astonishment.

Ten years before, at almost the same hour, I had crossed the path of a solitary woman. I had spoken to her and I had brought her back to the hotel where I was living a short distance away in the Rue Serpente.

Now, the one of today bore an extraordinary resemblance, in the facial features, simultaneously timid and anxious, the modest appearance and the humble and mild manner, to the one of old. She certainly could not be the same one, for

281

ten years ages al faces, especially those of women who seek adventures in the evening on the Boulevard Saint-Michel. But I recalled having once obtained a certain pleasure with the woman encountered. Perhaps the resemblance was a sign, the announcement of a benevolent consolation brought be chance. In my distress I resolved to relive an hour of my youth. I accosted the evening passer-by and understood from the first phrases exchanged that I was not mistaken about the meaning of her solitude and the objective of her stroll. I was only struck by her timidity, her confusion in accepting, which seemed to reveal a lack of habitude.

My old hotel was nearby and I saw with satisfaction that it had lost nothing of its sadness and dilapidation. The steps of the stairway were mildewed. A gas jet emitted a faint light. A bizarre damp sweated incessantly from the walls.

I found the keys lines up at the office door, with a number suspended from each ring, and dirty yellow metal candle-trays. The proprietors had not changed. They were motionless behind a table where the remains of a meal were always present. They were worthy *petits bourgeois*, out of place in that profession, not made to manage a hotel of that sort. They would have liked to have none but resident tenants, good students paying by the month, as I had once been; but that was not possible. It was also necessary to rent rooms by the hour to temporary couples who were made to pay in advance, because they might well slip away afterwards without being seen, forgetting to settle the bill.

I saw by the fashion in which Monsieur Mulet stretched out his arm that he still had the joint pains of which he had complained of old. He didn't recognize me. I asked him if number nine was free. That was the room I had lived in. By a fortunate chance, number nine was free. I exchanged five francs for a formidably old key that I had taken in my fingers so many times, in days of hope, when that key opened the door to unlimited life.

The sane tremulous light! The same stairway that I'm climbing! The same woman that I'm about to embrace! It really is an hour from the past that I'm about to relive.

I open the door. Almost all the items of furniture are the same. How faded, rickety and ridiculous they are! How much force and illusion is required to go to sleep and wake up among those shameful witnesses! The sofa is prodigiously caved in and the ink-stain that dishonors it is still there. The night-table is shaky. A nameless fabric is suspended from the shelf-unit. The curtains resemble two specters.

My companion had taken off her hat and something that served as a coat. Meekly, she sat down next to me on the sofa and I was obliged to catch her, for, not knowing that item of furniture like me, she nearly disappeared into it. And I had put my arms around her shoulders mechanically.

No! It wasn't possible! It was no longer possible! The image of Rise-Thé was before me. Not that of recent times but Rose-Thé of old, the woman of the cocktail in the Bois de Boulogne, the woman of the voyage, the woman of the daily return. Oh, how conscious I was now of my folly! And this was what had doomed me! This frame, this milieu, this woman, those memories!

This evening, again, I had wanted to relive an hour of my youth! Well, I had it, that hour! Exactly the same! It was something fine and proper. This rotting hotel, this room in ruins, devoured by mildew and bugs, in which generations of unfortunates had left their sweat, their odor and the phantom their misery. This woman, like the room, who had been with other passers-by and who would undress again for others before the evening was over.

My youth! Wasn't that the cause of everything? I had devoted a cult to it. Everything that it had brought me was admirable. All the men I had known at that time had been intelligent and charming. All its hours had been a garland of pleasures. Yes, I had been duped by my youth. It had abused me with its lies. What had it been, in sum, if not a time of indefinite idleness, with Bohemians and failures, with worthless women?

In cafés, in hotels, in ugly places, I had thought I was enjoying myself, far from everything that is truly desirable and beautiful. I had vegetated throughout my youth and it was only when I had begun to emerge from it that I had begun to work and to love. And that was what had followed me with its lying prestige, unknown to me. That was what had killed my happiness, what had bewitched me from afar, by means of their maleficent spell of past pleasure, the sorcery of memory.

But it was too late! The woman I loved had gone, my happiness was dead and his was what remained!

I don't remember whether I wept at that moment, but my distress was undoubtedly very visible. I had forgotten the woman who was beside me. I felt her hand caressing my forehead and I saw her beside me with a kind face and the wide eyes of a faithful animal. She was searching for a phrase that she couldn't find, and simply said: "There, there!" to console me.

I pulled myself together. She still had a hand on my forehead. She understood that I had a subject of dolor and was enveloping her in the mystery that is the chagrins of the amours of others.

Then she spoke to me. With the objective of consoling me she employed the means of simple individuals, which is to recount their own misfortunes. How had life had been for her! How she had been deceived! Everything had gone wrong! It was necessary not to believe that this was her métier. No, it was at hazard, from time to time, when the need of money was too urgent. She was the daughter of good provincial people, but they too had been deceived and ruined. She had started out as a typist, but when one is a typist it's necessary also to know shorthand, and she only knew how to type. Then a very distinguished young man had persuaded her not to work any longer. He had deceived her and left her. She could no longer even be a typist now. She had tried other kinds of work, but she had been deceived again. Men! There were such bad ones! They took women and discarded them afterwards. Several times, she had had a friend. It hadn't lasted. No one loved her, and the most terrible thing of all was that she didn't believe in God.

She spoke with sincerity and I perceived beneath her own story the eternal character of that story of so many women. I thought that those creatures of the street that I had brushed and followed, and considered as instruments of my pleasure, were perpetually struck by misfortune, incessantly deceived and humiliated. A great pity seized me, mingled with shame with regard to the woman who was before me, a pity and a shame that made me forget momentarily the dolor of having lost Rose-Thé.

"And my name is Félicité," she said. "Isn't that a joke?"

And she did indeed laugh at that irony of fate.

One only thinks about good deeds when it is too late to do them. In exchange for the caress on my forehead that that poor girl gave me, in exchange for her kind gaze, or her misery and her weakness, I ought to have given her something other than money and the few vague words I pronounced.

I had understood that what she needed above all was a little amity and consideration. I remember that I thanked her, that I even told her my name and address and invited her to come and see me one day, as if she was a friend, but I said it lightly, without attaching any importance to it, in such a way that she did not come. I did not know at that moment the importance of a sincere gaze when one is suffering, the beauty of a soul that offers itself, even if it is very humble.

It was only when a voice had resounded: "Number nine is free…," only when I had gone down the worm-eaten staircase, candle-tray in hand, only when Monsieur Mulet had stretched his joints with a slight groan, and having breathed in the night air after the abomination of the hotel, and I had said adieu to the woman named Félicité, that I understood that it had been given to me that evening to encounter an elite soul.

At the very moment when my true dolor was born and I became conscious of it, she had had pity and she had given birth to pity in me.

While walking, I had reached the Place Saint-Michel. I turned back abruptly and started to run in order to find her again. It was too late. She had disappeared into the infinity of the city.

Chapter XVI

In my apartment there was a little room without windows that I never went into. It had no furniture except for a big wardrobe; I had the custom of saying that it resembled a wooden tomb.

It happened that that room became for me the most beautiful in the apartment, because that wooden tomb contained Rose-Thé's remaining dresses. I can say that, as long as those dresses were there, I conserved hope.

Yes, opened the door of that magnificent sad wardrobe and I looked at those, where I found either a gesture or an inclination of my mistress' body.

There was the previous summer's blue dress, the one that was a little too short and which allowed her knees to be seen when she was sitting down and she crossed her legs familiarly. It was also a little too low in the neckline. It was the work of a very small couturier, naturally made on the model of a great fashion house.

There was a velvet dress that suited her so well and in regard to which Rose-Thé had been in great despair when I had obliged her to part with it. She had made a little hole in it with a lighted cigarette on the day when she had put it on for the first time.

"Fortunately, it wasn't me who did that!" I had said, immediately.

And the following day, I had run to a local mender in order to take it to her myself.

And there was the silk kimono, under which she was naked, and which she took off with so much facility.

I went to gaze at those motionless dresses, touched the fabric, respired the perfume. There were six of them, and because of the number they made me think of Bluebeard's wives. Perhaps he too sometimes went to open the secret room in order to look at the six dead women that he had loved and killed. We were somewhat similar. I had killed, by turns, the six charming Rose-Thés of my life.

But once, as I had just opened the little room, I heard a noise on the staircase like someone putting down something heavy outside my door. The doorbell rang, and my concierge brought in a large trunk. An unknown and arrogant chambermaid declared that she had me to fetch Madame's dresses.

I could have resisted, saying that I would give them to her myself, sending the hateful chambermaid away, but what was the point? Then too, the concierge was standing there, silently judging that it was only just to return the dresses to their owner without difficulty, especially since the trunk was there and he had brought it up.

I therefore took the six souvenirs of my happiness and deposited them in the trunk myself, with a thousand precautions in order not to crumple them. And when that was finished, I was gripped by a vertiginous discouragement, and I also added stockings, ankle-boots, lingerie and a box of power: everything that remained of her. The trunk was closed. I had it reopened because I found a little silk brassiere in a drawer.

The arrogant chambermaid showed no gratitude because I was giving up so many dear things. She was still looking at me as she would have looked at anyone who does not want to return what does not belong to them, who wanted to rob her mistress.

No, nothing remained any longer. There was no more to do than take away the trunk.

She hoped that I would charge her with a commission and had doubtless prepared a disagreeable response, but I was unable to speak.

She went away. I heard the sound of the trunk on the staircase, like the sound of a coffin being borne away.

I found another pair of small slippers. I had a desire to throw them out of the window on to the chambermaid's head.

No, I pressed them to my heart, weeping.

Chapter XVII

That day, beneath his frayed black pajamas, Hallu was wearing a pink silk chemise that he displayed with ostentation. His stiff hair was oiled in a greasy fashion that made it shine, and cheap perfume was exhaled strongly from his entire person.

He had greeted me in a distant and protective fashion. He sniggered. He knew that I was unhappy, and was rejoicing in it almost overtly. I had been driven to come by an insensate hope. Who could tell? Perhaps, I had said to myself, there was something veritable in Hallu's practices. Perhaps the amorous spell that he had mentioned to me, the force of a talisman, might bring Rose-Thé back to me.

But once I was in his apartment, disgust took possession of me. I thought about my friend's ridiculous pretensions, and his ever unrealized powers of seduction, about the vanity of all that, and I got up to leave after a few minutes.

He did not retain me. He gave the impression of being embarrassed by my visit. He had looked at his watch. He bid me a rapid *au revoir* on his threshold.

At the bottom of the staircase there was a long corridor. I had just traversed it and was about to go into the street when I bumped into a woman who was coming in rapidly.

We were face to face. I raised my eyes. It was Renée Stevens.

We chatted. We talked about this and that. I asked her if she had seen Jean Noël recently. She had only just left him.

The idea that a creature as fine, as proud and tender as her had any relationship whatsoever with Hallu was odious to me. It seemed to me to be a sort of profanation of grace.

"Can you imagine," she said to me, as if she had read my thought, "that there's a little milliner on the second floor of this frightful house who makes adorable hats for next to nothing. I've just tried one on that would be perfect."

It was quite possible. I sighed with relief. I told her that I had come to see a certain Hallu.

"A very ugly fellow, slightly lame," she said. "I know him vaguely."

A few more words, and she smiled and departed lightly. I listed to the rustle of her dress in the dark corridor and the staircase.

I wanted to light a cigarette and searched my pocket for a box of matches. I didn't find one. That took me half a minute. Instead of hearing the sound of a door in the stairwell I continued to perceive René Sevens' light footfalls, which were fading away. I took two or three steps backwards and listened. She was still going up. It was to Hallu's that she was going.

Should I not have warned her about the coarseness of what he had said about her? Should I not have told her the story of the wax figurines, and by what bizarre means, by what sorceries, he had striven to attract her? I had a desire to launch myself up the stairs, to call to her, to cry out to her that when one has a parcel of happiness it is necessary to keep it preciously and not to compromise it, not to act like the fool that I was.

But I could be mistaken. Perhaps she had rung at the door opposite, or she was going to see Hallu to seek information, or for a banal conversation.

I was gripped by a frightful curiosity. I hesitated. I waited. I went along the corridor again, and then I retraced my steps.

It was not my concern. I sensed that I was in the wrong, that I was accomplishing a rather vile action, but I could not do otherwise. I went back upstairs slowly. No milliner at any door. I arrived at the figure five traced in chalk, enormous on the wall.

Perhaps it was there, opposite, that Renée Stevens had gone in. One or two minutes went by, and then I heard a light plaint, a moan that dragged on, a song of voluptuousness and pleasure, which was filtering though Hallu's door and was the same, exactly the same, as the one I had once heard behind the partition of a house of rendezvous, and which had come from Renée Stevens swooning in the arms of Jean Noël.

There was no doubt about it. It was her—and already!

Hallu's pink chemise was explained, his perfume, and his haste to see me leave. I imagined him, faunesque, ridiculous, unkempt, with his little evil eyes and his gross lips, violating the charming grace and the modest and tender gestures of Renée Stevens.

Had he made her come by occult methods or had she ceded out of natural perversity, for the savor of giving herself to a man who desired her? What did it matter, in sum? The two hypotheses caused me an equal horror. I went down the stairs at a run, crossed the Rue Delta in a single bound, and started running very rapidly along the Avenue Trudaine, in order not to think about it any longer.

Chapter XVIII

Now I was escorted by despair. I went to the right and left to flee from it, but if I lost it for a moment, it caught up with me immediately.

I woke up very early with a start, my head frightfully empty and my mouth dry. I paced back and forth, for I had difficulty in interesting myself in reading, and I waited.

I waited for the postman. How late he came! He even arrived a little later every day. Sometimes, I stood at the window in order to see him coming in the distance. He didn't hurry. He chatted at the doors with the concierges who were sweeping and he sometimes disappeared for five minutes, when he went to take a registered letter.

At other times I didn't have the patience to wait and I went to meet him on the boulevard. I asked him, indifferently, like someone in a hurry who suddenly thinks about his mail: "Anything for me, postman?"

Yes, there were letters, newspapers, sometimes making a thick packet—but in reality, there was nothing.

Then began an interminable day. In the early days I went to see friends, I tried to struggle; but gradually, the evil that was eating me away grew, and I avoided encounters or visits because they prevented me from thinking about that evil, and I had an imperious need to remember it incessantly.

And the evil consisted of this.

By a surprising phenomenon of memory, I relived with a redoubtable exactitude the important hours of my life spent with Rose-Thé. I recapitulated the conversations, the kisses and the gestures; I saw again the places and the landscapes where all that had unfurled and I bitterly regretted that lost happiness. But that part of my thoughts was still the sweetest, in spite of the torture I experienced. For I had found that torture greater in imagining what it would have been necessary to do and say to modify destiny, and I inflicted it in myself like an untiring torturer. On such a day, at such a moment, if I had embraced her and taken her in my arm, some equivocation would not have been born, which had engendered some rancor, of which some event had been born. That first evening, at Martial's, when I had perceived the empty, obscene, monstrous eyes of the Russian Pavlichef, if I had fled with Rose-Thé, or if I had immediately spat in the man's face, nothing would have happened!

Sometimes, a verity appeared like an enlightenment. The exact text of the phrase that it was necessary to say, at the critical moment, the phrase that could prolong amour for several years, unfurled before me in dazzling characters. Yes, that was what it was necessary to say, and I would have been saved! But why had I not said it? What was the madness, the aberration, that had blinded me? It was quite simple, though. I had looked into the distance without deigning to look beside me. Was there not still time to pronounce those words? Could I not at least write them? No, there was no longer time. There are words that are profound and moving at a certain moment and which, at others, are nothing but risible stupidities.

I wrote those risible stupidities anyway, but at the moment of sending them I had the vision of Pavlichef holding my letter, which he had just found, in his hands, and reading it scornfully, and I fell into a desperate rage caused by my impotence. And I always recommenced the painful scaffolding of supposed events, the savant mathematics of everything that could have been, everything that had not been, and everything that never would be.

I searched out places where I might have encountered Rose-Thé by chance. I went to tea-rooms, to dance-halls, and sometimes, carried away by my feverishness, by my desire to see something happen, I went to several dance-halls in succession, only staying a few minutes and leaving, like a man in a hurry. I gazed at the couples, I had a desire to question the waiters and the errand-boys. When I presented myself at the entrance I was tempted to say to the cashier: "I'm only staying if Rose-Thé is there."

She was never there, and that without any reason, for she might well have been there, but in the immensity of Paris, destiny, which sometimes enables one to encounter the person for whom one is searching several times in one day, can, for amusement, keep you away from her for a lifetime.

I had not clear idea of what would have happened if I had encountered her. I did not imagine it. I was simply driven by the desire to see her, to feast my eyes on her mage.

And I took account, in the course of those excursions, that for a man who is not loved, a significant moral diminution is added to that dolor.

The first time I perceived that was one evening, at about six o'clock, at Bodega's. There were a lot of people there. I sat down and ordered a port from a passing waiter, but he came back shortly afterwards without bringing me anything. I expressed my desire for a port again. He gave the impression of not having heard me, and did not serve me, although he hastened toward clients who had arrived well after me. At the same time, a young man and a young woman came to occupy two chairs alongside mine. They drew gradually closer and leaned on my table just as if I did not exist, implicitly eliminating me from that table.

I was gripped by anger, but I suddenly reflected. I had become insignificant. They had scarcely noticed me. The waiter had neither seen me not heard me. I was almost endowed with invisibility. The man who has lost his love is no longer more than half of himself. He is only an ambulant incomplete body, a sort of paltry shadow devoid of strength.

Into how many places did I take that shadow, that soul in torment, that drifting wreck? How many times did I arrive at night at my door with the intention of going to bed, reading and going to sleep, and how many times did I set forth again, aimlessly, at random? How many times was I caught in passing by the warm breath of a Metro that drew me into one of its carriages, its light and its human diversity? How many times did I reach the fortifications, those sad vastnesses, like a Sahara to which extinct volcanoes have added their desolation and which, in spite of that—I have no idea why—always makes me think of Vauban?

I remember one evening, among others, when, under the empire of my obsession, having walked for a long time without knowing where I was going, I found myself in the saddest place on earth, in the vicinity of the Porte Maillot. An interminable file of vehicles rolled before me and seemed to be heading for the Arc de Triomphe. The cafés were shiny and noisy and the customers on their terraces were almost extending into the street. The air was still and the heat stifling. Groups of cyclists were passing, calling to one another, and I saw their headlamps going to the right and left like drunken flames. Entire families, seemingly weighed down by the dinner finished in the bright shadow, were flowing toward the Bois. Everything was horrible and solemn. The soul of all the nearby garages rose up with the dust.

I went into Luna Park in the hope of a distraction.

My throat was seized by an odor of human sweat. Restaurant servants in gala costume, maidservants in their Sunday clothes wearing their mistresses' hats and stockings, were dancing with apprentice chauffeurs, childlike pimps and men devoid of profession. Others of the same species were displayed at tables, in front of peppermint and cherry liqueurs, and beverages that no language can define.

I sat down among them, regretting having come but not having the courage to leave without having savored the entire spectacle. And then, alongside me, at the next table, I saw, with the power of a hallucination, in spite of the implausibility of their presence in that place, Rose-Thé sitting with Pavlichef.

But it was a different Rose-Thé from the one I had known and loved. She had thickened and diminished. Her hands had become red, as if she employed every minute of her life washing dishes, and she was displaying them with pride. She had a double chin that she caused to project further by leaning on it.

Next to her stood Pavlichef, with the same eyes, in truth, but of which the expression, the intimate depths, had changed, for he was looking at that Rose-Thé with a timidity and an infinite kindness.

At first I felt my heart stop on recognizing the two individuals who were the unique objective of my thoughts, and a painful sensation of cold ran through my brain, with the impossibility of making any movement

It really was them! It was their gestures, their form, I even recognized the color of Rose-Thé's dress and a large ring on Pavlichef's finger. But how changed they were! Yes, too changed, too changed for it really to be them.

With a great effort of my frozen mind I recognized that hazard had placed beside me two individuals rather similar to Rose-Thé and Pavlichef, who were like caricatures of them, and my suggestion had augmented the resemblance.

I uttered a sigh of deliverance and I observed them without them noticing me, because of the insignificance that my mental poverty and solitude conferred upon me. I observed them passionately and dolorously until the moment that they got up to go toward a naked negro, deformed and mechanical, immobile on a pedestal, bearing in the middle of his chest a bizarre apparatus for measuring the strength of a fist. And I saw them hitting the negro's belly with all their strength and guffawing with joy at the comparison of their strength, while three or four circulating wrecks stopped and formed a little circle around that minimal event.

Then I went past the shooting range, a game of massacre in which the dolls were German emperors and generals, and a seller of bonbons and barley sugar, and plunged back into the eternal popular fête of the Porte Maillot.

Once, I was sitting down in a bar in Montmartre, on a stool. A woman came in who must have been a regular, for she made little signs with her head to the barman, the waiters and a few clients, and immediately started twirling on her own, without any music, sometimes sketching comic entrechats. I thought that there must be a great force of joy within her to act thus without the provocation of an orchestra and a group of friends. Afterwards, she headed toward me and unceremoniously, while laughing, spoke to me in English, asking me to buy her a cocktail.

Discontented at being mistaken for an American, I replied coldly that she could have a cocktail, and turned away. She drank it joyfully, while continuing to laugh and talk in a loud voice. Jokingly, she threw the slice of lemon that was in her glass at the head of a man wearing a monocle, who was delighted by that, and she recommenced twirling all alone, only stopping to launch her foot high in the air or to fall momentarily on to someone's knees.

I was exasperated by that irrational joy, but a little later, when the woman sat down on a chair to catch her breath, I understood by the forward slump of her head, the weight of her arms and the stupid expression n hr face that she was struck like me by the vertigo of dolor.

I had a desire to go and talk to her, to try to console her, but my pity was limited by my timidity and I left in order not to have to think about her any longer.

Another time, I was sitting in a tram facing a man who was talking to himself, and, as the tram was traveling slowly, I had all the leisure required to hear the words he was murmuring and to examine his features.

Another time, I followed a drunkard, and I happened to sit down on a bench beside a young man who was struck by immobility and who was staring at the toes of his boots with a mortal attention, untiringly.

And gradually, I acquired the habit of recognizing, in the street, in restaurants, at the theater, all the obsessive individuals of the same family, who were staring within themselves at the image of their lost happiness, making the gesture with their hands of embracing it in the void and who could not accustom themselves to their solitude.

And thus I had in life a few companions, to whom I did not speak, but who were the only people with whom I could exchange some sympathy.

Less penetrating than me, they were unaware of our kinship. I did not make them any sign because they would not have understood. But I accompanied, in silence, those poor brothers devoid of hope, and when I saw them close the door of their houses, I said to myself: *Friend, may the tomb of your bed not be populated tonight by any words, may the face not appear, may the memories not lacerate you, many slumber come with forgetfulness!*

Summer had passed and autumn came with its power of memories. I had hesitated so much to quit Paris, and all the seaside towns of which I had thought had seemed so tedious, that in the end I had stayed. The first rains and the first chill brought me a surplus of sadness because they reminded me of other first rains and other cold spells.

Often, in the evening in the hope of encountering Félicité, I walked along the Boulevard Saint-Michel, not far from the Rue Serpente. I remembered her hand on my forehead and she was, among all creatures, the only one who would not have been insupportable to me. I even thought that the simplicity of her soul would have brought me a certain consolation. I searched for her ardently. I thought that the place where I had the best chance of encountering her was where I had encountered her before, but hazard is rarely amicable.

I regretted bitterly not having asked her for her address. I had given her mine, but so distractedly, insisting so little on her visit, that I was certain that the humble person would never dare to come.

Gradually, I gave up trying to find her and no longer thought about her. Days passed, and only then, in the course of my excursions, did an idea occur to me that I should, logically, have had much sooner, if I has not possessed, like almost all men, an unlimited vanity.

Now, on the boulevards, and in the streets, I adopted the habit of stopping in front of shop windows when there was a mirror therein. I made a semblance of either straightening my hat, or examining my eye, as if a speck of dust had fallen into it.

In reality, my hat was in its place and my eye was luminous, without the intrusion of any foreign body, but it was my face that I was looking at. I perceived for the first time that I had aged. Perhaps it was not so much because of my abandonment, because of the power of Pavlichef's seduction that Rose-Thé had left me, but because she had tired of living with a man who as rapidly losing his youth.

Yes, nature preceded by abrupt leaps. There was a moment in life when slow progression changed into a kind of race. Hair began to fall out with more abundance and grow back with less ardor, inexorable wrinkles were hollowed out in the corners of the youth, the undersides of the eyes formed bags, the skin became brittle and it as only the hands that did not have a wrinkled appearance. At the same time, fatigue came more rapidly, one was less capable of walking, work and activity, ideas flowed less richly in the brain, one was less cheerful, less agreeable, less alive.

I had arrived at that period. I had not suspected it myself, for one always deceives oneself with regard to one's vigor and age, but that was why Rose-Thé had left.

Pavlichef was younger than me! Not much younger, to be sure, but at least he appeared so.

What would I not have given to know his exact age? He must rejuvenate himself, that was certain. I conceived the project of writing to Russia. But where/ What folly!

I assessed photographs of myself dating back a few years. What a difference there was with my present visage! Oh, I was much better before. But it is a photographer's métier to embellish. I had never been as good at that moment, and if I had my photograph taken today, I would still have the same appearance.

There was no doubt about it, however. The image that the mirror sent back was different. Something had changed. I saw a more jaundiced complexion, more prominent bone-structure, a gravity and a heaviness in a thicker contour.

But if it was for that reason that I had lost Rose-Thé, nothing could ever remedy it. The days would only aggravate my case. Hair would continue to fall, wrinkles to form, bags to swell, youth to fly away, and Rose-Thé was more lost with every passing minute.

Then it was a new illusion that took possession of me. When I went past the redoubtable mirrors in shop windows, at a more rapid pace, because I no longer wanted to pause in front of them, what I perceived as I darted an oblique glance at them was a silhouette entirely old, a caricature of a man.

I told myself that that was exaggerated, that suggestion was deforming my image and that the individual glimpsed had been created by my terror of old age, but all the same, I also told myself that Rose-Thé had doubtless thought like me, that she had spotted my wrinkles and my silhouette, and my despair increased endlessly with the sentiment of the inexorable.

Chapter XIX

At Cauterets I once knew a man who appeared on the promenade at seven o'clock in the morning clad in a tuxedo, with varnished shoes and a white cravat. He was a modest man drunk of elegance. All year long he had led a mediocre life, waiting for the splendors of one month in summer at a seaside resort. So, at dawn, during that month, he put on his costume and his dreams in order to be ready to realize the worldly adventures for which he hoped.

I was now like that man, who had once made me laugh. At seven o'clock in the morning, clad in the tuxedo of hoe and seven-league patent leather shoes, which make you go so swiftly along the road of desired things, I paced back and forth in my apartment, seeking the cleverest and most decisive phrases, and waited for the most beautiful adventure of my life.

A local florist had the mission of bringing a large basket of flowers every day, with which I garnished all the vases myself, with consummate artistry, varying the colors in accordance with the proximity of fabrics. The cushions on the divan were deployed harmoniously. All the books, by a further miracle, were in order. There was no place anywhere for a crumpled piece of paper or a speck of dust. Armed with a vaporizer, I went through the rooms from time to time in order that a light artificial perfume would mingle with that of the flowers. And the ash of my cigarettes no longer fell anywhere but in the ash-trays

Happiness was to pass through. It might only stop for a moment and leave again. It had to find a frame worthy of it, in order to settle and remain.

Zette and Martial had brought me the news. Rose-Thé had the intention of coming to see me. Oh, as a comrade, naturally, as a friend, to chat. She had simply told them that, and had not added anything.

301

But Zette and Martial were, it appeared great psychologists. They had understood that things were no longer so good between Rose-Thé and Pavlichef. They had seen them quite often, firstly because Pavlichef was a buyer of paintings, and secondly because of me.

"There are things about which a woman isn't mistaken," Zette had said.

"In sum, he's a flashy foreigner," Martial had said, in a profound voice. "He's not of our world."

Very agreeable words to hear!

And other words, even more agreeable, had been the story of what those excellent beings had said to Rose-Thé about Pavlichef and me.

"You see, I'm a brute," Martial—whose mildness was known to me—had affirmed. "I told her what I thought brutally. I made a comparison between you and him. And I didn't mince my words. I don't regret anything, because I don't like that Russian, and if it's necessary, I'm ready to give him back the money for his paintings and his dinners."

The last words had a chimerical character, but all the others were true, and even below the reality, for there are a small number of friends who can divine unhappiness and accomplish of their own accord, in order to help you, the necessary action

I had not made them any confidence; one is accustomed in life to hide one's pain, and a stupid self-esteem makes you affect not to have any. An amicable instinct had impelled them.

"She'll come to see you and you'll sort it out," Martial had concluded.

And as he was a simple individual, he had added, shaking my hand forcefully: "I congratulate you."

The day of Rose-Thé's visit was not fixed, but that was of no importance. I was ready to wait indefinitely and there was a relative happiness in that waiting.

As life followed its natural course, many people continue to come to see me, unaware of the dangerous emotion they caused me by ringing the doorbell. But I could not explain to the early milkman, nor the postman bearing a registered letter, nor the idle friend, that it would have been better if they had gone on their way without leaving the milk, the letter or the amity.

A melancholy and foggy All Saints' Day came in its turn to inscribe itself on the inexorably calendar of the days. Experience informed me that, that day, people seem to lose all social sense and are reluctant to go and see one another. Personally, I did not go out, still waiting, in spite of the taste for mortuary things that are developed in humans, firstly by sensuality and then by dolor.

And at about five o'clock, there was a little ring at the door, a very tiny ring, the ring of a person full of delicacy who has been at home in an apartment and who wants to show right away, on returning after a long absence, that it is only a timid visit.

With one bound I was at the door. It was not Rose-Thé. It was a hesitant woman whom I did not recognize at first in the dim light of the stairway and who, in truth, after a second of uncertainty, began to go back downstairs in order to go away.

I retained her. I had her come in. It was Félicité.

I was disappointed, but glad to see her nevertheless. I no longer had any need of the hidden treasure of pity that she was capable of giving me, but I rendered homage in my mind to that unnecessary wealth.

She apologized at length for having come, recalling what I had said to her. In any case, she did not want to disturb me, she had said bonjour, that was sufficient; she would depart right away.

Again I was obliged to retain her.

It was necessary not to hold this audacity against her. All Saints Day was so sad, so damp, she felt abandoned then, she had such a chill in her heart, she had so much need to flee men and their desire for a moment, Oh, I couldn't know!

But yes, I knew, I divined, I knew the life well enough for that. I read in her gaze the hunted beast, in the crumpled pleats of her dress and her dirty ankle-boots from which a fragment of the heel protruded. I knew what her condition was, that her course through the streets commenced every evening, and that the pursuers were pitiless. The image of a hunt was so clear that I started listening momentarily to see whether I could hear the hunters and the dogs outside the house and the sound of a horn filling the stairway.

I made her sit down by the fire and I tried to comfort her by playing the part of someone receiving in his home a agreeable friend, whom he is glad to see, but who is like any other. For I sensed that that was what was capable of doing her the most good.

She was now a little less nervous; her fear of disturbing me had calmed, and she gazed at the objects, the furniture and the wallpaper, which, in spite of their modesty, gave her the sensation of a splendid luxury.

And the impression of intimacy, the fire and the light, and above all the amity that I lavished upon her, gradually had an effect, dissipating the terrors of the street, the fear of pursuit. She had found a refuge for an hour and her heart melted. Her eyes suddenly became troubled and she began to weep.

Yes, in truth, she was a worthy and unfortunate young woman. Mentally, I saw a few scenes of her life. Seamstress, restaurant maid, perhaps even worse. She only knew hotel rooms and lodgings and the sidewalk as a promenade. I thought of her terrible remark: "The most frightful thing of all is that I don't believe in God."

So, she had nothing. Nothing remained to her. And I understood that what I was giving her at that moment, the sensation of amity, was a great deal. She needed words, moral support, the idea that she was not scorned, but treated as an equal. Yes, that was it. I had contracted a debt relative to her because she had consoled me one evening with pity. I could pay her generously. I placed my hand on her forehead and I returned the caress that she had given me.

Then the doorbell rang.

And impatient ring, full of authority, the rung of some-one who is going home and is ringing because they have forgotten their key. Félicité got up from the armchair into which she had fallen, terrified, and I saw her kind eyes fill with dread.

I knew as I went to open the door who was behind it. I reflected on what was about to happen. All the movements of my blood had slowed. I weighed the pros and cons, and, full of calm, I astonished myself with a second consciousness of the irony of destiny.

I was surprised now to be able, in the few seconds that preceded the moment when I opened the door and those that followed, to contemplate scenes so diverse, to envisage hy-potheses so different. It seemed that the ring of the doorbell had triggered in my brain a dazzling and infinitely rapid cine-matograph.

Yes, it was Rose-Thé. She was on the threshold, tranquil and smiling, without emotion, and she simply said: "It's me."

Ah! I understood immediately that she was in that period of unstable equilibrium, that torment of existence, when a woman belongs to whoever opens his arms to her, who insists and who keeps her. And I also understood everything that it was necessary to say and do, how it was necessary to welcome her, to invite her in, and the astonishingly clever and sincere phrases presented themselves to my lips, and I sensed that in my life, those phrases were immortal. I saw the divan where she would sit down as before and I was delighted to have her before my eyes, clad in a seventh unknown and charming dress, that of the wife that Bluebeard has not killed.

But then I thought of the woman who did not believe in God, who was there, who possessed nothing but the illusory dust of amity that I had just given her. I imagined how it was necessary to ask her to go away immediately, with what a scornful gaze Rose-Thé would look her up and down, first to affirm her power and then because she had always affected to establish a profound demarcation between herself and woman she judged inferior. Thus would crumble the little edifice of good that I had just built. I would waste those few drops of verity and pity that had been able to trickle into my mental misery, the information of so many evening marches that had taken my voyage back to the wretched region where the woman struggled.

So, I was like all the rest! Always whipped, always chased away! A minute's truce, and one throws them out to make way for those who are beautiful and rich.

Rose-Thé was radiant, more elegant than before, with a fur coat that was unfamiliar to me and an enormous ring with a glaucous stone that made me think of one of Pavlichef's eyes fixed upon me. She was about to come in and the other would go out, with her thin coat and her worn boots from which a little of the sole was sticking out.

No, Félicité, you will not have come in vain to ask me for the happiness of being received as a friend in an abode where there is nothing to fear, neither a bad welcome nor an insult, where one can savor after so much pain, a little consideration, under an intimate lamp.

"Excuse me," I said. "I'm very sorry, but I can't let you in."

"What?" Rose-Thé's face filled with amazement and anger.

I repeated: "I'm very sorry, but I can't let you in."

There was a second of silence, during which we stood there, facing one another, in the dim light of the stairway, where the special and annual light of the Festival of the Dead filtered through the window.

I sensed that I had killed my happiness, at a stroke, without any compensation, and in an irrevocable fashion, but I could not act otherwise.

Rose-Thé made a movement of her shoulders, a gesture of the arms that rose up and signified: *As you please! I've done my best! The die is cast! So much the worse for you!*

And she went downstairs.

I listened to the sound of her fur coat decreasing, heard her say a few words to the concierge, then nothing more, nothing more than the sentiment of the inanity of everything and a great void in my head and around me.

And a little later, when I found myself alone again, definitively alone, when the poor friend of an hour had departed in her turn, forever, I knew that my happiness was lost, that in that corner of my life, something had ended, which must have been my youth.

I started pacing back and forth, quite rapidly at first, and then more slowly, prey to a great disarray in my thoughts.

But then I was surprised to suffer less than I would have thought. I perceived myself in the mirror and was less shocked by the little wrinkles around me eyes and the ash that was born in my hair at the temples.

I stopped, astonished not to experience, more keenly than usual, the laceration that I knew so well.

Yes, my youth had ended, but perhaps there was another, behind that precious youth, another, which commences at thirty, another, which is not foolish, which is better and truer.

Perhaps I had just understood the meaning of that youth with gray hair, and had accomplished the first action demanded by it, which was to sacrifice personal amour to a more general pity.